BOOK 1

DEAD Rockstar

LILLAH LAWSON

Midnight Tide
PUBLISHING

DEAD ROCKSTAR

2nd edition

Copyright © 2024 by Lillah Lawson

Published by Midnight Tide Publishing.

www.midnighttidepublishing.com

Cover designed by

Shayne Leighton

Edited by

Jennia Herold d'Lima

Formatted by

Book Savvy Services

For Ellen,
my soul twinner

ONE

Oh, you think your life is complicated? Try falling in love with a dead rock star. One *you've* brought back — totally on accident - from the dead.

I mean, a good man is hard to find, right? Sometimes you've gotta get a little creative.

Let me start over.

My name is Stormy Spooner. I'm a lifelong atheist, a vegan, a librarian - and I'm a necromancer.

How did I get into this mess? I wear glasses, for fuck's sake. I'd like to say that your guess is as good as mine, but it was my own fault.

You wouldn't be the first to tell me that it's impossible to be a necromancer and an atheist. As my best friend, Sloan, loves to tell me, "You don't even, like, believe in anything. How can you practice magic if you don't believe in it?"

And once I would have agreed. I didn't believe in magic, and I sure as hell didn't practice it. What I did was more of a pathetic, drunken fumbling that accidentally hit the mark. It was supposed to be a *joke*.

When I announced to Sloan, between sips of our dark-mint-and-mocha iced coffees, that sweltering, humid summer day, that I was going to become a necromancer and raise the dead – well, *one* dead, specifically – I was just kidding around. I have a dark, twisted sense of humor. It gets me into trouble a lot. But this time, it got me some dead guy with pretty green eyes and hair so black it absorbs the light.

Oh, come on. Haven't you ever had a crush on a dead guy? You know you have. Jim Morrison, maybe? Jimi Hendrix? James Dean?

All the hot dead guys have names that start with J, seems like. Except for *my* dead guy. The guy whose green eyes stared down at me from the posters on my wall all throughout my lusty teenage years, the guy whose voice ignited a million fantasies, the guy whose death at the maddeningly-young age of 38 had haunted me for years. The guy who had faded into an enigma, just another dead rock star in a sea of dead rock stars. Pick your poison, they're a dime a dozen. My dead guy was never really famous, not the kind of famous that John Lennon was (another "J"), or Madonna or Prince. He was a blip, a cult-favorite, a moment in time. More people these days haven't heard of him than have. My dead guy is what you call "obscure" (and why Sloan loves to joke that I'm a hipster). My dead guy, the enigmatic, dark and mildly terrifying Philip Deville, former lead singer and bassist (and sometime harmonica player) of the Bloomer Demons, is my favorite musician of all time and the orchestrator of my sexuality. I can't put too fine a point on it, really. He was *the guy. My* dead guy.

Well, until he wasn't. Dead, I mean.

You're going to have to just trust me on this, and I'll tell you the story, but let's just get it out of the way right out of the gate. There's no hiding the dude; he did his best, it's just not in his essence to be hidden, and honestly? What's the point? My dead guy is no longer dead. He's very much alive – or undead, which I think he'd prefer, because it has that gothic sort of feel to it, and that's what gets him all hot and bothered, and that's how I like him.

Believe it or don't, but I raised the dead. I'm a necromancer. And unfortunately, because of a certain hot, (un)dead rock star, I'm going to have to do it again.

I REMEMBER the moment when the thought first came to me. I was guzzling my mint-mocha whatever on my lunch break, enjoying the sweet iciness on my tongue, letting it flow down my throat until I felt the first pangs of brain-freeze in my temple.

"I'm going to become a necromancer," I announced. Sloan, my best friend since childhood, was sitting across from me at the Jitter Bug, our favorite coffee shop and the place where we usually met on our breaks, which we always took together. It was the only place in town that made a reasonable knock-off of a Frappuccino that's vegan.

"Well, that's fucking stupid," she replied without missing a beat.

"Why?" I demanded.

"For starters, genius, you're an atheist. A *smug* atheist. It's all you talk about, Sagan and Hawking and shit and how religion is the opiate of the masses. Necromancy is magic. How many times have you told me you don't believe in anything remotely spiritual or paranormal?"

"It's all about intention," I countered. She, as a relapsed Christian – her term –couldn't be more knowledgeable on this subject than me. I'm a tad haughty about my intellect. It's a librarian thing.

"But how can you have the intention if you don't *believe* in it?" she argued, and I sniffed. "Not to mention it's utter hock-and-booey."

"Hock and *what?*"

"Hock-and-booey." She smirked at me from beneath her perfectly coiffed blonde bangs. Sloan is your usual nightmare – long blonde hair, blue eyes, her parents loved her enough to get her braces, blah blah blah. All of that and her ass is absolutely *huge*. She has the gall to complain about it, too. Meanwhile, I'm sitting on my pancake bottom, hating her.

"Ok, you were either going for cock-and-bull or boo-hockey and you didn't land on either."

"Fuck you," she said, popping a chocolate covered espresso bean in her mouth. Caffeine junkies, the both of us. We lived at the Jitter Bug year-round. We'd decided back in college, while in the midst of the 90s *Friends* craze, that we needed our own Central Perk. While the shenanigans of Phoebe and Chandler had become dated and cheesy, Sloan and I had retained our love for coffee and snark at our favorite artsy table. People write song lyrics on it in sharpie and that's the kind of overly sincere kitsch that I can appreciate, especially since we're right on the outskirts of bumfuck, aka Brunswick, Georgia, where creativity goes to die.

I decided to change tactics. "If you could bring one dead celebrity back to earth for one night," I asked her, scooping a dollop of chocolate-tinted coconut cream on my spoon and plopping it on my tongue, "who would it be and why?"

She didn't miss a beat. "Mister Rogers," she said, taking a somehow prim sip of her drink. "He likes me just the way I am. And I bet he gives the *best* hugs."

"I was thinking more along the line of dead rock stars, you

girl scout." I spooned up more cream. "Like one you'd want to fuck."

"Oh. Hard pass, then," she said, pulling out her chap-stick and running it over her lips. She did that about fifty times a day. Chap-stick addiction is a real thing and it's weird.

"Come on, you're a slut. You must have one."

She smirked. "Be that as it may, I have no desire for a night with some bloated, booze-soaked addict who croons in my ear off-key while he's trying to get his flaccid dick up. I've dated enough live musicians to know I don't want a dead one."

This was horribly unfair, but I let it slide. Sloan is a mean bitch at heart, and it does no good to point it out. She gets worse by the hour. I swear, she wakes up Suzy Sunshine and by the time she uses her withered claws to pull down her bedclothes she's turned into a cackling old crone. Why she'd want to meet Mister Rogers I'd never know. She'd have him running, screaming for the hills. She eats gentlemen for break-fast and burps up their bones. She's the perfect muse for an angsty, boy-man songwriter, which is why it was so irritating that she wouldn't play along.

"I actually have someone in mind," I began again. I don't like being derailed when I'm on a thought-bender.

"Of course you do," Sloan said with a groan. "Philip Deville, aka the Turquoise Devil, aka the Robert Plant wannabe that you've been wanting to bone since you were fourteen years old. Who has been rotting in his grave for over twenty years, and newsflash, Stormy, wasn't even that famous when he was *alive,*" she said, smirking. "God, if you're gonna be one of those obsessive fan-girls about this shit, couldn't you pick somebody everybody likes so that we can at least relate?"

"Like who?" I demanded. "John Lennon?"

She rolled her eyes. "Get with this decade, man. No, he's too sincere - too serious, just like you. You need somebody fun, somebody to dust the cobwebs from your ass. How about a live person? Hmm. What about Steven Tyler?"

I glared at her. "Steven was an androgynous fox back in the day, I'll give you that, but he's what, seventy? He's old enough to be my grandfather."

"It's not like Phillip Deville was a millennial," she pointed out. "If he was in his late thirties when he died, and it's 2019 now..."

"You are missing the point entirely," I said, irritated. "It isn't what age he'd be now – he's been on ice, so to speak, for over twenty years. If I raised him – you know, from the dead – he'd still be thirty-eight. That's older than me, but not, like, Woody Allen level creepy." I flashed her a look. "*Some* people I know don't mind a little May-December, but-"

"So you're going to become the world's first atheist vegan necromancer," she interrupted me. I didn't like her tone. She made it sound crazy. "And you're trying to make it *non-creepy?*"

"Yes." I smiled. "Precisely." I sucked the dregs of the icy coffee from my cup and tossed it across the table toward the trash bin where it bounced off the lid and hit the floor, spraying mint-mocha everywhere. This kind of stuff happens to me a lot. I jumped up, muttering apologies to the bored-looking cashier, and grabbed a handful of napkins. "I'm going to raise the dead."

"You're going to reanimate all 6'5" of Phillip Deville's mostly decomposed, festering corpse?"

"You understand rightly." I grabbed another wad of napkins.

"You're an idiot, Spooner." She peered at me sideways. "Did you bring the flask to work today? Nipping a little Jim Beam in between shelving boring textbooks?"

"I resent that." I did have my flask with me that day, but she didn't need to know that. "Remember that vinyl I got? I just found these weird printed lyrics and I thought maybe-" I shrugged, mopping up puddled coffee. "It'd be fun. To try. You in?"

"If it means I have to listen to fucking Bloomer Demons one more time – on my *night off* – then no. I am decidedly not in." She finished her own beverage and tossed it at the bin. As expected, it sailed right in. "Nah, I love you, Stormy, but I'm out. Anyway, I've got a date tonight. I plan to get laid. By, you know, a live dude."

"Killjoy."

"Sorry. I've been trying to cinch this guy forever. He's in med school. Studying to be a surgeon. He might actually be able to find the-"

"Dude," I interrupted her, gesturing with my head toward the legging-clad soccer mom at the counter, holding up her gold Amex like a trophy. "You're kinda loud."

"I think even Karen would agree that men should know basic female anatomy," Sloan retorted, but she lowered her voice. After another moment watching me clean up my mess, she moved off her chair and started to help me. "Maybe I'll come by in the morning. Bring you a celebratory bagel. One for you and your zombie. Think he'd want a schmear?"

"I think he'd rather have donuts." I'd read once that in his tour rider he'd always asked for powdered-sugar donuts. There was a joke there, a whole *is-that-cocaine-on-his-upper-lip-or-powdered-sugar* thing that some tabloid had printed once, but I preferred to think he just really liked his sweets.

She looked at me and shook her head. There was mocha on my shoe. "I've got to get back to work."

"Yeah, me too."

"Try not to get too blitzed and attempt to summon a dementor in the card catalog."

"That doesn't even make sense. First of all, we haven't had card catalogs, since, like, twenty years ago. Where have you been? And they weren't a place you could go, like a room. It was literally just a cabinet with...oh, forget it. And if you'd actually read Harry Potter, you'd know that dementors aren't summoned-"

But she was already halfway out the door of the coffee shop. She turned back to me with a grin. "Catch you later, necromancer. Hope he rises to the occasion." I could still hear her cackling as the heavy glass door shut behind her.

Sometimes I hated Sloan. You're joking around, just trying to get a rise out of her, and she refuses to be ruffled. So you end up taking your whole shit seriously and you end up doing all sorts of failed-jokes out of spite, just to prove you *can*, even though you never meant to to begin with.

Which is how I got into all this trouble in the first place. Fucking Sloan.

JUST AS I was hopping into my truck, breathing a sigh of relief to be done for the day, my phone rang. It isn't like my job is hard or anything, not compared to some, but I was just...weary. Most days I'd come home from work bone tired and fall into bed. I wasn't exercising much anymore, something that I always used to enjoy. All I wanted to do was sleep, ever since my life had fallen spectacularly apart.

I glanced at my phone as I put the truck in reverse and sighed. Sloan. I didn't really feel like talking to anyone right now, even her, but I knew she'd call me back every two minutes until I finally picked up. She had a sixth sense when it came to my black moods. Without fail, any time the curtain was beginning to fall over my eyes, she'd call within a few minutes. She wouldn't let me dwell. It was both maddening and a lifeline.

"Yo," I answered, easing out of the parking lot and extending a wave to Jean, the head librarian and my boss. She nodded her gray-curled head at me and resumed fishing for her keys.

"Hey, I'm in a rush, but I wanted to let you know..." I could hear the rattle of Sloan's makeup case in the background. She must be getting ready for her date. Sloan was a makeup junkie; I'd never seen her without perfectly applied, thick black, winged eyeliner. Not even when we were teenagers and she'd spend the night. "...Tess called me today."

"Tess?" I parroted dumbly. "Called you? Today? Why?"

"It was after we had coffee, when I went back to work," she said. "When I saw his name on the caller ID, I almost sent it to voicemail, but I was curious-"

"What did he want?" I demanded.

"You're not going to like it."

"Spill. Now."

"He wanted a freebie. What else?" Sloan is a hairdresser. She pays booth rent at The Curling Dervish and half the people in town ask her for freebies, or for trades. I have no idea how she makes enough to pay rent.

"Why would he go to a women's salon to get a haircut? I didn't even know he was back in town."

"Not for him, goober. For his..." She lowered her voice to a disgusted whisper. "For his *girlfriend*."

I kept my eyes on the road and concentrated on driving carefully as I'd just noticed a cop pulling into the lane behind me. But my instincts were screaming at me to drive off the road and into the nearest dumpster. A girlfriend? Since when?

"Oh."

"That's all you've gotta say? *Oh?*" Sloan demanded. I could hear her slamming makeup down on the counter. "Your ex-husband pops up out of nowhere after months of radio silence, calls your best friend, and asks her to give his girlfriend a freebie? And she wants a cut *and* color, mind you. We're talking a hundred bucks, at least. The nerve-"

"It doesn't matter," I said in a pained voice. My throat felt a little closed up. "Let him do whatever he wants."

"It certainly does matter," Sloan argued. "I told him, politely of course, because I was on the clock, to go fuck himself. I don't do freebies for anybody anymore. But especially not him and his skank of the month. After all he did to you. I wish he'd been here in person. I would have got right up in his face-"

I managed to smile. Sloan's protectiveness of me was one of her finer qualities. But I just wanted to get off the phone. I'd already been in a dark place and her call had only put fresh hurt on top of what was already a festering wound. "So is it a new girlfriend? Or is he back with *her?*" I didn't want to ask, but I had to.

"He's still seeing *her,*" she said, her voice full of pity. "Don't sweat it, Storm. If he wants to have a mid-life crisis and start dating a Jennifer Lopez wannabe, that's not your problem-"

"It's not a mid-life crisis," I argued, clutching at my stomach. "He's only thirty-three."

"It hit him early," she said pertly. "Along with the male pattern baldness."

I frowned. "Oh, his hair's fine. Hey, Sloan? I'm driving. Gotta go, okay? Talk later."

"Okay, yeah. I've got to slip into my dress, anyway. Still trying to decide on shoes. This guy is major buttoned up. NO idea what he sees in me." She was silent for a moment, and I could hear the rattle of mascaras in her bag. "Hey, you aren't still planning on doing that stupid spell, are you?"

For a moment I'd forgotten what she was talking about, then I remembered. The necromancy spell. I'd mainly just been winding her up. Right now, my plans consisted of climbing into bed in my rattiest pajamas and doing my best to forgot about Tess and his gorgeous Latina lover by upending a bottle of red wine. "I was just trying to be funny. I wasn't serious." But even as I said the words, a tendril of excitement began to work its way up my back...it might be fun...

"Okay, good." Her tone turned serious. "It's just...you're in a vulnerable place right now. And I know it's all just hock-and-booey-" there was that word again- "-but sometimes our intentions, like you said - they get away from us. I don't want you playing around with any of that stuff, getting hurt."

"I don't believe in 'that stuff', Sloan," I said irritably. "I was just kidding, anyway." In my mind, I was already mentally stockpiling supplies. I had most of them in the cupboard already. Joke, my ass. I was such a liar. A liar and a fraud.

"Fine," she said. "Good. Go home, get some sleep, and don't think about Tess, okay? He's not worth it, believe me. You'll find some cuter, hotter piece of ass soon, one that isn't a-"

"Okay, Sloan," I said. "Love you, bye." And I hung up.

Sloan would understand my shortness. Talking about Tess – even thinking about him–still caused too much pain. She was probably cursing herself for even telling me now. Of course, I would have found out eventually anyway.

If Tess had had a *new* girlfriend, it would have hurt less. I assumed he'd been seeing various women ever since our divorce. After all, he'd been seeing them *before* we'd split up, I'd discovered. But the fact that he was still with *her,* the one who had broken up our marriage, felt like a punch in the heart. Considering I was still stuck in the holding pattern, paying off both the monetary debt he'd left me with and the mental, emotional debt I couldn't seem to shake, it was unfair that he had been able to move on. I'd comforted myself by assuming they'd be broken up within a week. When I heard the rumor that she'd dumped him, I had giggled with glee. Served him right. But now, they were back on and back on my stomping grounds. It was bad enough that apparently they were a real item, but now I would have to dodge seeing them in town and hearing all about them trying to swindle my best friend. This was my turf and I'd explicitly told him to stay away. Did Tess seriously not think I'd find out if he came back?

I gripped the wheel, my mouth setting into a hard line. I knew Tess better than anyone, knew his little tricks.

It was bait. He knew I'd hear about it, that Sloan would dutifully let me know. This was on purpose, this little bit of intel. I wondered what he wanted from me.

Money, probably. Well, unfortunately for both of us, I didn't have any. And I had no plans to take his bait. But once Tess realized that going through Sloan wouldn't work, he'd be contacting me directly. I could count on it.

I'd deal with that when I came to it. I'd lock my doors and pretend I wasn't home if he came knocking. I couldn't deal with Tess tonight. Or any night. My days of dealing with him were over, even if I secretly wanted to see him so bad it made me ache.

I wanted to hate him, just like any good, newly-divorced young woman who had been made a fool of would. I wanted to bash his head with a frying pan, run him over with my car, set fire to his clothes on the lawn. I wanted to humiliate him, hurt him, make him suffer for what he'd done – filling my house with drugs, losing his job, cheating on me – but simmering beneath the hatred and hurt was love. I hated myself for it, but there it was.

Never again would I wake in the middle of the night with Tess' fine brown hair tickling my face. Never again would we take snacks and wine to Driftwood Beach, getting blissfully drunk while feeding the seagulls. Never again would I feel the light touch of his hand on my leg as we went for a drive in his dusty old pickup. That part of my life was over, and I didn't want it to, but it *hurt*.

Fumbling with one hand, I managed to locate the auxiliary cable, plug it into my phone, and press the 'shuffle' button on Spotify without crashing the car. Phillip Deville's sultry, velvet voice came through the speakers and I turned it up loud, drowning out all thoughts of Tess Spooner and my replacement.

Two

The first thing I did when I got home was kick off my weather-beaten burgundy chucks, followed by my equally weathered bra, and throw them in the corner. When Tess first moved out it was agony being alone all the time, but I soon assimilated to life on my own. I'd turned into a full-fledged slob. There was nobody around to judge me except Blinken, my cat, and he was thankfully silent. I looked at my purse, thrown haphazardly onto the chair, not bothering to take my phone out since I didn't feel like talking to anybody. Instead, I walked into the tiny kitchen, pulling my dishwater hair into a messy ponytail as I went. I flipped on the dim overhead light and started rummaging for the makings of a cocktail.

Gin, rum, half a shot's worth of tequila. Ancient sour mix, a jar of maraschinos soaked in brandy. Things were looking dire. I'd been drinking far too much lately, and my measly salary wasn't enough to replenish the top shelf stuff. My eye fell on the giant bottle of Merlot that Sloan had left the last time she'd been over for one of our slumber parties. Yes, we were grown women who still had slumber parties. One of the perks of being two single women in our early thirties, with no attachments and no real lives to speak of. Once a month or so we'd throw on our jammies, order takeout, and get shitfaced while watching romcoms and listening to 80s metal and new wave.

I'd hoped for one of our slumber parties tonight; being alone wasn't a good idea when I felt like this. But I didn't begrudge Sloan her date. Sloan was happy being perpetually single, but she started to get salty when she didn't have regular boning. She liked her boys, Sloan. Still, I was lonely and wished she was around. I grabbed the bottle of wine and popped out the cork, marveling at my own talent for doing so. I took a swig out of the bottle, deciding not to waste a glass on little old me, then sighed and grabbed one from the cabinet. Being lonely and sad was no excuse for trashy.

I ventured into the living room, which wasn't really much of a room, just a small square in the middle of the trailer. My bedroom, off to the left, was even smaller, and the bathroom was so tiny you had to turn sideways to use the toilet. One day I planned to move. The thought that I'd shared such a stifling, dusty place with Tess seemed unbelievable now. He was the one who had talked me into renting it. I'd scoffed at the thought of living in a trailer, much less a miniscule singlewide that had been standing crooked since the early 90s. But he had won out in the end – as he had for most of our short-lived, pitiful marriage. "Don't be such a snob," he had admonished me. "There's nothing wrong with living in a mobile home." While that was true, now I was stuck living in this rusted tin can on my own, with nobody to fix the constantly broken faucet in the tub or reinforce the sagging beams in the kitchen floor. At least I had a wooded, private yard.

I was lucky, really, if I could stop the pity party long enough to admit it. Just a few miles down the road, over the bridge, was the ocean. I lived a hop and a skip from Jekyll Island, one of the most beautiful stretches of beach in Georgia.

The weather was always mild, the sand soft and pale, the slate-blue sky calming and beautiful. Even when the sun bore down in the dead of summer, the beach held a dark aspect that never failed to calm me. The sand was always cool to the touch, the stark, stripped driftwood beckoning to me like kindly skeleton fingers. Even having grown up here, I wasn't immune to its charms, but it had been a long time since I'd ventured out to the water. I used to go running on Driftwood Beach every day. Now, I'd do anything to avoid thinking about the place.

I stayed on the mainland, went to work at the library, and came home to my cat and my solitary life in the little trailer, weather-beaten by the damp sea air more and more every day. Before long, it would crumble into the ground, hidden by pine trees as the earth reclaimed it, and I'd have to move to a shitty apartment.

Blinken was lounging on his cat bed, licking at a paw. He blinked his yellow-green eyes at me. "Hello, Mr. Blink," I said to him, and he resumed his bath, unfussed. I sat the glass of wine down on the coffee table and perched on the couch, feeling like a buoy, full of air, unable to relax. I had smelled the salty brine of sea-rain on my drive home; the pinging of an oncoming migraine and the ominous gray of the sky ocean-side had only confirmed my suspicion – a storm was coming, and it was going to be a doozy.

I was having trouble keeping Tess out of my mind. I wondered if I'd ever forget the shock of brown hair that fell over his blue eyes, the way he always slouched, tall and skinny, too skinny near the end. Of course, that had been because of drugs, but I'd stupidly fallen for his excuse that he was just working too hard. All that supposed overtime, all those late nights. The musty smell coming off his skin as he'd lay with his back to me, seemingly too tired for closeness. I'd just assumed that any unfamiliar smells were from the chemi-cals at the plant, that the extra cash in his wallet was overtime pay. I never guessed that the money was from selling drugs, the weight loss was from using, or that he'd lost his job months before and the musty smell was the perfume of another woman, a voluptuous, dark haired confection named Roberta who only lived a few miles down the road at St. Simons.

I wish I could say that I'd figured it all out, confronted him and kicked him to the curb, but I hadn't. Even after I knew the whole truth, I still loved him, believed his apologies and assurances that he wouldn't do it again. I hadn't even waited a respectable week before taking him back, letting him back into my house and my heart. I'd believed his lies, hook, line and sinker because I hadn't known what else to do. Where would I be without Tess? My relationship with both of my parents was strained and I hardly ever saw them. I had no siblings to speak of, only a toddler half-sister who I barely knew and didn't much care about, and not many friends other than Sloan. Without Tess, I didn't know who I was, or worse, what I might become.

It took Sloan sitting me down and telling me point blank what everyone else had known for months: my husband was cheating on me (still), and worse, he and his side piece were running drugs. There had been a raid on Roberta's place, and the rumor was that the police would be coming for Tess soon. That's the thing about the "salt life" - living in a small coastal town, news travels fast, and it doesn't take long for your demons to come for you.

Still in shock, I'd taken no justifiable pleasure or humor in the situation as I sat in the corner of the room, on the same couch I sat drinking on now, and watched them cuff my husband and take him away. I hadn't cried or yelled or done anything other than just watch. After he was gone, I carefully packed his things in boxes and sat them gingerly on the front stoop. I went down to the jail and used the last of our savings to pay his bail. This time there were no reassurances, no pleading, no *"I'll change, I promise."* He only gave me a pained look, a small, brotherly pat on the shoulder, then used the pay phone to call Roberta's brother, who came and picked him up – or I assume he did, because I'd fled in tears soon after. That *he* could reject *me* at such a moment was a humiliation I could not get over.

I'd barely spoken to Tess since it'd happened, other than one ill-thought-out text where I'd commanded him to *"Never come back, if you know what's good for you,"* though I had no idea how I'd make good on that threat. He'd seemingly taken it to heart, though, because I hadn't seen or heard from him since. I'd had to file for divorce and get the lawyers to serve the papers. Tess was nowhere to be found. He'd just disappeared. Like he'd left *me,* which, I suppose, he had.

I took a sip of my red wine, settling back on the cushions, reaching over to grab my phone out of my bag. I was tempted to call him; I assumed the number would be the same. Tempted to tell him to leave my best friend alone, and if he knew what was good for him, to leave town. I'd heard through the grapevine that he was living in Savannah now, which gave me an ache in my chest – Savannah was no place for a drug addict with a sordid past. But that wasn't my business now, and he didn't deserve my worry.

I decided against calling. I knew once he picked up and I heard his voice, I'd lose my nerve. Not worth it. And why give him the satisfaction?

I grabbed the remote and turned on my ancient disc-changer stereo, which I'd had since I was a teenager in the late 90s. It was a wonder the old dinosaur still worked. Iggy Pop and the Stooges ran loud and rambunctious through the speakers. "I Wanna Be Your Dog." It seemed appropriate. I settled back against the cushions and closed my eyes. I wished I had some pot – before, Tess and I had smoked most days, and after he'd left, I swore it off, determined not to be like him in any way. But hell, what was a little spliff now and again? Sloan got the good shit, medical grade, but not the kind that makes your brain fall into a reverse spiral; rather the kind that takes away pain and fills you with fuzzy bliss. But it was expensive, and I was broke. I tipped the bottle up instead, toasting my poverty and broken heart.

Two thirds of the Merlot gone, and I was still laying against the couch cushions, but I was a lot less anxious. I felt muddy and numb. Blinken had taken his leave of me, off to the bedroom to steal my pillow. I was too grim, even for him, tonight. I'd gone through the entire Stooges record. The CD clicked as it changed, and then it was onto the Bloomer Demons album *God is Dead.* One of my favorites, and the one most likely to make Sloan groan and get up to leave. Dark and gritty and full of existential angst, it was an acquired taste. But, like I told her, "You can't fight true love."

I'd had it on CD since I was a teen and had a digital copy on my iPhone. But it was the super-rare turquoise vinyl edition that I'd found scouring the flea market recently that was the real treasure. With my heart in my throat, I'd managed to haggle the pimply, leather jacket-clad guy into selling it to me for twenty-five bucks. It was such a rarity that only a few of them existed. The guy, admitting to me that he wasn't a fan - "I'm more of a Megadeth person" - had no idea what he had. The outer sleeve had been pockmarked with ancient grains of dirt, and the sea-air had slightly warped the record, but there were no real scratches, and I suspected it would still play. I would have bought it no matter the condition, though. My hands were shaking as I handed him the money.

I had called Sloan on my way home with it, screeching in excitement - "Oh my god, oh my GOD, I found it, I found it," and she'd yawned and said, "Jesus Christ, you're a loser." And hung up on me.

The album starts out with crickets chirping. Then the soft

slush of waves lapping in a body of water. The croak of bull-frogs. Then, after what feels like an age, the gentle, melodious sound of a violin. By the time the fuzzy, nuclear sound of the bass kicks in, followed by the pounding drums, you're a minute and thirteen seconds into the track. When Phillip Deville's smooth-but-razor sharp baritone makes its introduction, it's been another two minutes and five seconds.

Part of Sloan's problem is that she hates songs that are in "parts." Those long, epic, sweeping saga songs that tell a story, that have more than just two verses, a bridge and a chorus, are dead to her. She hates them. "I just want to listen to a good song, maybe dance a little. I don't need fucking Lord of the Rings on my Spotify playlist. Bands like Rush make me want to kill myself. It's musical diarrhea. When do we get off the toilet?" I love Sloan because I have to at this point, but some-times I want to kick her in the face. The saga songs – musical novels - are the *best*.

Bring Me Back, the first song on the *God is Dead* album, was definitely a saga. As I drank the last drop of wine from my glass, the music was churning its way toward the third part, where Phillip almost sounds like a demented monk, reciting lines of poetry, monotone and devoid of vibrato. I wrenched myself awkwardly off the couch, feeling just how drunk I was as I stood up, and grabbed my phone. Over in the corner, propped up against my bookshelf, was the album. Weathered a little around the edges, with a faded circle on the front where the record itself had started to wear through, it was pretty worse for wear, but I didn't care. I sat down on my old brown carpet and gingerly pulled the liner notes from the sleeve. They were delicate and had been ripped a little by some previous owner; I cursed them inwardly.

Bring Me Back was a weird song. I'd read in an interview with Philip that it was inspired by T.S. Eliot's "Prufrock" and was all about man's preoccupation with death – how we fear death more than anything else while simultaneously flirting with the thrill of it. And it made sense, since Phillip was thirty-six when the album was recorded and coming off some pretty serious drug addiction and a divorce (I knew a little something about that myself) and confronting middle age. But what puzzled fans was the single line he sang in Italian, his deep voice skipping over the words in a clipped, clinical baritone as though his voice itself was the record needle. It's just one line, but it's strange, a weird one-off in a sea of darkness. Translated, it meant something like, "Find the spell and bring me back (at least, that's what it said in his obit from *Rolling Stone*. I don't speak Italian)". But there was no spell. The lyrics of the song were just reworkings of the Eliot poem, musing on death and middle age.

Bless and curse the glorious beast that is the internet; a buzz started on Reddit or somewhere a few years back that proved helpful. Someone had snagged their mom's old vinyl copy of *God is Dead,* the rare one with the turquoise record, just like mine. They were practicing sketching by tracing the artwork on the liner notes, an elaborate Celtic pattern with dragons, snakes, flowers and a crescent moon, when they discovered that it was actually letters they were sketching. *Olde English* letters, hidden in the artwork. When written out on paper, they formed four lines of poetry. Since then, the rumor had spread like wildfire among Bloomer Demons fans and people had started snapping up the remaining *God is Dead* albums, desperate to get their hands on Phillip's last unknown lyric. And I had been lucky enough to find one at the flea market from some stoned guy who preferred Megadeth. Imagine my luck.

I traced my hands over the old letters, then opened my cyan-colored composition book, the closest I'd found to turquoise, where I'd written out the poem in my own script a few nights ago. Any good witch needed a grimoire, right? This would be mine. I read over the lines a few times, smiling. I was sure there were other fans who had figured it out by now, but I still felt smug. This wasn't a poem or a lyric. Phillip Deville had left it right under our noses. *Find the spell and bring me back.*

And Sloan didn't think I'd really do it.

I'd told her it was a joke so many times, but I'd collected all the supplies and written out a spell, hadn't I? Now that I was certifiably sloshed, I allowed myself to sit back and brood a little on just *how* funny my best friend had found the whole thing. She'd always found my obsession with the Bloomer Demons hilarious, and I supposed it kind of was, the level of fandom that I rose to. God knows I'd taken it to some spectacular heights over the years. That's just who I was...I took to the things I loved – my music, my books, even Tess – to the extreme. I loved hard. Sloan could always be relied upon to bring me back down to earth – but shit, sometimes I didn't *want* to come back down. Didn't I deserve to enjoy things?

I'd record myself performing the spell. Send it to her. After all, she pulled no punches, so why couldn't I troll her back a little while she was on her date?

So I set to making everything perfect. Conducting a spell, after all, was a serious business that involved ritual. I didn't have any candles, but I had a wax melt burner that Tess' mom had guilted me into buying on one of our "mother-daughter-dates" at TJ Maxx (Tess' mother was sweet, and I missed those excursions with her. I wondered if she took Roberta out for lunch and home décor shopping trips now that I'd been cast aside) along with four or five packets of scented wax. I plugged it in near my makeshift altar and broke off a square of "Cinnamon and Clove" to put in. I cleared off my narrow glass side table and set the record, sleeve and paper on it, along with a picture of Phillip I'd ripped out of a music magazine, chest muscles rippling beneath his flowing black hair (*"Blaze - the*

Goth Issue"). Rummaging through my jewelry box, I found an old gemstone – sapphire – that was once part of a now-broken necklace and a pentagram on a string that an old boyfriend had given me in high school. I sat them in a row on the glass table along with a smooth, black stone I'd pulled from the creek behind my trailer and a piece of weather-bleached sea wood I'd found the last time I was on Driftwood Beach.

Now for the last preparation. I had recently bought a bundle of sage at the Brunswick farmer's market. A woman there had called hello to me and I'd stopped at her booth to be polite. She sold sweet-smelling goat's milk soap and perfumed lotions, but it was her "pagan priorities" that caught my eye. Among them were sage, candles, what looked like jewelry made of twigs, different cloths and little jars that appeared to hold sand, dirt, shell, and maybe even bone. I didn't believe in that sort of crap, but I was intrigued. The red-haired lady had pressed a bundle in my hand, saying softly, "To clear the air, honey," and on a whim, I decided to buy the little bundle of sage and try it. I might not believe in it, but there were plenty of things I *had* believed in, like my marriage, that had turned out to be horseshit, so what the hell. Plus, I'd seen a few acquaintances in a local Facebook group I belonged to making fun of the woman – they called her "Goat's Milk Soap Lady" and joked about how "woo" she was. That stuck in my craw, so it made me grin to throw a few bucks her way. Trust me to always go against the grain. I wondered when I'd ever stop letting it get me into trouble.

I sat down in front of the table and rummaged in my bag for a lighter just as Phillip began to sing his Italian verse. *"Trova l'incantesimo e riportami indietro."* He could have said it over and over in his regular speaking voice and it would have sounded like music. A chill crept up my spine and I resisted the urge to melt into the carpet. His baritone seemed to slip over me like silk; both cool and warm at the same time. I lit the sage, turned on the wax burner, and poured another glass of wine, feeling both important and impossibly silly all at once.

I grabbed a box of tarot cards from my bag. In the "New Age" section at work we had a few things like that. Mainly books by Sylvia Browne, the psychic, a couple of ghost stories, a withered, donated copy of the *Necrocomicon* with a giant coffee ring on the cover, and a few assorted boxes of tarot cards that the stoner teenagers liked to check out. I'd start with the tarot and go from there.

I scanned the back of the box and decided to do a simple spread, just four cards; that seemed easy enough. I shuffled the deck, laid out the cards, and pondered. The box said to, "ask a question in your mind," but nothing was coming to me. Instead, I thought *This is stupid. I am drunk. Find the spell and bring me back.* With a shrug, I turned over the first card.

Judgment. I smirked. Okay, that was fitting. I was definitely full of judgment when it came to shit like this. I thumbed through the crumbling book to find out more.

The Judgment card may indicate the beginning of a new phase. The Questioner should feel that they have accomplished all they can and leave old phases with a sense of purpose, moving forward with the freedom to begin a fresh and unfettered start. New beginnings. Reanimation of long-dead feelings. Autumn leaves may die, but new life emerges from the barren tree.

I gaped at the card, which depicted a trumpet-bearing figure from the heavens playing for three barely-clad androgynous beings, who appeared to be dancing themselves out of shallow graves, then put it down in disgust. "These things are always like this," I said aloud, ignoring the rising of my gorge. "They seem super specific but really you just read yourself into it."

Reluctantly, I turned over the next card.

Death.

"Oh, fuck this." I wasn't drunk enough for *that*. After what I'd read of the judgment card, I was in no mood for whatever the death card had to tell me. Nope. I glanced briefly at the illustration on the card - a grinning skeleton holding a skinny scythe, tipping forward as though holding an imaginary hat - and put it on top of the pile. I shuffled the cards back in the deck and shoved the lot in my purse, spilling wine on my skirt in the process.

A card slipped out of the deck as I was putting them back. I turned it over and groaned. The death card again. This time I all but crammed it into the box and shoved my purse, deck and all, under the couch. Fuck you very much, no thanks, I'm good.

I should have taken it for the sign it was and put the kibosh on the whole plan, but I was stupid, drunk, and I get myself in trouble a lot due to those two aforementioned conditions. I sucked down the rest of the wine and decided to start the spell before I lost my nerve, threw up, or both.

Once the phone was propped up and filming, I held up the paper. "Sloan, you bitch. Look what you've made me do. You didn't believe. And now I'm here, sitting by myself, drunk on a Friday night, and what am I about to do? I'm going to raise the dead." I winked at the phone and turned back to the paper. A giggle escaped my lips, but suddenly it didn't seem all that funny. My arms were erupting with goosebumps.

I realized, as I began to read, that this was the first time I'd said the words out loud. The spell seemed simplistic; it rhymed, and it seemed so *basic* somehow. Cheesy or not, though, I couldn't deny the chill creeping up my back. I stubbornly continued anyway, inserting Phillip's name in the last line as I suspected I was supposed to do.

With salt in air and water in veins

> I call the pale rider to loosen his reins
> I call for death to loosen his chains
> I call for air to return to the breast
> I call for fire to ignite the rest
> Let what was earthside return once more
> Restart the clock, and settle the score
> Reanimate the dead flesh of man
> Render **Phillip Deville** alive again.

As I uttered the last word, the song abruptly stopped, and the lights went out. I was pitched into darkness.

Three

Startled, I fell backward. "What the fuck?" I felt like I'd been hit with a jolt of electricity right as the power had flickered off. My trailer was pitch black, and the air felt like it was thrumming. The hint of acrid smoke drifting past my nostrils smelled faintly of sulfur, but how could that be? I had only burned cinnamon clove scented wax and sage. Was it the breaker? Had the trailer been hit by lightning? I dusted myself off and got up off the floor, cursing. The bundle of sage was still smoldering on the table, so I grabbed it for light and stood up, feeling my way toward the kitchen.

The light was no longer blinking on my stove as I fumbled my way into the room, knocking over the broom that I'd stupidly propped up in the doorway. "Hey witch, there's your broom. Time to get the fuck outta Dodge," I joked, my voice shaky. I made my way by feel over to the control panel, opened the metal door and flipped the main breaker switch, then flipped it back. Nothing happened.

Had I forgotten to pay my power bill? It had happened before. Back before Tess had left, it got shut off every other month for non-payment. No, I was sure I'd paid it just a couple of weeks ago, and the power company wouldn't turn me off in the middle of the night anyway. As I made my way back to the living room, I heard little drops hitting the tin roof of the trailer. Rain. So the storm had made its way inland already. I sighed with relief; it was just a power outage. The wind was kicking up; I could hear it rattling the windows. Knowing my luck, we were in the middle of a hurricane. I hoped my small trailer could withstand it.

My phone was still recording. I could see the little red light by the camera, blinking away as I entered the room. Fumbling in the dark, I made my way back to it. "Sorry, Sloan," I said in a goofy voice, picking up the phone. "Looks like my spell was a little too powerful. I knocked the power out. See, that's why you shouldn't doubt my powers. Byeeee!"

I turned off the recording and called the power company. "Your call has been logged," the automated voice said. "A crew will be dispatched shortly. We will assist your address as soon as possible. In case of an emergency, dial 911." I flicked the phone off and sat on the couch. The place was quiet as a tomb, save for the sound of the deepening rain pinging on the tin roof and the howl of the wind. The bundle of sage was strong and fragrant in my hand, so strong it was giving me a headache. I blew it out and set it on the coffee table, then thought better of it and ran to grab a saucer. The last thing I needed was to burn down my house.

I was very drunk. My head was suddenly pounding, and my mouth was insanely dry. My entire body felt cold and numb, like I'd been sitting out in the snow for hours without a coat.

Fumbling my way back into the kitchen again, I grabbed a glass of water from the tap, careful to turn it off firmly in case it was a while before the power came back on. Being on well water, flushing toilets and running water was a luxury I didn't have in a power outage. Living right at the beach, you got used to these things. I'd been through so many sea storms and hurricanes I'd lost count. More than one tornado had raced right through this stretch of woods, which was directly between the sea and Brunswick. I'd been lucky so far, but tonight I didn't feel brave. It wasn't the storm – those were old hat, growing up in Coastal Georgia, especially after coming within feet of getting struck by lightning on Driftwood Beach last year – but rather the storm within *me.* I was so lonely, so adrift, that I'd just cast a spell and was now wandering around my trailer alone in the dark. Back in the early days, when we were happy, Tess and I would snuggle when the power went out. We didn't bother with candles. We'd just let the darkness claim us. Now, I'd give anything for a little light.

I greedily drank from the glass, deciding I might as well go to bed; it'd likely be the middle of the night before the power came back on. In these parts, a woman in a lowly singlewide trailer on the edge of town wasn't likely to be a priority. They'd be focused on the island and would get to the mainland later. I padded down my dark hallway into the bedroom and threw myself on the bed, pulling the bedclothes around me, shivering. I needed to wash my sheets; they felt gritty and wrinkled. I tucked my phone up under my pillow in case of emergency and was drifting off into sleep in seconds, thanks to the booze.

I woke up the next morning to the overhead light blaring bright above me. My head was still pounding and the taste of stale, rancid grapes was all over my tongue, which felt a size too big. I pulled myself up from the bed and groaned as I made my way into the bathroom. Through the little window in the living room, I could see a tree down in the front yard. Likely there were more.

I peed, washed my hands and brushed my teeth, remembering the night before. My lips were stained, a line of dark red dividing my bottom lip in half. I searched my booze-drenched brain, trying to remember last night's events. I'd drunk a whole bottle of wine and had the bright idea to try and cast a spell. Then the power had gone out.

As I walked to the kitchen to make a pot of industrial strength coffee, I realized that I'd never sent the video to Sloan. That had been the whole point of doing the damn thing, and I'd totally forgotten. As the coffee percolated, I scrolled through my phone, opening our text history and tapping "add attachment." As I searched for the video, I frowned. It wasn't there. Maybe the file was too big. I'd have to send it through Facebook or upload it to YouTube. I went into my picture gallery and looked through my most recent photos and videos. Pictures of Blinken, a few screen shots, and that was it. Nothing from the night before. It was as if I'd never taken the video, though I knew I had, clearly remembering the little blinking red light in the dark. But there was no video in my camera gallery. Had I deleted it somehow?

I slammed my phone down on the table, angry. I'd done that entire stupid spell for absolutely fucking nothing.

IN THE BRIGHT MORNING LIGHT, the humidity of the storm still lingering in the air, my house looked like a hot mess. I could see trails of dust on my counters and I hadn't done dishes in days. It was disgraceful, I thought, as I drank the last dregs of cold coffee from my favorite Snoopy cup. I couldn't keep living like this. Hungover, haggard, lonely, bored.

When Tess had been around, I'd been a dutiful little homemaker, the kind of woman that I despised, but I'd justified it.

I'd cleaned up his messes, cooked his dinner most nights, washed his skid-marked underwear. And for what? He'd cheated on me not once, but many times, had brought drugs into our house, squandered our money and left me like a chump. And who was I now? Just a loser sitting in a singlewide trailer that faintly smelled of trash with a kitchen floor that hadn't been mopped since the day before he left, doing spells to try and raise the dead. Oh, of course it was all *hock-and-booey,* but just the fact that I'd done it was proof that I was not the person I once was. The person I used to be snickered and left the room in disgust if Tess even turned on *Ancient Aliens.*

The truth, I suspected, was that I was starting to lose it. Left to my own devices, I was headed full swing toward a nervous breakdown. I had to take charge before it was too late, and I became some daft hippie smelling of raw milk. I snorted, then remembered the way the perfectly coifed, fancy Brunswick Moms had made fun of the Goat's Milk Soap Lady in our group. It bothered me the way they mocked her, had little in-jokes at her expense. Sloan and I had our share of gossip and snark, but I liked to think it wasn't from a place of malice. I was going to have to work on not becoming one of those bitter women I hated.

I tied up my blonde hair in a messy bun, threw on an old work shirt, and set out to do the chores I'd been neglecting for weeks. I started with my disgusting sheets, which I threw in the washer. Then I mopped the floor, did the dishes, vacuumed the rugs and my couches, washed out the coffee pot with vinegar, and cleaned the toilets. It took me most of the day, but I felt better, albeit sweaty and grimy, when it was done. I hopped in the shower, feeling brighter than I had in weeks. I ventured outside in my rain boots and picked up the debris from the fallen trees that I was able to get on my own and made a mental note to ask Sloan to send her uncle over to get the rest.

He had a logging business and would collect it free of charge. He might even chop some of it into firewood for me if I asked. Tasks done, I felt much better. Before I knew it, I was in my car and heading for the farmer's market.

I decided I would make vegan flautas for dinner. Something about rolling up the little corn flutes and deep frying the crap out of them always calmed me, even if it did fill my house with the smell of grease. I'd make some guacamole, too, maybe stop on the way back and grab another bottle of that Merlot - see if Sloan wanted to drop by. I still needed to hear how her date had gone. We could have one of our slumber parties. It'd be a nice way to cap off a productive day, and maybe when I went back to work on Monday things would still be looking up and I could truly forget about my shitty ex-husband who I still craved.

It's all about intention, I told myself.

The farmer's market was bustling as usual; it always was on Saturdays. There was a line snaked around the booth that sold fresh-baked chocolate croissants and an even longer one at the coffee station. There was a band playing on the small wooden makeshift stage over by the playground, and a group of children were drawing in chalk on the pavement. A mom with a stroller took a discreet sip of something from a lemonade bottle, and when she saw me notice, she winked. I headed toward the grocer booths, laughing to myself. I wasn't the only one with problems.

I grabbed a few ripe avocados, handing exact change to the farmer, who was about my age and despite wearing old-man overalls, fairly adorable. He had clear, bright eyes and an easy smile. He handed me a bag. "Do you come to here every weekend? I don't think I've seen you before."

I opened my mouth to answer, but then something caught my eye and the words died in my throat.

A few booths down, over by Goat's Milk Soap lady and her

sage bundles, was a man. Clad in a tight black t-shirt and black jeans reminiscent of the mid-90s, military boots, and a black coat, he was an imposing figure, with rippling hair that flew behind him in the morning breeze. He stared at me intently from behind the soaps, his expression unreadable. He was overdressed – it was late September, but hot and humid as all get-out – this was Georgia, after all. He didn't need a coat. His hair was a glossy jet black, pulled back in a severe ponytail, but it was so long it still blew in the coastal air. He was tall - no, tall didn't do it justice - *hulking*, standing a foot over the woman, who was trying pretty hard to make a sale. She looked like a waif next to him, standing there in a light pink sundress with her neck craned, holding up a rosy colored square for him to smell. He reached down gingerly and took it from her hands with the grace of a cat, his hands huge with thin fingers. He put the soap to his nose, smiling at her politely, but he was still looking at *me*.

My breath caught and I forgot all about the avocados, the cute young farmer and the bag he was holding out to me. It couldn't be. It was impossible.

I was looking at *Phillip Deville*.

"Um, miss? Your bag?"

I shook my head and smiled goofily, wrenching my eyes away. "I'm sorry," I said. "I thought I saw someone I knew." I took the bag from him and moved to go. His face fell a little.

"I was just asking if you come here every weekend-"

But I was staring back toward the soap booth, looking for the tall black-haired man who had just been standing there. He was gone. Had I imagined him?

"I'm sorry," I said again, turning to the blond guy in the overalls, vaguely aware that I'd been rude. "You were saying?"

"Never mind." He smiled good-naturedly, giving up. "You have a nice day, now."

Damn. He'd been flirting with me. There I went, imagining

dead rock stars and ignoring the cute hipster farmer trying to pick me up. Another chance lost. I gave him a sweet smile, hoping it hid my embarrassment, and walked out of the booth, kicking myself. What had come over me? Had my drunken tarot night really fucked with my head that much?

I scanned the crowd, my eyes falling briefly on a soft, matte black leather jacket in the crowd. Then it was gone, lost among the throng. The band had started playing, and folks were gathering near the stage. Kids were crouched down on the pavement, making chalk figures. Dogs with bandannas and monogrammed t-shirts led their owners through the aisles. I forced myself to smile, but I couldn't shake the feeling that whatever, whoever I was trying to see, was watching *me*.

I stopped at another booth to buy a bunch of bright-green collards that looked inviting. I was reaching for my wallet when out of the corner of my eye I saw him again. I looked up, slowly, and he smiled. Standing there in the avocado booth, where I'd just been, he was unmistakable. It *had* to be Philip Deville; the man was a dead ringer. Down to the flashing green eyes, the cupid's bow mouth, the dark, heavy brows. *But it couldn't be.* I shoved my money at the woman with the collards, and squaring my shoulders, stepped out into the mass of people, trying to decide if I should approach the man or run.

The band onstage was a ukulele-and-banjo playing duo - brothers, folksy guys who played here often. They were doing a cover of a Mr. Bungle tune I hadn't heard in forever. It was giving me a weird feeling of deja vu. My brain searched for the title and came up blank. I tried to assure myself that I wasn't going crazy, but with my ears swimming and my head ringing, it was hard to believe it. *Retrovertigo.* That was the song. A fitting title, considering how I felt right now. My eyes searched for the mysterious man, lost again in the crowd.

I stumbled over to the bread booth, hoping they might have corn tortillas for my flautas, still trying to shake myself out of the trance, caused by what had to be the world's worst hangover. Could you hallucinate from drinking too much? Fuck, I had to get ahold of myself; it was too much. *I* was too much.

There was a man standing in front of me, tall with dark, pulled back brown hair and a black t-shirt emblazoned with the Metallica logo. He was wearing a light black jacket, rolled up to his forearms, and was quite handsome. *He's the guy I saw,* I told myself. *You just saw the tall guy with dark hair and your imagination filled in the rest.* I smiled at him and reached for a bag of tortillas. He gave me a warm smile in return and went back to picking out his bread. He was holding the hand of a little girl in a green dress, explaining to her the different types – rye, pumpernickel, ciabatta. I sighed with relief, the mystery solved, willing my heartbeat to slow down and making myself the sincere promise that I would not drink a single drop of alcohol tonight.

The taller of the brothers on the stage was singing, his voice light and airy and full of sugared irony and I stood there a moment, taking it in. Then a flash of glimmering black hair, absorbing a ray of sunlight, a tall, rigid back rounding a corner and ducking behind a booth. I blinked; there was nothing in front of me but cottony, homemade handbags and buckwheat pasta. It was time to go home.

I headed toward the exit, my shopping done. I felt oddly cheerful, considering my wooziness and what had to be some serious dehydration-induced hallucinations. It might be a good idea to go home and grab a nap before starting dinner. And I'd drink at least a gallon of water. No more wine. At least for a couple of days. I was drinking too damn much, and it was making my brain weird.

Someone knocked into me, hard. I dropped my bag full of food.

"Oh, damn. I'm sorry!" The young man reached down and

grabbed the bag and handed it back to me. "I didn't mean to just mow over you there."

He had run smack into me while holding a huge bouquet of flowers, and now I had white and yellow petals all over me. I brushed off my shirt and looked at him. His wide silver-blue eyes were a little frantic. "It's fine." I held out my hand for the bag, masking my irritation, and he handed it over. I'd never seen a grown man with so many freckles. His hair was sandy colored with threads of silver, most of it tucked under a ball cap. He was wearing a red polo shirt with the Georgia "G" on it, which made his flushed baby face appear even pinker. Despite the silver strands of hair, I guessed he couldn't be more than twenty or so. "Thanks."

He stood there a moment, seemingly ready to say something else, but I moved past him and kept walking out toward the parking lot and my car. So I'd struck out twice due to my own social ineptitude, but it just wasn't my day. My stomach was rumbling angrily, and I realized I hadn't eaten since the day before. No wonder I felt half insane. Bumping into freckled frat boys and floating obliviously past cute farmer guys were the least of my worries. My blood sugar was so low I was hallucinating dead rock stars.

On the drive home, I blasted Pantera loud enough to wake the dead and shook my head clear of all the nonsense – both from the night before and at the farmer's market. I told myself that I was being silly, that I was letting my imagination get away from me, that it was just a good old-fashioned dose of anxiety combined with loneliness and that I needed to decompress. A long talk with Sloan full of her acerbic, rough-around-the-edges support combined with a good bang (I decided I'd go back to the farmer's market tomorrow and give cute avocado guy my number) should do the trick. I'd eat a good meal. I'd go to bed early. *It's all about intention.*

I'd managed to finally convince myself that it was all a

bunch of hock-and-booey right up until I walked up onto my front porch. My foot stuck for a moment on the welcome mat, and when I moved it, a string of turquoise-colored gum stretched out from my shoe to the carpet. Fuck, my favorite burgundy chucks. Groaning, I pulled my foot upward to remove the gum and had to brace myself against the door when I saw the tarot card stuck to the sole. I knew which card it was before I pulled it off. *Death.*

Four

"Stormy, you've lost your goddamn mind." Sloan dipped a chip into the guacamole and grimaced as it broke. "Fuck, man overboard." She grabbed another chip, rescuing the first one, and popped it all in her mouth. "You are batshit, woman."

"Don't talk with your mouth full," I said irritably, but I was laughing. "I'm telling you, it happened. I did the spell, and the lights went out, like, immediately. And the video that *I know* I took, wasn't in my gallery."

"You probably deleted it by accident when you turned it off," she said in a logical voice that I loathed. She broke a chip in half and dipped it. "And that storm was a doozy last night. I heard there was a tornado in Glynn Haven and that's not far from here. The lights actually flickered at the bar where Dan and I were-"

"I noticed the storm," I interjected, "I'm just saying it's weird, that's all."

"Well, anyway, point being, your little spell didn't work." She gestured around my tiny trailer. "I see no middle-aged rock stars lurking around."

"Yeah, too bad." I'd been getting ready to tell her about the man I'd seen watching me at the farmers market and changed my mind. Sloan had an edge to her tonight, more than usual. I decided she wouldn't find it funny. Instead, she might give me a lecture, or worse, bring up Tess. "So what about the death card turning up everywhere?"

"It's an old deck. The box won't even shut properly. See?" She grabbed the little cardboard box off the table and demonstrated how the top wouldn't stay folded down. "You said you pulled the death card last night, right? When you put it back, it probably didn't go all the way in the box. It just fell out. And we both know how bad you are about throwing away your gum without wrapping it in paper first."

"That doesn't explain-"

"It does, though," she cut me off.

I poured a glass of Merlot and held it out to her. She waved it away.

"You seem bitchy," I remarked, taking the glass for myself despite my vows from before. I hadn't yet eaten anything. With the way Sloan was murdering my guacamole I might not get to. I had, at least, managed to down a ton of water. I'd been peeing all evening. "You know, more so than usual." She gave me a sharp look, then laughed.

"You know me too well." She grimaced. "I guess I am kinda salty."

"Date not go well?"

"Oh, that. No, it went great, actually. Jeez, Stormy, you wouldn't guess it from looking at him – he's so cute, but he's got this pinched up expression he does, like he's wound up so tight a fart couldn't escape – but once I got his clothes off, he warmed up rather nicely. And hung like a-"

"Stop!" I protested, laughing.

"The date was fine," she went on. "I had fun, actually. But I probably won't see him again."

"Why not?"

The doorbell rang.

"Saved by the bell. I'll get it." Sloan stood up. "You stay there and have another drink. I'll need you to figure out my life when I get back."

I did as I was told. So much for not drinking tonight. Sloan had shown up with a bottle of my favorite wine and I'd barely even resisted. I drained the glass as she reached the front door, peered through the peephole, muttered, and opened it. "Weird." I could see her from my vantage point at the table as she poked her head out, then walked out onto the porch, her hand over her eyes. It was after seven and already dark. "Weird," she said again, walking down the steps and into the yard.

"Nobody there?" I asked when she returned.

"Not a soul." She came back inside, shut the door and locked both the deadbolt and the lock on the handle. "I heard that knock as clear as day, didn't you?"

"Yeah, definitely."

"Probably some stupid kid overeager for Halloween," she said, sitting down and digging into the guac again.

"Out here? I've only got the one neighbor and he's old as dust. No kids."

"Teenagers roam," she said. "But I'll stay over, just in case. You need looking after. You've been a hot mess lately."

"Oh, shut the fuck up." I laughed. "I have not. And Blinken could take better care of me than you could." The cat, sleeping in his kitty bed in the corner, gave one sassy swish of his tail. "So-you were starting to tell me why you're salty."

"Oh, it's nothing. Nothing good, anyway," she said with a grin. "No gossip. I'm just...I dunno. I guess I keep wondering how long I'm going to do this."

"Do what?"

She looked at me, one eyebrow raised.

"Oh, no, Sloan." I groaned. "Don't tell me you've gone back to *him.*"

For the past two years, Sloan had been having an on-and-off-again, very casual affair with a guy who was quite a bit her senior. I didn't know how much older, but I figured it must be a lot, judging by how cagey Sloan was about him. One thing I did know: he was married. From what little Sloan had told me, they'd met when she'd taken a second job tending bar at Beachy Keen, one of our local crawls. He'd flirted and she was unimpressed, telling him he was far too old for her. Then he'd tipped her a hundred bucks for one Miller Lite and she'd reconsidered. I didn't even know his real name – she called him Gus, but it was a nickname, I knew, taken from Disney's Cinderella – when I asked her, she laughed and said it was because he wore t-shirts to bed, but no pants. As disgusting a mental image as that was (and I suspected she was trolling me, hoping to gross me out so I wouldn't ask more questions), I'd never pressed her further.

She was my best friend and we shared *everything*, but she would not budge one inch when it came to Gus. She was ashamed of the affair, ashamed that she couldn't break it off. All I knew was that they'd go weeks or even months without speaking, and then, out of the blue, she'd be seeing him again every night, hot and heavy, until he inevitably got cold feet again and ended things. Any time I brought him up, Sloan started fidgeting and curling into herself and acting uncharacteristically shamed, and I didn't enjoy seeing her like that. Like a snail without a shell, covered in salt.

As funny as it was to think of my best friend as a slug, the entire situation left me with a case of the squicks, and I didn't like it one bit. Surely Sloan didn't love him, but even so, it messed with her head. Nobody's self-esteem could weather such hot-and-cold head games. And whatever money he threw her way wasn't enough to get her out of poverty, so to my thinking, he just wasn't fucking worth it.

Sloan told me *everything* and always had, so her silence on Gus told me all I needed to know.

"It's only been a couple of times lately," she said, peering into her wine glass like she'd lost something in it. "And now that I'm seeing Dan, I'm really tempted to just end it for good."

"You should."

"I know."

I had another sip of wine and wisely said nothing.

"I'll do that," she said with finality, looking up at me with a smile. But I could tell by the way her eyes shifted to the right that she was full of shit.

WHEN I GOT up the next morning, Sloan had made coffee and was sitting at the kitchen table, holding a cigarette in her hand. "I'm not smoking it," she rushed to explain when she saw me. "I know the rule. I'll go outside."

"I wish you wouldn't smoke at all," I lectured her.

"Yeah, yeah. One of these days I'll quit."

"Good," I said, walking over to the fridge to grab the creamer. "What time is it?"

"8:30. Shit, Stormy, you look like hell."

"Well, thanks, and fuck you very much, too."

"How much did you drink last night?"

"I dunno, a couple. You're the one who kept pushing glasses into my hand." I poured myself a cup and added two heaping teaspoons of sugar. "I haven't been sleeping well."

"Tess?"

No point in lying. "Yeah," I confessed. "Ever since you told me he's back I can't seem to stop thinking about him. I wonder if he's going to come back here."

"Don't take him back, Storm."

"I won't!" I said, irritated. "Anyway, he has *Roberta.*"

She leveled her eyes at me. "I'm serious, dude. You've been all over the place lately. Drinking too much, this weird spell shit..." I opened my mouth to protest and she cut me off. "I think you're allowed a little crisis after all that fucker put you through, but I'm just saying, you're vulnerable right now and people like him prey on weakness."

I sipped my coffee and said nothing. It chafed that she was talking as though she knew him better than I did. Like she knew me better than I knew myself. Like she didn't have her own giant turd of a situation to navigate. *People like him,* she'd said. Something about the judgement in that turn of phrase bothered me. "It's only been a few months," I said finally. "I'm doing the best I can."

"It's been the better part of a year," she argued. "Just don't leave yourself open. You know?" She looked at me thoughtfully. "Don't let bad stuff in."

I smiled at that and she brightened.

"So, what are we doing today, Brain? Trying to take over the world?"

"I hadn't got that far," I said, still drinking my coffee. "I'm barely awake."

She looked me up and down, taking in my rat's nest hair and worn, faded Motley Crue t-shirt. "Throw on some pants and let's head over to my booth," she said. "What you need is a makeover. It'll perk you right up. Cut and color, and I'll thread your brows, because they are a total mess-"

"No, no, Sloan," I protested. "Not the fucking brows again. For the last time, I don't want them threaded. You know I don't care about that stuff. And anyway, I can't afford you."

"Oh, shut the fuck up," she said. "You feed me every other day. It's free, dipshit."

"Sloan-"

"Fine, I won't thread the brows. Just let me pluck them a

little. I swear, it's like you're a cave person. I can't keep looking at them like that, I'm sorry." It was true, I never did anything to them. Didn't have the slightest notion how to use a brow brush or pencil and only plucked them once in a blue moon. They were thick and unkempt, and I really didn't give the first shit, which made Sloan crazy, since beauty was her business. Her own brows were perfectly arched and filled in with a specific shade of brown-black that she bought in bulk from the beauty store just in case it was ever discontinued.

I sighed. "Maybe just a little haircut. Just a trim." If I was going to ask out the avocado guy, I should spiff myself up some.

She nodded excitedly. "A trim, maybe some bangs? Add a few low-lights? And I've got this new gloss-"

I groaned. There wasn't enough coffee in the world.

HOURS LATER, I let myself back into the house and sighed, slumping down on the couch with my newly shaped brows, trimmed hair, bangs and violet low-lights, and a foundation on my face that seemed a shade too light for my skin, but Sloan insisted made me look "fresher." As much as I loved her, I was glad that she hadn't come back with me, instead opting to go out with Dan again (so much for her "I probably won't see him again"). I was tired, and more than a little down in the dumps. All my mantras from the day before had gone right down the drain. I'd never even made it back to the farmers market to flirt with avocado guy.

The entire time she'd been making me over I'd been thinking about Tess. What would he think of my hair, would he like the winged eyeliner, would he...? And hating myself for it. Who cared what he thought? He was a cheating, drugged-out bastard. And anyway, he had a girlfriend, and if he had brought her back to our hometown, he obviously was serious about her. I needed to just let go.

So why couldn't I?

I rarely allowed myself to think back to the time Tess and I met. I'd been a total mess then, having just emancipated myself from my parents' home (they would divorce less than a year later; turns out I had been the glue holding their dysfunction together), staying with Sloan and her parents and trying to figure out what to do with myself. Seventeen and newly homeless, I was vulnerable and scared.

When I'd seen the pool guy, shirtless and grinning, one afternoon at Sloan's house, his brown hair falling over one eye as he bent over to skim leaves from the water, it had been love at first sight. For me, anyway. It had taken a few weeks for Tess, who was nineteen at the time, to work up the nerve to ask me out. Once he did, we were inseparable. I'd never forget that summer, newly independent and full of possibility, cruising with Tess in his pickup to go bowling, play pool, frolic on the beach...he'd taken me to shows, out to dinner, and we'd spent more nights than most making out in the bed of his truck, parked in the pine trees, with only the stars to keep us company.

Only Tess and Sloan knew about my past, about my horrible, abusive parents and the abject poverty I'd grown up in. Only the two of them knew my darkest secrets and had loved me anyway. I'd never forget the first time I'd brought Tess home – first I'd taken him to my mom, who still lived in the trailer park where I'd spent most of my childhood, and he'd sat dutifully on her threadbare couch while she'd chain-smoked, chugged Natty Lights and regaled him with stories of my childhood. I'd been red-faced and embarrassed as she related how, at eight years old, I'd peed my pants from fright at a school assembly when I had to get up and speak. Tess had held my hand, laughing kindly, and leaned over to kiss my cheek. He'd drank several beers with Mom, let her bum smokes all afternoon, and left with her red-lipsticked seal of approval on his cheek. Shortly after, I'd taken him to Dad's to meet my glossy, born-again new stepmom, Dee, and the baby girl that had arrived two and half months before their wedding. Dad now lived with Dee and Shably (that poor kid, she'd spend her whole life telling folks that her name was *not* Shelby, but that she was named after a misspelled, cheap wine) in Panama City Beach, where they had an apartment just one street up from the water. Tess had been a good sport when I'd complained the whole time, mocking the clean white beaches and clear, blue expanse of ocean, preferring the murky, swamp-like seas of Jekyll, and insulting the tourists. He'd been well-behaved, respectful and engaging when Dad had taken us all to a fancy steakhouse for dinner, trying to show off his newfound money, and he'd hugged Dee goodbye when we left. They'd loved him, too. Even Sloan had loved him, and she didn't love much of anybody.

Tess had come into my life at a time when I'd needed him. He had embraced my family, my issues and quirks, and I'd loved him with my whole heart for over a decade. I thought back over those years, unable to make sense of how he'd become such a totally different person, and how on earth I hadn't noticed my husband slowly becoming another version of the past I'd run away from.

I shook my head, determined not to do this now. I wouldn't spend one more night in a shitty slump, brooding over my pain. I had a new 'do, my house was freshly cleaned, and I had a Sunday evening free with no plans. I'd make the most of it. I'd put on some music and do yoga. *Improving myself starts now.*

I threw on a pair of tight-fitting yoga capris and left on my faded, baggy Motley Crue shirt. I pulled my hair up in a loose ponytail, careful not to mess up Sloan's hard work. I always waited a day after a new hair-do before washing it, just to get some extra enjoyment out of it. I passed by my little makeshift altar on the way to the stereo and made a mental note to clear all of it away; my failed attempt at a spell. I felt mild shame that I'd even done it in the first place. I really had to get my shit together.

What to listen to...Outkast? Too upbeat for yoga. The Cure? Too depressing. Ah, I knew. Siousxie and the Banshees. But as I turned on the stereo and clicked through the changer, it was the Bloomer Demons I settled on, as usual.

Fire, Blood, and Candy was their third album, released after they'd started to wane a little in popularity, and while the lyrics were full of deep-seated angst, the melodies added a sort of pop-ambiance to their normal doom metal sound. A lot of their fans hated it, but I didn't. Didn't matter to me what direction they took – *you can't fight true love.*

I lay down on the rubber mat, which was gnawed a little on one side thanks to Blinken, and relaxed into corpse pose, controlling my breathing to the beat of the music. How Sloan would laugh at me if she saw me doing yoga. It was another thing – along with tarot reading and spells – that I'd always scoffed at. I'm not a very spiritual person. I'm pragmatic, logical. I believe in science. I'm that annoying person that retweets videos from Scientist Twitter and goes on drunken rants about the evils of organized religion. Just after my divorce, Sloan had set me up with a guy who had raved half the night about the Illuminati. He'd been surprised when I got up in the middle of dinner and left.

Why, I wondered as I settled down onto the mat, feeling my bones relax, did I feel the need to hide parts of myself? Despite my snark, I'd been secretly doing yoga for years. It relaxed me, made me feel less on edge. I'd been dabbling with tarot cards for a few months now, and I could feel part of me blossoming, taking to the new age, "woo" side of me like a parched plant to water. Why had I never told Sloan? Or anyone else, for that matter?

Tess left and I lost myself. I didn't know who I was anymore. The truth was, I had already begun to change long before he left, but the end of my marriage had pushed me over the edge. Whatever I was becoming had the feeling of something *big*. I didn't know if I was about to have a mid-life crisis of my own or if it was my new emancipation, but I could feel it coming, calling me, just on the edge of my awareness, in my peripheral vision.

I shifted into the snake pose and focused on stretching each muscle one by one. Next, downward dog. My shirt billowed down, exposing my belly, and I stretched my neck out, not looking, determined not to be critical of the softness around my waist band.

I went through some semblance of a routine, and by the time I was back in corpse pose, I was panting heavily, sweat running down my face and neck in rivulets. I was so out of shape. I'd been living on nothing but fried food, coffee and wine for weeks. It seemed like eons since I'd run on Driftwood Beach. My normal ritual was to do that every other day, riding my bike on the weekends. I had saved for two years to buy a beach-ready road bike. Now it sat out under the shed, collecting rust.

I grabbed a hoodie from the couch and mopped at my face – after all, there was nobody there to see me – and was standing up and reaching for my glass of water when I heard the doorbell. I stood there, wondering if I should even answer it. It was after dark, I was home alone, and after the night before with the pranksters, I was a little concerned.

"Who is it?" I asked, grabbing my phone and pushing it down into the waistband of my yoga pants. As if I'd have time to dial 911 if it was really someone intent on doing me harm. I craned my neck, listening for the answer.

"It's me."

It was a male voice, one I didn't immediately recognize. But "it's me" implied that I knew them. Against my better judgment, I went to the door, unlocked the deadbolt, turned the door handle, and pulled it open.

I stood there for a moment in the darkness, staring up at the man on my doorstep. He was so tall the door frame was almost level with his dark green eyes, which flashed in the dim light of the porch. He repeated, again, the voice soft but deep as a well, "It's me. Phillip."

The next thing I knew I was traveling downward toward the floor, which I hit with a loud *thud.*

Five

THE HANDS THAT WERE TOUCHING MY FACE WERE SOFT BUT cool, the fingers calloused. "Stormy Spooner, wake up. You okay?"

I was in arms that felt strong and were holding me tight. My eyes were closed. I surmised that I was lying on the floor where I'd fallen – no, fainted – and he had knelt down to check on me, cradling me in his arms. I'd had some kind of hallucination, some episode, probably because I hadn't eaten anything other than espresso beans and had exercised with no substance in me. I would open my eyes and it would be someone else holding me. Sloan, or even Tess. But Sloan didn't smell like woodsmoke and sandalwood, and Tess's arms weren't firm and strong like these...

I took a deep breath and opened my eyes, just peering a little at first. Then they opened wide, disbelieving.

Sitting above me, his long, ink-black hair falling into my face, with an expression of both concern and amusement, was Phillip Deville.

Phillip Deville.

THE Phillip Deville, lead singer, violinist, bassist and

sometime harmonica player for the Bloomer Demons, cult-famous rock star, poet, legend. And dead for– I tried to do the calculations in my woozy head – twenty-three years?

I lay there in his arms, my head buzzing, unable to sit up, though I wanted to. I wanted to flee from the house and run screaming into the trees. This could not be. It wasn't possible. I was seeing a ghost. I opened my mouth, but no sound came out. The eyes that stared down at me were like emeralds, a dark shining green, the expression in them kind. But I was terrified.

He brushed a hair from my face, then tucked his own behind his ears. "Are you okay?" he asked again.

"I... you died when I was in high school," I stammered stupidly. "It was on the news." As though this gave it more legitimacy.

"MTV News?"

I looked at him, befuddled, and managed to choke out. "Yes, but also the, er, evening news. NBC. CBS. All of them."

He looked pleased. Then he threw back his head and laughed. "Did Kurt Loder break in with a bulletin? I always hated that fucking guy. I hope he had to do it."

I tittered dumbly, this time the words unintelligible. It was entirely possible that I would pass out again.

He chuckled softly, his sharp white teeth shining in the dim room. "I've given you quite a shock," he said in a quiet voice that was very deep despite his low, soft tone. "Though you shouldn't be shocked, really, should you, Stormy Spooner?"

"I don't understand."

"Find the spell and bring me back," he said softly, and put a hand around my waist, pulling me up to a sitting position.

I stared at him. "Spells aren't real," I said incredulously, the blood roaring in my ears. "Especially not that one. A third-grader could have written it."

"I think I've just been insulted." His rosebud mouth curled into a dangerous grin. "And yet."

I shook my head dumbly. "No. I'm a fucking atheist for god's sake."

His laughter was like tinkling glass distorted through a bass pedal. He slapped a knee. "That was very good, Stormy Spooner."

"Stop calling me by both names." I shook my head, moving away from his arms, but they held me fast. "I don't understand. Are you really Phillip Deville?"

"Yeah, I am," he answered affably. "Or was."

"But how?" I took in his face – long, straight nose that came to a soft point, almond shaped eyes, hint of stubble on a squarish chin, elfin ears, long hair – he'd worn it several different ways back in the height of his career. Sometimes it had been copper red, wavy and shining, other times he'd worn it frizzy and spiky on his head, then the chestnut-brown phase when he'd kept it mid-length and tucked under a police cap (after he'd been arrested for the second time on drug charges and served a stint in jail), the "Cruella" phase, parted down the middle with one side black and the other bleached white, and then finally jet black, worn long, like a vampire. That was how it had looked when he'd died, and it was how it looked now. I reached out to touch a strand, still not believing he could be real. I hadn't had even one drink today. "You cannot seriously be saying that I did this, that I brought you back. It's not possible."

"How else could I be here?" he asked and pulled me upright. We rose to our feet. He towered over me. Those bios that boasted his height at 6'5" had not been false. At 5'9", I considered myself tall for a woman, but he dwarfed me.

"I'm hallucinating. I'm having a dream. I *have* lost my goddamn mind."

"You look fine to me."

"Sloan is playing a joke on me. She sent somebody here to pretend to be you-"

"I don't know any Sloan," he said thoughtfully. "But that'd be a good band name."

I stared. "How...how did you know where to go? How to find me?"

"You summoned me," he said simply. "It was like an impulse in my head. I just followed it."

"Like your own little GPS witch computer in your noggin'," I said, feeling hysterical and light-headed, and began to giggle.

"What's GPS?" he asked, dark brow furrowing.

"Never mind." I felt woozy and leaned into him without thinking. His arm was as solid and bulky as a rock.

"Do you have anything to drink?" he asked, an arm going around me like it was second nature. "It was a long trip. Evidently being dead makes you thirsty."

"W-what do you want?" I sputtered, in a state of disbelief. "Water, coffee, tea...?"

"Do you have any red wine?" he asked with a hint of a smile. "I haven't had red wine in so long."

"I do, actually," I said, and managed to smile back, though I was pretty sure I'd be in the loony bin by this time tomorrow and probably looked like a Muppet. "We – um, me and Sloan – drank most of it, but I have a couple glasses left."

"That's great. Thanks." His lips curled again. "It'll be like first communion."

I stared blankly. Finally, he nudged me forward, toward the kitchen.

"You said it was a long trip. Did you, um...fly?"

"Of course not," he said, amused, following me down the hall. "I took a bus. Turns out all those coins people throw in graves come in handy."

This time I was able to reach out for the wall to brace myself, before slumping to the floor.

I RUBBED AT MY EYES, but the vision in front of me was definitely there. I was propped up, sitting at my kitchen table, my head resting on my hands. Phillip Deville was standing over by my fridge holding a half-empty bottle of red, pulling the cork out with his fingers. I'd never seen anyone actually *look* thirsty, but he did. It was like something out of a commercial; wild, caveman looking guy with *deep, big thirst.* He took a whiff of the contents, his eyes closing in pleasure, then took a long swig from the bottle. I watched his lips move over the rim and caught my breath. He held it in his mouth, savoring it.

"It's not worth all that," I said. "We just buy it at the liquor store down the road. It's not, like, good stuff or anything."

"It's been years since I've tasted wine," he said in a moan of pleasure. "It could be Night-Train and I'd be in heaven. Oh, shit. Sorry. I should have poured it in a glass."

I waved a hand. "It's fine. Glasses are behind you, though."

I watched as he poured one for each of us. It was the last thing I needed, since I was still so woozy, but I accepted it politely. He sat down beside me and just stared, waiting for me to speak.

"Is that even a thing?" I asked incredulously. "Night-Train? I thought that was just a Guns 'n Roses song."

"It was real back in the day," he said, closing his eyes. "Cheap shit. Worst hangover of your life. Make you wish you were dead."

The word "dead" gave me a chill. "I can't...believe it's really you," I managed to say, leaning against the table for support. "I may die. Of a heart attack. Or possibly a stroke."

"Don't stroke out on me. I'm not sure if dead guys can do CPR." He grinned. "Though I do appear to be breathing."

"This is all a dream. Just a dream. I'm going to wake up any second." I shook my head back and forth, hard enough to make my cheeks jiggle. "I'm going to pick up the phone and dial and it won't ring. Or I'll try to scream, and no sound will come out. Or I'll run and run and never get anywhere. This is a panic dream."

He smiled. "You're funny. Hey, what year is it?"

My mouth fell open. "Seriously?"

"My clock seems to have stopped," he said with a wry smile.

"Um."

"You got it, right?"

Phillip Deville, my favorite dead rock star, told dad jokes. I rested my head on my hand, feeling tunnel vision set in. "2019," I said slowly.

"I died in...1997. So I've been dead what..." He thought. "Twenty-two years?"

"Closer to twenty-three," I said weakly, staring down at my glass. "I was in, um, my first year of high school."

"Christ," he muttered. "All those supposed die-hard fans and it took twenty-two years for somebody to do the fucking spell."

"Well, you did have it hidden pretty well," I said. "That rare vinyl goes for like five hundred bucks on Ebay these days. I just lucked out."

"That record seriously pulls five hundred bucks? Fucking gougers." He looked pleased with himself.

"Shouldn't surprise you. The second you died all that stuff skyrocketed in value. People love their dead rock stars."

Did he wince? "I guess they do." He took another sip of wine. "I guess it took my being dead to hit the big time. But still...five hundred bucks for that shitty record. I can't believe it, man."

"It's not a shitty record," I said defensively. "It's a piece of art."

He raised an eyebrow and laughed.

"It is," I insisted. When he didn't respond, I added, "I got it for a steal."

"Well, I'm glad for that." He was still smiling. "And obviously, you deciphered the spell on the back?"

"Kinda. I found some folks speculating about it online, on reddit-" He looked confused. "-and just sort of looked over it. Honestly, I don't even know how – I mean, I'm not a witch, I've never done a spell before, I didn't even have half of the proper supplies-"

His dark eyes settled on me, a question in them, and I had to look away, my words getting lost. He was too intense. "But you had the power, evidently."

"I didn't mean to." My cheeks burned. "I've been listening to your music a lot lately. It helps get me through-" I looked down. Famous people probably thought it was so cheesy when they heard that type of flowery, pathetic praise from fans. "I'm sure you were tired of hearing that from desperate, sad losers two decades ago."

"No," he said softly. "I'd never get tired of that."

I blushed. "I've been your biggest fan since longer than I'd care to admit."

"High school, at least," he said with a sly grin. "I'm not sure how to feel about that. I'd say I feel old, but." He sipped his wine. "I think that's pretty ungrateful, considering."

"How *do* you feel?" I asked, curious. "I mean, considering where you've, er, been..."

He put his long, muscled arms out in front of him and considered them. Somewhere between my front door and the kitchen he'd pulled off his black leather jacket and was now only clad in a faded black t-shirt that looked about a hundred years old. The skin of his arms was a soft, pale white, save for the tattoos on his bicep and forearms – a phoenix on one arm, and the number "7" on the other. I had the sudden thought I'd like to lick one of those arms and felt my face grow even hotter. He looked at me with a smirk, almost as if he'd heard my thoughts, then back down at his hands. He picked up his glass and as he raised it to his lips, I noticed his hands shook a little. "Now that I know you're okay, I'm starting to feel a little freaked myself." He took another deep drink of wine and looked at me intently as I sat across from him. "It's not every day someone brings you back from the dead. All things considered, though, I feel pretty damn good." He splayed out his fingers, made a fist, and ran his hands up and down the length of his arms.

"Really?"

"Yeah. Just before I passed...god, that feels weird to say...I wasn't in a very good place. I don't actually remember a lot." He looked at me. "Just curious, what was my cause of death?"

I looked at him, surprised. "A drug overdose," I said slowly. "They never came right out and said what from, just that it was a 'concoction.' But everybody knows what that means."

"And what does it mean?"

I thought for a moment that I'd offended him, but he was looking at me with actual curiosity. "I just always assumed it meant the person was on so much shit they didn't bother trying to find what actually did the job."

He did wince that time. "I'm sorry. I shouldn't have-"

"No, I asked," he said quietly.

"You don't...remember?" I questioned. "How it happened?"

"I remember," he said quietly. "I just wondered what the official story was." He looked around the kitchen. "This place suits you, but it's so small. I don't see how you ever shared it with someone. How long has your husband been gone?"

How the hell did he know about Tess? "A couple of months," I answered. "How did you know-"

"There's someone at your front door," he interrupted me. His rosebud mouth had turned into a hard line. He stood up and walked to the far corner of the kitchen, just out of sight. "I'll stay here, but if you need me -"

I hadn't heard anything. "Are you sure?" I asked, and just as I spoke, there was a knock at the door. I stood up and went to answer it, looking curiously at Phillip. He was standing there straight as an arrow, his dark features lined with tension. How had he known someone was there before they ever knocked?

It was probably just Sloan. Despite how disoriented and downright *weird* the whole thing was, I was incredibly excited to bring her in her and show her Phillip Deville, in all his gorgeous flesh, standing in my kitchen. "You owe me, like, a thousand apologies, you beyotch-" I began as I opened the door with a flourish. But it wasn't Sloan.

The man standing there was tall, though not nearly as tall as Phillip, with a face covered in freckles, pale blue eyes, and sandy blond hair. His eyes were partially hidden by a ball cap, but they were light, almost like glass, and somewhat unnerving, in an other-worldly kind of way. I looked at him for a moment, then remembered. "You're the guy I ran into at the farmers market," I said, puzzled. "What are you doing here?"

"Yeah, sorry about that. We didn't meet formally," he said, holding out his hand. "I'm Lee Courtenay."

I extended my own reluctantly and gave a limp shake. "Stormy." I didn't give my last name. "Can I help you?"

"I hope so," he said, taking off his ball cap and holding it over his chest, a move that seemed both weirdly gallant and boyish. "I'm a detective. Me and my partner here -" He gestured over his shoulder; a man suddenly came out from behind the shadows to his left. He was tall, tanned, with closely shorn dark brown hair and very dark eyes. He barely nodded at me. There was something menacing about him. "Shank's his name. Yeah, it's really his name." He rolled his eyes. "Anyway, we're investigating some things going on in this neck of the woods – pranks and stuff, a little light burglary – and I wondered if you'd had anything weird happen recently, or any strange visitors come out this way?"

My heart started to thump. I looked at him for a moment. He didn't look old enough to be a detective. He looked barely old enough to be out of college. "What kind of pranks?"

"Oh, anything. Strange people sniffing around, maybe you noticed something missing...?" I didn't say anything, and he went on. "Maybe a stranger knocking on the door..."

"Other than yourself? I can't say that I have, Mr. Courtenay," I replied. I felt sure that I didn't want to tell him about the weird knocks Sloan and I had heard the night before, and I *definitely* didn't want to tell him about the man standing in my kitchen. "Thanks for coming by to check, though."

I expected him to turn and go, but he lingered, making me uncomfortable. My voice came out harsher than I meant it to when I asked, "So why *did* you run into me at the farmers market? What's up with that?"

He gave a short laugh. "Oh, I was bringing flowers to my aunt. She has a booth there. I was in a hurry because I wanted to get home in time for the Georgia game. Again, I'm sorry about that."

I regarded him warily. Sounded like a line of BS to me – most men I knew these days barely brought flowers to their significant others or their own mothers, much less brought them to an aunt at work – but he *was* wearing an expensive UGA hat, and I wanted him gone, so I accepted the story with a shrug. "I see. Well, it was nice seeing you again. Goodbye."

He leaned in closer to me before I could move away and make for the door. I could smell his aftershave. It was a nice scent, musky, but there was something amateur about it, like Axe Body Spray's slightly older cousin. His freckles were a dark splotch on his high cheekbones. I gripped the door handle. "Okay, I didn't want to alarm you, Ms..." He seemed to wait, but I didn't offer my last name. "Stormy. But the truth is, there's an escaped convict from the prison in Knoxville, and the authorities have reason to believe he might've come this way. Family on Jekyll, you understand. You live out here alone – and frankly, this is the boonies - with only one elderly man off to the side over there. We already talked to him and he didn't see or hear much, but I'm just concerned for your welfare."

"I haven't seen or heard anything," I repeated firmly. "And anyway, I'm not alone most of the time. My friend often stays over. And my husband will be here, too." I felt safer telling the lie. Something about the dark man standing in the yard was giving me the heebies, even if Lee seemed genial enough. Genial or not, I didn't buy his story at all. It was too coinciden- tal, that the same man I'd literally run into at the market was now at my well-secluded hole in the wall. Something else was up, and I'd find out what it was, but right now my main priority was getting these men off my property and away from the handsome, mysterious man lurking in my kitchen. I'd already been standing out here far longer than I wanted to. "I'll be sure to tell them both to be on the lookout."

He seemed to want to say more but nodded. "Alright, then. You do that. Keep your doors locked, your phone charged up, and don't hesitate to call if you see or hear anything. Or if your, uh, husband does." His expression suggested he didn't believe my story. He handed me a card and I stuck it in my pocket without looking at it. "That's my direct line. Call 911 or the sheriff's department and they'll take an hour to get out here. You call me, and I'll come right away. If you see anything, *or anybody,* at all, you understand?"

"Yeah. Sure." I wished he'd leave; my entire body was tense with nerves.

He stood there for another minute, his eyes searching mine, and then finally he stepped backward and down from the porch, walking into the night with his partner in tow. I stood there watching as they got in a dark car and left. Weird, I hadn't noticed any headlights from the kitchen window when they'd pulled up.

I pulled the card out of my pocket and read it. "Detective Lee Courtenay." There was a number and email address, but why didn't it end in .gov? Even the font seemed unusual.

There was warm breath on the back of my neck suddenly, and I gasped. "He's gone, then?"

I turned to face Phillip, who was standing behind me, silent and hulking. "Jesus, you scared me half to death!"

A rueful smile. "Better than all the way to death, no?"

"Not funny."

"I thought it was."

I tried for my best pissed off face. "It was a detective. Apparently, there's an escaped convict in town-"

"Bullshit," he said, taking the card from my fingers. He examined it.

"Why do you say that?"

"Because he was looking for me," he said, handing the card back and shutting my door. He locked the deadbolt and the handle.

"And what if *you're* the escaped convict?" I demanded.

He leaned down, his face a few inches from mine, and his lips curved into a slow smile. "Then you're in big trouble, Stormy Spooner."

His eyes were so huge and glittering, I almost got lost. I

leaned back, gasping a little for breath, and laughed. "How do you do that?"

"Do what?"

"You, like, almost hypnotized me."

He shook his head. "I didn't do anything. I was just, you know, being weird." His face turned serious. "You do know that I'm not going to hurt you, right?"

"I guess so." He didn't seem dangerous. The thrill I felt in my stomach definitely wasn't from fear.

"This guy, whoever he is, he's hoping that you think just that – that I'm a danger to you. So you'll turn me in." He looked at me plainly. "And if you want to, you should. I'm not going to ask you to hide me."

"I'm not going to turn you in to some Boy Scout," I said, irritated. "Even if I should. None of this makes any fucking sense. I know that wine I buy at the gas station is cheap, but Jesus fuck, I didn't know it would make me hallucinate-"

"I'm grateful to you, Stormy," he interrupted. "You brought me back. I mean...damn. I kind of can't believe it. I never thought – the guys laughed when I designed the liner notes – said I was fuckin' nuts. If they could see now..." He seemed to be having some dialogue with himself. "But they'd be in their fifties by now, if they're all alive. I can't go to them. I'll have to change my-" He looked up at me, and grinned. "Sorry. I've been underground for a long time. Have a few things to think about."

"It's okay." I tried to muster up some semblance of sanity, though I was shaky as hell. "Why don't you sit on the couch and relax, and I'll bring your wine to you? I can tell you what I know about the band, what became of them after you, uh..."

"You don't have to serve me," he said.

"I know I don't. But I'm getting mine anyway," I said and disappeared into the kitchen before he could protest. My hands were shaking.

When I returned holding our glasses, he was standing over by my stereo, looking at a Bloomer Demons CD. "I kept them all," I said with a smile, sitting on the couch. "I have your whole discography on both vinyl and CD. I can't bear to throw them out, even though most of the time I listen on Spotify or iTunes."

"What the hell are those?" He looked at me, puzzled, and sat beside me on the couch.

I handed him the glass. "You know, like on my phone."

He shook his head.

"Like digital."

"But a CD *is* digital."

"No. Like MP3." Still nothing. I realized he'd died before that had really become a thing. "Sorry. The way most people listen to music now, it's like a digital file and you can just stream the song from your cell phone using different apps like Spotify, or Pandora or whatever, or download a copy from iTunes or Amazon." He looked really confused now, so I decided to shut up. "It doesn't matter, because vinyl is in again. Anyway, I have all your stuff. Even the really rare demos."

"Did you ever see us play?" he asked. "Live?"

I frowned. "No. I wish I had. It was always my dream. But I was so young when you passed, I never got the chance. My parents never let me go to your shows." I grimaced at the thought of my parents. It was weird to say, *when you passed,* like I wasn't sitting here talking to the man, looking as alive and healthy as possible. And he looked positively robust. His cheeks were flushed with life, and while he was pale, he looked remarkably well. It was very hard to believe that a few short days ago he was rotting away in a coffin somewhere. "They said I'd get into trouble. I think they suspected I'd find my way onto your tour bus and give you my underwear."

"Would you have?"

I flushed. "Probably."

The silence in the room was suddenly *very* silent.

"I'll play for you, then," he said after a moment, clearing his throat. "As a thank you."

"That would be amazing." But I couldn't think about that right now, though my teenage self would have died. "I have to tell you, I have a million questions. This is all so confusing. I just don't see how you can really be here."

He smiled slowly, like a cat. "I'll answer what I can, but *I* have to tell *you* that I'm in the dark too, on a lot of it." He took a deep breath. "It smells so good in here. Like cinnamon and cloves. It makes me think of Halloween. Are you burning incense?"

"It's my wax melt burner," I said. That look of confusion again. "It's like a candle, but in electric form."

"I don't know what that is." That slow smile reappeared. "I had these big candles once that I kept in the studio. They smelled sort of like that. I'd light them all and just sing my vocals in the dark." He looked thoughtful. "I was usually shit-faced. Once I actually caught my shirt on fire. I was halfway through a verse on *The Death of Love* before I realized." That grin. "I thought I was Jim Morrison reincarnated. I guess I took 'Light my Fire' a little too literally. What a douche."

"You or Jim?" I asked.

"Yes." He smirked.

"Is that where the scream comes from, at the end of that line?" I asked, excited. "On *The Death of Love*? Because your shirt was on fire?"

"Yeah."

"It's so fucking sexy when you do that," I said. I flushed crimson and clapped my hand over my mouth. "I had no idea."

"Thanks, sweetheart," he said with a big grin. "That's what I was going for. Well, until the second-degree burn." He pulled his shirt up to reveal a section of stomach, the skin taut and muscular but with a blotch of raised, shiny skin. I stared. His face turned wistful. "Of course, later that night I was in the toilet shitting my guts out from too much cheap wine and cocaine, wearing a sweaty shirt with a huge-ass hole burned in it. Not very sexy. Being a rock star is such bull shit, all smoke and mirrors."

"I think I prefer the smoke and mirrors," I said with a laugh. "Now you've ruined that song for me."

He grinned, then looked down at his lap, his face turning serious. "So - my band," he said. "Are they all..." He swallowed. "...still with us?"

"All but one," I said.

"Which one?"

I opened my mouth to answer, but he stopped me. "Never mind," he said, taking a long drink of wine. "I'm not sure I'm ready to know yet."

I realized both of our glasses were empty and moved to take his, but he held a hand out and stopped me. "I'm sorry, Stormy, I know it's rude, and you have so many questions, but I'm really tired. I think...this whole process...it's just worn me out. This body isn't used to walking upright again yet. Could I trouble you for somewhere to sleep? The couch here is fine, if you don't mind."

"Oh! Oh, of course!" I looked at the clock. It was after ten. Not terribly late, but just hours ago he'd been six feet under. "I'll take the couch, you can sleep on my bed. It's more comfortable."

"No, I don't want to do that," he said firmly. "I'm fine here, really."

I looked at him, dubious. He was 6'5" and my couch was little more than a love seat. "Let me at least get you a blanket and a pillow, then."

When I returned, he'd stripped down to his boxer shorts – black and tight-fitting, and I forced myself to look away – and his soft black t-shirt. He'd pulled his hair back and was holding it with his hand.

"Would you like a hair tie?"

"If you have one." He smiled at me. "So many little things about living to get used to. Like tying back your hair and brushing your teeth."

"There's a spare toothbrush in the cup in the bathroom," I said. "I'm a stickler for always having a spare toothbrush. You never know when you'll have a houseguest."

"Might even be a dead one," he joked, and headed toward the bathroom. I watched him retreat, then realized I was gawking at him in his underwear. Phillip Deville. In my house. In nothing but black boxer briefs. Alive. I clutched the pillow to my chest. How in the hell could this even be happening?

I made up the couch as bed-like as I could, fluffing the pillow and even spraying some Febreze on the blanket. I could hear him in the bathroom, running water, the *swish swish* of the toothbrush. He emerged from the bathroom as I was straightening the afghan on the couch and propping up my pillows, embarrassed at what meager means of comfort I had to offer him. He'd found a hair tie and now that his black, silky hair was out of his face, I could see just how sharp and fine his features were. I'd always assumed that he wore makeup in his photos, that some of them must be airbrushed, even though he'd come to fame in a time when airbrushing wasn't a huge thing yet. I'd always figured there was simply no way a man could be as beautiful as him in real life. Eyes simply weren't that deep green, brows heavy but with a delicate arch. A man's jawline couldn't be so angular, his teeth so blindingly white. His nose, while on the big side, was perfectly shaped, coming down at a long slope to a fine upturn. A genuine rosebud mouth without benefit of a lip pencil or a computer program to finesse it. He couldn't be real, but he was.

"Holy shit," I breathed, not realizing I was speaking out loud. "You're so beautiful."

He actually flushed. It only added to his beauty, gave him a reckless, boyish charm. "Really?" He seemed genuinely surprised. "I figured I probably looked the worse for wear. You know, considering." He came over and took the pillow from me. "I was afraid to look in the mirror. Thought I might have bolts coming out of my neck."

"No, not at all," I assured him, looking into his eyes. This was going to be trouble. "You're as gorgeous as ever. More so, I think."

"Stop it, you," he said softly, staring back at me. I'd read once in an interview that he'd always hated his appearance. It was why he'd done so many things with his hair over the years, to try and hide what he thought were his shortcomings. He'd called himself "Lurch" in interviews and referred to his "face even my mom couldn't love." I never could understand that, and definitely didn't now that I was seeing him in the flesh. He was so handsome it was almost supernatural.

"It's true." I suddenly had the sensation of falling. Alice down the rabbit hole. I felt woozy, and he reached out a hand to steady me.

"You've had a shock," he said in that quiet, low voice. "I know you have questions. I'll tell you what I can...tomorrow. Ok?"

"Yes." I was speaking in a whisper, marveling again at his intuitiveness. I had lots of questions; about him, about the magic that had brought this about, about the weird guy, Lee...and I felt more than a little shocked. He squeezed my shoulder and smiled. I smiled back. I felt stuck to the spot, still falling into his eyes. Finally, I wrenched myself away and pushed another blanket at him. "I'll go in my room so I won't disturb you." I knew I wouldn't be able to fall asleep any time soon. I had way too much to think about.

"Thanks, Stormy Spooner." He grinned. "I'll see you in the morning." I grabbed my phone off the coffee table and turned toward the hall. "And hey...Stormy?" I turned back. "Thanks again. For making me undead."

I managed to laugh and went to my room, shutting the door with a gentle click. I sat down on my bed in a whirl of nerves. My hands were still trembling. I heard my couch creak and could scarcely believe that it was actually Phillip Deville lying in there, under the afghan my grandma had crocheted for me. Philip Deville...no, it wasn't possible. I'd had some kind of psychotic break, brought on by grief over my divorce, or drinking on an empty stomach.

But no. I knew he was out there. I could still feel him, feel his aura, coursing through my house, through my own nervous system. I tapped out a text to Sloan, my head spinning.

"What's going on with you tomorrow? Need to see you — got to tell you something, but in person." I hit *send*.

She called me back immediately and I sent it to voicemail. She hated when I did that; I was apt to get cussed out, but it seemed clear enough that when somebody wanted to just text, you texted. Nobody talked on the phone these days except Sloan, and besides, Phillip was asleep out in the living room.

A second later, she pinged back. *"What is it, hooker? You know I hate it when I call you and you don't answer even though you're HOLDING your phone. What's so important?"*

"Going to bed," I typed. *"Tired. But I need to talk to you — have to show you something. Can you come by tomorrow?"*

"I'll try to around lunchtime."

"Awesome. TTFN," I typed back. *"Loves."*

"Loves, too," she responded. *"Now leave me alone so I can fuck Dan."* I was glad she hadn't said Gus. Maybe she was figuring her shit out.

I put my phone down on the nightstand and listened. The

trailer was quiet as a tomb, the thought of which gave me a chill. I dug through my hope chest for my cutest pair of pajamas, knowing that Phillip would see me in them in the morning. Normally I just slept in a loose-fitting tank top and underwear or gym shorts – but I couldn't let him see me like that, in all my no-bra, sagging glory, with pasty legs. I didn't have any decent lingerie, only a crotchless red monstrosity that Tess had bought me one Valentine's Day. But I managed to dig out a cute set of boy-style button up jammies in a silk-like material that had little skulls on them. I'd had them since high school. I pulled my hair up in a bun, then sat back on my bed. I counted to thirty-five, then counted backward to one. Unable to wait any longer, I stood up, opened my door, and quietly padded down the narrow hall.

The kitchen light was still on, a beam of light shining onto the back of Phillip's head. He was lying in the fetal position, long legs curled under him, the afghan barely covering him; he was too big. His hair was curled over one shoulder, his mouth in a little pout, and I imagined he'd slept the same way since he was a little boy. In the dim light, his inky eyelashes fluttered a bit; no doubt he was dreaming. His breathing was shallow, and he moved a little, throwing an arm over his eyes. He began to snore, and I suppressed a giggle. I glanced at him one more time, committing the image to memory, then went into the kitchen and turned off the light so he could sleep in peace.

I went back to the bedroom, heart pounding, turning off my own light and easing into bed. For a brief moment, I had the thought that I could climb onto the couch with him...or maybe he'd come visit me in the night...then I shook my head. *Stop being silly. Two nights ago, he was dead. He isn't coming in here. You just leave him alone, you weirdo.*

I figured I'd be up all night, tossing and turning, unable to quiet the excitement I felt over PHILLIP DEVILLE sleeping in my living room. But the events of the day had worn me out, and despite my wariness at the strange Lee Courtenay (not to mention his even odder, scarier partner), I felt safer knowing that Phillip was on my couch, keeping guard.

Six

I awoke, startled, to a tall, brooding man throwing open my door, his long, disheveled black hair streaming behind him. "He's outside again," Phillip seethed as I cracked one eye open, confused. "Do you want me to go deal with him?"

"Huh?" I sat up, trying to get my bearings. I'd been so sure I'd wake up and this would all be a dream. But there was Phillip, standing in my doorway, still in his tight boxer briefs that left little to the imagination, his face full of barely controlled fury. "Who?"

"The guy that was sniffing around here last night, with the phony story about the escaped convict."

"Oh. Lee." I rubbed at my eyes and patted my hair self-consciously. I knew I looked like busted ass. "Did he knock on the door? I'll go get it."

"No, he didn't knock," Phillip replied, coming over and sitting on my bed. I could smell him – smoke and sandalwood. His hair was in a tangle, and I noticed there was a small hole in the sleeve of his t-shirt. He needed to get some new clothes.

"He's out there snooping. In your barn. I saw him creep out of the woods and go in."

"There's nothing in there but Tess' old junk. Just a couple of shovels and some cans of paint," I said, but I was suddenly angry. Who the hell did that guy think he was, snooping on my property? "I'll call the cops. I don't think they'll take kindly to one of their own poking around without a warrant."

Phillip put a hand on my arm. "No, don't do that," he said. "Let me deal with him. I'll go out there and make sure he never comes around you again." He paused. "And he's not a cop. I told you, he's looking for me."

"If he's looking for you, it's probably best you don't go," I argued. "I don't want you to get hurt. What if he has a gun?"

He looked at me for a few beats, then threw back his head and laughed.

I smiled faintly. "What?"

"I don't think you need to worry about me, ma chere," he said, and bumped under my chin with a finger. I scowled. "I'm a big boy and I can take care of myself, I promise."

"Well, considering you were *dead* two days ago..."

"How long are you going to throw that in my face?"

"I've only known you for a few hours. I'm thinking a little while longer."

He was inches from my face, and I desperately wished I'd had a chance to get up and brush my teeth. "Let me just throw on some clothes and I'll go talk to him, tell him to get the fuck out of here." For some reason, I didn't want Phillip near Lee Courtenay. He was right, I knew, he could take care of himself, but...I didn't want it to come to that. I had a strong urge to keep him away from Courtenay at all costs. "I can handle it."

He cocked his head to the side and then smiled. "Actually, I don't think you need to – I think he's gone now."

"How do you know?"

"I can't really explain," he said. "I just know. He's gone. He didn't find anything."

"How do you know he didn't?"

"Because he's looking for me," Phillip said again with a devious look. "And I'm right here." He brushed a hair back from my face and stood up. "Stay right there. I'll bring you some coffee."

A FEW MINUTES later I was propped up on pillows in bed, my knees curled up under me, watching Phillip Deville serve me coffee from a pretty silver tray – one that I'd never used, a wedding present Tess and I had received; from whom I no longer remembered. It had sat on top of my cabinets for years. I smiled, enjoying the domestic feel of it all, as Phillip poured me a cup, added a teaspoon of sugar, then frowned at the creamer. "I looked for plain cream, or some milk, but all you had was this stuff. I remember coffee creamer, of course -" he made a face- "but what on earth is pumpkin spice?"

"Hey, don't judge." I took the cup from him. "They always start selling it in September and I only buy one bottle a year, I swear." I had only recently been able to find a vegan pumpkin spice creamer and I was still over the moon about it. Sloan told me I was a basic bitch, but I didn't care.

"But I mean. Why? Why would you want your coffee to taste like a pumpkin?"

"Not pumpkin, pumpkin spice. You know, like the flavor of pumpkin pie."

He poured himself a cup, and I wasn't at all surprised to see he drank it black, no cream or sugar. He shook his head. "No, thanks. That's fucking weird."

"I guess there are a lot of things you'll have to get used to,"

I mused. "Wait till you see how many flavors there are of Mountain Dew."

"I never drank that stuff in the first place," he said. "Well, except to mix with vodka when they didn't put fresh orange juice in my rider. I read somewhere that it makes your balls shrink."

"Did you guys do the whole crazy request thing?" I had always wondered this. "Like Van Halen and the all brown M&Ms? I know you always asked for donuts."

He laughed. "Nah, we just asked for everything we could think of," he said. "We were shits. We always wanted expensive crap like sushi and fresh fruit trays and top-shelf vodka and whiskey. Drugs. Condoms. Shit like that." He looked at me and shrugged. "And the donuts. I always did love those."

"I'm pretty sure that 'everything we could think of' is the epitome of crazy requests," I pointed out, and he laughed again.

I wanted to ask if he had sex with tons of groupies on tour, but I didn't. Anyway, I knew the answer to that already. Lots of them had talked after his death, gave interviews. One of his 'girls' had even posed for Playboy. I wondered how he'd feel about that. He'd find out soon enough, if he decided to ever go googling. First, though, he'd have to learn what Google was.

Instead, I said, "You need some new clothes, huh?"

He looked down at his worn shirt and boxers. "Oh. Oh, yeah. I guess I do." He picked at a thread on his shirt. "This is what I was buried in."

I must have looked horrified. He hastened to explain. "Oh, don't worry. They're not all...gross. They're clean. I guess they kind of, uh, rejuvenated when I did. They are old, though. I wore this just about every day on our last tour."

"You were buried in a t-shirt and jeans? And motorcycle boots?"

He looked surprised. "Well, yeah. What else? Can you imagine me in a suit?"

"I think you'd look very handsome in a suit." I'd kill to see it, now that I thought of it. His uniform his entire career had been pretty much what I saw before me – a sea of black, with the occasional army green or burgundy. T shirts, jeans, black boots. Black leather jackets. Black bandannas and hats.

"For now, I'd settle for a fresh t-shirt and a pair of pants that don't fall off my hips," he said. "I seem to have lost a few inches when I came back."

I smirked, and he grimaced at me. "Not there, thank you. There I'm good."

I raised an eyebrow.

"I mean my waist. I guess the beer pooch is gone." He slapped his belly, his shirt riding up to reveal bare skin. I tried not to stare at the dark hairs leading down to his navel.

"I think I can help," I said. "My friend Sloan is dropping by around lunch time. I could ask her to bring something with her. She's a hairdresser, so she could cut your hair, too." I sipped my coffee. "You know, if you were worried about being recognized or whatever."

A hand flew to his head and he looked alarmed. "Oh, no. I can't cut my hair, Stormy."

"Your vanity?" I teased.

He grinned. "Not exactly. I'll hide it under a cap or something if I go out. Until I figure all this out."

"Yeah, so what is your game plan, anyway?" I asked. "What are you going to do?"

"What do you mean?"

"Like, what's your purpose for coming back?"

"I don't have one," he said simply.

"But then why..." I fumbled. "Why did you – the liner notes, the spell..."

"I did it on a whim," he said. "It was just a joke. I used to try and do weird artwork in our liner notes, stuff for the fans to find. I was high for most of it; it seemed like a good idea at the time."

"So you put the spell out there as a joke," I said slowly, "And I recited it as a joke." I thought back to how intensely I had gone into the spell and shrugged it off. How could I have known what would happen?

"And here I am." His eyes dazzled. "My whole life was a joke, really, so I think it's pretty appropriate."

"I guess mine, too."

"Nah," he said. "You've got a good one."

I opened my mouth to tell him how wrong he was, then changed my mind. He didn't need to hear about all my pathetic crap right now.

He must have read it on my face, because he put a hand on my knee and gave it a squeeze. "The spell... if you want to know the truth, and this is kinda embarrassing, considering-" He leaned in close to me. "I got it off a drug dealer."

"What?" I said. "No way."

"Guthrie his name was. Guth. He was my fixer guy when I was home. He was this hippie guy who lived around the corner from my mom's and I knew him before I was famous. He was this peace n' love guy who also happened to sell drugs. He was on the up and up most of the time but one time he shorted me, and I went over there and said I was gonna rough him up. Who did he think he was, trying to short me just because I was famous now? I was drunk and pissed off and being a fucking asshole. He said to calm down, that he didn't have the money or the coke to make up for it, but he had something else. And he scribbled out what looked like a poem and gave it to me. I almost put him through the wall. But he kept swearing that it was a real spell, that it would really work. That he was a warlock, and it was legit."

"And you believed it?"

"No, I didn't. I just didn't feel all that great about roughing him up. I liked the guy. And I figured if he'd come up with a stupid ass story like that on the fly just to save his ass, he might be alright. So I took it and warned him never to short me again. He didn't." He smiled.

"What made you decide to leave it for the fans?" I asked.

His face darkened. "I dunno. Like I said, I was high. Drunk, too. I can't remember." I got the impression he wasn't telling the whole truth. "Anyway, turns out ol' Guthrie wasn't full of shit. Man, if he could see me now. Alive."

"And in my house, of all places."

"My witch lady, who brought me back to life." His eyes danced, but his face was a little sad. "As for my plans – since you asked – I haven't got any. I can't go home. If my family, my ex-wife, my bandmates, see me – how am I gonna explain? I can't resume any kind of life there. I've got to lay low. And I don't know how long I'll – how long I'll actually *be* here. I don't know if this is temporary. I don't know anything, really." He snickered. "I never believed for a second that this was real, and now I'm fucking here, and I have no idea what to do."

"I'm sorry," I said helplessly. "I should never have messed with that stupid spell."

"It's okay," he said easily. "I wasn't trying to blame you."

"You know what you should do?" I asked.

"What's that?"

"You could go see this guy, this Guthrie. He gave you the spell, right? It's likely he'd know the particulars, and maybe have an idea of what you should do next."

"I don't have a clue where he'd be," Phillip said, thoughtful. "I knew him twenty-five years ago, and he was a junkie then. Hell, he might not even be alive now."

"But what if he is?" I asked. "He might even be in the

same place. What was his last name? I could look for him on Facebook."

"What's Facebook?"

"It's like a social networking site, on the internet. Most people have a profile. I could search his name, and the location-"

"I don't know his full name," he said. "I don't even know if Guthrie is his first name or his last name. I think I'd have to go searching for him in person. The last I saw him was in Boston. That's where I'm from – my old stomping grounds."

"I know," I said. "Your biggest fan, remember?"

He smiled, but his eyes were faraway. "I guess you're right, Stormy. That's where I need to go to find Guthrie, if I can. There's a pit stop I can make on the way that'll ease my other problem."

"What other problem?" I asked.

"The financial one. If I'm alive, I need money. Can't survive without it."

I wondered how he'd get money without a bank account or credit card. I assumed his estate had long ago been willed to someone, though I had no idea who it might be, but I decided not to ask. It wasn't any of my business anyway.

"When will you go?"

"Tomorrow afternoon, maybe," he said. "The sooner the better, I guess."

I felt suddenly sad. I didn't want him to go. He seemed to read my mind. "Don't worry. I don't know much about the spell, but I do know that once summoned, I can't just disappear from the summoner. You'd have to release me, I think. I'll be bound to come back and see you."

"I have to release you? How do I do that?"

"I'm not quite sure. Another thing I'll have to ask Guthrie, if I can find him." He stood up and stretched, his faded t-shirt riding up again, revealing a flat stomach and a bit of raised, mottled skin – the burn scar he'd mentioned earlier. I tried not to stare, wondering how certain things had – what was the word he'd used? - rejuvenated, and others had not. "Could I use your shower, Stormy?"

"Of course. You'll find whatever you need in the bathroom closet. Just holler if you need me."

"I think I can manage on my own," he said, eyes twinkling. "But I'll bear it in mind if I get lonely."

"Wait, I didn't mean-"

He laughed softly and leaned down and kissed me on the cheek, his lips soft and warm against my skin. Then he was gone.

My phone buzzed on the nightstand. I picked it up. Sloan. "What's up?"

"Hey." She sounded annoyed. "I can't come by. My car's fucking dead. Can you come give me a jump?"

"I told you to replace that battery," I said.

"That takes money, and I'm broke as hell," she said. "Will you come?"

"Where are you?"

"I'm at the salon. I came in early to do a perm. Little old lady didn't even tip me. What a waste of a morning. Anyway, I'm stuck here."

"Nobody else there?"

"No, if there was, I wouldn't need you to give me a jump. Stormy, will you come or not?"

"Yes, yes, I'll come. Keep your pants on." I stretched and got out of bed. I could hear the shower running in the bathroom. "Might be half an hour or so, though. I'm just getting out of bed. I need to, ah – get ready."

"You sound weird," she said.

"Well, I told you I had something to show you..."

"Oh god," she said. "You've got a guy over."

"Y-e-e-e-s...." I said slowly. "Kinda. But it's not-"

"Stormy got laid, Stormy got laid...," she sang. "Who is he? Do I know him? Is he still there? Oh god, are y'all still in bed-"

"Stop!" I laughed. "I'll explain everything when I get there. But listen, Sloan, be prepared. You might be kind of surprised." That was an understatement.

"Oh shit, Stormy, no. Don't tell me it's Tess-"

"It isn't Tess," I said. "I swear."

"Okay, thank god. Anyway, I'm going to let you go. Gotta clean up my booth. But try to get here soon, okay? I want to go see Dan this afternoon."

So she was back to Dan. I couldn't keep up. "I told you I'll be as quick as I-"

"Byeeeeee!" She hung up the line. I groaned. Sloan was Sloan.

The shower had cut off. I took the tray with the coffee cups into the kitchen and could hear Phillip humming in the bathroom. It was eerie, listening to him – the same voice I'd heard through my speakers for the last two decades, amplified in my tiny bathroom. I was tempted to turn on my phone and record it, as much to prove to myself that he was here as anything else but decided not to. That was sketchy moral ground, even for the world's biggest Bloomer Demons fan. Besides, who would ever believe it was him anyway?

Phillip emerged from the bathroom in a cloud of steam. I blushed to my roots when I saw he was clad only in a towel, cinched around his waist. My yellow bathroom towels were tiny – I was too cheap to buy the big fluffy ones, and I just used them to tie up my wet hair – ending mid-thigh on Phillip and making him loom even taller. "Um...change of plans," I stuttered. "My friend Sloan can't come by after all. Her car's dead. She needs a jump. I need to go help her out."

"Oh, ok. No problem." It seemed like nothing bothered Phillip Deville. I supposed if I'd been brought back to life after twenty some years underground maybe nothing would bother me, either.

"I thought you might want to come?" I tried to keep the eagerness out of my voice.

"Is she cool?"

I knew what he meant. "Yes. She won't go blabbing, I swear."

"She knows who I am?"

I had to giggle. "Uh yeah, I'd say she does. I've only forced her to listen to the Bloomer Demons every day of her life since we were twelve. She's familiar with your work."

He grinned. "I'll just throw on some clothes and I'll be ready."

"Me, too." I went back to my bedroom and shut the door, my heart pounding. The longer he was here, the more nervous I felt. I threw on a pair of faded skinny jeans, black slip-on chucks and a Nirvana tank top, and threw a purple flannel over that. It wasn't very dressy, but I didn't want to appear like I was trying too hard. The jeans were tight, and my boobs looked good in the tank top. I took extra care with my dark blonde hair, which I braided in a side-braid, and put on a little mascara and bb cream in my vanity mirror.

I supposed what looked back at me wasn't terrible. I regarded myself; the dishwater hair, my wide-set light-brown eyes, my rosy cheeks. As a kid, I'd always hated how I blushed over any little thing, my cheeks always pink and flushed. It was humiliating. Now, as a woman in her thirties, I was mostly glad for them. Everybody my age was buying blush and dewy highlighters, and I had natural rosy cheeks. They still embarrassed me sometimes, though, since they tended to turn bright red anytime I felt anything intense. This meant they'd been permanently magenta ever since Phillip Deville had shown up at my door. I dabbed a little more bb cream on and swiped absently with my fingers, smoothing it over the few freckles that dotted the bridge of my nose. They were nothing like Lee Courtenay's, whose face was absolutely covered with them.

I rolled my eyes at myself in the mirror, setting the bb cream on the table. Why was I thinking of that guy, of all people, when I had a bona fide rock god waiting for me in the other room? I started out the door, then went back to the mirror again, dabbing on burgundy lip gloss Sloan had given me at Christmas. Phillip Deville was in my house for fuck's sake. I wanted to look good and according to Sloan, darker lip shades made me look sexy and dangerous.

When I emerged, he was already dressed in his same black outfit and was sitting on the couch plucking at a bass. "I forgot we had that," I said. The black bass had been Tess'. He barely played it. If I remembered correctly, a friend had let him borrow it forever ago and he'd never returned it. He cared so little about it he'd just left it with me. It was somewhat pathetic that I'd never moved it. "It can't be in tune after all this time."

"It isn't," he replied, looking at me. His eyes moved down the length of my body so quickly it was almost imperceptible, and I was glad I'd taken a little extra care with my clothes and makeup. "I'm tuning it. Do you play?"

"No," I answered. "I wish I did. I never took the time to learn." Tess hadn't been very amenable to teaching me the one time I had asked.

"Want me to teach you?"

"Sure," I responded, my heart lifting that he'd be around long enough to do so. Or maybe he was just being nice. "I'd love to learn that slide thing you do. But we should go — Sloan's waiting for me."

"Come here a second. I want to show you something," he said, beckoning to me with a finger. I raised an eyebrow and walked over to the couch.

He stood, holding the bass, and gestured for me to stand in front of him. He placed the strap over my shoulders and put the instrument in my hands while he adjusted it for my height. The bass was heavier than I'd have thought.

"I'll show you the basics later," he said, standing behind me, his voice dangerously close to my ear. "But the slide is easy." He placed his hands lightly over mine, moving one to the top of the neck, and the other onto the body. His skin was warm, and I could feel his long thighs pressed up against me. My entire body began to thrum along with the strings as he lightly tapped with his long, lean fingers. His hands were *huge* – one of mine fit entirely inside of his.

"I don't have any callouses built up," I said stupidly, trying to maintain a sense of calm. He was so close to me. His big arms were tight around me, his fingers entwined with my own. He smelled so good that it made me dizzy. I wasn't going to be able to learn a damn thing with such a distraction, unraveling my every thread of composure.

"You don't need those yet," he said, his voice low. "And anyway, the slide is really all about the amp. It won't sound like much just sitting around playing unplugged, but if you've got a decent pedal it'll sound fuzzy and distorted without having to use much pressure." He took my left hand in his and placed it on the strings. "Just start down here," he said, clasping my fingers. "Play whatever notes you're playing, then when you're ready for the slide just kind of lightly wrap your fingers around the neck and slide up. See?" His hands guided my own into the movement, and the strings gave a slight creak under my fingers.

I felt the blood rush to my face, and I blurted, "This is pornographic!"

"There's a reason people equate guitars with sex," he said with a hoarse, sexy laugh. His lips were so close that they brushed against my ear and my body erupted in gooseflesh.

"Just roll with it. The sexier you make it, the better it sounds." His breath caressed the sensitive skin behind my ear, fluttering my hair, and I gritted my teeth and closed my eyes. He had to know what he was doing to me. He had to feel it. "Don't be afraid to really grasp the thing; you'll look cool as fuck and it'll sound good, too." His fingers, still entwined with my own, guided my hand, wrapping around the base of the neck and sliding *upppp* – my body twanged right along with the strings.

I leaned into him, feeling his strong thighs pressed against me, relishing the way his big arms held mine down, and practiced it again, moving my fingers up the fretboard slowly and deliberately, hoping that it was half as sexy as when he did it. I felt his breath catch behind me, so I smiled and did it again, faster this time, and one of his hands strayed from the bass and down to my hip.

Oh shit, I'm in trouble.

His lips trailed against my ear, just the slightest movement. I couldn't tell if he was opening his mouth to speak or if it was the world's lightest kiss.

Phillip made a low noise in his throat and I moved to turn and face him, not able to wait any longer, needing to feel his lips on me – and my phone vibrated in my pocket. We both jumped. I flailed, turning around, eyes wide, and came dangerously close to hitting Phillip in the face with the bass.

"Whoa!" He backed up and almost fell over the couch. "Watch what you do with that thing!"

"Shit, sorry." My face was forty shades of red. I scrambled to remove the strap from my shoulders and propped the heavy bass in the corner, dying of embarrassment. I pulled my phone out of my pocket and peered at it a few beats longer than I had to because I was afraid to look at Phillip. She'd just had to text right then. *Damn.*

"It's Sloan," I said, tapping out a response. "She's getting impatient. I guess we'd better go. That is, if you still want to come?" I tore my eyes upward, and was met with a sweet, bemused smile.

"Of course," he said. "I used to work on cars, in my other life. The one before the one before this one." He laughed. "If you want, I'll take a look. Might could fix it." I realized that his own face was turning a little red and my heart flooded with tenderness. Even dead rock stars got embarrassed, it seemed.

"It's just her battery," I said. I almost started to say, "I knew you were a mechanic, I read all about it," but he'd probably get tired of hearing that really fast. And it made me sound like a freak. "It's died a couple of times recently. She just needs to buy a new one. She thinks she can just jump it off until the end of time."

"Something's draining it," he said. "What year's her car? If it's really new I might not know, since I haven't been around -" He looked like he'd never get used to saying that - "But if it's an older model I can check it out."

"She drives a '92 mustang," I said.

"Ha, that's funny," he said. "I had one of those. In fact, it was my last car."

I knew that, too, but said nothing.

"And hey," he said, following me out the door. "You're a natural on that bass." I felt a prickle of goosebumps start at my neck, where the ghost of his lips had been, all the way down my back.

I PULLED up at the Curling Dervish with Phillip sitting shotgun in my Blazer, wondering if he'd say anything about it. Neither Sloan nor I had nice cars, but hers was definitely nicer than mine, which had actually been Tess' old truck when we'd first gotten married. He'd only left it behind because it was a piece of junk – forget him trying to be nice. Phillip said nothing on the drive over; he appeared lost in thought. I hoped he wasn't thinking about our thwarted practice session and how I'd almost beaned him with the bass. I wondered how he planned to get up north. In fact, I wondered how he'd gotten to my house in the first place. He said he'd taken the bus. How had he not been recognized? And how had he gotten there so fast? I had so many questions.

Sloan was standing outside, the hood of her red mustang up, cussing up a storm. "Hey," she said as she heard me approach, not looking up. "I've been messing with the connections on this thing."

"Sloan, come here for a second," I said to her as Phillip exited the car. "I want you to meet someone."

She looked up with sudden delight, put out her cigarette and sauntered over. The hood had been blocking him, but once her eyes lit on Phillip she stopped and froze, her eyes going wide. "What the...*fuck?*"

Phillip stuck out a hand. "Hey. Nice to meet you."

I had to laugh, but it was mainly from nerves. "Sloan, this is-"

"You have got to be fucking kidding me," she said, still standing there, Phillip's hand extended unshaken. It occurred to me just how big his hands were, how long his arms were. He really was a huge guy. "You are shitting me."

"Sloan-"

"I knew you were a psycho fangirl, but only you could go out and find a guy that looks like an exact replica of Phillip fucking Deville. What, did you find some cover band or something? Holy shit dude, you look *exactly* like him! Down to the last detail. Not quite as hot as he was, but you know, close enough. Damn." She shook her head with a laugh, and finally shook his hand. "Stormy, you're a fucking mess, I swear."

"Sloan-"

"So this is what all that resurrection shit was about. The spell or whatever. This was the punchline."

I shook my head, but she kept on talking. Phillip stared at her, his lips curling into a very sexy smile. "What's your name? And where did you guys meet?" She looked back and forth from him to me expectantly, waiting for me to give her the 411.

"His name's Phillip," I said before he had a chance to speak. "And Sloan, he's not-"

"You're really committing, huh?" she said with a laugh. "I don't blame you. Probably good money in impersonations. Do you tour?" She shook her head at me. "Why didn't you tell me? I would have gone with you. I wouldn't mind a lookalike of that drummer, what was his name? I can't ever remember the names in that damn band. He had a girls' name, right?"

"Kim Rzeznick," Phillip said.

"Yeah. That's him. He was hot as fuck. I'm still pissed he died."

Phillip went pale and I instinctively reached an arm out to him. Kim Rzeznick had died only two years after Phillip, also from an overdose. I hadn't had a chance to fill him in yet, not after he'd stopped me the night before.

Sloan didn't notice his discomfort. She walked back over to the car. "I think I just need a jump, Storm, if you don't mind pulling the car up. I swear, as soon as I get my paycheck this week, I'll go buy a battery, but I just don't have a spare fifty bucks right now."

"Try a hundred, or the better part of it," I said, fishing my keys back out of my pocket. I glanced at Phillip again, worried. "I told you I'd loan you the money-"

"Shut the fuck up," she said from behind the hood.

"Hang on," Phillip interrupted. He looked like he'd somewhat recovered from his shock. "Let's try one thing first before you jump her off. Get behind the wheel, Sloan, and when I tell you to start it, give it a try, ok?"

"Ok," she said dubiously. "But it's dead as fuck."

She got behind the wheel and put the key in the ignition. Phillip got under the hood and looked at the engine. "Just like my old car, yep," he said. Then something interesting happened. He put his hands on the battery, and the moment his skin touched it there was a *ding, ding, ding* – the interior light came on and her radio began to play, blasting out Stone Temple Pilots.

"Hey, it's back!" Sloan exclaimed. "How did you do that? Just a cable loose or something?"

Phillip looked over at me. I was gawking, my mouth open. He gave me an imperceptible nod, and said, "Yeah, something like that."

She exited the car and gave me a bright smile. "I like this one. Keep him," she said to me, lighting another cigarette.

"Hey, could I bum one of those?" he asked her.

"Oh, sure." I watched him light the cigarette, his full lips closing over it, the flame illuminating his skin. "You can't have been dating long if you're smoking. That's one of Storm's deal breakers." Sloan really believed he was some impersonator. I supposed the mind would make any kind of mental gymnastics to explain the unexplainable. Watching her standing there, talking to Phillip, I decided maybe it'd be better this way. Better if Sloan didn't know the truth.

Her phone rang and she brightened, mouthing "Dan" to me, answered, and walked off in the direction of her shop.

I shuffled my feet and stood there, uncomfortable. Phillip was looking at me. "You sure you don't want a haircut?" I asked Phillip again. "That's what Sloan does for a living, so..."

He shook his head firmly. "No. Thanks."

"There's a Target not far from here," I told him. "If you wanted to go grab some clothes."

He frowned. "I do – I'd really like to get out of this shit. But I don't have any cash on me."

"I'll buy you some stuff." As I said it, I did the sums in my head. I wasn't exactly flush, but I had a little saved.

"I can't let you do that. It's not your place to buy me clothes."

"Phillip, don't be silly," I said. "I'm happy to. You need clothes, I've got cash. I just got paid. I don't mind."

"Only if you allow me to pay you back," he insisted. "Once I get on the road, I can get the money – assuming it's still there – and I'll pay you back with interest."

"If you want." I honestly didn't care. I was with Phillip Deville, for Christ's sake. I'd give my eyeteeth for him. I was curious where he was planning to get it, though. "I'm sorry about what she said. About Kim. I didn't mean for you to find out like that."

"It's alright." His eyes met mine, full of grief. "His death is even less surprising than mine was, you know? He was all kinds of fucked up back then."

"But still, it must be upsetting for you."

He nodded and put a hand on my arm. "Thanks."

I felt a jolt when he touched me, and a pang of yearning when he pulled his hand away.

"How did he go?" he asked after a beat. "I mean, I can guess, but..."

I decided to spare him the gory details, which Kim's girlfriend had leaked to the National Enquirer for a hefty sum. "It was an overdose."

"Right." His face was thoughtful. "The poor fucker. He never really stood a chance."

"I'm sorry." I didn't know what to say. I knew every detail of Kim Rzenik's tragic demise, had seen the leaked photos of his platinum blonde head, lying face down on his bedroom floor beside a puddle of vomit, many more times than I'd ever cared to. After getting fired from the band, and four unsuccessful stints in rehab, Kim had succumbed to his demons. He was found two days after he'd died, alone on his bedroom floor, clutching a letter in his fist. The letter had been written by his teenage friend Phillip Deville years before, outlining their dreams of starting a rock band and becoming famous. The letter, too, had been leaked to the press. *Forget the other bullshit – it's all about the music,* the letter had read. *No matter what happens, we Rock On.* Those words were on Kim's gravestone.

How would Phillip react when he discovered that, I wondered.

I hesitated, wanting to tell Phillip everything but knowing it wasn't the time. I looked at my phone. "If Sloan is done with us, we could head over, pick out a few things and then have lunch? My treat. When was the last time you ate?"

"When? I guess about twenty-two years ago, and some change."

FOR A SECOND, I just stared. I forgot to even be grossed out, which usually I was when people ate meat around me, and for far less than the massive T-bone steak on the plate across from me. The man tucking into it was doing so with such abandon that he hadn't even noticed his hair was falling into the lake of steak sauce on his plate.

He sliced a cube of steak, forked it, and brought it to his mouth. As he chewed, his eyes closed in an expression of bliss and he gave an audible moan. "Oh, my fucking god," he declared loudly. A couple of people turned to look at him, and I gave a shrug much like the one that Billy Crystal gives in the infamous diner scene in When Harry Met Sally. His scene with the wine the night before had been put to shame. "Forget sex. This is all I need right here. This steak. Jesus."

"That good?"

He exhaled with pleasure from his nose, then opened his eyes and looked at me like he'd forgotten I was there. "Good? Fuck yes. It's fucking great. Here." He stabbed another piece of the bloody meat with his fork and held it out to me. "You've got to try it."

"No, no thanks. I'm good." I waved the fork away. I was having Earl Grey tea and an avocado and portabella wrap, hold the swiss cheese.

"Come on," he insisted, pushing it at me. "It's the best steak I've ever had. In either life. You have to."

"No," I said firmly. "I actually don't eat meat."

He looked down at my plate with an expression of horror. "Someone brings me back to life and it's a bloody vegetarian."

I smirked at him and took a bite of my wrap. I was sure the portabella mushrooms in it were easily as good – no, better – than the bloody disgusting steak he was tucking into. "Actually, I'm vegan."

"What's the difference?" He picked up his glass and took a huge gulp of water. He'd already finished half his steak.

"I don't eat any animal products at all, so no cheese, eggs, dairy, honey-"

"You don't even put honey in your tea." He said it as a statement rather than a question, his eyebrows furrowing together as if to say *you are absurd.*

"I try not to."

"Now I see why you're so pale," he said with a smile, then went back to his steak.

"Oh, I've only heard that a gazillion times. And anyway - like you can talk." He was bone-white, and too skinny by a mile. "You could stand to gain a few, too."

"Hey," he said, dipping a finger into his steak sauce and

licking it off, clearly relishing it, "I've been dead. I have an excuse." He looked remarkably good, even if he was too skinny, especially now that he'd changed. Naturally, all he'd bought at Target were more black clothes – black t-shirt, fitted black jeans, black socks, even black underwear. I'd tried not to notice, but he'd bought more of the tight boxer briefs like the pair he was wearing earlier, and secretly I'd rejoiced – and he was still wearing the same black combat boots. I'd told him about the current style – lumbersexual – and showed him a few pairs of skinny cords, plaid shirts and skater shoes, and he'd just laughed. "This isn't a new style," he'd said with a guffaw. "This is the same shit grunge kids were wearing when I was alive in the 90s. The only difference is instead of JNCOs the jeans have skinny legs, but otherwise it's the same." I had realized he was right. Old was new again. The 90s were now considered "vintage". Oh my god, was I old?

I had to admit, staring at Phillip across the booth in the little diner, he looked amazing in all black. It suited him. It always had, and it still did.

"Your hair is in your steak sauce," I said with a laugh.

"Sweetheart, I don't even care." He took another bite and sighed with pleasure.

"You rock star," I said dryly.

He looked up at me and did the devil's sign with a grin, then turned back to his remaining steak.

"So," I suddenly felt my stomach do a loop, "Off to Boston? To get funds and visit that Guthrie guy? That's the plan, right?"

"Yes," he answered, popping a french fry into his mouth. "As for after, I have no idea. But I need money. And I have some – not a lot, but some – tucked away. Turns out being a paranoid junkie paid off, because I stashed cash. Otherwise I'd be fucked. If my will was honored, and I assume it was, all my estate went to my ex-wife." He ate another fry. "And yeah, I'm not sure I'll have any luck, but I'll try to find Guthrie. Ask him what the fuck I am, exactly, and how long I'll be here. I just need to get on a bus. If you could help me with that?" He rushed to add, "I'll pay you back."

"I can do better," I said with a bright smile. "I'd like to go with you."

"You would?" He sounded surprised.

"Sure," I answered. "I've got vacation time at work – two years' worth saved up, believe it or not. And I have a vehicle, even if it is an ugly piece of crap. You won't have to worry about some idiot on the bus recognizing you. And you'll have someone along for company."

"No offense, but why would you want to come with me?" he asked. "What's the appeal for you?"

"Only to go on a road trip with my favorite musician of all time," I said, incredulous. "Why wouldn't I want to go?"

He actually blushed. Then I blushed. He said quietly, "Well, as flattered as I am, I can't ask you to do that, Stormy. I don't know what this Guthrie guy is like now. He seemed harmless enough at the time, back when I was an idiot, but he had guns and shit. And with that weird Lee guy sniffing around your place, I don't know what kind of forces are at work here, you know? What if it puts you in danger?" He looked serious. "And anyway, it'd be lot of driving, and I can't ask you to-"

"You can drive, then," I said. "I assume you remember how. And won't I be safer with you than home alone? I've seen Lee Courtenay three times now. Twice at my house. If he's been there that many times, he'll come again. I'd feel better with someone around if that happens."

"I suspect you're capable of protecting yourself just fine," he said with a laugh. "And you can argue your way out of anything."

"All the more reason to bring me along," I said, "You need some brains with you."

"And beauty too," he said with a smile, and reached across the table to touch my cheek. I felt the blood rush to my face, hot.

"Alright, Stormy Spooner. You've twisted my arm. You can come with me, if you really want to."

Seven

WALKING INTO THE LIBRARY MONDAY MORNING, I FELT A spring in my step that hadn't been there in a long time. Holding my mint-mocha in one hand, I fished in my bag and pulled out my cell phone, looking at the screen.

I'd bought Phillip a burner smartphone at Target, shown him how to use it, telling him to call me if there were any issues. So far, he hadn't, but I'd only been gone from the house for an hour. Jeez, I had it bad.

That morning I'd woken up early, showered and got ready, and made him a full breakfast. After seeing the way he'd eaten at the diner and remembering how skinny he was in those damned boxer briefs, I decided he needed to be fed, well and often. When he'd come into the kitchen an hour later, he'd raised an eyebrow. "Get yourself a coffee," I said, gesturing to the pot. "Just brewed it."

He poured himself a cup, black, and regarded the table with a look of awe. "Do you do this every morning?"

"Ha. No. I don't ever do this, actually. I'm not a breakfast person," I said with a laugh. "This is all for you. I can't have you starving to death just two days after you've come back to life."

"Jesus, pancakes." He moaned. "I'd forgotten pancakes."

"Sorry there's no bacon," I said. "Or eggs. Pancakes, tofu scramble, and fresh fruit it is."

He smiled. "Are you going to hit me if I tell you I've never been a breakfast person either?"

I laughed. "Nah. Just save it for your lunch. I'm about to go to work."

He drank two cups of strong black coffee, tucked heartily into breakfast, and walked me to the doorway as I left for work. "I might write a song," he said, looking over at Tess' old bass.

My heart leapt at the thought of him sitting in my house, drinking my coffee, writing a song. Maybe it'd be about me? Our little practice session came to mind, and I felt the blood rush to various places. *Get a grip, you pathetic loser.*

I sat down at my desk, booted up the library computer, rummaged in my purse for my reading glasses, and busied myself signing in books from the overnight drop-off. Jean wasn't in yet and the library was quiet. I re-shelved the returned items then opened a program to check for overdue books. I wondered what Phillip was doing right now. Writing a song? Showering? The thought of that tall, chiseled body standing in my shower...

Stop, stop, stop. I was having a hard time thinking of anything else but him, even for a moment. The night before I'd lain awake half the night, just thinking about him in the next room, his long, athletic legs tucked under him. That beautiful black hair on the pillow, the rosebud mouth pursed. He was so beautiful. Maybe asking to go along with him on this trip was a bad idea, because just being around him was driving me totally insane. And it had barely been two days.

My phone dinged and I jumped, scrambling to pull it out of

my pocket, eager to see what Phillip needed. But it wasn't Phillip. A text from my dad – the first I'd heard from him in what seemed like forever – made me grimace. *"Was wondering if you were coming home for Thanksgiving this year,"* he had typed. *"Dee and Shay and I would love to have you."*

I made a gesture at the phone and placed it face down on my desk, not bothering to respond. Talking to my parents took a kind of mental energy that needed to be built up, prepared for. And when my dad started chattering about his new family and his fancy, happy little beach house in PCB, well, it was hard for me to keep my decorum, even when he was making the effort to include me. It was weird, being thirtysomething years old and having a baby sister. *Shay.* The cutesy nickname rolled around in my head as I tried to shake off the jealousy I felt. I didn't begrudge my baby sister her life; she was a sweet, dear little thing, what little I knew of her. Dee was okay, too – I secretly thought she was a bit dim, but she was nice enough, if a bit shallow. I was glad my dad had finally cleaned things up and could offer her something better. But it didn't mean I'd forgotten everything from my own childhood, either.

I sighed. I'd respond to Dad later, if I bothered to at all. I was grateful for the invitation, but I doubted I'd take it. Even if I could let go of my angsty feelings long enough to have Thanksgiving with Dad and his family, it wasn't worth the all-out war it would cause when Mom found out. God knew where she was – it had been even longer since I'd talked to her. I assumed she was doing fine; like any good narcissist she always knew how to land on her feet. I wondered if her last stint at rehab had stuck or if she was off the wagon again. Red wine had been her drink, too.

She'd been begging me for years to come see her for Thanksgiving and Christmas, to stay with her for a few days, and I never did, because I knew how it would go. The pair of us, wine-drunk and sad, either crying over her dusty records, tallying up points over our terrible ex-spouses (she would always win; there was no competition with Mom where she didn't emerge victorious), or worse: a screaming match. "You look down on me now," she'd accused me once when I'd made excuses not to come. "Because I'm still here." Whether she meant it literally, as in still in the trailer park, or metaphorically, as in, *still an alcoholic,* I never asked, because it didn't matter.

I didn't look down on her. Really, I didn't. After all, I lived in a mobile home, didn't I? I drank like a fish, especially now that Tess was gone. The life we'd had together turned out to be eerily similar to my own parents'. I didn't have a leg of judgment to stand on, with either of them, since I'd repeated every bad example they'd ever shown me. The truth was far sadder. It was just too painful to be near her, near either of them.

I didn't want to think about Mom right now.

I didn't care to think about either of my parents. I preferred to think about Phillip Deville, a vision in black, sitting on my couch, just waiting for me to come home. I banished thoughts of my parents and with a dreamy smile, resumed working.

In a wistful haze, I sent off a few emails to patrons with overdue books, warning them of late fees and fines, threw away a bunch of old magazines to make way for the newly donated pile, and helped an elderly customer use Google. When I returned to my desk, my phone was buzzing. When I saw "unknown caller," my heart skipped a beat. I wasn't supposed to use my cell phone for calls at work, but just this once...

"Hello?"

"Fucking motherfucker."

"Huh?"

"Stormy?"

"Phillip?"

"How in the Christ you people make phone calls by

tapping a little screen I will never know." His voice was loud in my ear; he was yelling. "I have been trying to call you for thirty minutes." I heard a loud thump and another, "Fuck! Please don't be cracked, please don't be cracked-"

"Are you ok?"

"Yeah, I'm ok!" he boomed.

"Stop yelling, Phillip," I said, stifling my laughter. "You don't have be so loud. Jesus, didn't you talk on the phone back in the dark ages?"

"Yeah, real phones, the kind where you press a button, and-" I heard a *thunk* and a stream of loud cuss words. "Goddamit. You there?"

"I'm here." I giggled. "All thumbs today?"

"It's just a damn glass rectangle, there's no receiver. I keep dropping it-" There was a rustling, then he was back. "Every time I tried to call, the phone would shut off. I rebooted it like you showed me, then I'd try again, I'd dial, and it would happen again."

"Perhaps I should get you a phone more suited to your generation," I said, suppressing a guffaw. "Like a rotary phone, or better yet, one that dials in to an operator who can connect you to Aunt Bea?"

"Well, that's just mean," he said coolly, then I heard another *thunk,* followed by a stream of expletives.

"What's going on?" I asked, still holding back laughter. "I mean, why did you call? Is something wrong?"

"No," he said, still talking too loudly. "I just wanted to say hi. You know, check in. I guess I missed your voice. And I wanted to try out this cell phone. Now that I have, I kind of want to stomp it with my sixteens."

"Don't stomp the phone, Phillip." My heart soared. He wanted to hear my voice. I looked over at the lone library patron to make sure they weren't listening in. "Did you write the song?"

"I got the melody down. You're out of paper though. What kind of librarian doesn't have any paper?" he said. "I thought I'd use your computer but every time I turned it on it just turned off. It's broken, I guess?"

"No," I said. That was weird. "It was working fine yesterday. And anyway, I do have paper. Second drawer in the nightstand by my bed. You can go grab some if you want."

"I'll do it while I've got you on the phone." I could hear him walking through the house. "Ok, first drawer of the nightstand..." I heard a drawer slide open.

"No, Phillip, the SECOND drawer! Don't open the first-"

It was too late. I heard muffled laughter and bit down hard on my lower lip. "Oh. Sorry." A quiet laugh, then, "I found the paper."

Fuck.

"We will never speak of what is in the top drawer, okay? If you mention it to me, I'll kill you all over again."

"Yes, ma'am. Or should I say, 'yes boss', judging from what I-"

"Phillip!" I yelled, and the person on the computer looked up at me, alarmed. "Sorry," I mouthed before speaking again to Phillip in a hot whisper. "Get out of my room."

"No need to get bitchy," he said. "We all gotta get off, don't we?"

I was going to die of embarrassment. I would just gently keel over and expire right on the library carpet. I could feel my cheeks burn. "I've got to go. I have work to do."

"Nice to see some things haven't changed since the 90s."

"Phillip Patrick Deville, I swear to Lucifer-"

He was still laughing. "You middle named me! Okay, fine. It might take me a minute to figure out how to hang up this thing. My fucking fingers can't seem to-" I didn't wait for him to finish. I hung up on him, my face uncomfortably hot. I thought back to the pumpkin spice lube Sloan had given me last Christmas as a joke, wondering if he'd seen that, too; I had to giggle a little, imagining explaining the term "basic bitch" to Phillip Deville. Or was I a basic *witch?*

I was still mulling over how mortified I was as I locked up at 5pm and stepped out of the library. I patted my pockets to make sure I had everything, threw my purse over my shoulder and headed toward the car. Halfway down the ramp, I tripped and almost went sprawling onto the concrete. I grabbed the metal rail and hoisted myself back up, cursing under my breath. My shoe was untied. I bent down, still muttering, tied it quickly, and shifted on my haunches, ready to head back to the car, when something caught my eye.

It was starting toward dusk already, so the natural light wasn't great, but even before I turned the little rectangular card over, I knew what it would be. A tarot card. A quick flip with my fingers revealed just what I expected. The death card.

I left the card where it lay and sauntered off to my car. Whoever or whatever was trying to rattle me wouldn't succeed. The one thing I knew was that I wanted to leave with Phillip more than ever.

I CAME in the house praying that Phillip had forgotten his wayward discovery from earlier, or at least wouldn't mention it. I had bigger problems to worry about. I'd gone back and forth several times in the car as to whether I should tell him about the tarot cards. The entire situation was fucked up and weird enough as it was without me adding more kooky shit into the mix. I was equal parts pleased and annoyed to find Sloan sitting with him on the couch when I came in.

"I didn't see your car," I said to her.

"Hello to you, too," she said. "Dan's got it. He dropped me

off. He was going to get me a new battery, and then run it by the car wash. Isn't that sweet? He's coming back for me in a few." She certainly was smitten with Dan. If she was happy, I was happy, especially if it meant she was staying away from that Gus guy.

I looked at Phillip, wondering what he'd told her about where we were going and why. He was plucking at the bass, an unlit cigarette hanging out of his mouth. "I won't smoke it," he said, seeming to read my mind. "It just helps me think. I can't write without one."

"So you guys are going on a little road trip," Sloan stated, meeting my eyes. I tried to reassure her with a glance. "How long for?"

"Not long," Phillip answered for me, still plucking away. "Just a couple of days."

"Did Jean give you shit for taking off work?"

"Nah," I said. "I think she was glad to get rid of me, honestly." That wasn't really fair. We got along well, and she was always kind to me, especially after my divorce. But I knew I got on her nerves sometimes - my anxious energy could be a lot to deal with.

"Well, the reason I came by," Sloan said, rummaging in her pocket for her ChapStick glancing at Phillip and then at me to make sure it was okay to talk in front of him. I nodded and she went on. "I didn't want to tell you over the phone, especially while you were at work. But...I saw Tess today. And his girlfriend."

"Oh really?" I was surprised at how okay I felt hearing this. "Roberta?"

"I think that's the first time I've heard you say her name without turning green," Sloan answered, gliding cherry Chap-Stick onto her lips. "They came by the Curling Dervish. You just missed them, they were there literally five minutes after you. With money, believe it or not. I told them to fuck off."

"You didn't do her hair?"

"Fuck no I didn't." She smirked. "I told them I was all booked up."

"You didn't have to do that. I know you've got to make a living." I sniffed, wishing they weren't both looking at me. Phillip's expression was strange. "How was he?"

"Ugly. Strung out. The usual."

"Sloan-"

"Fuck him, Stormy. Stop defending him. He showed up with that skank and was asking about you right in front of her. It was just so gross."

"He was asking about me? What did he ask?"

"What do you think? Wanting to know if you were seeing anybody-" She looked at Phillip, then at me with a wink, "-and I was quick to say YES, you are. And that he'd better leave you the hell alone if he knew what was good for him. I'll kick his ass myself if I have to. He wanted to know who, and I told him to mind his own fucking beeswax. Asking if you were still driving the truck, how long you'd been seeing your guy, all this weird, nosy stuff. Finally, I got fed up and threw him out. He flipped me off before they finally left." She looked at Phillip. "Classy guy, her ex."

Phillip, who had once flipped off Kurt Loder and told him to, "lick my asshole, you fucking corporate stooge" on live TV, clearly realized he had no legs to stand on and resumed plucking the bass with a shrug.

"I wish you wouldn't have caused a scene," I said with a sigh.

"There was nobody there but us," she argued. "Calm down, Church Lady."

"What was she like?" I asked. "Roberta?"

She raised an eyebrow. "Nice, actually. She's really pretty, but she looked kinda miserable. Tess was hanging all over her with his tongue hanging out. I think he was doing it to make you jealous, because he knew I'd tell you. I felt kind of sorry for her." She looked at me. "But only so much. She knew what she was doing, you know?"

I bit my lip. On the one hand, it was heartening to hear that Tess was still asking about me, even if he'd had a girl on his arm while he did it. Did it mean he still cared? That he missed me, that he had regrets? Or was he just being a nosy douchebag? Probably the latter. Still, it was nice to hear, on some level, that maybe he cared. At least a little.

For a moment I allowed myself the fantasy of what it might be like to call him, his voice on the other line eager and friendly, the apology he'd give me, sincere and meaningful. He'd tell me about how he'd changed, how he missed me, how he'd forgotten how much we loved each other but he knew now, he knew, and he wanted to come home...

"Don't go there," Phillip said in a low voice, still plucking away. He was playing the opening bars of *"I Could Die with You,"* one of my favorites from their first album.

"I beg your pardon?"

"You're thinking he must still care about you on some level if he bothered to ask about you," he said, pulling the unlit cigarette from his mouth and rolling it around his fingers. "You're mulling over calling him. But I can tell you, Stormy. I've been that guy. It's about ownership, a piss-on-my-hydrant thing. Don't take it for love, because it ain't love."

Sloan's eyebrows raised into her hairline.

"Okay, well thanks." I was embarrassed, and suddenly very close to tears. I didn't need the two of them ganging up on me. Divorce was hard. What did they expect?

"Divorce *is* hard," he said, repeating my thoughts. It was beginning to freak me out, the way he did that.

I decided to change the subject. "Anybody hungry?"

"Yes," they both said in unison.

"I haven't been grocery shopping in a while. And if we're about to leave I don't see the point in doing it now. Pizza?"

"Let's get Mazzios," Sloan agreed.

"I'll have to go pick it up," I said. "They don't deliver out here anymore. I live too far out, I guess it costs them too much in gas."

"I'll go with you, if you want to call in the order," Sloan said. She looked at Phillip. "So what are we thinking, the usual? Just a large vegan meat lovers to share?" He stared at her, eyes wide, as though she'd just insulted his mother.

I laughed. "Right." I knew he'd be asking me later what in the actual hell a "vegan meat lovers" consisted of, and I relished the thought of what his face would do when I began to explain fake pepperoni and sausage to Mr. Rare-Steak.

I picked up my cell and called in the order, our usual vegan pie and a large triple meat for Phillip. Sloan looked shocked. I'd never done such a thing for anyone before, not even Tess. But Phillip needed his strength, and besides, he hadn't given me any grief about my lifestyle, and Tess had constantly. It seemed a simple enough concept – you respect me, I'll respect you. Even if I hoped I never had to see another bloody steak for the rest of my life. Maybe eventually I'd turn Phillip Deville vegan. Ha!

IN THE TRUCK, Sloan had a million questions, as I had known she would.

"So what's his real name?"

"Phillip," I said, not wanting to get into a spiral of lies. They were too hard to keep up with.

"Come on, that can't really be his name."

"It really is."

"I guess that's not an uncommon name. But it seems a little too on the nose," she said. "And you guys met at a show?"

"I never said that," I replied. "You just assumed."

"So where, then?"

"You won't believe me even if I tell you." I had planned to lie, to let Sloan assume whatever she wanted, because it'd be easier, and safer, too. But I'd stopped myself. I was rattled. I needed Sloan as my sounding board, and anyway, we never lied to each other. She'd be able to read right through it, and besides, all that had happened made me feel crazy, and I wanted to tell *someone.* Even if she didn't believe me. "Anyway, I tried to once already, and you didn't believe me."

"Try me now," she said.

"OK, fine. The other night, when I told you I was going to do the spell, I did it. I got drunk and I read the spell and lit some sage and other shit, and well...something happened."

"The power went out," she said. "You told me."

"Not just that. I recorded the whole thing, and it just magically disappeared off my phone, remember? The power went out, but other stuff has happened too." I swallowed. "But the most important thing is that he showed up."

"Who did?"

"Phillip," I said. "Sloan, I know you're going to tell me I'm fucking insane and try to drive me to the hospital to have me committed, but I'm telling you the truth. The guy in my house right now is Phillip Deville. THE Phillip Deville. He's not some impersonator or singer for a cover band, it's not a big joke or a huge coincidence. He looks so much like Phillip Deville because he IS him. He showed up at my house two nights ago because I summoned him."

"You summoned Phillip Deville with a spell," she said slowly, as though talking to a confused child. "You uh... brought him back."

"Yes. I know it sounds fucking crazy-"

"You think?" she asked. "Have you gone completely loopy? This shit with Tess has rotted out your brain. First of all, you have told me how many gazillion times that you don't even *believe* in that crap-"

"I know, but-"

"And putting aside that fact, Phillip Deville has been dead for over twenty years. I remember when he died. You came into math class in 9th grade with your blue mascara running down your cheeks, hysterical. You cried for weeks."

"I know."

"People don't come back from the dead, Stormy," she said. She looked kind of mad. "They just don't. You can't expect me to believe this. This is some kind of crazy...I don't even know. You're cracking up. This is...like some next level delusional shit. Trying to pretend this impersonator guy or whatever he is is real? I mean, I like him – he seems cool, and I'm glad you're moving on. God knows you need to get laid. But I think you should see someone. A professional."

"Look, I know how it seems. How it looks," I said, trying to stay calm. We were almost at Mazzios. "But think about it. Isn't it kind of eerie how much he looks like Phillip Deville? And what about your car? We both know that battery was dead as fuck. He put a hand on it and your car came on without you even having to turn the ignition. Explain that!"

"He wiggled a wire," she said.

"I was watching him," I said. "He didn't wiggle any wire. He literally just put his hand on the battery for a second."

"This is stupid," Sloan said. "If you want to have a fling with a guy who looks like your favorite dead rock star, fine by me. But why all this theatrical shit? Why the big show, trying to convince me?"

"I'm not making this up."

"Fuck you. Stop it, right now. This isn't funny, Stormy, I'm worried."

"There's no reason to worry. I'm telling you the truth."

"The fuck you are."

"Don't get angry, Sloan-"

She put up a hand to silence me. "Don't pull that shit with me, Stormy Spooner. I *am* angry. I am." I knew better than to argue with that tone of voice. Sloan in a rage was a thing to behold. I sighed and turned my face back toward the road. I could see Sloan reapplying her ChapStick out of the corner of my eye, her face a black cloud.

Moments later, I pulled into the parking lot and into a space right in front of the doors. Sloan got out and slammed the door behind her. I sat there for a few moments, taking in some deep breaths, then followed. She might want to slap me right now, but I didn't want her to have to pay for the pizza. She was broke. We rarely ever fought, and I hadn't seen her so angry at me in a long time. For the second time that day I felt like crying. I had the sense that whatever I'd done, whatever magic had happened in my living room, I'd unleashed something much bigger than myself. Much bigger than even Phillip Deville. There were forces at work here, and I hadn't the first idea how to control them. Until I did learn, they were going to wreak havoc all over my personal life.

It was hard to believe, I knew, but couldn't Sloan see right in front of her? It was obvious that the man was Phillip – the resemblance was too uncanny. There were plenty of guys around going for that look, but none of them were six five and full of rock-hard muscles or had green eyes the color of gems. I supposed that when a thing seems too preposterous, you find a way to explain it away, to dismiss it. That was what Sloan was doing. But I knew a way to convince her. When we got back with the pizzas, I'd have Phillip sing for her. He could do one of his most familiar songs and once she heard that unmistakable razor-velvet voice, she'd know I was telling the truth.

Once she was back in the car, though, still treating me to

stony silence, I soon forgot all about having Phillip play for her.

I pulled out into the highway, the fragrance of hot pizza making my mouth water. I opened my mouth to say something to Sloan, to make her smile – I really couldn't handle it when people were angry at me – but my words died in my throat as I saw a car pull out of the parking lot right behind us. It was a burgundy colored Mazda, old and beat up, and just the sight of it filled me with dread. I couldn't make out the two figures inside the car, but both were wearing ball caps pulled down over their eyes. As they followed me down the street, I knew that they were up to no good. A shiver went up my back, and I instinctively crouched down in my seat, as if that would be any help.

They were following me. Whoever they were, I wouldn't lead them to Phillip. I passed the turn off for my road and went further into town, toward the library. Sloan turned to look at me. "Where are you going?" she asked.

I replied in a low voice, "I'm being followed."

She gave me an incredulous look. "Why on earth would somebody follow you? Girl, you are seriously losing it."

"Look in the mirror," I said. "That car. They're following us. Watch."

I veered right suddenly, turning onto a side street at a hard angle, and the car immediately followed. "They aren't even trying to hide it, see?"

"You're crazy," she said, but she looked nervous.

"I'm going to try to lose them," I said.

"You're not going to do that in the middle of town. You need to get out on the open road, and then just gun it."

I did as I was told. I turned again, watching the burgundy car in the rearview turn with me, and headed toward a rural street that didn't have much but farm houses on it. It was pitch dark on this stretch of road, and I usually avoided it because of deer that always seemed to jump out in front of me at night, especially in the fall. I hoped none were in the road tonight.

I passed a few houses, and once I was out of the line of sight, passing by nothing but coastal farmland and trees, I stepped down on the gas. My little truck was a piece of crap, but it still had plenty of get up and go. I floored it and we shot forward, racing around a curve, gaining speed. For a moment there was only darkness behind me, and I felt my heartrate start to slow. Then after a second or two their headlights became visible. I hadn't lost them yet. "Fuck."

"What the fuck is going *on* today?" Sloan said, her irritation giving way to fear. I knew she was worried now. "Go faster, Storm."

"This road is so twisty, I'm afraid-"

"Just go," she said. She was gripping the seat with both hands.

I gunned it harder, and we sped around another curve. The lights were still behind me, but further away. They didn't know these roads like I did, evidently. I sped around another curve, then another, going faster and faster, and then finally it appeared that I'd lost them. There was a four-way stop up ahead, but I barely paused, instead veering left and driving straight through. I hoped they'd assume I'd gone right, which led to Jekyll Island, rather than back the way I'd come. I couldn't see the hint of headlights in the rearview, and the road was dark and deserted.

"Don't slow down," Sloan said. "They could still be behind us. I doubt they turned around."

"I think we lost them-" I started to say, then suddenly the headlights were behind me again. I sped up, zooming down-hill, toward a bridge up ahead. I knew this area; below the bridge was a creek, connecting to Turtle River. It was pretty shallow, but I didn't want to be speeding over the rickety little two-lane bridge in the dark. I instinctively touched the brake.

As I did, the headlights got closer and closer – they were bearing down on us. I could hear the Mazda's old engine rumbling loudly behind me.

"They're going to rear end us!" Sloan screamed, and I braced my shoulders, waiting for the impact.

But the car didn't rear end us. Instead, it got closer and closer, then moved into the center of the road to pass. As the car came up beside me, I looked over, unable to help myself, catching a glimpse of a younger looking man with a hat pulled down low over his eyes. As he passed on my left, the driver suddenly rammed the car into my side of the truck, hard. I'd lost a lot of speed but was still going fast enough to fly off the road. There was no ditch to break our fall, so we propelled forward, down the hill and toward the creek, the old truck screeching as I hit the brakes, trying desperately to stop before impact, Sloan and I both screaming.

As we careened toward the water, I felt a jolt and then heard a loud, metallic smack. The front left of my car had hit one of the huge concrete girders that held up the bridge, my head slamming into the steering wheel and my leg jamming into the dash. I let out a cry of pain. I sat there for a beat, trying to catch my breath, my leg throbbing, and peered out the window to see if the attack was over. The burgundy car gunned its engine and kept going, over the bridge, up the hill, and into the night without slowing.

I sat there, stunned, reeling from the shock and the pain in my head and leg, and felt something wet on my face.

Sloan's voice was quietly shocked in the darkness. "Stormy, are you okay?"

"I think so," I said in a shaky voice. "Are you?"

"Yeah," she said. "It shook my neck pretty hard. I'll probably have whiplash in the morning. But I'm fine."

"I hit my head," I said, raising a hand to feel the goose egg forming on my forehead. My vision felt blurred; I wasn't sure if it was a blood pressure thing or from hitting my head. "And my leg is killing me. It got jammed up against the dash."

"I'll call 911," she said, reaching for her phone.

"No." I reached out a hand to stop her. "Don't."

"Why not?" she said. "Somebody just ran us off the fucking road. We've had an accident. And you're hurt! You need an EMT!"

I couldn't explain why I didn't want her to call them, only that I didn't. Luckily, she cussed and threw the phone down. "I don't have a signal anyway. Fuck. You said your leg is messed up? I guess I'd better get out and walk, go find somebody. We need help down here."

I looked at my own phone, thinking I could try to call Phillip. But mine was dead too. A no-reception area. "Let me try to start the truck," I said, putting my hand on the key. "It felt like a hard impact, but I bet it's still drivable."

"Are you sure that's safe?"

I shrugged. "This truck has been rumbling along for a decade. It's solid as they come. Might as well try."

To my luck, the old pickup started up with no trouble. I patted the dash, grateful that at least one thing Tess had left behind was doing me some good. I hoped and prayed there was no real damage to the truck, other than the banged-up front end. If I could just get home, get to safety, everything would be okay. Damage could be assessed, and so could our injuries. Phillip would help. He'd make it right, somehow. It had only been fifteen minutes since I'd seen him, but suddenly the desire to be near him was so strong it took my breath away.

"If you can scoot over here, we'll switch places," Sloan said. "You shouldn't drive, not if you're injured. But maybe we should take you to the hospital first, Stormy. Your head looks bad, even in the dark."

"Home first," I said. I wanted to see Phillip. Everything

else could wait. I scooted over, gingerly, trying to ignore the screaming pain in my leg, and let her take the wheel.

"Can you drive a stick?" I mumbled, pressing my head against the passenger window, suddenly tired.

"What do you think I am, an idiot?" She laughed, then her voice turned serious. "Stormy. Don't fall asleep." She put the truck in reverse and maneuvered it away from the concrete bridge with a loud, metallic screech. I opened my mouth to tell her that there was no chance of me sleeping, not now, and probably not later, but I couldn't seem to find my voice. My head was in turmoil with the chaos and terror of knowing that someone had just caused me to wreck my truck. Who was after me, and why did they seem to want me dead?

Eight

As we pulled into the driveway, I saw Phillip standing on the porch, his face set with worry. I wondered how bad the truck looked. Sloan came around to the passenger side and started to help me out, but Phillip was down the steps in a flash, scooping me into his arms.

"What happened to you?" he asked, his voice crackling with electricity. "I knew something was wrong. I could feel it."

"Let's go inside," I said weakly. "And then I'll explain." I wanted to get inside, lock the door, and check out my injuries. I really hoped I wouldn't have to go to the hospital.

"Are you alright?" he asked Sloan, and she must have nodded yes, because he turned without another word and carried me inside the house. Now that I was back home and in his arms, I felt safer, and more than a little sleepy. I laid my head against his shoulder, marveling at how warm he was. You'd think he'd be cold, but he was like a furnace, brimming with heat. I closed my eyes and breathed in the smell of woodsmoke.

"Don't let her go to sleep," I heard.

"Stormy." Phillip sat me down on the couch and I groaned,

not wanting to give up the warmth of his strong arms. "Wake up, sweetheart. Don't go to sleep."

"Would you guys stop harping on me? I'm not going to sleep. Jeez." I reluctantly opened my eyes again. Sloan was holding out a slice of pizza to me. I was no longer hungry, but I took it dutifully.

"So what happened?" Phillip said, looking at me carefully. His eyes moved over me, assessing my injuries. "Who did this?"

I explained briefly what had happened – the men following us out of Mazzios parking lot, losing them, then being run off the road – and when I was done, his eyes flashed with anger.

"I'll find them," he said. "Find them and kill them."

"Calm down," Sloan said. "We don't know why they did it, or who they even were."

"They were just trying to intimidate me, I think," I said, still woozy. "Now that I'm thinking about it, I don't think they actually intended to hurt me. If they'd wanted to kill me, they could have done worse. It was like they were passing on a message."

"A message for me," he said, as if it were the most obvious thing in the world. "And they *did* hurt you."

"Why for you?" Sloan asked him. "Is this some kind of mob situation or something? Are you into drugs? And what does any of it have to do with Storm? What's going on?"

Phillip looked at me. "I tried to tell her the truth about you," I said weakly, biting into my pizza. "She didn't believe me." It tasted like cardboard. "And honestly, I don't know why, either. Why *are* they after you, Phillip? And who are they, exactly?"

"I don't actually know yet," he admitted, running a hand through his dark hair. "I just know that they're looking for me."

I smiled weakly. "It's the paranormal po-po," I said, with a small laugh. "They're going to throw you in psychic jail for coming back from the dead without a permit."

"Ha." His eyes swept over me again, still concerned. "Eat that. You're pale. I'm worried you need a doctor."

"I'm fine."

Sloan had wolfed down two slices already. She was regarding us both silently, but her face conveyed a number of emotions, and none of them were good. She was worried and confused, but she was also still angry with me. "Who the fuck are you?" she demanded finally, looking at Phillip. "Really."

"Phillip," he said simply, staring back at her.

"Please don't tell me you're taking part in this delusion of hers," she said, exasperated. "Because I've got to tell you, I can't take much more of this."

"There's no delusion here," he said. He looked down at me again, making sure I was eating. I obediently took a bite. "But I'll tell you what you want to know."

"Good," Sloan said, picking the peppers off her pizza, something I knew she only did when she was nervous. She arranged them in a little pile on her plate. "Well? Who are you then?"

"I'm Phillip," he said with a slow smile. "Phillip Deville."

"For fuck's sake-"

He held up a hand to beg her for silence. "Wait. Let me explain. Just listen, before you decide we're both nuts."

"I've already decided that," she said moodily, but went back to her pizza.

"I *am* Phillip Deville," he went on. "But it's not what you think." He looked at me briefly, then back to Sloan. He seemed to have reached some decision. "Whatever Stormy told you, it was an exaggeration of the truth. Because she didn't know how else to explain it without betraying my confidence. She was protecting me. She didn't bring me back from the dead with some spell. She couldn't have, because I never died."

I almost choked on my pizza. A look from Phillip silenced me, though. What was he doing? I was trying to be honest, here, and he was just feeding her more lies.

"What are you talking about?" Sloan looked more confused than ever.

"I faked it."

"You pulled an Elvis," Sloan said dryly. "I'm going to need more of an explanation."

"When I overdosed, they pronounced me dead," Phillip said smoothly. "They were able to revive me at the hospital. But by the time I came to, somebody had already leaked the news that I'd died. All my fans, half my friends thought I was gone. And I was in a bad place. Really bad – drugs, alcohol, depressed to the point of being suicidal – I was in no shape to leave, not without some serious medical and psychiatric care. I needed a break, a stint in rehab, and some serious therapy. The band and my family got together and decided that it might be for the best if everybody continued to think I was dead for a while. It'd give me a chance to get well."

"So you just let people think you were dead?" She was baffled. "I kind of get it, doing that for a short time. But I mean...it's been like twenty-five years!"

"Twenty-three. Almost," I piped up. Sloan glared at me.

"After I kicked the drugs and booze and had some time to decompress, it had already been over a year," Phillip continued, the lie appearing to come to him easily. "And I found that I wasn't really interested in the band or playing music anymore. I waited for a long time to feel ready. But I just wasn't into that life anymore. And the more I thought about the poor fans, all of them who had grieved for me and everything, who were putting flowers on my phony grave and getting tattoos and shit...I just didn't want to rip the rug out from under them. I thought it might be best to stay buried."

"Frankly, that's fucked," Sloan said bluntly. "First of all, who are you to make those assumptions? To keep your fans in the dark like that? And not to mention, faking your own death is a hell of a fucking undertaking. Wouldn't it have been easier to announce that you were leaving the business and quietly go on with your life?"

"I couldn't have left without a big, clean break," Phillip said. "They wouldn't have let me."

"Arrogant." Sloan snorted with indignation, and Phillip's eyes blazed with fury. A laugh escaped my lips and I clapped a hand to my mouth.

"Anyway, have you seen yourself?" Sloan asked incredulously. "How have you not been recognized?" I rolled my eyes at her. An hour ago I'd been wondering the same thing about her.

"I have," he said. "From time to time. I usually use the 'impersonator' excuse. You were just too smart to fall for it." I smirked behind my pizza at how smoothly he lied. Sloan apparently swallowed it, though, because she looked pleased with herself. I fought the urge to roll my eyes again.

"So you never did the spell?" she asked me. "That was all bullshit?"

"No, I did the spell," I said. "Mainly just to wind you up, but the recording got deleted. So it turned out to be useless."

"I knew it. I knew it was all hock-and-booey," she said in a satisfied tone.

I gave her a little smile and took a bite of pizza, hoping she'd let it go now. No such luck. "But none of this explains how the two of you hooked up," she pointed out, picking more peppers off her pizza. "Or why Stormy didn't tell me the *moment* she met you." She looked at me, her face full of irritation; she was used to me telling her literally everything. How many times had she said to me, "just get to the point, I don't need the details?"

"The spell *is* how we met," Phillip answered for me,

sensing my discomfort at lying. Sloan's eyebrows furrowed in confusion. "You know that album she bought, the rare one? It's so special because it's got the spell buried in the liner notes. I guess she's told you all that already."

Sloan nodded.

"There's a whole thread on reddit about the spell." I was suddenly glad I'd told Phillip all about reddit and the wormhole that it was. "People sharing theories, trying out the spell and posting pictures, stuff like that. I read it from time to time, just to keep up with what the fans are doing. Makes me laugh. And it's nice to see I still have my dedicated fans." He smiled at me. "Stormy posted about the spell a while back, and I don't know...I just was drawn to her, somehow. She seemed too interesting, and so invested in the music. I liked her. It gets lonely, being dead. On a whim, I emailed her."

"And we got to talking," I said, seeing where he was going.

"I felt bad for her, going through a divorce and everything. We talked a lot, got to be friends. I was flattered. She was such a huge fan of mine. She knows every single song. Knows me better than I know myself." He winked at me. Okay, he was laying it on pretty thick now. "I couldn't help myself. Against my better judgment I decided to tell her the truth. About who I was."

"When was this?" Sloan asked.

"About a week ago," I said. "I didn't believe him. I told him I needed proof."

"So here I am," he said, with a casual shrug. "I came down to Jekyll Island to meet her in person and show her I am, in fact, Phillip Deville."

"This is so weird," Sloan said finally. "But there's one more thing I don't understand. Who the fuck are the guys who were after Stormy and me?"

"We don't know," I said, thinking quickly. "But we have our suspicions that it's two guys from the reddit group. I know there were a couple of guys in there who wrote for GOTHZine, you know, that metal/doom online mag? It's like Vice meets Rolling Stone? I think maybe they uncovered Phillip's secret. They found him somehow and now they know for sure that he's not dead. That he never died. They want to break the story." I was surprised at myself, now that I'd gotten into it, how easily the lies came.

"Some of my fans are crazy as fuck," Phillip explained with a sympathetic look. "I mean, I get it, but damn. We think these guys are onto me, and they followed me down here to catch a glimpse. They want to get my photo, or better yet, confront me and get proof that I'm alive. Can you imagine the payout if they broke that story with some exclusive? They obviously know who Stormy is, and that she's made contact with me. They're hoping to expose me through her."

"Is that why you're leaving?" Sloan asked us.

"Yeah." I nodded.

"It seems awfully impulsive, to risk outing yourself like that just to meet some girl you met online," Sloan said, a hint of judgment in her voice.

"What can I say." Phillip shrugged, his voice taking on a wistful quality. "It's been a lonely twenty years." I fought the urge to guffaw. He really was too much.

"Well." It seemed Sloan was out of questions, at least for the moment.

Phillip sat down beside me, satisfied, and finally took his own piece of pizza, looking smug. He had managed to mollify Sloan with that ridiculous story, god only knew how. I'd known Sloan most of my life and she was like a dog with a bone. I'd never been able to lie to her. I wondered if one of the apparently many magical powers Phillip possessed included the ability to spin a tale that even the biggest cynic would swallow without trouble.

My head ached. The car crash nagged at me; who had

chased us? Was it Lee? I didn't think it was a coincidence that he'd shown up at the exact same time as Phillip. They *were* looking for him. Had we hit on something – was it possible he really was a fan with a hunch? Was I in danger? Was Phillip? I barely knew him, but I already felt protective. I'd brought him back, and it felt like it was my duty to keep him safe. Though looking at him, devouring his pizza with wolf-like bites, his huge shoulders practically busting through his thin black t-shirt, his long, muscular legs almost the length of my couch, I had no doubt that he could take care of himself and then some. *I wouldn't want to be on his wrong side*, I thought to myself with a small shiver.

PHILLIP WAS BROODING. Both pizzas were gone, Dan had picked up Sloan – he'd stayed and chatted just long enough for me to decide that I liked him, despite the fact that he was a totally vanilla frat boy - and they'd left Phillip and me sitting on the couch at opposite ends. My leg was still throbbing, but it wasn't anything an ibuprofen or two couldn't fix. I felt remarkably okay, though my nerves were still frayed. I watched Phillip silently, the way his jaw twitched – he was biting the inside of his mouth or grinding his teeth or something. He was obviously anxious.

"What is it?" I asked finally.

"I'm worried that I've put you in danger," he said, turning to look at me. God, his eyes were beautiful.

"You? I'm pretty sure *I'm* the one who started this whole thing," I said with a grin, but he didn't return my smile. "I've just been thinking on that myself. I'm the one who said the spell and brought you back, right?"

"But I put it in the liner notes," he said. "Honestly, Stormy, it was just a fucking joke. I was so strung out back then, it seemed like a good idea at the time. Just something funny, to watch the fans pick through my words and try to make a legend out of them. You know, like the whole 'Paul McCartney is dead' thing, or Ozzy biting the head off that bat. It wasn't supposed to be taken seriously."

"Ozzy really did bite the head off that bat," I said, but he didn't seem to hear me.

"When Guthrie gave me that spell, I was amused that he seemed to believe in it. Part of it was just me taking the piss out of him. I know it probably seems like this whole orchestrated thing, that I put the spell there on purpose so someone would bring me back, that if I actually went through with it, I knew I'd have a second chance, but-"

"Wait, what?"

He stopped. "What?"

"Went through with what?" I asked. "What do you mean?"

"Nothing," he said. "I was just talking."

"You died of an overdose," I said slowly. "At least that's always been the official story, the one your estate..." I trailed off, noting the look on his face, my stomach doing a flip flop.

"It doesn't matter," he said softly. "Whatever they printed, it doesn't concern me now."

"Phillip, did you-"

He cut me off. "I'm just saying that I didn't know the spell was real. If I'd known, I never would have put the stupid fucking thing on the album. I never would have put someone in harm's way just to bring me back." He took my hand in his. His skin was so warm. "I'm so sorry, Stormy."

"You don't have anything to apologize for," I said.

"I do," he insisted. "And I want to make it up to you. I don't know how, but I will. Somehow. And in the meantime, I'm going to keep you safe. From whatever it is that's hunting me."

"We'll figure out who that is," I promised.

He gave my hand a squeeze. "How long have you and Sloan been friends?" he asked, changing the subject.

"God, since we were kids," I answered, smiling at the memory. "I've known her since 6th grade or so, but I guess it was around 9th grade that we became really close. Why?"

"That's how me and Kim were," he said, and my smile deepened, thinking of him and his guitarist as teenagers, going through puberty, learning to play guitar together. I'd kill to see a picture from that period. "Those lifelong friends, those are the best ones." His eyes met mine. "If they're true."

"True?" I asked.

"You know. Loyal." He squeezed my hand again. "A friend you can trust with your life. True."

I looked at him curiously, and he grinned. "Don't mind me," he said with a laugh. "I think I'm in one of my moods. Barb used to call it the Nihilist Hour, when I'd get like this. Next thing you know I'll be locking myself in your bathroom, holed-up reading T.S. Eliot."

"Sloan's true," I said, his hand still warm in mine. On impulse, I reached forward and enveloped him in a hug. He tensed for a moment, then relaxed into me, his shirt soft and smelling of my soap, his shoulders wide and solid. His hair tickled my face. My heart pounded at the memory of that morning, his arms around me, teaching me to play bass.

"Do you still want to leave in the morning? For Boston?" I asked, reluctantly pulling away.

"Yeah. I've got to sort all this shit out. Do you still want to go?"

I nodded. The thought of him going and leaving me behind was impossible.

"Ok, then. But before we go, you need to do one thing," he said. "It's probably stupid and won't work anyway, but I want to try it."

"What is it?" I was curious.

"Guthrie told me almost nothing about that damn spell. And I didn't ask." He was still holding my hand. "But there's one thing I *do* remember."

"What is it?"

"I heard him say something to somebody else once. This strung out hippie type he gave a spell to – a different spell. He told him when he summoned someone to make sure he had salt sprinkled all over the place."

"Salt? Why?"

"He said that the practitioner should bathe in salt. That it would help protect them, to counter-balance the black magic they'd performed. I guess kind of a reversal, maybe? A cleansing?"

I took a deep breath. Until he'd said the words 'black magic' it hadn't even occurred to me that that's what I'd done. Not the good kind of magic. Not the benign kind. Black magic. I'd opened myself up to all kinds of bad things, and I hadn't even bothered to think about it. I shuddered. "Okay, so. How do we do it?"

"I'm not really sure. We'll just wing it," he said. "Do you have salt?"

"Yeah, I've got one of those huge cylinders of Morton salt with the pourable spout," I said. "Top cabinet, above the stove. With the spices."

Wordlessly, he went into the kitchen and returned with the salt.

"Do you think it'll work?" I asked.

"I hope so," he said. "Another thing I used to hear Guthrie say, is that magic is all about intention. If you believe, that's 75% of the battle." I nodded. I'd been saying the same thing to myself for days, which was a serendipitous little detail I didn't want to think about just now. But it was true, if the fact that he was standing in front of me was any indication. "Come on.

Let's get this over with. See if we can't cleanse some of the evil off you." His grin was wolfish and impossibly sexy.

"Leave a little of the salt," I said, standing up, feeling suddenly coy. I came just under his chin; near him, I felt so short. There was a heat coming off him, something electric. He stared down at me, his eyes on fire. "Not much, but just a sprinkle. It might come in handy."

"Careful what you wish for." He gave me a long, slow smile. He leaned in toward me, and for an achingly long moment it seemed like he was going to kiss me, but then he leaned back and touched my arm. "Come on. Let's get you cleaned up."

I followed him into the bathroom and held out my hand for the salt. "Do I just, like, pour a ton of it into the bath, or what?" I asked. "Would it be better to use epsom salt?"

"No, the plain stuff. Table salt," he answered. I was still holding out my hand, and he shook his head. "If it's okay with you, I want to be the one to do it. I feel like that will make it more potent."

"You're going to bathe me?" I was incredulous.

"Yes." He gave me another one of those slow smiles. "Is that okay? May I?"

"I mean, I guess..." I said, my thoughts racing. Had I shaved...areas...recently? Oh god.

"I have seen naked women before," he said dryly, noting my discomfort.

"Oh, I know," I said. "And therein lies the problem." I imagined a bevy of impossibly thin and toned, busty super-models, strippers and groupies parading around him, and wished I could hide my belly and stretch marks.

"If you're not comfortable, you could leave your underwear on," he said helpfully.

"Okay," I said, nervous. "The washcloths are under the cabinet there." He turned to grab one, and I undressed quickly, leaving on my underwear and bra, which thankfully matched, though I realized as I settled down in the steaming water that they were both white and would become see through in a few short moments. The hot water hit my scraped leg and I yelped. Phillip was by my side in a flash.

"You ok?"

I nodded. He glanced down at my underwear but met my eyes again in seconds. Smooth, this one. Despite the pain in my leg, the hot water felt amazing and I felt my limbs relax. Phillip dipped the washcloth in the steamy water and dabbed it at my head. It felt like a little of the swelling had gone down. Without thinking, I closed my eyes and settled down in the water as he ran the washcloth over my shoulders, my arms. How long had it been since someone had bathed me? It felt so good, calming and primal at the same time.

"I'm going to do the salt now," he said in a quiet voice, and I opened my eyes. He was pouring it onto the washcloth, rubbing it into some kind of body scrub. "I have no idea if this is the right way, but we'll see. Can you sit up a little?"

I leaned forward, closing my eyes again, and felt the washcloth caress my skin. It was grainy and rough with the salt; it felt like sandpaper, but in a good way. I sighed with pleasure. He moved it back and forth over my back in circles, scrubbing me methodically, then down to my lower back, then my hips and legs, taking special care with the scrape, back up to my arms, over my stomach and breasts, my shoulders and neck, and finally my face, which he washed very slowly and gently. "Lean back," he said, "So I can do your head."

I eased back into the water, feeling my hair fan around my face. My skin seemed to be alive; it was thrumming. He washed my hair with the cloth, his fingers moving through the wet strands, his thumbs resting on my face. As he touched me, I felt something strange happen.

I felt unnaturally light, almost as if I'd left my body. The sensation of warmth from the water, from *him,* had pooled into a delicious liquid gold feeling, and I felt like I was fluid myself, floating all over, everywhere. Like I was looking down on the both of us. My limbs throbbed with pleasure, but at the same time I couldn't feel them. I was in two places at once, feeling two feelings at once. Pleasure and pain. Numbness and warmth. Dark and light.

His hands moved over me, touching each place a second time, moving over every inch of me. His black hair was loose from its ponytail, falling into his eyes, a few tendrils making their way into the water to mingle with my own. Black and dark blonde. At some point I had opened my eyes, but I wasn't sure when. His were now closed; we'd switched places. I memorized the lines in his face, so intent with the job at hand, and marveled at his soft, inky black eyelashes. A rock star on a grand stage, tall, imposing, a bona fide sex god, former junkie, legend in his own right, back from the dead, and with eyelashes as soft as down, as dark as ink.

After another few agonizingly sweet moments, he leaned back, sat on the edge of the tub and smiled. "I think I got you," he said. "Every place there was to get." His smile was boyish.

I was floating; I didn't want to move.

"You look like an angel," he said. "With your hair floating all around your face like that."

"Angel or devil, I don't care," I sang in a warbling, off-key murmur.

"For in front of the door, there is you." His voice was husky and razor-sharp, echoing in the small, steamy room. Familiar and yet other-worldly with the bathroom acoustics. A chill went up my spine. "Bowie."

I sat up, droplets of water cascading off my shoulders. "Get in." I said.

He looked at me dubiously. "What?"

"Get in. The water is still hot." I smiled at him invitingly. "You could use a good scrub yourself."

He stared at me, unsure.

"The tub is too small," he said.

"We'll fit."

He stared.

"Are you scared of me?" I asked. It was meant to be flirty, but I realized the question had other implications.

He looked at me for another moment, then wordlessly stripped off his shirt. The muscles in his arms and chest twitched. His skin looked like china under the harsh bathroom light. He leaned down and took off his pants, then smiled at me. "You wear your underwear, I wear mine."

"Fair enough." I scooted to the far end of the tub, giving him room as he stepped into the tub and eased down. He wrapped his legs around mine.

"Sorry," he said. "I've got really long legs."

"No kidding."

He wrapped his arms around me, too, and instinctively, I leaned against his chest, resting my head in the crook of his neck like a lover. I wondered if he'd flinch, but he didn't; rather, he set his chin down on top of my head, cradling me, and let out a sigh. The room was quiet except for the *drip-drop* from the leaky faucet. It was strange, but the tub wasn't all that cramped, I realized, my eyes closed, letting my limbs do the assessing for me, noticing that it was almost as though the tub had expanded. I stretched out my legs, feeling his skin against mine, and marveled that I could unfurl them all the way without having to bend my knees. What magic was this, and had I done it?

I could feel the thump of his pulse against my back where his chest was pressed up against me. His heartbeat was steady, strong. I pressed in closer, feeling the hardness of him against my lower back, and his breath caught in his throat. I tried to ignore the way my very blood seemed to be singing as it rushed to my extremities. My chest was flushed with desire, and I could tell by his shallow breaths that he was feeling it, too. But it wasn't about that right now – as much as I wanted him, wanted to turn around and devour him whole, this was about cleansing, about taking back control, taking back the power over us. I relaxed against him with a sigh. His arms were strong and held me fast, and I knew if he ever were to truly become predatory, there would be no hope in hell of getting away from him. As it happened, I had no desire to.

Phillip was singing again, his voice low. *"My death waits like a witch at night...and surely as our love is bright. Let's laugh for us and the passing time..."* He laughed low and murmured in my ear. "That you would think to sing that song right now."

"It just came to me," I said.

"Bowie was always my favorite," he said.

"You were always mine," I whispered.

"I KNOW we need to get on the road," I said to Phillip as we coasted up onto the bridge that led to Jekyll Island, "but we won't stay long, and I really want you to see this place."

"I've been to the beach before," he said with a smile, staring out the window. I could see why he was unimpressed so far. The sky was gray and dreary – the sun hadn't been back out since that big storm that had brought him to my door – and the water was dull and dirty against the mud of the marsh. Even the grass, in the dull light of the fall, was muted and colorless. A lone seagull crested against the wind and flew off into the horizon.

"But Jekyll is special," I insisted. "You'll see."

The truth was that I wasn't quite sure why I wanted to bring Phillip here. I'd woken up that morning with a new vigor, the excitement and energy in my limbs almost palpable, and I'd thought before my head had even risen off the pillow that I wanted to take Philip to Driftwood Beach. I knew he was in a hurry to get going, so I'd packed quickly and loaded up the truck, figuring we'd leave for Boston right after – no point in stopping back at home first. I had arranged for Sloan to take care of Blinken until I got back, and things were all tied up with work for the next week. Everything was set to go. But I just had to show Phillip Driftwood first. It felt right somehow.

"If it's special to you, I'm sure it will be special to me, too," he said, putting a hand briefly on my knee. It was a simple gesture, but it brought back memories of how Tess had once done the same thing, and I felt an immediate jolt at his touch. But this was different. "How far is it?"

"Five minutes' drive," I answered, changing gears and grimacing as my old Blazer made a rusty, clanging noise. God knew what that was. "Jekyll Island is quite small. And Driftwood is on this side of the island, anyway. Once we go through the toll bridge it's less than a mile to the main road, we'll take a left at the roundabout, another mile, and we're there. It's really close. We could walk if we had more time."

"I wish we did," he said, still smiling. "That sounds nice."

"Maybe on a sunnier day," I said, wondering if he'd be around long enough to see it through.

"Yeah," he agreed. "Let's do that."

Five minutes later I pulled onto the side of the deserted road and got out of the truck. The wind had picked up; it looked like rain. Phillip got out of the passenger side and stood beside me. "Well, here it is," I said, pointing to the narrow trail within the trees. "These little cut throughs are all up and down this road for a couple of miles, but I always take this one. I'm a creature of habit."

"After you," he said, and I started down the winding trail, thick with brush and sand, hoping it wouldn't rain on us. Phillip had to duck to follow me, the trees were so low. We shuffled through the soft, billowy sand, pushing dead limbs out of our way, passing by dunes, getting grit in our shoes.

"Venomous snake nesting ground," Phillip read as we passed a faded old sign. "Well, that bodes well."

"You let them be, they'll let you be," I said, still dodging limbs.

"Sage advice."

We walked through the clearing and came out onto the beach, which was totally deserted except for one older couple picking up shells several yards away. They gave us a little wave and went back to their task. The horizon had a gray look to it, the water churning with a dirty, weak froth. "It's going to rain," I said, holding a hand over my eyes and craning to see beyond the water. "But I don't think it's going to be a storm. Just a drizzle, probably."

"It's beautiful out here, even overcast," Phillip said, standing beside me with his own hand over his eyes. "I've never seen anything like this. So many trees."

The entire span of the beach was covered in bleached, dead trees. Each of them was unique, gnarled and twisted and stripped into its own grotesque, sloping shape. I pulled myself up onto a J-shaped piece of driftwood into a sitting position. "Aren't they gorgeous?"

"Eerie," he said. "Beautiful."

"Like something out of a Tim Burton movie," I agreed.

"I don't know any of his movies besides Edward Scissorhands," he said with a smile. "But I could totally see this on one of our album covers." Looking out at the expanse of gray beach and gnarled, bleached trees, I had to agree.

"I used to come out here every day and go for a run," I confessed, smiling as he pulled himself onto the driftwood beside me, lowering into a crouch, his head resting beside my right leg. "It's always been my favorite place. Was my favorite place. This is the first time I've been in months."

"Why did you stop coming?" he asked, staring out at the water. The wind whipped his black hair into a frenzy around his face.

"Because of Tess," I said. "My ex-husband." I sighed, and ran my hands over the smooth, stripped bark. "We had our wedding reception here, what seems like a million years ago. It was such a beautiful night. Everything was perfect. We hung paper lanterns from the driftwood, and we set up tables with all different colored tablecloths. People brought dishes to share, and we had sangria and s'mores and after dark we lit a bonfire and sang and danced around it."

"That sounds cool."

"It was. It was perfect." I felt sad at the memory. "I remember sitting there on the sand, in my white sundress, and the sea air was cold on my shoulders. Tess came and put his suit jacket over me, and it smelled like him, and I remember thinking I was the happiest I'd ever been." I swallowed. "I'm pretty sure he was already cheating on me by then."

Phillip was quiet, listening.

"We used to come out here all the time together. It was our place. I guess once he left...it was just too hard, to come out here. Among all those memories. It feels like it's his place now."

"No," Phillip said, resting his cheek briefly against my leg, a movement that was friendly and tender but somehow felt sensual. "It's *your* place. Don't let him take it away from you, not if it means so much to you."

"You're right," I said. "But sometimes it's just so hard to let go. Of pain. You know?"

"I do know." He paused for a moment, and I watched as his

face lit up with a sardonic smile. "Did you ever read anything about my wedding?"

"A little bit," I said. "But I'd love to hear your version."

He scratched at a speck on his black jeans, his face thoughtful as he remembered. "Barb hired a camera crew from a metal mag to film the day, even though I told her I didn't want that. They followed me everywhere, even into the bathroom while I was getting ready. I was a ball of fucking nerves and I wanted a drink, but I wasn't going to start mainlining shots with a camera in my face." He shook his head. "I finally yelled at them to get the hell out, and that was the portion of the video that made MTV. Me, standing in a bathroom half-dressed in a tux that didn't fit right, yelling at a cameraman, my stupid hair flying all over the place, because somebody made off with my comb. On my *wedding day*. Meanwhile, Barb and her mother got into a screaming match just outside the chapel, and somehow Barb's veil got ripped off her head and stomped on. All the guests, who were already seated, heard them carrying on, and when I walked up to the pulpit to get into position, everybody was giggling. Barb comes out on her dad's arm, and there's a giant shoeprint from her mom's Manolo right in front of her face."

"Yikes," I said. "But still, it could be worse."

"Oh, it got worse," he said with a choked laugh. "We got through the ceremony okay, even though I forgot half my vows. But the at the reception everybody got rip-roaring drunk – having an open bar for a bunch of musicians and junkies is a mistake, just FYI – and Kim actually passed out *on top* of the ice sculpture. He sort of stumbled into it, knocked it over, and was out cold on top of it. Almost looked like he'd passed out trying to hump the thing. Then he just laid there in a puddle of melted ice and everybody danced around him, dodging the wet spots."

I stifled a laugh as he went on.

"He came to, soaking wet, tried to stand up and give a toast, called me a bastard, then threw up all over his tux, threatened to punch everybody's lights out, then passed out again." He sighed. "After that the party was pretty much over. I got so blitzed, trying to forget how mortifying the whole thing was, that I barely remember my honeymoon." He turned to me with a smile.

"Christ," I said, embarrassed for him.

"Yeah," he said. "At least you don't have a wedding story like that to contend with, despite whatever came after. I'd love to get married at a peaceful spot like this, out on the beach."

I hesitated, then said, "There's another reason, too, that I don't like coming out here much anymore. I…. almost got struck by lightning here. Last year."

He looked at me in surprise. "Holy shit! What happened?"

"I came out here to run one Saturday," I said. "I could see that it was going to storm, but Tess and I were arguing, and I just wanted to get out of the house. I didn't get a mile down the beach before the rain let loose. I hadn't brought a slicker or anything, so I got drenched. I was trying to make my way back to my car when the thunder and lightning started up." I thought back to that day, remembering the ominous gray of the sky, the huge, fat storm clouds directly over my head, and the tumultuous churning of both the sea and my heart. That had been the day I'd begun to realize that my marriage was ending, and my usual level-headed, cautious attitude toward bad weather had taken a backseat to my heartbreak. "I was almost at the dunes that mark the entrance of the trail, and I turned one more time to look at the water. I've always liked the way it churns during a storm, bringing all the debris onto the shore, all dark and frothy."

"Like a purging," Phillip said thoughtfully.

"Exactly." I nodded. "I watched it for a second, caught up in the beauty of it, but then I noticed there was a man down the beach, several yards away. He was running too, I guess trying to get back to his own car. But then he stopped and was just standing there, looking back at me, like he was frozen. I called out to ask him if he needed help, but he couldn't hear me – the rain was so loud, and I was far away. Then there was this massive thunderclap that shook the ground, and it started to hail. I turned and ran toward the dunes to my car, giving up on trying to help the guy - but just before I hit the trail, the lightning struck less than a foot away. It hit one of these pieces of driftwood and split it in half right in front of me."

"Damn," Phillip breathed. "That's insane."

"I don't *think* it hit me – I'd be dead – but I swear, I could *feel* the electricity, thrumming in the ground and in the air around me. The force of it knocked me into the sand, and when my fingers went into the dirt, it *shocked* me. I felt it jolt through my hands. Somehow, I managed to scramble back up and get to my car, but I was shaking like a leaf." I shivered. "If I'd been holding onto that piece of driftwood, I'd have been smoke."

"Sounds like you used up one of your nine lives," Phillip joked, but his face was grim.

"And I used another one last night, when I got run off the road," I said. "Now I'm down to seven." I realized as I said the words that Phillip had the number "7" tattooed on his arm. I felt a chill and wrapped my arms tighter around myself.

If he saw the significance, too, he gave no sign. "I'm glad you're okay," he said softly. "It's pretty fitting, your name – Stormy - isn't it? There's always a storm raging around you." Then he was silent, staring out at the water.

After a moment, I felt a need to fill the silence, to put my thoughts at bay. "Do you think it will be hard?" I asked. "Giving up your old life? Fame, fortune, being up on the stage?"

"Right now, it's the last thing in the world I want," he

answered honestly, still looking out at the water. "Whether or not that'll change, I don't know. I hope not. It was fun, playing music. It was my dream once, and I was lucky enough to see it come true. But with all that shit comes the drinking and drugs, and the fractured relationships, and the fish eye lenses, you know? By the time I died, my life was a shell of what I'd thought it would be. I didn't know who I was anymore. By that point I didn't even want it."

I was silent, watching him stare out at the water. The wind blew his hair into his eyes, but he didn't push it away.

"It's like being on a rollercoaster, but long past the point of being fun. And you keep telling yourself 'this is fun, this is fun, it's a ride' – you know, like the Bill Hicks quote?" I didn't, but I nodded. "But you're really ready to go home. You've got a stomachache and you've ridden it for hours and you just want to go home. Go back to normal. But you can't get off the ride once you get on. Not unless you just jump."

"Is that what you did?" I asked softly, reaching out to touch his shoulder. "You jumped?"

He paused. "In a manner of speaking."

"What do you miss the most?" I asked. "About that life?"

"I don't think I've been away from it long enough to miss anything," he said, then added, "I miss my bass. It was custom made – I spent years on it. Designed it, built it, painted it, spent years customizing my pedal board."

"I know," I said. "I've seen it in the guitar mags."

"I wonder who ended up with it," he said. "I doubt it sold at auction or anything. I was never famous enough for that."

"Not true," I said with a snort. "It did sell at auction. I can't remember who got it, but it was in the hundreds of thousands. It was a charity thing. C'mon, Phillip. You have a cult following now. Your fame rose exponentially after your death." It touched me how humble he was, how he didn't seem to realize how much people loved him.

"I guess that makes sense," he said. "Thinking back to, like, Morrison, Lennon and all. But it's weird to think about. I don't hold myself in the same esteem, you know."

"You deserve it," I told him. "Fame and adoration. Even if you had to die and rise again to see it."

He laughed. "That's such a weird sentence."

"Well, you're a weird guy."

We both stood, sliding off the large piece of bleached driftwood, and began to walk down the beach. The sand was gritty in my shoes, so I reached down and took them off, and Phillip did the same, sitting down on the damp sand to remove his laced-up combat boots. He rolled up his black jeans and I chuckled to myself, watching him – this tall, goth drink of water carefully rolling up his pants so he could walk in the surf. It occurred to me that a moment like this might never happen again, so I took a mental snapshot of him, sitting there in the sand, heavy, dark boots sitting beside him, his long fingers deftly rolling up his pant legs, hair streaming around his face. "You're so handsome," I said softly, feeling overcome with an emotion I couldn't identify. "All of this feels like a dream."

He looked up at me with a slow, sexy smile, and pinched the skin of his arm. "Nope, no dream," he said with a laugh, rising on his haunches and standing. "I'm as undead as they come, Stormy Spooner. I'm afraid you're the real deal, a real-life necromancer. Fuckin' weird, huh?"

"Very fuckin' weird," I repeated.

"What's weirder is that I've never set foot in Georgia in my life until a few days ago, but I can't shake the feeling that I've been here before, y'all."

He stood there, grinning, then he pitched forward and enclosed me in an awkward but very warm hug. His arms were strong and warm and held me tight. I wrapped my arms around his neck and hugged him back, inhaling the woodsy, clean scent of him, feeling his tangled hair brush against my cheek. The sound of the water lapping up on the shore was behind us, soothing and calm.

He gave me one more quick squeeze and pulled away, his pretty green eyes catching the dull light. "I don't want you to worry. We'll figure all this shit out, and it's going to be fine. I promise."

"How do you know?" I asked as we began to walk along the water, our shoes left behind in the sand. "What if it's all a giant clusterfuck and I've opened a huge can of worms and we have to somehow fix it?"

"I've already died," he said. "What's the worst that could possibly happen now?"

Nine

THE ONLY NOISE WAS THE LOUD RUMBLING OF MY ENGINE. I couldn't get Spotify to work; it kept saying "no connection," and Phillip was oddly silent as he navigated the truck on the highway. He was leaned back, switching gears like the truck was his. Even though I hated myself for it, it gave me a little thrill to see him driving it. And it gave me plenty of opportunities to sit back and look at him.

He felt my eyes on him and gave me a small smile but said nothing.

I could hardly believe the night before had actually happened– the salt bath, lying against him in the warm water, the tub seeming to expand to fit us both, my head in the crook of his neck, his hair soft and damp against my skin, his voice in my ear as he sang to me. Never in my wildest imaginings could I have conjured up such a perfect moment. I'd never forget the way his breath felt on my forehead, how he smelled, how it felt to have his long, muscular legs wrapped around mine, the feel of his skin against my own, wet from the tub, coarse with salt. It was an odd thing, but sensual and private and perfect.

So perfect that I'd ached with wanting when I had gone to bed a little later, alone. Once the water started to cool to luke-warm, we'd exited the tub, and I'd stood there in the steamy room, staring up at him, waiting for him to say or do something. A signal, a hint of a flush, a look in his eye. But instead he handed me a towel and ran his finger over my cheek. "You still have salt on you," he'd said.

I held the towel away from me, not wanting to cover up yet, craving more intimacy. "I don't care," I said softly.

He had leaned down then, his face inches from mine, breathing deeply, and I felt the thought on his lips. But he seemed to think better of it, and pulled back slightly with a smile, then drew a towel around his waist and left the bathroom.

I'd gone into my room without saying goodnight, confused, slightly hurt and incredibly turned on, and pulled on my pajamas in the dark. I half expected to hear him knock on the door, but he didn't. I heard the creak of the couch springs, then his light snoring, and after about an hour I'd finally gone to sleep, frustrated but oddly satisfied. Then, an equally perfect but bittersweet moment out on Driftwood Beach, when he'd talked about himself and enveloped me in that warm hug that just felt *right*.

Now, in the truck, it felt like it all must have been a dream. If not for the little flecks of salt I was still finding stuck to my skin from both the tub and the beach, I would have believed it was. The energy had changed within both of us, and whatever dream-like, magical bonding had taken place had given way to anxious, worried energy.

I didn't know what to say to him now and figured I probably shouldn't bring up anything that would only make him worry more. So I stayed quiet. I wished I could have some music, though. The silence was more than deafening and I was starting to feel acutely embarrassed. I fiddled with my phone, closing the app and reopening it, but Spotify still wouldn't work. Neither would iTunes. It made no sense; I usually had stellar internet connection on the open road. Of course, I knew, in the back of my mind, what it was. The same thing that had rendered my laptop useless and had caused Phillip's burner phone to keep going off. It was Phillip.

Something – his brainwaves, maybe - fucked with technology. As if this whole thing wasn't weird enough.

"Sorry."

"What?"

"None of your shit works around me," he said.

"Stop doing that!" I said, with mock irritation. "Reading my mind!"

"It's not on purpose," he said. "It just sort of happens."

"One of these days you'll catch me thinking something I don't necessarily want you to know, and then I'll have to throw myself off a building." He only grinned in response. "Oh god, it's already happened."

"It's been enlightening." He smirked. "I know that you still crave McDonald's cheeseburgers, and that your friend with the cool band name is banging an old dude who dresses like Winnie the Pooh-"

"Oh, god, stop." I groaned, then started to laugh. "Don't ever tell anybody about the Mickey D's."

"I'll buy you one," he said in a sly voice. "We're out on the road, it's a vacation. Nobody will ever know."

"No!"

He laughed. I fiddled with the radio and managed to pick up one channel. Through the static I could hear George Jones' booze-soaked crooning of White Lightnin'. Phillip began to sing along in his velvety baritone, and the hair on my arms stood up. It was such a weird juxtaposition – his doom-metal voice lilting along to one of the country greats – but it was absolutely beautiful.

"I know what you're feeling," he said, staring at the road, picking up our pre-song conversation. I busied myself looking at a truck we were passing, just like mine but blue. "But don't worry. I'm not trying to pick up on anything you don't want me to. I'm working on controlling it. And I'd never knowingly invade your privacy." He glanced over at me and smiled. "Please don't be scared of me."

"I'm not scared of you," I said.

"You're wary of me, then," he said. "I can feel it. It bums me out."

"I'm not," I argued. "I swear."

"Why can't you look at me, then?" he asked.

I opened my mouth to say, *that's all I've been doing.* Or, *if I look at you, I won't be able to stop.* But both of those things were pathetic, and I was embarrassed enough without being a failure to feminists everywhere. Instead, I changed the subject. "Tell me about where we're going. Who we're seeing. The plan."

"My old neighborhood. I squirreled some money away there once, after our first album went platinum. I had this paranoid idea that banks were evil, or that some accountant at the record label – or one of my bandmates – was going to cheat me. After a while, I was so strung out I forgot about it. I guess it's a good thing I did, huh?" He looked over at me. "I hope to fuck it's still there."

"Where is it?"

"Buried under a tree in my old backyard."

"Did anybody know it was there? Your family or anybody?"

"Just Jason," he answered.

"Jason? As in Jason Langley?"

He nodded. There were two remaining members of the band. Nathan "Ollie" Green, the band's rhythm guitarist, who had totally quit playing music after the deaths of Phillip and

Kim but turned up from time to time in skating competitions and also held a monthly column in a local indie rock magazine, where he wrote about the intersection of politics and rock music. Jason Langley, head guitarist and co-founder of Bloomer Demons, was Phillip's best friend from childhood and was still very much alive but kept a low profile and had done so for over a decade after his last stint in rehab. He'd done the Dr. Drew show, and after that he'd disappeared into the ether. I hadn't seen any interviews with him or heard of his where-abouts in a long, long time. I had always assumed that was good news, that maybe it meant he was sober. His name still cropped up from time to time on message boards and reddit, but nobody had seen him in the flesh in over a decade. I told this to Phillip, and he nodded with a grim smile.

"Doesn't surprise me. He always said if he was ever going to truly kick that shit, he'd have to leave the business." He smiled sadly. "He was so strung out – more so than any of the rest of us, really. We all loved our cocaine and wine, but he was doing heroin and shit, and well...you know the way it goes."

"After Kurt, it became old hat," I said.

"Kurt? As in Cobain? What happened to him?" he asked.

"Oh," I said, realizing. Phillip had died in 1993, a year before Kurt's very public and very tragic demise. "He uh-"

"Don't worry about it," he said, waving a hand. "I can guess. Damn. I liked him. He was so talented. Hell of a nice guy, too nice, really, just very sincere. I was really rooting for him to get it together."

The irony of this struck me. "It was a whole thing," I said. "People still have conspiracy theories. There are whole docu-mentaries trying to blame Courtney for what happened." I didn't mention that Sloan and I had been embroiled in a decade long argument about that very subject, and that we were now sworn to never talk about it again, lest I revoke her feminist card *and* bestie card. I fucking loved Courtney Love. Anyone who didn't could eat a dick.

"I'm sure people tried to blame Barb, too. For my downfall," he said thoughtfully. "Did they?"

They had. There were whole groups of fans who hated Phillip's ex-wife, even though she'd never gone public with any stories or tried to profit off his death. She was another one who kept a low-profile. I knew she was remarried and had children, but she rarely gave interviews and it was an unspoken agreement between the fans – the true ones, anyway - that she was to be left alone. I gave him a curt nod but didn't elaborate. I loathed the jealousy that brewed in my gut at the mention of her name. "I hate that you all struggled so much," I said finally, not sure what else to say, not wanting to bombard him with upsetting stories of his peers or his fans. Or his ex. "I know it must be hard."

He gave a non-committal shrug, but I wasn't going to let him off so easy.

"You said Kurt was sincere," I said, looking at him. "Now that I've met you, I could say the same for you."

"What do you mean?"

"The real you," I said. "Beneath the hair and the clothes and the persona – oh, I have no doubt you really are that guy – the tall vampire type with the sardonic wit and the animal charm, that's really who you are, but there's another you, behind the...the smoke and mirrors, as you say. It's ironic to me that you'd use the word 'sincere.' Because that's what I see in you. Sincerity." I looked at his sharp profile, his pursed mouth, the way the hair fell over his ear. "So much of it that you had to hide."

He didn't answer, but he glanced at me, and his face was sad. "That's very astute of you, Stormy."

"Not really. It's just what I see." Without thinking, I

reached over and tucked his hair behind his ear. He looked surprised. "Is it hard? Being two people?"

"Yes," he answered. "It was. Not at first, maybe. It's fun, acting, playing a part. Seeing what you can get away with. And it's easier to be a larger than life version of yourself, to put a dramatic face out there, when you're newly famous. But after a while..." He swallowed. "It hurt. I wanted to go back to the life I had before, but I couldn't. It was impossible." He sighed. "I belonged to them now."

"It's bullshit," I said, angry. "It's like our society has made sincerity unpalatable. Any kind of vulnerability, it's repugnant to us, especially in men. So you guys force yourselves to wear masks, to cloak yourself in sarcasm, in bravado, and it works at first, because that's what we want, you know, a tough guy. But then you go to take off the mask, and it's stuck to your face. It's there forever, and you can't get it off."

"Not without pain," he said.

"It's bullshit," I repeated. "Is that what happened, Phillip? To you?"

"Sure," he said, his face stony. "We're all just out there trying to be that guy. Scratch the surface of any strung-out rock star and you'll find a little boy who just wants to please his mama who abandoned him. Win her love. The public becomes a version of that same feeling – we just want to please you, win you over. That's all any of us are doing out there – drugs, groupies, stardom – it's all just us trying to climb back in the womb, trying to win our mother's approval, and everyone else's."

"So that's your story, then? It's that simple?"

He nodded. "Yep. Jason's, too. My mom was around though – you read the biography?" I had. "She was there, but she was a drunk, blah blah. Different stepdad every year, but at least she was around. And she was proud of me when I made it. In her own way, you know. Jason's mom, though...." He made a noise in his throat. "She was something else. She neglected him, left him alone for months at a time. Would come back strung out and beat the shit out of him. The whole reason he got into music was because she had this stupid idea that he'd be a child prodigy, like the next Mozart. Like every other boy on the block isn't picking up a fucking guitar. All he ever did was disappoint her. Once we started making money she tried to come back around, and it got real ugly."

I had read about some of this. A fight that had come to blows, Jason serving time for battery after punching his new stepfather in the face. The band had fired him over it, but hired him back a year later, after yet another stint in rehab. I didn't bring this up. "Do you think he's okay? You know, these days?"

"No idea," he said. "No idea at all. I hope so. I guess we'll find out."

"What about your mom?" I asked. "And your...Barb?" I almost didn't want to bring her up again. "Have you thought about where they all might be? How they're doing? Do you plan to..."

"No," he said succinctly, not letting me finish my question. "I won't be visiting anyone from my – my other life. My life before." He cleared his throat. "For one, it's too risky. For me and for them. But also, I don't want to disrupt anything. It would be an ordeal. How would I explain? How could we go back? I've been dead for over twenty years. I can't expect any of them to -" He seemed to be having a hard time. "And I don't know that I even *want* to go back, to see them all. Before I died, it was so bad, so much shit. What if some of them have died? And Barb..." He trailed off, looking uncomfortable. "Well, you don't want to hear about all that. About her."

"I don't mind," I lied. "I've read a lot of it anyway. If the magazines can be believed."

He laughed. "They can't, but it's probably all true in my case."

"I always thought it was funny that you were married so long," I admitted. "You don't seem like the marrying kind. Especially not back then."

"I wasn't," he admitted. "Barb would be the first person to tell you that." He shrugged. "But we were just kids when we got married, and it was right before Bloomer Demons hit it really big, so I had no idea what was in store, and neither did she. We thought we were in love. Whatever...it is what it is, I guess."

"So what happened?"

"Same old story. Drugs. Cheating. I did all kinds of dumb shit and she put up with it because the checks were rolling in. We weren't right for each other and everybody told us that, but we wouldn't listen. She was so hot then, you have no idea. And she had an attitude on her that I just loved. Most girls, the groupies, were all docile and sweet, sucked up to the band. Even before we made it. And I liked that, too, but what I liked about Barb was that she just didn't give a fuck. She wasn't impressed by me. She let me know fast she could do better elsewhere if she chose to. And that's what kept me around. I knew she meant it.

"But even after we got married, her attitude was the same. I never felt like she really loved me. It always seemed like she was just waiting for the next, better opportunity." He looked at me. "Don't get me wrong – I'm not making excuses or blaming her. I was cheating on her every stop of the tour, and I was on drugs and not very good company when I was around. I was a terrible husband. I treated her like shit. She had every right to think I was a piece of crap, because I was."

"Sounds like she and I have some things in common," I said. "I also stuck by a man I knew was no good for me. He didn't have any money, though."

"I'm sorry," he said. "That he treated you badly."

"It's okay."

"You didn't deserve that."

"I know."

He went on, "After our divorce she got a pretty big settle-ment, I didn't dispute it, and we went our separate ways. She was heavy into drugs too, and I hope to god she got off them. It's a blessing that we never had any kids. I wouldn't be able to bear the thought of leaving somebody alone in that world." He looked sad, distraught even, and I wondered if I should tell him that Barb had indeed cleaned herself up, remarried and had children of her own now. Would he be happy for her, to know that her life had gone on, or would he grieve over all he had missed? I wasn't sure it was my place to delve into such heavi-ness - something so personal – but I knew what it felt like, to watch the life you thought you'd have go up in smoke, with nothing to show for it after. His pain was my pain. I stared at him for a beat, watching him bite the inside of his cheek, his face set in a painful grimace, and decided he'd rather know.

"If it makes you feel any better…" I said, "From what I've read, she's okay. Remarried, kids, the whole bit."

"Well, that's great," he said, his face breaking into a genuine smile, but there was a darkness behind his eyes. "I'm glad. Glad she's doing okay, has a family. But…I still don't want to see her." He sighed heavily. "Is that awful?"

"I don't know," I said honestly. "My ex is kind of a weak point with me. He hasn't been gone very long and he…well, he still has power over me. I'm a fucking idiot around him."

"No, you aren't," he said. "Love is complicated. Sometimes we give people more chances than they deserve." He paused, then asked, "Do you still love him?"

"No," I said quickly. "At least not the way I used to. But I hate being alone, and when I get *really* lonely, it feels like I love him. I just want him near me. He's one of very few people who really knows me. I get confused, you know. Lose sight of what it is I really need."

"Stormy," he said quietly, his eyes back on the road. "That's no good, girl."

I suddenly wanted to tell him everything. So I did. About Tess' infidelity, the drug use, how I had given him a second chance, only for him to be arrested without even giving me the dignity of coming home from jail with me. How he'd left me nothing but our pitiful trailer and a truck on its last leg. How I still waited by the phone for him to call, which he hadn't, not until he'd come breezing back into town with Roberta, asking for favors from my best friend.

Phillip listened in silence, but his hand was still on my arm. It felt good, telling him. Just getting it off my chest, I felt lighter. "I guess for a long time I thought he was all I could get. Guys don't hit on me much; they never did. I know I'm not a knockout. Tess was the first guy to show a real interest, and he seemed so hot for me-" I blushed a little. "-and I responded to that, because it didn't happen much. When he started to drift from me, I kept clinging to him even though I knew it was over, because I was scared. Scared of not being wanted, of going back to that invisible place again. Scared I might not ever get anybody else."

He looked at me again, frowning. "You're insane. You're beautiful, Stormy."

I shrugged.

"No, it's true. You have something about you," he said. "A vibe that I've never gotten off anybody else. It's, like, pure, but also sly. You have hidden depths...and beautiful eyes. I could get lost in them." I looked down at my lap, embarrassed, but he went on. "This Tess guy sounds like a massive dick, but he obviously saw the same things that I see."

"He just used me," I said bitterly.

"People are shit," he replied. I nodded in agreement. "But you know...I loved Barb. I really loved her. I knew deep down she wasn't right for me, though. And even if she had been 'the one,' I don't think we would have lasted because of all the shit she and I were doing, you know? I treated her bad, and she treated me bad, but I did love her, and I believe she loved me as much as she could."

I stared out the window.

"Maybe it's the same for you and this Tess guy. You could look at it like that. You loved each other, but it just wasn't a good fit in the end. Life got in the way, mistakes were made, and it isn't meant to be but...you both loved." He gave my arm a gentle, warm squeeze. "Maybe a nicer way to look at it?"

"But it doesn't change what he put me through."

"No," he agreed. "It couldn't."

I smiled and gave his hand a squeeze back, feeling better than I had in a long time. I let my fingers linger on his skin, enjoying the warmth and closeness.

His face went tense and he pulled it away. Crestfallen, I said, "Sorry. I didn't mean-"

"No, it's not you," he said, his expression grim. "I didn't want to say anything until I was sure, but there's somebody on our tail."

"Fucking seriously? Not again!" I looked in my side mirror but didn't notice anything out of the ordinary. We were on a major highway, so there were cars everywhere. "Where?"

"The car behind us, two cars back," he said. "The maroon one. He's been keeping his distance, but I've been noticing it for an hour now. He always stays two cars back. No matter where we turn, he turns. He's going our speed."

"But most of the cars are. It's a highway," I pointed out.

"I have a feeling about that one," he said. "Watch."

He waited a few moments, then drifted into the left lane without signaling. In the rearview, I could see the maroon car take notice; the driver's head turned sharply. He didn't change lanes – that would have been too obvious – but the driver was definitely watching us. He had also picked up a cell phone and was talking into it.

"Should we try to get off the highway?"

"Yeah," he said. "But not to lose them. I want them to follow me. See what I can figure out. We'll stop for a drink, yeah?"

He waited two more exits, then drifted back into the right lane and exited quickly without signaling. He crested over the hill toward the red light, going fast, to see if the maroon car would try to catch up with us, thinking they'd lost us. It worked. The maroon car careened over the hill at breakneck speed, coming up behind us much too fast; he had to slam on his brakes. The driver looked angry now that we'd noticed him. He had miscalculated, a rookie move.

"He obviously doesn't do this often," Phillip said with a short laugh.

"I think that's Lee Courtenay," I said, sneaking another covert glance. "He's got a different hat on, but from what I can see, it looks like him. Unless he's got a twin brother."

"Why is this fucker following me?" Phillip demanded, quickly looking at me. "What does he want?"

"Well, you keep saying he's looking for you," I replied with a hollow laugh. "Looks like he's found you." I bit at a fingernail. "But, Phillip? What if it's me he's following? I met him before I ever even saw you, at the farmers market. I can't help but wonder if his interest has nothing to do with you at all. Maybe he's one of Tess' buddies or something. Maybe he's investigating the drug ring-"

"It isn't that," Phillip said as the light turned green. He

hung left and took off fast. "And anyway, that day at the farmers market – I was there, too."

I remembered seeing the man with the dusty black jacket that day, darting behind booths, staring a hole through me, the way his black ponytail had rippled in the late-morning sun. I had thought I was going mad, leftover jitters from the stupid spell I'd done, and the hangover I'd brought on myself. "You asshole. I thought I was going crazy."

He laughed despite how tense we both were. "I had to see you for myself. I couldn't wait till you were back home. I had to check you out."

"How on earth…how did you know…" I flailed. "How did you find me there, of all places?"

"When you summoned me, I just knew where you'd be," he said. "It's like…I could feel you. I followed you there, but I didn't know how to approach you in public, with all those people there. So I just watched. I knew you saw me, too, but it was kind of a thrill, honestly." He grinned, catlike, and my heart started to race. But then his face turned dark. "And then I saw *him*." He glowered. "That phony act, spilling flowers all over you. He was there for a reason. He was there because *I* was there."

"But how could he have known you'd be there? That either of us would be there?" A half-formed thought began to form in my consciousness and then faded away before I could pinpoint it.

"I don't know," he answered honestly. "The next time he dares to show his face, we'll ask him. You're right, though; it's definitely Lee in that car. So let's give him the opportunity to 'catch' us; just see what the coward does." He pulled into a Chevron station and parked by the door. "Want a Coke or something?"

I wasn't sure I liked this idea. "I'll go in and get the drinks and you stay in the car," I suggested. "We can't risk you being recognized. Especially not if we're already being followed." I grabbed my purse and went inside before Phillip could argue, picking out two seltzer waters and a Coke, paying the cashier with shaking fingers. As I waited for my change, I saw the maroon car from the window, coasting slowly through the parking lot. It looked like he was thinking about stopping. But as he passed the storefront, I saw him turn his head, glance into the store, and then he stepped on the gas and sped away from the store, turning onto the street and away from us.

I came back out to the truck, holding the drinks, and got in wordlessly. Phillip was looking in the rear-view mirror, his face a black cloud. "Fucking coward," he seethed, taking his Coke and unscrewing the lid. "He knew I was sitting right here, waiting for him, and the motherfucker just drove on." He grunted. "Sure did get an eyeful of you before he did, though. Did you see the way he was staring at you?"

"I can't imagine what he wants with us," I said. "Phillip, what if...I was joking before, but what if he's some kind of cop for real, but like a...don't laugh, but...like a paranormal cop? What if we broke a rule? What I did...it wasn't white magic. That's why you did the salt ritual, right? What if he's coming after us because I wasn't supposed to summon you? Like I've upset the balance or something, broken a rule, and now I have to pay the price. Maybe this Lee guy is just trying to bring me to justice."

Phillip didn't reply, but the look on his face revealed that he'd already considered this. He reached a hand out and touched me on the shoulder. "I don't think that's likely – he's had plenty of opportunities to dole out justice if he was gonna - but...well, whatever it is, I'm not going to let anything happen to you, Stormy. I owe you my life – literally," he said with tenderness. "I'll be damned if you meet some punishment for giving me that gift. I won't have it."

I took a long drink of my seltzer, trying to give him a

bright smile, but I felt queasy. I'd gone and gotten myself – and Phillip – into a world of trouble. It was obvious that Lee, whoever he was, was not going to stop following us. He wouldn't leave us alone until he got what he wanted, and I would find out what that was soon enough.

Ten

"I'm exhausted," Phillip said, pulling into the parking lot and choosing a space in front of Room 604. He had already been to the front desk to reserve it, after I'd insisted we pay in advance. "This place looks like a dive, but as long as I'm taking charity from you, I want to spend as little as possible.

"Phillip, I told you I don't mind-"

"I know," he said firmly. "But I don't like taking your money. I'll be glad when I can pay it back."

"Anyway, this place doesn't look all that bad," I said hopefully, stepping out of the truck. We stood on the curb. "It's old, that's for sure, but it isn't dirty. And this is an okay neighborhood, from the looks of it. They even have Wi-Fi and a pool."

"Fancy a dip later?"

"Maybe. It's so cold, though." I smiled at him, a genuine smile. Now that we were out of the cramped truck, things felt a little brighter. "I just hope a certain someone stays away."

"Shh," he said, putting a playful finger to my lips. "We're on vacation, Stormy, let's not ruin it with bad thoughts."

"Vacation. Ha." But I was smiling. It sort of *did* feel like a vacation. A road trip upstate with a handsome, thrilling man, staying in a motel in the middle of the week. It was all so spur of the moment. Something I never did. It felt kind of good. I realized, guilty, that I hadn't checked in with Sloan all day. I hadn't sent so much as a text. Then again, she hadn't contacted me, either.

"Let's go see this dump of a room," Phillip said, and grabbed my hand as if it were the most natural thing in the world. I followed him up the steps to the second floor, and he fished the key out of the pocket of his dark black jeans. "I'm sorry I couldn't get us two beds. They only had one queen left."

"You expect me to believe that?" I teased as he fiddled with the room key, trying to get the handle to click open. "Don't you read romance novels? That's the oldest trope in the book. Couple forced to travel together under weird circumstances, there's all this sexual tension, then they get a room and they're *forced* to share a bed because the one motel within miles miraculously has no double beds despite being, you know, literally a place full of beds."

"Sexual tension, huh?" he interrupted, turning to me with a sly smile. "Are you saying we have that?"

I met his eye. "Are you denying that we do, Phillip Deville?"

"Hey, I'm not denying anything at all. But you're the one calling me a liar, here."

"I'm just saying that it's…convenient." I smirked up at him. We stared at each other, the sound of the ancient AC unit clunking behind us, until finally he looked away. He pushed the motel room door open and gestured for me to enter.

The room was dark, so Phillip flicked on the light. It was sparse, a little old and dusty, but clean, with green carpet, green drapes and a patchwork bedspread on the queen bed. It smelled of lavender cleaning solution and stale coffee, which I figured was better than most. There was a bathroom with a bathtub and shower, much to my relief. My salt bath the night before was wearing off and I felt more than a little ripe. I took off my jacket and purse and laid them on the bed, then turned to Phillip. "Well, what n-"

I didn't get a chance to finish the sentence. Phillip grabbed me, pulled me close and placed his huge hands on my shoulders. "Stormy," he said in a fierce whisper, his face inches from mine. "I want to kiss you so bad. I've been wanting to since I first laid eyes on you. Tell me you want me to. Because I can't stand it anymore."

For a minute I just looked at him, eyes wide, forgetting how to form words. "I do want you to," I said finally, in an equally fierce whisper. I stared up at his beautiful face, his flashing eyes, and smiled. "Duh."

Then his lips were crushing mine, tasting of cloves and of Coca Cola, very sweet, soft and rough at the same time. The stubble from his chin was scratchy against my face, but it felt good. His arms gripped me, his hair brushed against my cheeks and I was filled with the essence of him, dark and warm and bright. I kissed him back, giving myself up to it immediately, stopping the racing thoughts in my brain. There would be plenty of time later for rehashing, replaying, and screaming to myself in disbelief that this really happened. But right now, it was *happening,* and it felt so good that my knees went weak, so I leaned into him, my hands resting on his hard chest, my fingers splaying out, wanting to touch him tenderly, to memorize him completely. He was an amazing kisser. He tasted so good, and I opened my mouth fully to his, wanting to explore him, devour the delicious wetness of his tongue, the crushing firmness of his mouth. His kiss felt somehow sacred, and also profane, and tantalizingly delicious. I never wanted it to end.

But he pulled away, leaving me aching, hanging by a thread.

He smiled at me, long and slow, pushing his hands through

his hair and back out of his face. His eyes ran over me and I felt scorched by the heat in his gaze. "I've been thinking about this since last night when I had you in the bathtub," he confessed with a drawn-out grin. "And it was every bit worth the wait."

"I've been thinking about it since you put that bass in my hands," I growled, and pulled him toward me.

I put a hand on his chest, feeling his heartbeat, the warmth of him. I wanted to finish what we'd started, taste more of him, feel his breath on me, his mouth on me, but I didn't want to push. There was something agonizing and exquisite about the waiting, the postponing of the inevitable. We both knew it would happen, but when? Where? How? Each of these questions had weight, and the weight was heady and full of mouth-watering, thrilling tension. I felt my breath catch as we stared at each other, both breathing hard. I felt my lips curl into what felt like the thousandth smile of the day, my cheeks hurting with the effort, and as I started to pull away, he pulled me close, his face achingly close to mine, his lips barely brushing against my mouth, his breath feather light against my lips, his dark, long lashes soft and ticklish against my face. I put my arms around his neck, and his went around my waist as he picked me up easily, pressing his mouth against mine with agonizing slowness. We would draw this out, make it last, make it build and build until it took us under...

"Is it true about rock stars and hotel rooms?" I murmured against his mouth.

He groaned and chuckled in a low voice. "Is what true?"

"That they get up to all kinds of nefarious things in them."

"Depends," he answered, his lips trailing down to my collar bone. "On what you consider nefarious."

"I don't know." I laughed, relishing the feel of his mouth on my skin. It was all I could do not to collapse; my knees felt so weak. "I'd like to think I'm up for anything, but I do happen to know that you toured with Motley Crue, and I figure Nikki Sixx might've taught you some really bad habits..."

"I guess you'll just have to find out." His mouth was on mine again, and I was kissing him back, my arms around his warm neck, my hands buried in his tangle of long black hair.

"If you're up for it, I am." I giggled into his neck.

"Believe me, I'm up for it." He growled, grabbing me by the hips, and I almost started purring right there in his arms. Forget waiting; I wanted him right here, right now.

I was just resigning myself to, *it's going to happen it's going to happen,* when there was a knock on the door.

Phillip put me down instantly and we stared at each other, startled, both still breathing hard. My hands were still on Phillip's chest. His heart was beating fast.

"Nobody knows we're here," I whispered. "It's got to be him." Lee.

"I'll take care of it." Phillip brushed past me and went to the door, gesturing for me to hide in the bathroom. I went in reluctantly, pushing the door shut but leaving it open a crack as I heard Phillip fumbling with the door handle. I heard him say, "Who are you?" and the voice that replied, "I'm here to see Stormy," was not Lee Courtney, but rather someone else. Someone whose voice I'd know anywhere. I emerged from the bathroom, confused.

Tess, my ex-husband, was standing in the doorway.

"What are you doing here?" I demanded.

"Hey, hey, darlin'," Tess said with a big smile, coming into the room and sweeping me into a hug like an old friend. After the pleasure of Phillip's hands – and mouth – all over me, it was an unwelcome sensation and I recoiled. "I knew it was you! At first, I was like, 'nah, it can't be her, why would she be all the way out here, with some weird looking joker like that'…but it *is* you.'" He grinned at me. He'd cut his hair, and looked oddly tanned, which was weird since it was fall. He was also either baked out of his mind, or drunk, from the way he was stumbling, leaning up against the wall. Knowing him, it was probably both.

"What are you doing here?" I demanded again, gaping at him. "Did you follow us?"

He shook his head. "Well, I did, but only from the Chevron station up the road. I was pumping gas and I saw you come out with a bunch of drinks and I couldn't believe it was you. I didn't know why you'd be out of state, especially out this far, and my curiosity got the better of me."

"Why didn't you just say hi at the store?" I asked, suspicious.

He laughed. "You were pulling out in too big of a hurry. I had to finish pumping my gas, didn't I?"

I stared at him, disbelieving, and he stared back at me, all wide-eyed innocence. We'd done this when we were married...he'd jokingly called it the redneck standoff. But I wasn't in the mood today.

"Well, as, uh, nice as it was to see you," I said, trying to keep my voice polite, my rage simmering underneath, "I'm really tired. It's been a long day. I was just getting ready to go to bed." Something wasn't right. I didn't believe that Tess, who just a few days before was sniffing around my Sloan, just happened to see me at a gas station hundreds of miles from home. Or that he'd follow me to a motel on a whim and knock on the right door. Or that this grand coincidence would happen less than twenty minutes after we'd seen Lee Courtenay follow us. It was all beyond fishy. But I wasn't about to waste any time trying to solve the mystery. The truth was, I didn't care. I didn't have any more patience for unwelcome stalkers; not tonight. I wanted to get back to Phillip and finish what we'd started. "Bye, Tess." I said, gesturing toward the door. "I suggest you don't come back and tell your friend the same. I'm officially out of patience, got it?"

Tess ignored this, turning to Phillip with a look of what could only be described as misguided self-confidence. "I don't believe we've been introduced." He extended his hand. "Tess Spooner. Stormy's *husband*."

If he was waiting for recognition, embarrassment or shame to show on Phillip's face, he was disappointed. Phillip stared at his outstretched hand and made a point of putting his own large hands in his pockets. He didn't offer his name in return, but instead looked at me, waiting for my cue.

"You look kinda familiar," Tess continued, peering up at him. "We meet before? Did you go to our high school?"

Phillip still didn't respond but gestured his head toward the door in an unmistakable command. *Leave.*

I had told Tess to go, and here he was, still standing around, clogging up space. After years of being ignored and ill-treated by him, something in me finally snapped. "Get the fuck OUT, Tess!" I yelled, my face turning red. "Do you fucking hear me? Out. Now."

"What's wrong, darlin'?" His face was a picture of innocence.

"Don't play dumb with me," I thundered, inching closer to him. "You show up in town less than a week ago, calling Sloan, asking her for favors, trying to get information out of her. And now I happen to go out of town and you miraculously show up at the same motel within five minutes of me arriving? How dumb exactly do you think I am?"

"I swear, darlin'." He put his hands up in mock surrender. "It's a coincidence. I came back to Brunswick to get some of my stuff, after I got out of rehab. Roberta and I left the next day."

I didn't even know he had been to rehab. I hated myself for the pang I felt at being cut out of his life. It was a joke, was what it was. This man wasn't *shit*. That was clear as day. And yet, I still felt sad. We'd had something, once. If nothing else, he'd kept me from feeling alone. Years of security, comfort, companionship, after my shitty, isolated childhood…He had given me that much. I bristled against those feelings and settled instead with the rage. I set a firm eye on him. "I'm glad to hear it, but you still need to go. And don't come back, Tess. This is messed up."

"It *is* a coincidence," he insisted. "My girlfriend – you remember Roberta - has family out this way. We were in town last week, but we came back here this mornin' to stay with her aunt for a few days. She's real sick."

"Whatever." I put a hand on his shoulder and pushed him to the door. "Just go."

"You sure do look pretty, darlin'," he said with a smile as I jostled him out. "Whatever you're doin'," he winked at me, "it agrees with you."

Suddenly Phillip was in front of me, clearly furious. "Stop fucking with Stormy and go. Or I'll *make* you go."

"Calm down, dude." Tess put his hands up in surrender. "Don't worry, I'm not trying to get a piece. I had my fill when we were married, and believe me, there's plenty of better ass-"

He didn't finish his sentence because Phillip's fist connected with his face with a loud *thwack*.

Tess' nose immediately began to gush blood. For a second, he just stared at us, wide-eyed, then a childlike wail came from him. "Oh, you fuckin' ASSHOLE. You broke my fuckin' NOSE-"

Phillip slammed the door in his face. We heard Tess continue to curse and wail outside for a minute, then silence.

I went over to the bed and sat down, putting my face in my hands. My shoulders shook with laughter, but my fingers were wiping away tears. It was official; I was losing it.

"You ok?"

"Yeah."

"You're crying."

"Yeah, well, I'm laughing, too." I looked up defiantly, wiping at a cheek.

He cracked a smile. "I'm sorry," he said, sitting down beside me. "I shouldn't have hit the guy."

"I'm glad you did. He deserved it." I tried for another smile, but I was humiliated. "I asked him to leave, what, fifty times? You saw how he ignored me; he was always like that. And what he said about me – about how he had his fill-"

"That's just shit guys say when they're outmatched," Phillip said easily with a kind look. "Don't pay him any attention, Stormy. If he wasn't still hung up on you, why would he be here?"

"I don't know," I said glumly. "I don't know anything anymore."

He put an arm around me, but it felt brotherly. The mood from a few minutes before had drained away. "I might go for a swim," he said after a moment, and I hated myself for how deflated I felt. I wanted him to stay there with me.

"You'll be cold."

"It's a heated pool." He smiled at me. "Come join me, if you feel like it. I'd really like it if you did." He paused, pulling my head toward his, his lips brushing against my temple. His chin was scratchy against my cheek. He stayed there just for a beat, long enough for me to feel his breath as he sighed, then got up.

He grabbed a towel from the tiny bathroom and exited the room without saying anything else. I managed to keep it together until the door shut and then dissolved into tears.

Here I was, on a road trip with the man of my dreams – literally. We'd just been sharing an amazing kiss, our first kiss, and I'd managed to let Tess get to me. What was wrong with me? Just looking at the two side by side, Tess' sneering, idiot face and dumb accent and cocky, shitty personality, contrasted with Phillip's tall, strong gracefulness, swift, sharp mind and beautiful face, there was no contest. Phillip had been right to knock his block off. That was one 'redneck standoff' the good ol' boy had decidedly lost. He'd always been vain, preening in the mirror twice as long as I ever had – well, let him catch a glance of his face tomorrow morning. It'd be twice its normal size with a lovely blue-black hue to go with it. Try to snort a line with that nose; it'd hurt like the dickens. In another life, I would have laughed about it, would already be texting Sloan; she'd find the whole thing hysterical. But all I could feel was emptiness. Tess was my husband. Well, had been. When he'd left me, everything I thought was true about my life had fallen apart. I couldn't put a funny face on it. Not after seeing the way he still dismissed me to nothing, not when his cruel mockery still sounded in my ears.

The way he'd stood there smirking, making jokes, acting as though he still casually owned me but didn't give a crap about me at the same time, stung. How could such a no-count jerk face still have the power to reduce me to nothing with a glance?

He was definitely following me, but it wasn't because he loved me or wanted me back. That was clear. No, he must have some other purpose, some reason for suddenly reappearing in my life. The fact that he was reappearing at the same time Phillip had entered the picture didn't seem like a coincidence, either. I remembered what Phillip had said back at the house about how men sometimes acted around women - "like pissing on a fire hydrant. It's an ownership thing."

What did Tess want? Was he just here to pee on his hydrant, or was something else going on?

I sat for a few more moments, thinking, trying to get my brain together, then got up and washed my face in the sink. I patted my skin dry, hoping the puffiness wouldn't be too noticeable. My face always swelled up like dough when I cried. I reapplied a little of my makeup and re-braided my hair, which was silly if I was going swimming. I realized I didn't have a bathing suit. Phillip could probably get away with swimming in his black boxer briefs, but I couldn't swim in my undies. I remembered back to the night before, sitting in the bath in our underwear, and how see-through my white panties and bra had been, and felt myself go warm. I really did want to join him for that swim...I'd join him anywhere, if it meant I got to feel his hands on me, and taste those delicious, full lips...

Maybe, if nobody else was at the pool, it wouldn't hurt to just jump in for a second in my undies...what was the harm?

I grabbed a towel and headed for the door, remembering to grab the motel key, sliding it into my pocket. I opened the door, stepped out, and shut it. I only felt a split second of unease before I was grabbed by a pair of strong arms and yanked backward, into the shadows.

"DON'T MAKE ANY NOISE." There was a hand over my mouth and an arm over my throat, so it would have been hard to make much noise even if I'd wanted to. I struggled, but whoever it was held me fast. He was strong. Maybe not as strong as Phillip, but close. "Stop struggling. I'm not going to hurt you."

Yeah, right. Like I was going to believe that.

My immediate thought was that it was Tess, back for revenge for the nose incident, but the voice was all wrong, and honestly, Tess wasn't very strong.

"I have a little message to pass on to Mr. Deville." His hot breath was in my ear, his lips brushing against my neck. "I don't mean you any harm, Stormy. Just pass along the message, and you head on back to Jekyll and I swear I won't bother you again."

I kept struggling against him, uninterested in what he had to say, only interested in getting away.

"If I ease up on your neck and take my hand off your mouth, will you cooperate?" I didn't answer, only thrashed against him. "Stormy, come on. Stop. Look, I'll let go of you, but just hear what I have to say. I don't want to have to hurt you. I saw what Phillip did to that fucker's nose. I'd rather things not get physical if they don't have to." And suddenly the weight was off my neck, the hand was off my mouth, and I was spun around to the impossibly young face of Lee Courtenay.

His eyes shone pale blue under his baseball cap, and he managed a smile that almost looked genuine. His freckles were stark against his flushed cheeks. "I'm sorry for strong-arming you like that," he said. He managed to look contrite.

I rummaged blindly for my phone. "Why the fuck are you following us? And how dare you put your hands on me!" Where the fuck was my damned phone? Had I left it in the room? I deliberated; could I make a run for it and get past him, or should I stall him, keep him talking? Should I yell for Phillip?

"I'm sorry," he said. "I have been following you."

"No shit. Since the day I saw you at the farmers market. Bringing flowers to your aunt – yeah right."

"My aunt actually does work there," he said.

I took a step back, my hands clenched into fists. "I'm about two seconds from screaming, Lee. Do you understand me?"

"Okay, Stormy. Calm down." He held his hands out. "Just let me talk to you for a second and I'll go, and I won't bother you again. I swear."

"Like I'd believe a word you say."

He rubbed at his brow. For someone with such a babyface, he had a lot of mannerisms that seemed much older, like someone who had seen a lot and was just plain bone-tired. And

Lord, was he *strong*. There was no way I would have been able to get out of his grip if he hadn't decided to let go. "Stormy, there are…people that aren't too happy with Phillip being…back. Let's put it like that."

"I don't know what you're talking about."

"We don't have time for you to play dumb," he said, still rubbing at his brow. "I know exactly what and who Phillip is, and I'm the least of your worries. I've been trying to warn you for days, but there's always somebody around who…" he trailed off, rubbing his brow again, then resumed talking. "Now, Phillip can exist peacefully if he doesn't draw too much attention to himself but going back to his stomping grounds is a very bad idea. Like, the opposite of what he should be doing. Traipsing around his old house looking for buried treasure and trying to look up old friends is the opposite of laying low. Better for him – and for you - to get in your truck and head back to Jekyll Island. Keep a low profile, find a way to blend into the scenery."

"How do you even know that's what he's doing?" I demanded, angry.

"It's pretty obvious, isn't he? Why else would you two be here?" He smiled, not unkindly. "Just tell him to go back to Jekyll for a while. He'll listen to you. If he does that, he'll be left alone." His face darkened. "If he doesn't, well…nobody wants to die twice, do they? At least not after a measly week."

"Is that a threat?" My blood felt hot in my veins. I'd rip him apart myself if I had to.

He laughed. "Hell, no. Do you think I could take that guy? I might be strong, but he's stronger. I'm only the messenger, and I'm just telling him – through you - how it's got to be. If he wants to stay safe and keep *you* safe."

"What the fuck does it matter if he goes to see an old friend?"

"Best not to meddle in it, Stormy," he answered. "You're in enough trouble as it is."

"Why? And who the hell are you to give me advice?"

"A friend," he said, his pale eyes looking into mine. "Probably the only one you've got."

I snorted. "Then I really *am* in trouble. What kind of friend works with my ex and follows me halfway across the country-"

He scoffed. "Tess? I hate that guy."

"Oh, well in that case, that changes *everything,*" I sneered. I was seething. "You ran me off the road. You're lucky we didn't run into the creek. I could have been killed. Some friend. Anyway, I barely fucking know you."

"I didn't run you off the road," he said, his eyes wide and perplexed. "Why would I do that?"

"For the same reason you'd rummage through my barn, break into my house, and follow me to a motel and kidnap me from the stairwell."

He shook his head, two bright spots appearing on his freckled cheeks. "Just give Phillip that message. And it wasn't me that ran you off the road. I swear."

"The guy I saw in my rearview right before I crashed into the river sure looked a lot like you," I snapped.

He shook his head, his light eyes still wide, and took a step back, appearing unsure. I took the opportunity and bolted. I didn't need to look back to see if he was following me; I could somehow feel that he wasn't. My heart was beating hard in my chest, and cold sweat collected under my armpits. Whatever Lee might say about not wanting to harm me, I knew that whatever he was mixed up in was no joke. I had to get to Phillip and warn him, fast.

Phillip was oblivious, happily doing laps in the steaming pool, swimming the length with long, measured strokes. Despite my frenzied state, I took a second to just stand there and watch him, in awe of his graceful physicality, the sheer power of him. His arms and legs were impossibly long and lean. I collapsed into a deck chair, still sweating from fear and exertion, and waited for him to get back to my end of the pool, marveling at the almost super-human power he seemed to possess, wrapping the dry towel around my shoulders because I'd forgotten to bring a jacket. I was shaky, my heartbeat wild from my encounter with Lee. Watching Phillip swim was calming, though, as I counted each stroke, his arms coming in and out of the water, the tattoos on his left arm stark in the blue water and the cold steam coming off it. He had many tattoos, most of which I knew about from pictures, a couple of which I didn't. There was the band logo, a serpent on his thigh. But it was the one on his right arm that I'd always wondered about – the number seven, crowned, behind a locked gate, a human skull as the padlock. There was a beam of sunlight streaming down from the heavens, illuminating the numeric figure. It was a strange tattoo, one that fans had spent a lot of time theorizing about, and I made a mental note to ask him how it had come to pass later.

"Coming in?" He'd noticed me sitting there and swam over to the edge of the pool with an eager smile.

"I thought about it, but I guess not," I said. "No swimsuit." I no longer felt like swimming.

"You don't need one," he said, and his eyes met mine, still full of delicious heat.

"Don't tempt me," I said, looking him in the eye. "Anyway, something's come up." I related what had just happened with Lee in the stairwell, my heart still hammering. I twisted my hands in my lap as I recounted everything, wondering how on earth any of it could be happening. I didn't know how many more late-night followings I could take, how many more jolts to my nervous system. Between Lee and Tess, I was a mess.

As I told him, Phillip swam over to the steps and came out

of the pool, wrapping a motel towel around his waist. Steam came off his huge shoulders. He sat beside me on the deck chair, the bright smile from before replaced with a look of anger. "Did he hurt you?"

"No," I said. "I don't think he ever intended to. I think he just wanted to scare me a little, to warn us." I had gotten the impression that what little power he'd exerted over me, Lee found detestable. It seemed like the entire thing had left a bad taste in his mouth. Shady dealings didn't seem to come naturally to him. I told Phillip this, and he nodded.

"Maybe not, but we still need to be careful. We don't know who he works for, and what he's willing to do to stop us. It might be that he doesn't have much choice in the matter."

"Will we go back, then?" I asked. "To Jekyll?"

He shook his head. "I won't. But I think you should."

"No, I'm not leaving you."

He sighed. "Stormy, I know you want to help, and I'm really touched. I like having you around. Not just because you summoned me and I'm drawn to you and all that, but because I really like you." His eyes burned into mine. "I really do. But this...it's dangerous. Tonight alone you've had two guys show up that could have done you harm. We've been followed. Somebody ran you off the road. People are showing up at your house in the dead of night, snooping. I can't keep putting you in danger. It's not right."

"You just proved my point. I'd be in just as much danger at home, by myself," I argued. "Maybe more. And anyway, I'm the one who started the whole-"

"I really don't think so," he said. "This is about me. Some rule must have been broken, some taboo has been breached, like you said. Whoever it is I've angered, they don't like that I'm here, just like Lee said. I won't know what's up exactly until I can talk to Guthrie. But I feel like if you went home and went back to your life like nothing was wrong, they'd leave you be. That's clearly what they want you to do. Lee told you as much."

"But what about Tess?" I asked.

"I don't want to hurt your feelings when I say this," he said. "But I don't think Tess is following you because he cares about you. I think he works for, or maybe with, this Lee guy. I think he's wrapped up in all this somehow."

I knew that already – Lee confirming that he knew Tess had made that obvious. But it still stung to hear it. "How, though? How would he even know any of these people? And he was back in town before I did the spell. Before you were ever in my life." I wasn't sure why I was arguing. I knew he was right.

"Just one of my hunches," he said. "I'll just get a feeling about something, a vibe or whatever, and so far, they've been right every time. You know, you've seen me do it. I wouldn't call it full-fledged psychic or anything, but I get, like, impressions. I just sort of have general ideas about things and I can trust them." He put his hand on mine. "I think there are other people out there who can do the same thing. What if maybe the fact that you were going to do the spell was already out there, before you ever did it. And whoever these folks are, they felt that intention, they could read it. And they've sent out their...whoever they are...to try and either stop you, or at least curb you somehow. I think Lee is one of those people, and so is Tess."

"My intention..." I trailed off. I had been pretty clear on my intentions. I'd even joked with Sloan about it beforehand. Could it really be possible that somebody, somehow, had picked up on my plans – even though at first they'd been a joke – before I'd even started?

"I'm the one who brought you back. I'm the one who read the spell. I'm the one who did the magic," I said finally. "You're driving my car and we're on my dime, at least for the time being. You've been with me every step of the way since you came back. Do you really think after all that, if I just turn around and go back to my shitty trailer that they'll leave me be? I'm a liability!"

"Not if you release me," he said quietly.

I looked at him, confused. "What do you mean, 'release you'?"

"You summoned me. So I came," he answered. "But if you release me of that duty, so to speak, I am no longer summoned to you. I can go and do whatever. And the tie between us is severed."

"That sounds like some idiot bullshit from a YA vampire novel," I said, irritated. It hurt my feelings that he'd suggest such a thing. And I wasn't sure I believed it could be that simple, anyway. "How do you know it'd even work? You said you didn't know about the spell."

"I don't," he said. "Not really. There's a lot Guthrie needs to answer. But this is just a thing I-"

"That you just know, right?" I snapped. "Seems like you conveniently just know a lot of things."

He was annoyingly calm. "Why are you upset with me?"

"I'm not." I couldn't look at him, so instead I stared at the steam coming off the pool. The tendrils of white fog almost looked like ghosts floating on the water. "You could have just said that you wanted me gone."

He was quiet for a minute, then he picked up my hand, brought it to his mouth, and kissed it. "No, Stormy," he murmured. "I don't want you to go home. I want you to stay. So bad I'm tempted to just say forget it, come with me. But I'm trying to keep you safe."

"I don't enjoy being treated like a child," I said angrily. "I can make my own decisions. You've been back, what, three days? And you're trying to boss me around."

"No, Stormy, I just want-"

"Yeah, yeah, to keep me safe," I said, standing up, wrapping the towel tighter around my shoulders. I was freezing, and so very tired. And very hurt, and very angry, though I wasn't sure I had the right to be those last two things. "Funny, that's just what Lee said, too, right after he had his arm over my throat." I sighed. "Fine. I'll release you. If you want me gone so bad, you don't have to tell me twice. I'll do it in the morning, okay? Right now I'm tired, and I'm going to bed." I pulled the towel from around my shoulders and handed it to him, ignoring his stricken expression. "For your hair. Enjoy the rest of your swim."

I stalked off back to the motel room, hoping he'd come after me, stop me, kiss me. Anything. But he didn't follow. Instead, I fell asleep wrapped up in the stiff, scratchy motel sheets, trying to swallow my angry tears. When Phillip woke me some time later, sliding in beside me, his damp hair brushing against my face, I rolled over on my side and put my back to him.

Eleven

We got into Boston around noon the next day and immediately stopped for lunch. I insisted; Phillip kept saying he'd spent enough of my money, but I reminded him that we were very near the home stretch now and besides, I was starving. Finding a restaurant that served vegan fare seemed impossible since I didn't know my way around town and neither did Phillip, not anymore, so we stopped at a Philly Cheesesteak place and I ordered two large fries, a water and an apple pie and hoped none of it was cooked in beef fat. I was silent, still sullen about the night before, as he went to the counter and checked with the cook, but secretly, I was touched, despite my sour mood.

I kept busy, drowning my fries in sriracha, trying to ignore the looks Phillip kept giving me. He'd been trying to make me laugh, cracking jokes – he said there was a pasture nearby with some high grass, should I feel like a salad - but I wasn't in the mood. We hadn't said much since the night before when we'd argued out by the pool. I had gotten up early, visited the motel lobby, and poured us two cups of scalding, watery coffee and brought them back to the room as an olive branch. He was just sitting up in bed when I got back, his black hair a halo around his face, the sheets bunched up around him, shirtless and breathtaking. I tried not to look.

I handed him his coffee, and with an *I mean business* look, I'd told him, "I thought about what you said, but I've decided I'm coming with you anyway. And I don't want to argue about it. It's my decision. My days of doing whatever a man tells me are over."

I had expected him to protest, but instead he'd just nodded, looking equal parts defeated and relieved. He'd sipped his coffee in silence, watching me as I rummaged through my bag looking for something to wear. If all went well, I'd be meeting Guthrie and who knew who else, and my faded old band t-shirts and jeans wouldn't cut it. I'd retreated to the bathroom and come out wearing a long, pencil thin black skirt, black boots and a green flowing top that I hoped didn't show too much cleavage. It had been a long time since I dressed up. As I was doing my makeup in the tiny mirror, Phillip had come up behind me, still shirtless, and wrapped his arms around my waist. He leaned down – he had to – and rested his head on my shoulder.

"I'm glad you're coming with me," he said in his low voice. "And I don't like arguing with you. It's best for us both if we're not at odds, don't you think? Especially since we're heading into the danger zone."

"I agree." I finished applying my eyeliner and turned to face him, his hands still resting on my middle.

"You look beautiful," he said, smiling at me. "Not that you didn't before, but you clean up nice. I like the dark eye makeup."

"If I'm gonna be a witch, I guess I'd better look the part," I joked.

We had both kind of swayed there for a minute. Then he'd pulled back a little reluctantly. "I'll go get a shower and get dressed, then," he said. "So we can hit the road." I had watched his retreating back as he went into the bathroom, wishing I hadn't been in such a rush to dress. I was tempted to follow him into the shower and have my way with him. My body ached for him, longed for his touch, and I could tell by the way his eyes burned when he looked at me that he felt the same. We'd had so many false starts. But every time something almost happened, something *else* happened to ruin it. Maybe the two of us just weren't meant to be. After all, who did I think I was, trying to get sexy with Phillip Deville? He was famous, gorgeous, six foot five of pure trouble. And who was I, but some lowly stupid librarian living in a singlewide in bumfuck? I didn't relish the thought of being some discarded groupie who Phillip tired of and sent packing after one hot night. But then again… I thought of his huge, muscular arms, his strong, lean legs and the delicate hair on his chest and taut stomach and shivered. Whatever happened afterward, it would be worth it just to have him one time.

I'd stood in front of the bathroom door for a good five minutes, listening to the water run, deliberating. Should I slide into the shower with him and make up? But what if everything had changed now that I'd refused to release him and shut down his attempts to protect me? Despite the lust in those dark eyes of his, even a small chance that I'd be rejected made me hesitate. If he turned me down, I'd die a thousand deaths.

So now here we were, at a diner in Boston, me shoveling too-salty fries into my face and trying not to look at the perfect specimen of man in front of me - those inky black lashes, the strong, almost square jaw, his impossibly white teeth, his chiseled nose. Trying not to undress him with my eyes or think any illicit thought that he might pick up. He had ordered coffee and a burger, and he was sipping the coffee slowly, savoring it, his eyes closed. He felt me watching, and opened his eyes, giving me a slow smile.

"You had no way of knowing, but picking this place was kind of funny," he said, sitting his cup down, wrapping his huge hands around it, absorbing the warmth. "I used to come here all the time when I was a teenager. Before I joined the band and lit out of town."

"Oh yeah?"

"Yeah." He nodded. "I even worked here one summer. They have the best coffee in town."

"You don't usually hear that about diners." Our local Waffle House served sludge that might as well be dirty motor oil.

"They have one of those old school machines, like a huge monster of a coffee maker, it's all steel." He took another sip. "They just use Maxwell House coffee, like the cheapest of the cheap, but that machine makes it just right."

"The food looks pretty good," I said magnanimously, gesturing to his burger, which was toasty with butter.

"Best in town," he agreed, holding out his plate. "Want a bite?"

"Nope," I groaned, but gave him a wink to show I wasn't miffed. "Just because you crave something occasionally doesn't mean you have to give in."

"That's true. But then, sometimes you should." His lips curled into a huge smile before he took another long sip of coffee, his eyes boring into mine over the rim of the cup. My heart skipped in my chest. Fuck. I should have followed him into the shower. "Sometimes you should just give in to the impulse."

"Phillip," I warned, feeling my face warm.

His smile deepened as he put down his cup. "Hindsight is 20/20."

"Get out of my head, you loser." I gave him my best glare, determined not to let my cheeks flush, and wiped my hands on a napkin. "Where to first?" If I didn't change the subject fast, we might end up back at the motel.

"You're no fun," he said in a mock pout, picking his cup back up. "First, I'm going to go get my money, if it's still there. And I'm handing you a huge wad of it right off the bat, so find somewhere to put it in that giant bag of yours."

Every time he mentioned that damn money it hurt my feelings, even though it shouldn't. He'd told me right from the beginning that he wanted to pay me back, and I'd agreed. But it felt wrong to me; after all, I was the reason he was here. And I was happy to come with him on this journey, to help him make heads or tails of what to do now, and I didn't need to be paid to do it. But I knew his pride and honor would never let up, and he wouldn't rest until he'd given me my money back. I took a sip of my water. "Okay."

"There's a park across from my old place, or there was," he said. "If it's still there, you could hang out for a while, if you don't mind, while I get the money. Probably best for you to be somewhere else while I do it. I have no idea who's living in the house now, and it'll be risky enough with just me. Two of us would be a really bad idea."

"Had you considered that someone from your family might still be living there?" I asked.

He didn't answer, but his look showed me that he had. Of course. He'd probably thought of nothing else. I imagined the wondering, the worry, had probably eaten him up with nerves. He took another long sip of his coffee and gestured to the waitress for another one. His face was sad, suddenly, and very tired. I didn't think he had gotten much sleep the past few nights. Whether it was from worry, or something else, I didn't know and was afraid to ask. Not that he'd answer me truthfully anyway. He had a very stubborn and annoying need to keep me "safe." Something I planned to bring up to him again once all this madness was over - if he was in my life after that.

I'd release him, if that's what he wanted. If he asked me again to do it, I would. He could be free to go on and live the life he wanted to live, now that he had another chance. I knew that just because I'd summoned him didn't mean I had some claim over him. Just because I'd been his "biggest fan" in his other life didn't mean that he was obligated to me in this one. For all I knew the attraction between us, at least on his end, was just part of the spell. What if he didn't even really like me that much? Maybe I was just a means to an end, and he'd be glad to be rid of me.

I dug another fry into the puddle of sriracha on my plate – it almost looked like blood - and tried to push the thoughts out of my head. No point in worrying about it now.

"Don't do that, Stormy." His voice penetrated my dark thoughts. "You're driving yourself nuts."

I nodded, but didn't look up at him, content to keep shoveling in fries. If I looked at him, I might cry. "I told you before to get out of my head."

"I'm not in your head. Anybody looking at you could see it."

"And you're not worried? At all?"

"A little," he said. "Mostly for you. Once you've been dead, everything else just seems kind of unimportant. I guess it puts it—*life*—in perspective."

"You're like a Goth Dr. Phil," I said with a laugh, wiping at my eyes, getting salt in them, and beginning to cry in earnest.

"Who is Dr. Phil?"

"Like a self-help guru, psychologist guy," I said. "He's on TV. He's bald and has an obnoxious southern accent. He gives wayward people the tough-love thing and convinces them to turn their lives around." He looked so affronted I started to laugh. "Dr. Phil Deville, Scare-apist."

THE AIR WAS CRISP, slightly cold, and there was a smell on the light breeze – the faint acridness that only came from old, well-used wood stoves. I smiled, recognizing it as one of Phillip's signature smells– woodsmoke from his home town. The sky was a bright, sun-drenched blue, not a cloud in sight. But straight above, I saw the silver-white needle point of a jet slowly streak across the sky, leaving its fine pen line behind it, growing fainter as it moved. I sat down on a park bench and pulled out a magazine and my cell phone, planning to pass at least an hour, if not more.

Phillip said the house was near this park, but he figured it'd take him a while to case the place, make sure nobody was home, get into the backyard and dig. It was going to be tricky. Regardless of who lived there – whether it was his family, strangers or nobody at all – it was breaking and entering, and he could get in big trouble if caught. He would eventually be recognized if he was. This was Boston, his hometown, and he was more famous here than anywhere else. He'd tucked all his dark hair up under a military style green cap and thrown on a royal blue hoodie over his signature black shirt and jeans, but he still looked like Phillip Deville. I'd given him my glasses – 80s style aviators with mirrored lenses- but even that hadn't helped.

I flipped idly through the magazine, scrolled through my cell phone, and was bored after ten minutes. I sent Sloan a text – my phone seemed to be working okay, now that Phillip wasn't nearby. *"Just checking in. What's going on with you? Haven't heard from you in a while. We just got into town. Phillip is taking care of biz."* I checked my voice-mails and looked through Facebook and Twitter. But all the while I was worried about Phillip. I hoped he'd make quick work of this.

Sloan pinged back after a few moments. *"Same old shit here. Jealous of you and your guy, sexing up in a hotel."*

Ha. If only. I wrote back. *"Motel, not Hotel. Big difference. Just a biz trip. I told you that."*

"Whatever you say. Liar."

"How's Dan?"

"Dunno."

Uh oh. And things had been going so well.

"Trouble in Paradise?"

After five minutes she hadn't responded, and I knew I'd pissed her off. I shouldn't have been so flippant, I should have been more empathetic. Sloan could dish it out but couldn't always take it. I sent another text.

"Sorry, bad attempt at humor. Are you guys ok? Are YOU ok?"

Five more minutes and nothing. I put the phone back in my purse with a frown. I didn't have much battery left and Phillip might try to call me if there was an emergency, but I didn't like leaving things like that with Sloan. I hadn't talked to her in days, and now I'd pissed her off. I bit at my fingernails, worried.

Another twenty minutes went by, and finally an hour, and after an hour and thirty minutes I started to get anxious. I'd read the magazine cover to cover, people watched, surfed the web and for the past twenty minutes I'd been staring at a squirrel scurry along a fence post. Phillip needed to hurry up before I died of nerves or old age. Didn't he know how frantic I'd be?

The sun was directly overhead, bathing me in welcome warmth on the cool day. My hair was pulled in a side-pony and lay on my left shoulder, catching the rays and seeming to glow like white-fire. The ends tickled my chin and I looked down, momentarily captivated by the little white tips of my hair and how they seemed to glow, until I realized that I was staring at a mess of split ends. Ten minutes later, and I was still hunting through them with disgusted determination, pulling each one apart with the fervor of a serial killer.

"What in the fuck are you doing, picking for lice?" I heard a familiar laugh, and saw a figure running toward me, holding a plastic bag. He was still wearing the blue hoodie and his dark green military cap was askew, black hair streaming from it.

"Jesus, he's shit at disguises," I murmured to myself, but I was standing up and running to him before I knew it, split ends forgotten.

"I got it." He gave me a triumphant look and handed me the bag, almost shoving it at me, like he was afraid of it. Then he pulled me into a clumsy hug. He was out of breath, but his face was full of glee. "It was all still there, after all this time, can you believe that?"

"Wow," I said. I didn't know why he was handing it to me. I pushed it back at him. "I was beginning to get really worried, you were gone so long. I was scared you ran into trouble. Was it hard to get in there and get it?"

"No. I just walked around back, dug it up and took it. The reason I took so long is a whole other – well..." He hesitated and looked around the park. "Can we go somewhere? To the car? I don't want to stand here and tell you the story. Somebody might recognize me."

"Okay," I said.

"I parked the truck right around the corner." I followed him to the parking lot, got in, and buckled up without a word. I wasn't sure why my heart was pounding so hard. He was obviously okay. He had gotten the money. He had achieved one of his goals, and now we could move onto the second without the specter of his poverty hanging over him.

"How much money is that?" I asked. "If you don't mind telling me."

"I don't even know exactly. I don't remember. I was high as hell when I buried it, and I collected it over the course of several months. But it's at least thirty grand, maybe closer to fifty."

"Wow," I breathed. I had never been in possession of even a quarter of that much money all at once. "And that's just from a few *months?*"

"It was during our heyday, when I was still young and hot enough to make a few coins." He laughed. "That's a lot to me now, but I have to say, it wasn't back then. It's a drop in the bucket compared to what I used to be worth." He shook his head. "All in other hands now, though. That's what happens when you die."

"I just can't imagine," I said in awe, staring down at the bag. "The life you lived..."

"It wasn't all that great, Stormy," he said quietly. "Even with the money. It was a lot more hassle than it ever was good, I can tell you that." I noticed his hands on the wheel shook a little; something had upset him.

"Still, you have to feel...nostalgic, if nothing else, being here," I said. "It must have been hard, seeing your old house. I imagine you must miss this place, and the people you loved."

"Yes," he said, growing even more quiet. "Yes, I do." Then he was silent.

He didn't say much else until we were at the motel. He seemed to be lost in thought. We pulled round to the room, parked, and Phillip followed me inside, the cash tucked under his arm like a bag of groceries. He pushed it under the double bed and sat down on it, wiping his brow.

I sat beside him silently, giving him a minute. He seemed really rattled; all his triumphant excitement from before had disappeared. But he still didn't speak, only stared at the wall, silently brooding, his hands working over themselves in his lap. He hadn't taken the bait before in the truck, so I decided to just be direct.

I put a hand on his leg. "Let me guess," I began. "You saw someone from your family and that's why you're so shaken."

He shook his head and put his large hand over mine. "No, but it's a good guess. I didn't see anybody in my family, but I did see someone I knew." He swallowed. "I saw Jason."

"What?" I gasped. "Jason Langley?"

"The one and only."

I gaped at him, and he sighed.

"My family...they all moved out of the house. They're long gone. I guess after I died ownership passed to Barb, and she in turn gifted it to my youngest brother – you know I owned that house, I had bought it from my parents when I first came into money – and he didn't want it, so he sold it to Jason. And he's lived there all these years."

"How do you know all this?" I asked. "And how did you happen to see him?"

"I did more than see him," Phillip said. "And I know all of that because...well, he told me."

"What?" I looked at him in surprise. "I thought you were going to lay low!"

"I did, I swear. I cased the place from the truck, I was inconspicuous, I took my time. Didn't seem like anybody was home. I'm a fuckin' idiot. He was in the backyard the whole time, on the back porch – I didn't see him because he was slumped over in the chair, half dead. I come walking around back with my shovel and bag, and I didn't even see him. Just started digging. No idea the man was there until he said, 'Phillip.' And I stopped digging and my blood just ran cold and I almost passed the fuck out. I knew his voice without having to turn around."

"Oh shit," I said. "What did you do?"

"What could I do? I went up to the porch and sat down. Asked him how he was." He shook his head. "He wasn't good, Stormy. He's so strung out –he smelled like shit and I'd be shocked if he weighed a hundred and thirty pounds. He looks like he's a hundred years old. But he knew me. And he was glad to see me." He shook his head. "Weirdest part is that he didn't seem surprised at all."

"He didn't freak out when you told him?"

"Nope, I was the one who was freaked," he said, running a hand nervously through his snarled hair. "I started gibbering like a parrot, I told him that I'd faked my death all those years ago to get away from the fame and drugs and that I'd been living down south all this time, but I'd hit a run of bad luck and needed my money. I thought I was doing pretty good, too, but he just fixed one glazed eye on me and laughed. I said what was so fuckin' funny and he was like, 'I know I'm strung the fuck out and it's been twenty goddamn years, but don't think for a second that I forgot Guthrie or that damn spell in the liner notes.'"

I didn't know how to respond.

"And I just kinda went white and was like, 'Don't be stupid, man, magic and spells aren't real.' And he says, 'I knew this was going to happen long before you ever stepped foot out of the grave.' He says, 'I've been waiting for you.'"

"What did he mean by that?"

"No fucking idea. I couldn't tell if he was just that high, or if he was serious. I was so freaked I didn't ask him to explain." He put his head in his hands. I squeezed his leg, and rested my head on his shoulder, trying to comfort him. His body was tense. "I tried to convince him that he was just hallucinating, how dumb is that? That it was all some drug induced mania. But he saw me, and he'll remember."

"I'm sorry," I said quietly, stroking his arm. "I'm sorry you had to see him like that. I know it must have been horrible. But

I'm glad you at least got your money. And you know he's alive. That's...something, right?"

"He said that to me," Phillip said, shaking his head. "That's what he said – 'I'm still alive, and now so are you.' I didn't know what the fuck to say. God, he was the last person I expected to see. He's living in my house now. It's too much."

I rubbed his arm. His skin was warm and soft. I ran a finger over his '7' tattoo and pressed against him. "I'm sorry," I said again. "I wish I knew how to help."

"You already are," he said, looking at me. "More than you know."

I pulled him backward, and we both laid back on the bed, staring up at the ceiling. I nuzzled into the crook of his arm, and it felt as natural as if we'd been doing this for years. He smelled so good. His silky hair brushed against my face, a sensation I was starting to get used to.

He made a move to rise. "Let me get you that money-"

"If you say one more thing about that damned money, I'm going to put my studded Doc Marten in your ass," I said irritably. "Phillip, for the last time, I couldn't give a fresh fuck about the money. Are you trying to piss me off on purpose?"

"I don't like owing you," he said stubbornly. "It makes me feel like we aren't on even footing. It makes it hard to-"

"By that logic we'll never be square," I said petulantly, poking him in the chest. "Since you owe me your *life.*"

"Believe me, I know it," he said. "Why do you think I want to at least give you back a couple hundred bucks?"

"I don't want it," I said. "It means nothing compared to what I've gained."

I laid there and waited for the inevitable stubborn, pigheaded argument that was sure to follow, or a steady stream of cuss words, but he shocked me by propping himself up on one elbow and planting a sweet, slow kiss on my lips. His dark green eyes bored into mine, a question in them. I reached up and smoothed his hair behind his ears and smiled. "That's better," I said. "Kiss me again."

Leaning down gingerly, he pressed his lips against mine, and made a soft humming sound. His voice was like velvet. I ran my hands behind his head, pushing them into his hair, tugging it a little, as his mouth opened on mine. He still tasted like coffee. He was bearing all his weight on his propped-up arm, so I pulled him onto me, wanting to feel him crushing me. He made another sound in his throat and I could feel his teeth against my lips, his hands on my neck, the delicious warm weight of him on my chest and legs.

He felt so good, tasted so good. He didn't seem real. His hair too soft, his skin too warm, those eyes too dark and beautiful. But he was. Real and here and I didn't want the moment to end. Nothing was going to interrupt us this time; I didn't care *who* knocked at the door, we were not answering. I tugged at his shirt, pulling it upward and over his head, and ran my hands over his warm chest, savoring the feel of him. His breathing was hard and fast.

"Let's see how you treat groupies in hotel rooms, then," I whispered, giving him a devious look.

"No way." He shook his head, grinning. "For one thing, I'm stone cold sober. And I'm glad that I am. I want to remember this, to remember you."

"I'm not going anywhere," I said, looking into his deep green eyes.

"Good." He placed a rough kiss on my bottom lip, his hands roaming over my stomach. He inched my shirt up, his skin warm and rough on mine. "I plan to be a Boy Scout, on my best behavior."

"Don't do that," I said, nibbling on his ear. "I think I like you just a little bit bad."

"Don't worry." His hands were still moving upward under my shirt. "That guy's still in there, too."

"I'm looking forward to meeting him," I said, and let my hand trail downward, touching him lightly, then harder. He groaned.

"I want you," he whispered in my ear. "So bad. I don't think I can hold out any longer, Stormy."

"Me, either."

"So many false starts," he said, brushing against my cheek with his thumb, a tender, innocent gesture that made my skin erupt into flame. "Are we really going to do this now? I need to hear that you really want it – that you want me."

"Yes," I said firmly, placing a hot, messy kiss on his lips. "I want you, Phillip."

I didn't have to tell him twice. His mouth brushed against mine as he helped me tug off my own shirt and his long, graceful hands toyed with my bra. His lips trailed down my neck and to my collarbone, and he was making low, gruff noises in his throat that were better than anything he'd ever done on an album. I thought I might combust from the sound.

My brain could always be relied on to poor cold water on any good moment, and it didn't disappoint. As his lips trailed down my collarbone to my chest, a little voice in my head said, *You're about to have sex with a dead guy.*

Shut up, I told it. *I don't care.* It's Phillip Deville and he's wonderful and he's mine, and we could literally be rolling around *in* a coffin and I wouldn't give a flying fuck.

I could feel his lips curl into a smile against my skin and he emitted a low chuckle, his hands still roaming over me, making me shiver and moan. *Get out of my head,* I thought with a laugh, and he chuckled again and nibbled at my neck.

Every inch of him was alive and warm under my hands. The places where his lips had touched felt like scorched earth; hot and aching. I pulled at his belt buckle, needing him to be free of his jeans, needing to touch him all over. He shook out of them, and instead of removing my skirt, he pushed it up around my waist. His hands were caught up in the material. "Silky", he murmured against me, and I wasn't sure if he was talking about the fabric or me.

I tugged off his black boxers and ran my hands tentatively up his thighs, feeling the coarse dark hair there, enjoying the sighs of pleasure in my ear. I took him in my hand, gently, then a little rougher, and he drew in his breath sharply. "Jesus," I said, unable to stop myself. "I figured you were big all over, but..."

He laughed, his breath tickling my ear. "Flatterer," he said, his tongue darting out and touching my earlobe. "If you keep touching me like that, I might not be able to contain myself. It's been a long time."

"I don't want you to contain yourself," I whispered. I guided him down between my legs, where I was ready for him. With a quick movement, he pushed his way inside me, and I gasped; so did he. I had expected a little pain, but there was none. He moved in me with delicious thrusts, looking into my eyes, his arms holding mine above my head, but not in a show of dominance; rather a *surrender to me, let me serve you.*

No awkwardness like there had been with Tess, that furtive, almost embarrassing sort of bump-bump and me lying there with my eyes closed, wishing it were better. No, this felt right and perfect and like it had been written in the stars. Maybe it was the spell, maybe there was some invisible, mystical cord attaching us, and the attraction between us would be severed once I released him. But right now, it didn't matter, because all I could focus on was how good he felt between my legs, warm and full and lusty, his thighs rough and strong against my own, the weight of him strong and alive and heady. I bucked my hips against his, unable to lie still, unable to let him fully take control, wanting to dominate him as he was dominating me. His hair fluttered against my face, his rosebud lips placing kisses on my cheeks, my eyes, my forehead, making my entire face feel ticklish.

Only a few blessed moments and it was over. He hadn't been kidding. I supposed twenty-three years was a long time, even if he had been dead. I smiled into his shoulder as he groaned and muttered an apology and ran my hands up his back. He felt so good lying on me, a weight that I relished, that made me feel secure and calm. "Stop," I said, laughing. "You'll have other opportunities."

"I will?" His face glowed in the moonlight, his eyes bright.

"What did you think?" I asked, tracing a circle on his cheek. "That I'd love you and leave you? That seems more your M.O."

"Why?"

"You know, rock star and all..."

"Not all the stereotypes are true." He leaned down and pecked my cheek.

"I've read a few interviews, my dear."

"Well," he said, having the decency to turn a little red, "I'd like to think I wasn't quite as bad as some others. But anyway, that part of my life is over. That life in its entirety is over. I'm a different person now – truth be told, I was *before* I died."

"So you're not going to kick me out of your room to do the walk of shame now that you've had your way with me?"

"Never," he said, then his face turned thoughtful. "I just thought...it's blurry for me, you know, because of the spell. I didn't know how much I was just assuming and how much you might actually – you know, *like* me."

"Of course I like you," I said, incredulous. "Fuck the spell. Phillip, for god's sake, I had pictures of you on my wall when I was fourteen, standing around in nothing but tight purple underwear and combat boots. To say I'm attracted to you is the understatement of the decade."

"Oh jeez, I remember that photoshoot." He groaned. "It

seemed like a good idea at the time, until I saw the magazine. There was one shot where they actually had me turned over, with my ass in the air-"

"Leaning up against the couch," I finished for him. "With one hand tucked into your waistband, pulling it down." I remembered it all too well. "Just one hint of butt cheek showing. It was pretty hot."

He rolled off me and pulled me into his arms, nestling his chin in my neck. "It was humiliating, is what it was. The guys gave me shit about it for months. They called me pinup girl."

"It sold a lot of records."

"I guess it did." He laughed. "I have to tell you, Stormy, it's kind of nerve wracking, being with a woman who fell in love with your persona. You know, so much of that was just..."

"I know, smoke and mirrors." I sat up. "You live up to expectations just fine. If anything, I like you even more than I thought possible." I smiled and brushed a strand of his hair off his face, noting his pleased expression. "I might just keep you around."

He kissed me gently on the lips, his mouth still pursed in a smile. "I like it when you do that."

"Do what?"

"Touch my hair." He bent down and nuzzled his face against mine. "I always used to hate it when people touched my hair. And it was always the first thing women went for." He shrugged. "It's weird – when you do it, it feels so good."

I reached up and caressed his cheek, gently pushing his hair behind his ears. "I wonder why that is."

"I don't know," he said, his face buried in my neck. "It just feels good, you touching me."

His lips met mine again, and I wrapped my arms around his neck, pulling his face close to me, running my hands through his dark mane, letting my fingertips graze his scalp. He had so much hair – silky but tangled. I gathered it in my hands and pulled it back from his face as he kissed me. He made a noise in his throat as his mouth moved against mine. We were locked in place, our bodies a perfect fit, his weight surprisingly comfortable on top of me as he held himself slightly upright with an arm.

"Can I have another chance?" he murmured, pulling back to look at me. I still held his hair, pulled tight from his face, giving his jaw an angular, wild look. His eyes flashed in the dim room. "The first time was a fluke. I can do so much better."

"I have no doubt," I said with a slow smile.

In one quick motion, he was inside me again, moving against me in a glorious rhythm, while I held his hair back from his face, memorizing the lines of his jaw and chin. We cried out together and I let go, watching the strands fall around his cheeks, over his forehead, and down to his shoulders like black rain.

"I COULD USE a glass of wine. You?"

"Sure." I felt drowsy and contented, and was halfway to falling asleep, but I would have agreed to anything. I lay in the crook of his warm, muscular arm, half dozing, my body pleasantly singing with the last dying embers of pleasure.

"Can I take your truck? I'll run to the liquor store, buy us a bottle. There's one on the corner."

"Are you sure you want to risk it?" I asked lazily, tracing a pattern on his chest with my finger. "What if someone recognizes you?"

"I'll wear the hat and that hoodie," he said. "I'll keep my head down. Hell, they might even have a drive through."

"Sure you don't want me to go?"

"No," he said, planting a kiss on the tip of my nose. "You lie here and relax. I'll just be a minute." He pulled the shirt over his head. "You just be ready for when I get back."

"Are you telling me that the third time's the charm?" I asked with a lazy laugh. "Because the second time was pretty much perfect."

"You have no idea what you're in for, pretty lady." He winked at me and turned to leave.

I was dozing off before he even got out the door, dreaming about what he had in store for me.

I WOKE up a short while later to a gentle knock on the door, and groggily pulled myself out of bed. Phillip must've forgotten to take his motel key. I was still naked, and it was cold, so I threw a t-shirt on as I walked to the door. "Phillip, is that you?"

There was no response, just a sing-songy little "tap-tap" again. He probably couldn't hear me through the thick walls.

I opened the door, still half asleep, with a dreamy smile on my face. Suddenly I was wide awake. It was not Phillip standing there, but Lee Courtenay.

"What the fuck are you doing here?" I demanded, putting my arms over my bra-less chest, wishing for once I'd used some common sense and hadn't just opened the door like a foolhardy moron. "Jesus, Lee, again?"

"I saw him leave," Lee said with an easy smile, as though he were an old friend just coming to say what's up. I didn't like the bulge in his pocket though. It looked like it could be a gun. And I didn't trust that smile. "I'm not here to hurt you, Stormy."

"You say that every time I see you," I said. "Which is far

too damn often. If I wasn't 100% sure I could defend myself against you, I'd be concerned. You know – thou protest too much and all that."

He laughed. "I just don't want you to be ill at ease."

"You said that you'd leave me alone," I seethed.

"I know, and I'm sorry. But I don't think you understand-"

"You always show up when Phillip isn't around," I said. "You're scared of him."

He shook his head. "No."

"What do you want? I was asleep. I don't appreciate being woken up or having to look over my shoulder every time Phillip goes to the bathroom."

"What I warned you about – you didn't listen," he said accusingly.

I leaned against the door frame. "I passed the message along, Lee, but I'm afraid that Phillip didn't give a rat's ass. So why don't you take your ugly hat and your beat-up car and go bother somebody who gives a damn."

He winced. "Damn, you're mean."

"Yeah? Well, I don't like being followed, or having weird guys prowling around my house, or threatening me and my boyfriend-"

"So you guys are 'on', then," he said.

"That's none of your business." I started to shut the door. "Now fuck off."

"I had to try one more time. To tell you. You don't seem to understand the gravity of this situation."

"I understand just fine, Lee." I moved again to shut the door, and he stopped it with his foot.

"Your life is in danger," he said, then moved his foot. I slammed the door.

I sighed, leaning my forehead against the door. He was baiting me, and I knew it, but there was no way I couldn't hear what he had to say now. I opened the door again and looked at him expectantly. "Spit it out. Ten words or less."

"The man who gave Phillip the spell," he said. "If he finds out what you guys are doing, he'll kill Phillip."

"That makes no sense," I said. "*He* gave Phillip the spell. He obviously knows what it's for. He knew that someone might use it."

"Things are different now," he said. "You'll see. You don't understand. Guthrie-"

"Thanks for the tip, Lee," I cut in. "Now I'm going back to bed."

"I don't understand why you're not listening to me."

"Because you're a stalker and a liar and I don't know the first thing about you, maybe?"

"Surely that guy isn't such a great fuck that it's worth risking your life," he said.

"That's just it," I said, rearing my arm back. "He is." I slammed the door in his face for the second time.

Twelve

When Phillip returned twenty minutes later, I was still in just a t-shirt, sitting there fretting, holding ice on my knuckles. After I'd slammed the door on Lee, I'd punched the wall in a fit of rage. I was relieved when Phillip walked through the door holding a brown paper bag.

"Those coffee cups over on the fridge will have to do," he said, walking over and popping the cork on the wine. "I forgot to get cups."

"It's fine."

He glanced over at me. "What the hell happened to your hand?"

I relayed Lee's visit and my subsequent rage punch. He chuckled and shook his head.

"I'm gone half an hour..."

"He just makes me so mad," I said.

"That guy is an A+ creep. If he comes around here again, I'll deal with him."

"That's just it. I don't think he *is* a creep," I said, blowing on my fingers. "But he's definitely a coward. He doesn't come around unless you're gone."

"Then you'll stay by my side at all times," he said, sitting on the bed and pulling me close. He ran a hand up my thigh and I sighed with pleasure. "I can't believe you said that to him."

"It's true."

"When I saw those knuckles, I thought you'd punched *him.*"

"Next time I will," I said. I meant it. I reached up with my bruised hand and ran a finger down his jaw, which was stubbly and coarse; he hadn't been shaving. "But let's not think about him anymore."

"I'm still on cloud nine from before," he said, placing a soft, sensual kiss on my lips. "And I'm going to take you back to bed in a minute, believe me. But Stormy-" His face turned serious. "Don't risk yourself for me. Ever. I know you can take care of yourself, you've proven that. But no heroics. Not on my account."

"I have an obligation to you," I said. "I brought you back."

"That doesn't obligate you. You had no idea what would happen. I won't have you risking your neck for me." He brushed my hair back from my face. "I like you way too much for that."

"Fine," I said stubbornly. "But the same goes for you. No stupid heroics just for my benefit, either, understand? You need to lay low and keep yourself safe."

He nodded, his eyes full of bemusement and affection and something else I couldn't place. He was lying, but so was I, so what did it matter?

I held out my hand. "Where's my wine, you handsome devil, you?"

"It's the cheap stuff," he said, pouring me some and handing it over. "Hope you're okay with red."

"That's all I drink."

"Me, too."

We sipped in silence for a few moments, both of us lost in thought. I wasn't scared, exactly, but I was nervous. Anxious. Lee was a weirdo, but some of what he said seemed to have a ring of truth to it. Seeking out this guy Guthrie did seem risky. Just because he'd given Phillip a spell years back when they were both high as a kite didn't mean he'd take kindly to seeing him in the flesh all these years later, nor would he necessarily be thrilled to see a random girl from the sticks who just happened to accidentally perform necromancy. He might be really offended, or worse, want to squelch my black magic – which meant squelching me. I was out of my depth here, with no idea about magic, how to counteract it, or whether or not I'd gotten myself or Philip into serious trouble. We wouldn't know until we saw Guthrie, and once we did, it'd be too late to run.

We were taking a risk, but it was a necessary one. I just hoped we'd come out of it unscathed.

I guzzled down the dregs of the cheap wine and poured a little more. I wanted to have a nice buzz to help me forget my nerves. Phillip seemed to be of the same mind, because he discarded his cheap coffee mug and took a long swig straight from the bottle. Then he handed it to me. We drank that way, just staring at each other, saying nothing, until the bottle was about half gone. Then he took me in his arms and leaned me back on the pillows. He placed a gentle, wet kiss on my lips.

"I feel pretty lucky," he said, smiling at me. "To have you. I really don't deserve you, not after the life I've lived."

"That life is over," I said, wrapping my legs around him. "This is a whole different life."

"LET ME DO THE TALKING," Phillip had said to me before we exited the truck to knock on the door of the little house. As if I had any plans to chat up this mystery person.

It hadn't taken us long to find the place; apparently Phillip still knew the location by heart, even after twenty-three years. It wasn't far from his old family home, where Jason now lived (I knew another conversation about that would have to be had soon), just a couple of blocks, though in those couple of blocks the neighborhood had changed dramatically. Gone were the nicely manicured lawns, clean painted shutters and flower box windows. The houses on this street were full of peeling paint, sparse, dry lawns, and beat up vehicles. The house we were about to enter, if anyone was home and agreeable, was a tiny place that looked to be only one bedroom, with ancient powder blue siding and a roof that was in ill repair. The front porch wasn't much more than a stoop, and it was covered in boxes of what appeared to be junk. A sullen-looking yellow cat saun-tered out from one of the boxes, making me smile, and with a nonplussed swish of his eaten-looking tail, went around to the back of the house.

I was tempted to just wait in the truck, but felt I'd be safer by Phillip's side. Just the idea of Guthrie scared me. If Lee was to be believed, he would not be happy to find out who I was or what I had done: I did not like the idea of what he might say or do to me. I planned to tell him that if didn't want people doing spells, he ought not to give them out like candy to trick or treaters, but behind all my attitude, I was scared shitless.

Despite never having met him, something about Guthrie reminded me of a guy my parents had been friends with when I was a kid. He had lived in the same trailer park, in a singlewide off to the very end, secluded and nearest to the woods. His name had been something weird and old fashioned like Eldred or Elvin – my folks had insisted I call him "Uncle El" - and he had always frightened me. Now that I was grown, I knew he'd just been your usual run of the mill pot dealer, somebody who sold my drunk parents dime bags of weed and the occasional bump of coke; just a tragic, middle-aged guy who was probably harmless.

And yet he had creeped me out so much when I was little that I'd avoided going to his house with my parents whenever I could, begging to stay home in my bedroom with my books. When I was forced to go along, I'd cower in his living room, sitting on the very edge of his dark, scratchy couch, almost sliding off onto the floor, trying not to look up at the dream-catchers he had suspended from the dingy, smoke-stained ceiling. He'd had dozens of them, all sizes and colors, some of them huge, with elaborate, colored feathers, others small and cheaply made, likely bought from the dollar store. They'd catch the light from his streaky, dusty windows and the breeze from his box fan, and I'd try not to watch them dance, because I was afraid that the spirits attached to those dreamcatchers would catch my eyes and not let them go, that they would follow me – follow me home, follow me to bed, haunt me in my dreams, and I'd wake up blind.

As a child, I had no awareness of why it scared me, but now, standing with Phillip outside the truck, I had an inkling. "Uncle El" had co-opted something that didn't belong to him, that wasn't his…the magic that he'd contained within his little singlewide was too large and too *real* to be contained within that small, dirty space, commandeered by someone who had no tie to it, and no real idea of its significance. It was magic for magic's sake; false magic. Playing with things that weren't yours to play with. It had just felt *wrong*.

And that's how it felt now, too. It felt wrong. It wasn't Phillip that felt wrong, or even the spell I'd done; no, something about that felt *right* to me, as though I had been meant to do what I did in that drunken moment. It was all the rest – the specter of Guthrie, the shifty beings following me, so many variables – that felt out of place, wrong and dangerous.

I waited, pulling my black hoodie around me tightly, like a

cocoon, determined to shake my dreadful thoughts. I was certain that Phillip had been fumbling around in my head – I wasn't sure he could even help it most of the time – but thankfully, he said nothing, only placed an arm gently around my shoulders and gave me an optimistic smile.

Phillip wasn't nervous or full of dread, just eager. Now that one piece of business had been concluded, he was anxious to get the second out of the way. I envied him his lack of fear, his logical attitude toward it all. What he planned to do next I supposed relied upon whatever Guthrie had to tell him, if he told him anything at all.

I imagined his questions were the same as mine, though we hadn't discussed it. Instead, they hung unasked in the air between us. What exactly *was* Phillip? A zombie? A Frankenstein monster? A reanimated corpse? How had the spell worked? Was I a witch or was it just a fluke, a spell that would have worked for anyone? Was it indeed black magic? Could Phillip be hurt or killed? What happened if I released him? Was his incredible strength, almost-psychic "vibes" and the fact that electronics didn't work around him all part of his super-human abilities? How long did he have before he died again? Would he go on to live a normal human lifespan? Or was he immortal?

Those were just a few of the questions I wanted to ask. A few I hoped Phillip would get the answers to. Many I was content to never know, if I could help it. The thought of something happening to Phillip now filled me with terror. I was falling in love with him. I had no excuse. I hadn't even tried to stop it. How could I not have? I'd lusted after him since I was a teen, and he was bound to me – there were forces stronger than me at work. What would Guthrie say about *that?*

Phillip rang the door bell, and after about thirty seconds when there was no answer, he knocked. I wrapped my arms around myself tighter. It was very cold in Boston, and windy, too. I wished I had thought to bring an actual coat and not just a jacket. I was too accustomed to southern winters, where it would be forty degrees one day and seventy the next, where the only snow we ever got was like a dusting of powdered sugar on a cake. Phillip was only wearing his black t-shirt. He had to be cold. I resisted the urge to lean into him, to try and warm him up. He sighed and knocked again, louder this time. There were no sounds of movement from within.

"He must not be home," I said, but just as the words left my lips, we both heard footsteps from inside the house. My teeth began to chatter, and not just from the cold. "Phillip, it's not too late – we could just hop in the truck and leave-"

He shook his head at me, and we heard the lock rattling on the door. It opened gingerly, and a pair of blue eyes set in wrinkled skin peered out at us. Whoever it was had a mop of frizzy gray hair.

"What do you want?"

"We're here to see Guthrie," Phillip said. "Please."

"Guthrie?" the voice said, its owner still peering at us through the crack in the door. It repeated, "Guthrie?"

"Do you know him?" Phillip asked. "I'm an old friend of his but haven't seen him in a very long time. Does he live here, or have we come in error?" He was talking very properly, trying to keep the patience in his voice. Maybe he *was* a little nervous.

"Guthrie," the voice said again, and then the door swung open. It was a little old woman in a housecoat with birds of paradise all over it, and blue house shoes, the same shade of blue as the house. Her hair was in tufts all over her head; it looked like it had been years since she'd seen a hairbrush. "Yah, I know Guthrie." She chuckled. Her voice had a heavy accent. "Not a lot of folks asking after *him* these days. He hasn't lived here in ten years."

"And you are..."

"Lydia." She offered no other explanation.

"Nice to meet you, Lydia." He offered his hand, but she just looked at it. "I'm Phi-"

"Phillip Deville," she stated, giving him a steady look. "Yah, I know who you are. Don't you remember me?"

He obviously didn't. He blinked for a moment, then turned to me. "This here is-"

She interrupted him again. "Stormy Fiona Spooner."

I felt the blood drain from my face. How did she know my name? I never even used Fiona; my mother had given me that middle name after herself, and I hated it.

"How do you know Stormy?" Phillip demanded.

"Why don't the both of you come off the porch and get out of the cold before I'm forced to give explanations," she said with a dry cackle, and pulled us both inside.

The house was so tiny, the living room and kitchen were basically one room. I couldn't imagine Phillip here in his rock star days, even if he'd only come by to pick up dope. It seemed almost too small for him, his head near the ceiling. Another inch and he'd be brushing up against it. We both sat down on a mauve couch and a puff of dust rose in the air when I sat.

"I don't use this room much," she explained, sitting across from us. "I mainly stay in the back bedroom. I'm sick and have a bad back and prefer to lie down most of the time. I rarely get company anyway. I'm afraid I don't have any refreshments to offer you."

"That's okay," Phillip said. "We don't plan to stay long. I really just wanted to find Guthrie. I assume you know a little about-"

She laughed again, the sound as dry as bone buried in sand. "I would surely hope so. Since I'm his wife."

"But you two live apart?" Phillip asked, evident confusion in his voice. "You said you hadn't seen him in ten years."

"He just up and left you?" I asked, incredulous. "But you said you're ill…"

"I'm better off without him. Guthrie couldn't take care of a plant," she said bitterly, then fixed her eyes on Phillip. "I wish I could tell you where he is, dearie, but I can't. I've not seen him in years, and that suits me fine. Whatever you need to ask, you'll have to ask me, I'm afraid."

"I'm not sure you can help me," he said, unsure. He was tense and disappointed, the muscles in his arms rigid.

"Sit down, Sidhe," she said, and I looked at her, confused, wondering what word she'd just called him. I'd never heard it before. She looked back at me with clear eyes, then uttered another laugh. "You sit down, too, Fee. Let's see what we can do."

We both sat down dutifully, but I was confused. "Sidhe and Fee," she said, and it sounded like shee-n-fee. "I like the ring of that, don't you?"

"What does it mean?"

She took another puff of the cigarette, ignoring the question. "So, Sidhe, I assume you have questions about the spell. About what you are, among other things."

"I do." His voice had gone low. He didn't particularly care for this woman, even though it seemed she was being helpful enough. After all, she could have turned us away once she realized we were looking for Guthrie.

"Ask, then," she said. "I'll answer what I can."

"A spell," he began, then told her about the spell Guthrie had given him, how he'd put it on his album, and how I'd recited it. "Obviously it was a real spell, because it worked. Stormy here brought me back."

"Fee," she said again, looking at me. "That'll be short for Fiona, dear. You might dislike it, but it's part of you, and you should learn to embrace even the parts of yourself you don't understand or care for." She gave me a grizzled old smile, then turned back to Phillip. "Fee brought you back. Good job, dearie."

It struck me that she was giving a performance, almost a caricature, barely real. The woman was one warted nose away from a fairy tale villain. I tried to smile at her, but I felt like Dorothy faced with the Wicked Witch; I wanted to throw a bucket of water at her and run away. Instead, I steeled my gaze and spoke. "I didn't know the spell was real. I was drunk and reading an album cover. It was a total fluke." This was a stretch of the truth, but I wasn't quite ready to admit just how far I'd gone with it. "When he showed up on my doorstep it was a hell of a shock."

"And then you were pleased as punch," she said, her eyes gleaming with amusement. "Right?"

I looked down and didn't answer. She was poking fun at me.

"How did it work?" Phillip demanded. "How could it have? When Guthrie gave me the spell, he owed me money. I never took it seriously for a second, and when I printed the damn lyrics in my liner notes-"

"Not lyrics, a spell," she corrected him.

"Right, fine, the spell – when I printed them in the liner notes I had no idea that it was a real thing, that I'd be sealing my fate as this, this -" he gestured with his hands, "-whatever I am."

"Didn't you?" she asked. "Didn't you have some idea it might be real? Otherwise, why would you have bothered?"

"It's not like I knew I was going to die in two years," he said petulantly.

"Didn't you?" she repeated.

This was not going well.

"The spell – is it permanent?" I asked, deciding to go with a direct question. "Or can it be reversed?" Phillip looked at me with alarm – apparently, he had not thought of this.

"It's permanent, yes, but it can also be reversed," she answered. This was maddening. I had a sudden vision of her as the tuft-haired caterpillar in *Alice in Wonderland,* puffing away on her Virginia Slim, talking in riddles. "You can reverse it, except-" She stopped, then shook her head. "-you wouldn't do that to poor Sidhe, would you?"

"No," I answered. "Unless he asked me to."

"Maybe not even then," she said with a smile. *You're wrong,* I thought to myself, hating her smugness. *I'm not selfish like you.* She turned to Phillip. "Whether or not Fee cooperates, dear Sidhe, you can always reverse the spell yourself."

"How?"

"Can you not think of anything?" She raised an eyebrow.

I grimaced. "So if it's permanent, that means he won't, like, keel over tomorrow. But otherwise, is he a normal mortal guy? Can he be hurt or killed?"

"Yes," she answered, her cigarette dangling from her lips. "He can be hurt and killed, both. But it will be harder to do either to him than most. He has a bit of extra strength, you see."

"Yes." I'd seen that for myself.

"Why did Guthrie give me the spell?" Phillip asked.

"You just said yourself," she answered in surprise, "he owed you money. He did that from time to time back then. Idiot, foolish thing to do, but he never was very smart."

"I don't believe that, not anymore," Phillip answered. "He didn't have to give me that spell to placate me. He chose to, for some reason. He picked me for this...he knew that it would happen. The same as I know you're holding something back." He fixed his gaze on her, and his hands were clasped tightly in my own, squeezing my fingers harder than he realized. "Why did he pick me for this?"

"I can't say I know, Sidhe."

"Stop calling me that," he snapped.

"You're very tense," she said. "Relax, Phillip. You have nothing to fear. It's a blessing, a gift. Count your lucky stars. Not every man has the opportunity to shake off the mortal coil on a temporary basis."

"What do I have to give in return?" he asked. "That's what I want to know. My soul? Something else? Will I end up sacrificing someone I love or having to serve some-" He stopped and shook his head. "What kind of price do I have to pay for this 'blessing'?"

"None at all," she answered easily. "Magic doesn't work that way."

"Then *she,*" he gestured at me, emphasizing the word, since it sounded so much like the one she kept using for him, "will have to pay the price."

She looked at me dreamily. "Nothing she hasn't already paid."

Phillip's face twitched.

"This magic," I said, stepping in to diffuse the situation. "Is it white or black?"

"What?" Her forehead crinkled.

"The spell," I said. "White or black magic?"

She smiled. "Fee means White Lady. White Witch. Magic is all about intention and what you use it for, what's in your heart."

"That's not an answer," Phillip thundered. "And you just said it was short for Fiona."

"So it is." She puffed away, her watery eyes working over us. "And Sidhe is an old Gaelic word that roughly translates to 'tall fairy.' The Sidhe were a mythical race of faeries that were able to walk among the heavens and the earth in kind. They had much magic," she said with a clever smile, looking at Phillip. "Just looking at you, hulking around, so full of misplaced pride and concern you try to hide; it suits you. So

tall and strong – all the trappings of a brute, but such a femi-
nine face and a tender heart."

Phillip glowered beside me and I hid my smile behind my
hand.

"Fee and Sidhe. My white witch and my tall fairy man."

"We're not yours," Phillip growled. "And I'm sure as hell
not a fucking fairy."

"Oh, down boy." She chuckled. "He really can be like a
dog with a bone," she said to me, her eyes sparkling. "I don't
know how you contain him."

I ignored this, though inside, I wanted to chuckle. She
wasn't wrong. "From everything I've read, necromancy is
black magic," I changed the subject, uneasy.

"Sidhe and Fee, so worried." That smile again. "So it is.
Black magic. What of it? So many misconceptions about good
and evil." She sighed. "Nobody has any real understanding of
the practice, of what white and black magic entail. They work
in conjunction with each other, you see. Two halves of one
coin, two very necessary halves. You must find the balance."

"She's not going to tell us anything real," Phillip muttered
to me.

"Oh, I suppose now you've been earth-side for a whole
four days you suddenly know everything," she said. "Not real?
Look at your flesh, restored. Feel the breath in your lungs.
Mere days ago, you were rotting in the ground. And you want
to talk about what's real?"

"I didn't ask for this," he said, angry. "Neither did she."

"Yes, you did. Yes, you *both* did." She puffed her cigarette.
"Now shall we put away our egos and talk plainly?"

"I didn't intend to be a witch," I said. "I know that much."

"Well, don't worry sweetie, because you aren't one." She
laughed, smug. "Not yet. Nor will you be with that attitude.
Any fool can do a bit of magic if they say the right words
and have the right talismans. But to be a true witch, you

have to believe – in your power and in yourself. You don't believe much in either." Her words stung. "Intention, as I said. If you don't value what it is to be a witch, you'll never be one." I reared back, feeling as if she'd just slapped me. How many times had I said the very same thing to Sloan, half joking, half resentful of the way she always dismissed me? Now that the word was on Lydia's lips, it felt aggressive and mocking.

I looked down at my feet, angry. Even though I'd just told her I wasn't interested, who was she to suggest otherwise?

"We'll be going now." Phillip stood up again. "Thanks for nothing."

"You're being very unfair," she said calmly. "I've answered everything you've asked."

She flicked ashes into the ashtray and stood on shaking legs. "I can tell you one more thing. You asked how the spell can be reversed. There's one way, but you should know – it's immediate."

"What is it?" Phillip asked warily. We were both meandering slowly toward the door, eager to get away from her. Something was off; among the dusty, stale, oppressed air of the house there was a new electricity, something humming, something chaotic and anxious. I knew Phillip felt it too, because the hairs on his arm, where I was clutching him with white fingers, were raised.

"You've heard of Samson and Delilah?"

"Of course," Phillip said. "I was raised Catholic. Samson's strength was in his hair, and when Delilah cut it in his sleep, he lost it."

"Guthrie used to call that spell the 'Samson spell'." She grimaced. "It always irritated me. Christians take everything from pagans. Everything. Your hair, Sidhe. If you get tired and want to shuffle off, cut it. That's it."

"Just cut my hair? And the spell reverses? I die?"

"You cease to be in this realm," she answered. "Put it that way." Then she laughed.

Phillip looked a bit green. "We're going now."

"Goodbye, then, Sidhe and Fee. See yourself out. Lock the door behind you." And she was gone to the back of the house, seemingly without giving us a second thought, confident that we'd let ourselves out. We heard a door shut and Phillip turned to me.

"What a waste of fucking time."

"She did tell us a few things," I said.

"All she did was talk in riddles and throw us a whole hell of a lot of attitude." He put his hand on my back. "Let's get out of here before the cigarette stench absorbs into our clothes."

We were at the truck when the screen door opened, and Lydia stuck her frizzy head out. "Sidhe…look after her." She gestured at me with a gnarled hand. "She's in far more danger than you are."

Phillip's face twisted in disgust, and he opened his mouth to reply, but I stopped him with a hand. Something about the expression on her face told me not to tangle with this woman, and anyway, she was right. Phillip had been saying all along that the ragtag group of guys following us were after *him,* but it was just as I'd suspected -they were really after *me.*

"Let's just go," I said in a low voice. Lydia had already retreated inside in a cloud of smoke, the screen door slamming behind her. I could hear the deadbolts locking on the other side of the heavy door.

Phillip trudged over to the driver's side of the truck and opened the door. He climbed in and put the key in the ignition. Nothing happened. "Storm," he called to me. "The truck won't fucking start." I was still standing outside the truck, unlocking my cell phone to check for messages from Sloan, who still had not responded to my earlier text. I peered through the truck window.

"What do you think it-" I began, then something at my feet caught my eye. I crouched down to pick it up, hearing the blood rushing in my ears, knowing without really looking what it would be. Of course, it was another tarot card. What else would it be? The Death card, no doubt. Well, I wasn't going to touch the damned thing. Not here in this creepy ass yard, after talking to that creepy ass woman.

I stood back up, my stomach lurching, turning back toward Phillip, who was still fiddling with the ignition, cussing up a storm. I opened my mouth to tell him what I'd just seen, but no sound came out. Suddenly I was overcome with dizziness, an unwelcome, nauseating feeling of being *bound* – I tried to call out again, to move my arms, to wave, to shuffle my feet forward, but I was stuck to the spot. I couldn't even reach forward a couple of inches to open the truck door or tap on the glass and get Phillip's attention. I watched helplessly as Phillip continued to fiddle with the keys, not looking at me, not sensing my sudden terror. How was it that for once he couldn't feel me? Why wasn't he in my head?

I had the sensation of something looming heavy behind me, creeping up like a black cloud of smoke over my eyes, nose and mouth. I could feel the thud of Phillip's heartbeat – he was full of the same sense of foreboding and I could *feel it* – and realized, staring in mute horror, he wasn't actually fiddling with the keys at all, but was rather staring straight ahead at the steering wheel, one hand suspended in the air, clutching the keys, the other in his lap. He wasn't moving. He was *bound* - terrified and paralyzed, just as I was. I tried to scream but I could do nothing but stare ahead, voiceless, trapped in the immobile cage that was my body. I heard a sudden rustling of feet behind me, and that was the last thing I knew before my world went black.

Thirteen

Drip, drip, drip. My eyes opened, but all I could see was pitch black dark. Wherever I was, it was very quiet, except for that incessant dripping. It sounded like a faucet, but I couldn't be sure. I tried to move, gingerly – I was afraid that something might be broken. I didn't know what had happened to me, I had no memory of it. But my head ached something fierce, and it felt tight up top, like a wound that had opened and scabbed over. If I tried to make an expression, it pulled and hurt. There was something wet on the side of my face; was it blood?

I tried to roll myself up. At least I could move again, but I was afraid to test out my voice in case someone heard me. I managed to sit up, and my head began to pound. Okay, so I'd lie back down. The floor beneath me was cold; I was pretty sure it was tile. I felt around in the dark with my hands and felt a cabinet, a threadbare rug, and finally a large chunk of porcelain - a toilet. So I was locked in a bathroom. But where?

I focused myself, trying to pay attention to my surroundings, positioning my head in a way where I might be able to hear something. At first, there was nothing but the *drip drip drip* of the faucet and the slow rumble of the pipes under the floor. But as my eyes began to adjust to the dark, I thought I could make out the smallest crack of light. I inched my way slowly toward it, which wasn't easy lying down, and tried to crane my head toward it. Silence.

But then, I heard a very muffled sound that seemed to be a man's voice. I listened for several frustrating minutes but couldn't make out a word that was being said, nor whose voice it was. I hoped to god it was Phillip and that he would find me any minute. What had happened to him? The last I'd seen he was sitting in our dead truck, his hand on the keys, immobile. Then someone had bashed my head in, and I'd seen no more. I knew Phillip, and I knew he'd have moved mountains to rescue me if he'd been able to. The fact that I was wherever I was meant that maybe – probably – Phillip was not okay.

I tried not to think about that possibility. I swallowed the bowling ball in my throat and pressed my face up against the door, struggling to listen, to hear anything that might give me a clue.

Another muffled voice. This time it was closer, and it sounded angry. I craned my neck to the crack in the door, ignoring the pounding pain in my head.

"Shut the fuck up. Like hell I'm listening to you, after the way you fucked that up."

"I didn't fuck it up. She's here, isn't she? And that big fucking lumberjack of a motherfucker is right where you want him."

"I didn't tell you to hit her. In fact, you fucking numb nuts, I specifically told you *not* to hit her. She was bound, she couldn't have fought you. Your orders were to do no harm."

"Aw, how sweet, Lee's got a crush." The voice was taunting. "Hate to tell you bro, but you're not getting in there. That bitch fucking hates you."

"Don't call her a bitch."

"Why do you care? She's with him, isn't she? She summoned him. Do you really think she's-"

"You know, Shank, I've had just about enough of your mouth. Guthrie might have let you have free rein over his affairs, but I'm not Guthrie. And if you don't fucking like the way I give orders you don't have to work for me. Got it?"

"Work for you? I think you might be overstating your position."

The voices faded away and I heard a stifled slam; they'd gone to another room or outside. I felt cold with horror. Lee and the creepy, ominous Shank, who I remembered standing behind Lee, like a hovering, dark storm cloud, in my yard. So they'd kidnapped me, then, and brought me somewhere. And what did they mean about Phillip? "Where they wanted him." Where was that? Was he safe? What were they going to do to him, and how on earth, knowing his strength, had they managed to subdue him?

It was silent for a long while as I lay there trying to get my bearings. My head hurt so bad I could hardly think. Shank had dealt me a righteous blow. I made a vow to get my revenge on him, one way or the other. Bastard.

The *drip drip drip* was driving me crazy. I gingerly tried to sit up again, and the pain was still there, but not quite as bad. I grabbed onto the cabinet and pulled myself up, little by little, until I was in a crouching position, and felt around for the sink. Once I found it, I tightened each knob as hard as I could. *Now that I'm standing,* I thought nervously, *I could try opening the door. Just a little bit.*

It was risky, but I had to. I felt around for the door and finally grabbed the handle, turning it gently. I half expected it to be locked from the outside, but it wasn't - the knob turned easily. I opened the door just a crack, praying it wouldn't squeak. It was dark outside, and the only light was coming from what I figured was a muted TV in another room, emitting an occasional flash in the hall. I peered out, trying to get a feel for where I was. It was definitely a house, and a nice one from the look of the ornate, darkened hallway. In the shadows, I thought it looked like there was a rug on the floor. I opened the door a little wider. At one end of the hall there was a series of doors, all closed. The other end opened into a large room, likely a living room, where the TV was. I could only make out a third of the room. The rest of it was hidden behind the wall, so I didn't know if there was anyone in there or not, making it much too risky to try and leave.

But what else could I do? I certainly wasn't going to lie in the bathroom with my head bashed in, waiting for Lee and Shank to come back. What if it was Shank by himself? I got the impression if he was willing to smack me over the head, he'd be willing to hurt me in other ways. There was no love lost there. No, I wasn't going to wait around to see what else they had in store. Besides, I had to find Phillip. He might need me.

So which way? To the left, with the TV, or the right, with the doors? I took my chances and turned left, stumbling down the hall, trying my best to be quiet. The floor was creaky, and I held my breath the entire way. When I reached the room, I stepped slowly, on tiptoe, and let my head just peer around the wall, only one eye visible.

There was nobody in the room, but there were two open beers on the coffee table, both dripping with condensation. Shank and Lee were probably just having a smoke break or outside finishing their argument. They'd be back soon. I needed to split, and now.

I could suddenly hear voices on the other side of the door by the TV, and I froze. They were coming back in. I bounded back down the hall as fast as I could without making noise and into one of the rooms at the end. I heard them come through the door, still throwing obscenities at each other, as I pulled the door shut behind me. I prayed they wouldn't go directly to the bathroom to check on me.

"So what do we do now?" Shank asked. "Do you even have a plan?"

"I have a plan, but I'm not going to tell you the fuck about it." Lee was grumpy.

"She's bound to wake up soon. Might want to figure it out. She's only good for another hour at best."

"It doesn't concern you either way."

"I'm just sayin', you're crazy if you think she's gonna do your bidding after all you've-"

"Yeah, I KNOW, and no thanks to you, since you made it a thousand times worse. She was *bound,* dude. It's bad enough that you hit her, then you had to go and give her the drugs too-"

Drugs? What drugs? That would explain the throbbing behind my eyes.

I could hear footsteps coming down the hall. Just one set, from the sound of it. I retreated further into the dark room. I couldn't see anything, but it had the open feel of a bedroom. I fled backward, stumbling and almost falling over a bed. I fell to my knees and tried to crouch underneath, but there was no room. Stumbling, insane with fear, I found a door handle and yanked it open. A closet. I retreated inside, closing the door behind me, and crouched in the corner behind what felt like a coat.

I heard a door open and shut. Then a stream of curses. It was Lee.

The footsteps were back in the hallway, harder this time. "Where is she?"

"What? Who?"

Now there were two sets of feet in the hall. I began to shake.

"Stormy, you fucking idiot. She's gone!" He sounded furious. "Did you lock the door when you left last time?"

"I did, I told you I did!" If I hadn't been so terrified, I would have smiled. He definitely had not locked the door.

"So she just came to after being drugged and hit over the head, picked the lock and went...where?"

"She's here somewhere. She couldn't've gone far. We been here the whole time."

I clenched my teeth in terror. If either of them had to find me, I'd rather it be Lee. He was scary, but Shank was violent. At least I knew Lee wouldn't hurt me physically – though maybe he would now, considering how angry he sounded.

I heard another door slam.

Trying to be as quiet as possible, I patted my pockets to see if my cell phone was still there. I couldn't text Phillip's burner phone in case someone intercepted it, but I could try to text Sloan. Maybe even dial 911 if I hurried. The phone wasn't there. They'd taken it. I started to silently cry.

The footsteps were still sounding all over the house, along with the occasional slamming door and expletive. It sounded like they were methodically searching every room. Whether it would be Lee or Shank, I didn't know, but one of them would find me any minute. I tried to stop shaking and couldn't. There was no way to escape.

Silence fell. I didn't hear the footsteps anymore or any slamming doors. Were they searching outside? I retreated further into the corner, hoping the coat covered me. It seemed like hours passed, but it was probably only minutes. The silence was so loud, the walls of the closet seemed to be closing in, and I began to panic. Oh crap, what if I started hyperventilating? Silence and more silence. I sat like a statue, the only sign of life the trembling in my limbs. Time seemed to suspend itself as I waited, afraid to breathe.

Without warning, the closet door was wrenched open and I shrank back in fear, pulling the coat down from the hanger and exposing myself to the figure standing in the doorway. He reached into his pocket and pulled out a phone, pressed a button, and held it up to let the light expose me. It was my phone; I recognized the familiar turquoise Bloomer Demons case and began to laugh despite myself, the ridiculousness of the situation I was in overriding my terror. I was in shock, I was out of my mind. I cowered, obliterated by the light in front of him, unable to tell who it was, the only thing visible his large, hulking shoulders and what looked like dark hair. I threw an arm up over my eyes and waited for the inevitable violence, biting my lip to try and stop the mad laughter that wouldn't stop coming.

After a moment, I heard a voice, quiet in the darkness. "Stormy, come on out. It's me." Lee. Startled, I blinked in front of me, realizing that what I thought had been Shank's dark hair was a black beanie, pulled down low over Lee's light-blonde head. His expression was anxious.

I blinked again, unsure. My head was still pounding; I couldn't think straight.

He reached into the closet and pulled me out by my jacket, bracing me as I tried to stand. My legs were shaky. "You fucked things up," he said. "I was planning on letting you go just as soon as I could get Shank out of here, but then you had to try and escape. Now it's going to be harder. You need to be quick and do exactly as I say."

I nodded dumbly, a strange mix of sludgy drugs and pure adrenaline coursing through my veins. I thought I might lean over and yak on the carpet at any moment.

"Buck up. Now listen." He pointed at the door. "When you go out of here, take a right and go down the hallway and right out the front door. If you stay to the edge of the yard and run straight down the driveway till you get to the wooded area then head straight for the trees, you might have a chance of getting away while Shank's around back. You're only about a mile away from the road. If you hurry, you might make it. From there you're on your own. I'll try to detain him, but he knows he can't trust me." He shook me a little. "Got it? Can you remember?"

I cleared my throat and glared at him. "Down the hallway, out the front door, head for the trees. Even full of drugs and with a head wound, I'm not a fucking idiot."

"Go, then," he said, pushing me toward the door.

I hesitated, looking at his slight frame and short stature. He really didn't look a day over twenty, even as winded and sweaty as he was. How was he mixed up in all this and why? His every pore seemed to scream resistance. "Appearances can be deceiving," he said, an expression of irritation briefly flashing on his freckled cheeks. "Go *now* and don't look back." As I reached the door, he called after me, "And for the love of hell, pack up your shit and go *home*."

My legs felt like Jell-O but I managed to scurry down the dark hallway, past the kitchen and living room and out the front door, which thankfully was not locked. The rickety wrap-around porch creaked under my weight as I made my way down the stairs and I hoped that Shank was nowhere within earshot. The yard was an expanse of perfectly coifed grass and flowers, but not many trees to provide cover. I could see, as I rushed toward the edge of the yard, where the graveled driveway began, why Lee was worried I'd be seen. Anyone coming around the side of the house would spot me in a second. Luckily, it was very dark, with a milky sheen of light cloud cover that didn't fully cover the bright stars, like a puff of smoke. The crescent moon overhead gave off just enough light to cast shadows around the yard – just enough light to see by, if you squinted. I needed to hurry. I crouched down low as I reached the driveway, carefully staying off to the side as instructed, as much to avoid the sound of my feet on the gravel as to avoid being spotted. As I ran, my foot went into a mudhole and my ankle rolled. I had to clamp my hand over my mouth to not cry out in pain. Pulling myself back up, I hobbled down the driveway, forcing myself not to look back. If Shank was behind me, it wouldn't matter anyway. I picked up my pace as I saw the little grove of trees that gave way to a larger forest of pines up ahead on my right.

As I reached the end of the driveway a thick pillow of cloud drifted over the moon, blocking what little light there was. I kept running blindly. I was almost at the end of the driveway and into the trees when a figure came out of the woods and crashed into me, hard. I was knocked down to the gravel.

I fought immediately, bringing up my arms and driving them into the hard chest. "Let me go! I'll fucking kill you!" I screamed, my eyes shut tight with fear. I brought my hands up, my fingers forming into claws, ready to tear at skin, draw blood, inflict pain. I would fight to the death if I had to.

"Stormy. Stormy, stop. It's me." The voice was breathless, but unmistakable. Phillip.

I opened my eyes, still struggling against him. He seemed to realize he was holding me down and let me up instantly, helping me to my feet. I was out of breath and panting. For a moment he just looked at me, then he grabbed my arm and propelled me forward. "Let's go."

He ran fast, so fast I almost couldn't keep up with him. It was no surprise that he'd be faster since he was also stronger. I held tightly to his arm, forcing my legs forward, ignoring the burn in my muscles and the rapidly growing cramp in my side. I had no idea where we were going. I hoped he did.

He pulled me through the woods, past tall, ancient pines and redwoods, our feet crunching over the leaves. A frightened deer fled from us and a raccoon stood and stared as we made our way past. I could smell smoke on the breeze. There was no light other than the pale glare of the full moon, the clouds drifting across it and casting a weird, darkened glow over the ground. I was breathing hard, having a difficult time getting air. Tree branches whipped into my face, stinging and sharp. "Phillip," I wheezed after a few more minutes of trying to keep pace with him. "You're going too fast. I have to stop for a second to catch my breath."

"We have to get you to safety." His voice was urgent.

"I know, but I'm going to have a heart attack. Not all of us are part werewolf."

We stopped. I leaned against a tree, still wheezing. He watched me silently, his face full of emotions I couldn't identify. He looked all around us, eyes darting, alert for any threat. Finding none, he finally asked me softly, "Are you alright?"

"Kind of." I didn't know how to answer him. "You?"

He laughed. "I'm fine. Now that I've found you, anyway. I was worried sick."

"I've got a head wound," I said and touched a hand to it. "I think it might be bleeding."

"You were right," he said, breathing hard. "They were never after me. They've always been after you."

"I know." Hot tears stung my eyes. "I told you."

"I've got to get you somewhere safe," he said, biting at his lip.

"I don't think I can run like that anymore," I said weakly. "I'm not just out of shape, they drugged me, too."

"I never thought for a minute you were out of shape," he said with a smile. "Come here."

He extended his arms to me and I rushed into them. He was warm and solid and strong, drenched with sweat. The next thing I knew he had picked me up and thrown me over his shoulder. I felt like I was flying as he ran, pine needles whipping past as he brushed by tree limbs, the moon looking down on us, as cold and silent and ambivalent as a ghost.

"Phillip, I'm too heavy," I protested weakly, but he just laughed. The deep, velvety sound echoed through the quiet woods like the crackle of embers in a warm autumn fire. "I got you, girl," he said with a growl, darting through the trees. "Not even a silver bullet can bring me down."

SOME TIME LATER, I came to, lying on the rickety bed in our motel room and Phillip was leaning over me, his face lined with worry. When I opened my eyes, his face lit up into a bright smile.

"What happened?"

"You passed out," he said. "I think there were still drugs in your system."

"I have no idea what they gave me."

"I wish I could get you to a hospital, have you checked out." He reached out and tucked a piece of my hair behind an ear. "Maybe we should go."

"No," I croaked. "I'm fine. Are you?"

Before I'd passed out, Phillip had filled me in on what happened to him while I was with Lee. He'd described the experience the same way as I'd felt it – he'd put the key in the ignition and groaned when the car hadn't turned over. He'd yelled out to me that the battery was dead, then fiddled with the keys, cussing all the while, hoping that it might still start up. But as he held the keys in his hand, he'd been filled with an eerie sense of foreboding, as though the daylight had suddenly shrunk down into a dark void, the air crackling with electricity. He'd been struck by a piercing terror, and opened his mouth to warn me, to tell me to get in the truck. But he couldn't speak, couldn't get words to come. He couldn't move;

it was like he was bound by an invisible cord. Just as I had been.

He'd been powerless to stop it as he'd heard the commotion outside – someone had come up and hit me. He'd heard the thwack and my bellow of pain, and had been unable to move, tears streaming down his immovable face as he'd heard me being carried off, the start of an engine, the squealing of tires.

For ten minutes he'd sat there, still as a statue, crying with frustration and fury. Then he'd noticed Lydia's front door open again, her old, wispy head peeking out. He could feel the power of her dark eyes peering at him from the porch, and as he stared back at her, he felt the pins and needles come back into his limbs. He could move again.

Just as soon as he'd been able to get life into his limbs, to think straight, he'd exited the truck and bounded up the stairs, demanding Lydia tell him what happened. Her old face had been full of emotions – fury, fear, and sadness – but she'd refused to give him any information.

"It's for the best, Sidhe," she'd said sadly, hanging onto the door frame as though she'd collapse without its support. "Neither of you heeded the warnings. It's best you're apart, anyhow. Too much power concentrated in one place can be dangerous. And the two of you…you're just like Guthrie and I, you are. When you're together, the passion is undeniable. But then you look up and realize the world has collapsed around you."

He'd begged and begged, but she'd refused to tell him anything. Had just stared at him with sad eyes. All her mysterious power from before had seemingly dried up and shriveled away; now she looked impossibly old and very tired. Resigned, Phillip had let her retreat inside to her dusty haven and had gone back to the truck, full of terror for me.

To his surprise, the truck had started back up without a

hitch. So he'd backed out of the rocky driveway, and from there he just drove. Drove and drove around Boston, winding through little neighborhoods, meandering down city streets, staring into storefronts, even into his old neighborhood, where he saw Jason Langley smoking a cigarette in his old front yard. For hours he drove, but he found no sign of me. No sign at all.

"So how did you find me in the end, then?" I had asked.

"I stopped looking," he'd said simply.

"How…?"

"I parked my truck on the side of a random street and closed my eyes and just sat there," he said, stroking the side of my face with a calloused finger. "…and eventually, I just felt you. I guess you woke up, and I felt it. I followed the feeling. And there you were." I'd never forget his face, the way his eyes had lit up with tenderness, with…love.

"Everything just keeps..." I trailed off, my head muddy, "...getting weirder." That's when I had passed out. The weirdness of the world I was now living in was just too damn weird to stay conscious any longer.

Now, Phillip's face was less elated, and more furious. "Stop being so stubborn, Stormy," he thundered. "You might have a concussion."

"I just need rest."

"The best place to rest is in a hospital. With doctors nearby."

"But I just need a little time," I argued. "To get my story together. To get *our* story together," I argued. "If you take me there, they *will* call the police, don't you get that?"

"I don't care," he said. "I don't give a fuck about the story at this point."

"Please, Phillip," I begged. "I can't risk-"

"Fine," he conceded, looking irritated. "One hour. We'll figure out our story, then we're going. Like it or not, even if I have to drag you." He didn't look pleased. "Now. What can I get you? You must be thirsty."

"I am." I cleared my throat as I lay back on the pillows. "I'd love some water, and a coffee, too. Maybe it would pep me up. They have some in the lobby, don't they?"

"Yeah, but it tastes like shit."

"It'll be fine." I really just wanted the caffeine. "And a pack of crackers or something if they have it. Maybe the nausea will go away if I eat something."

He frowned. "I'm reluctant to leave you."

"I'll be okay," I said. "The door is locked and I'm not going to let anybody in."

He nodded. "I'll be back in two minutes. Don't open the door for anybody. I have my key. And don't go to sleep again."

"I won't."

As he left, I watched his retreating back, the sag of his shoulders. He was unhappy with me. I knew I was being infuriating, but I didn't see any way around it. A trip to the hospital would mean cops, and cops ask questions. They might assume from my head wound that Phillip had hurt me. Even if they didn't, one of them might recognize him.

One thing I knew for sure – just as soon as Phillip was satisfied that I was alright, we'd be heading back to Jekyll. I'd drag him if I had to. Lee and Lydia were right. I was in danger here. I wasn't so sure I'd be as lucky next time.

I was determined not to doze off, to be a good little patient. I rummaged through the bag beside the bed and pulled out my reading glasses – Phillip had finally seen them on me, and had made several quips about how I looked like a sexy therapist who drank chardonnay on her lunch break and whose couch was covered in yappy dog fur - and a magazine that I'd bought at a gas station. It was the most recent Rolling Stone. Phillip had already looked through it, marveling and laughing at all the new rock bands he'd never heard of and the clothes they wore. He was definitely from another time. I flipped through it idly, not really reading, just looking at the pictures. They were a little blurry. That whack to the head had been pretty brutal. I hoped the coffee would help steady me.

I wished I had my phone, but it was in Lee's possession and I'd probably never see it again. I didn't like the idea of him looking through my contacts, my private messages. I was filled with the sudden urge to check in with everyone, even the people I usually tried to keep at arm's length. I wanted to text Sloan, my boss, even my parents. I thought back to the Thanksgiving invitation my dad had extended to me a few days prior and hung my head in shame. I'd never even responded. How long would I continue to punish them, to push them all away?

I heard Phillip swiping his key outside, and the door whooshed open a crack. "That was fast," I said, putting down the magazine with a bright smile. He was serious when he'd said two minutes.

My blood ran cold when I saw who was entering the hotel room. It wasn't Phillip. It was Shank.

Fourteen

"When we took your cell phone, I also took this," he said, holding up my room key. Oh, shit. "Wasn't nice of you to run from us, Spooner. I reckon it's time you come back with me."

"I didn't run. He let me go." I kept the tremor from my voice. "Does he know you're here?" I didn't have to say who. He knew I meant Lee.

"None of your fucking business," he barked, with an antsy look back to the door. "Now get up off your ass and come on. Best do it without a fight, unless you want things to get ugly. I've had enough of you and your zombie boyfriend fucking shit up."

"I'm not going anywhere." I couldn't stand up if I wanted to. I felt more nauseated than ever, and my head was killing me. Adrenaline was coursing through my body, and I would run if I had to, but just the thought of getting off the bed made me feel sick.

He was at my bedside in two swift steps. He grabbed me by my arm and wrenched me up and I yelped in pain. "Shut up," he whispered hotly in my ear. "Now march." He gave me a shove. I felt something cold and hard at my back; I hadn't seen a gun, but I couldn't rule it out. He was clearly trying to march me out before Phillip returned, which wasn't the worst idea. What Phillip would do to him would have given me a shudder if I didn't hate and fear Shank so much.

I stumbled, almost face planting on the floor, and went down on one knee, feeling the rug scrape my skin through my pants. I stumbled toward the door, tears starting in my eyes. I was so sick of this, so damn *sick* of it. When would they leave me in peace? I opened my mouth to tell Shank that we were planning to leave, to go back home to Jekyll like we'd been told, if he'd just let me go, but the cold sharpness against my back and the rough, ragged breath behind me told me that it'd do no good.

"You shit," I seethed through my pain, too angry to keep my mouth shut. "Mark my words, I will make you pay for this. And when I'm done, you'll be taking meals through a straw in a face that's even uglier than it already is."

"Shut up, bitch." He pushed me to the door none too gently and I stumbled again. I fiddled with the door handle, trying to wrench it open with shaking hands. My head felt fuzzy and I had tunnel vision. The gun pressed harder into my back and I began to whimper, finally managing to get the heavy old door open. Shank gave me another shove and I lurched forward, bracing myself for the inevitable fall when my knees would hit the concrete hallway.

Instead, I fell into a pair of strong arms, and almost wept with joy when I looked up to see Phillip's face. He caught me, instantly appraised the situation, and propped me up against the door frame.

"Stay here," he advised.

Shank had already started backing into the room, holding out the gun, aiming it at Phillip. He was cornered, but he wasn't going to surrender easily. I clung to the door frame, fighting the waves of nausea and the aching in my head.

"Phillip, be careful!"

He took no notice of my warning and advanced on Shank. "I'd say you were the stupidest fucking person alive for daring to come here," he said, his voice full of acid. "But you're actually doing me a favor. Going to the police is probably the right thing to do, but where's the satisfaction in that? I'm going to enjoy beating you to a fucking pulp."

"Stay the fuck away from me, you dead piece of shit." Shank was waving the gun around erratically. I was paralyzed with fear. "My orders come from Guthrie and it ain't a good idea to fuck with him-"

"I don't give a fuck, man." Phillip reached Shank in a few short steps, and before the words were fully out of his mouth, he reared back and punched him right in the face. Blood spurted from Shank's nose and he went down like a lead balloon.

It was the second time in a couple of days that I'd seen Phillip break somebody's nose. He did it with ease, like popping a piece of bubble wrap. My mouth filled with saliva, and my gorge rose at the vivid visual before me. I swallowed hard, and slow-blinked, surveying the blood all over Shank and the floor, and exhaled slowly.

The gun was on the floor and Shank was reaching for it, but he couldn't really see because his eyes were swelling up. Blood poured on the carpeted floor. "I'm going to kill you, you dead fucking bastard."

"Like to see you try." Phillip's voice was eerily calm as he reared back with one massive leg and kicked Shank hard in the chest. He kicked him again, leveling him out on the floor. Then he was on him, pummeling him with his fists. Shank was trying to put up a fight, but he was no match for someone of Philip's size and strength. I had no doubt that Phillip was going to kill him. Because of me, Phillip was going to have a death on his hands. I wanted to yell, to scream at Phillip to stop, but I couldn't find my voice. A small part of me wanted him to keep going, to rip the scourge away from us. One less specter looming over our lives. I felt faint. Before I knew what was happening, I was going down, my vision tunneling and blackness rising to meet me.

A pair of arms caught me just before my head hit the concrete. Phillip. God, how did he move so fast? Just moments before he'd been pinning Shank down, beating his face to a pulp. He cradled my head in his arms, which were streaked with blood. "We can't let you get another head injury, sweetheart," he said, his voice full of tenderness. He paused just long enough to place a kiss on my forehead, prop me up against the door, then he straightened up and turned, ready to finish off his work.

Neither of us were aware that Shank had stood. How, I didn't know, since Phillip had beaten him senseless. He was covered in so much blood he looked like something from a Rob Zombie movie. *House of a Thousand Pricks,* I thought with a ludicrous, swimmy-headed giggle. *Except in this one the corpse has a heart of gold.*

Shank had found the gun, aimed it at Phillip and fired. Phillip recoiled, his left hand raising up to clutch at his right shoulder, and then he staggered and went down on one knee, onto the floor, blood seeping from his arm. I screamed.

Shank lowered the gun, took a look at us through his swollen, blood crusted eyes, and made a beeline for the door.

I couldn't let him get away. He had fucked with us enough; they all had. Through my pain and dizziness, I managed to get myself up off the floor and I hobbled in front of the door, blocking it. He made no move to slow down, like he planned to barrel right through me. I rallied my strength and tackled him as hard as I could, using my body weight to propel him forward, both of us falling into a heap on the concrete floor. My head split into shards of pain that seemed to come from all directions. The gun flew out of Shank's hand. I rolled him over, pinning him, and managed to grab the gun before he could reach for it. He struggled against me, but most of the fight had left him.

"You stupid bitch," he spat, his hateful eyes fixed on my face. "I should have broken your arms when I had the chance."

"You should have," I agreed. "I've had enough of your limp-dick bullshit." I cradled his head in my hands, picked it up, and cracked it as hard as I could against the floor. His skull made a wet, thick sound as it hit the concrete beneath the thin layer of carpet. He screamed out in pain, but I wouldn't let go. *Thud.* I did it again, and he was still.

"Jesus," said Phillip in a weak voice from the corner of the room. I looked up in surprise. He was lying against the wall, clutching his arm, his face pale. "Remind me never to piss you off. You just cracked his head like a fucking egg."

I managed to stumble over to the bed and eased down on it, my head an odd mixture of horror, nausea, elation, and pounding-hot migraine. I turned to Phillip, dazed. "I told you I'd protect you," I said stupidly, then passed out cold.

THE NURSE ATTENDING me had an unsmiling mouth and squeaky white shoes. She was professional, but I could tell she wanted to roll her eyes when I asked for the fifth time to see Phillip.

"He's in with the doctor right now," she said to me, which was more information than she'd given before. "You can't see him right now. Neither of you have been cleared for visitors."

She tucked the sheets in around my legs. "Now please, try to get some rest."

As it turned out, I did have a concussion, and I was also dangerously dehydrated as a result of whatever drug I'd been given. We were still waiting for the results to come back to find out exactly what it was.

After I'd dealt the blow to Shank and then passed out on the bed, Phillip had managed to crawl over to the phone and call 911. I had come to shortly afterward and seen him struggling at the mirror with a useless, bloody arm, trying to put his hair up in what appeared to be a man-bun. I tried to sit up, recoiling with horror when I saw Shank still lying on the floor. "Is he...dead?" I asked slowly, the memory of cracking his head on the floor rushing back. "Oh no, Phillip, did I kill him?"

"No," he told me hastily, turning around with a grimace. "He's breathing. You just cleaned his clock, that's all. Just lie down, Stormy. I called 911. They're on the way."

"Come sit with me."

He did. His arm was bloody and hanging at a strange angle. I could tell he was in pain but trying to pretend he wasn't. He'd done a half-assed job of tying a towel around it to stop the bleeding. "Let me," I said, ignoring the woozy feeling in my head.

"It's okay, Stormy," he said, shaking me off. "Just rest."

"Shut up, you stubborn ass." I took off the towel, folded it into a strip, and wrapped it around Phillip's arm, trying not to look too closely at the wound, which was still gushing blood. "We need to stop the bleeding." I pulled it taut, which wasn't easy among the slick blood and the fact that his arms were so huge, and the motel towels so tiny. I pulled it tighter, pretending not to see him wince. "There," I said finally, looking over my work, hoping the EMTs would get here quickly. It was still bleeding; the towel was already turning pink from the blood seeping through.

"I'll be okay," he reassured me, his good arm reaching out toward me. "It's you I'm worried about. Your head, the drugs..."

"I'll be okay, too." I looked in his wild green eyes and tried for a queasy smile. "I'm a fucking witch, remember?"

He tried to cradle me in his good arm, but his clothes were damp with blood and I was nauseated when I tried to close my eyes, so we both sat back up, laughing nervously, both in pain and freaked out and trying to look strong for the other. I wondered if my own eyes looked half as wild as Phillip's bright green ones did.

My eyes went to his hair and I laughed harder. It was definitely a man bun. "Your hair," I croaked. "What's going on there?"

"I thought it'd be a better disguise, maybe. I saw it in that magazine you had. I guess this is how we're wearing it now?" He licked his lips. "Do they call this a half-Leia?"

"That was a really shitty attempt at a joke, Deville," I said. "God, you're white as a ghost. Do you think you could bear to change your shirt before they get here? I could help you. That towel really isn't doing anything." He was still losing so much blood.

"No," he said, wincing in pain. "They'll just rip it off me anyway."

"At least let me fix your hair. I can't stand it, Phillip. You look like Jared Leto on a meth-bender."

"I don't know who that is," he said, but he pulled the band from his hair and let it fall free. It rained down on his shoulders in a long, sweaty cascade.

"I just hope your doctors aren't Bloomer Demon fans," I said, feeling another woozy spell coming on. I slumped back down on the bed and waited for the ambulance.

SOMEWHERE, in another part of the hospital, Shank was being treated for his injuries. He'd woken up while the paramedics were loading him onto the stretcher, and we had heard him screaming and hollering all the way to the ambulance. Knowing he was alive was a relief, because I didn't fancy being a murderer, or turning a guy into a vegetable – but I wondered what type of revenge he might try to unleash on me when he recovered. It was no use asking the nurse how he was doing; she wouldn't tell me.

"Will you let me know," I asked her as she retreated from the room, "when Frank is able to see people?"

I was glad Phillip had had the foresight to come up with a fake name before the paramedics had shown up. He'd suggested Frank Stein, but I'd pointed out how glaringly, ridiculously obvious that was. For a goth rockstar, he sure had the dad jokes. Frank Sloan was the name he'd given them in the end. Sloan would cackle with delight when she heard that later, though for some reason, I wasn't sure I quite liked it.

The police had already come and gone twice, peppering me with questions about Shank and Phillip, needing my official story. I'd recounted it the best I could, careful to give them the same story I'd quickly rehearsed with Phillip. It was a vague, general story full of holes and discrepancies, if the police bothered to take the time to look into it, but to my relief, neither of the deputies I'd spoken with seemed particularly interested. They were just glad to sign off on the report for what I'd told them it was: a simple robbery. I'd let my eyes fill with the appropriate amount of tears while telling them all about how Shank had demanded money, and when I'd told him I didn't have any, he had told me to give him all my jewelry and valuables. Phillip had burst in on the scene at just the right time, and he and I had defended ourselves against Shank the best we could.

They'd bought it, I knew they had. So far nobody had thought to ask why I had drugs in my system; I hoped they would continue to overlook that detail, just assume I was a user. They were tired, and overworked, and why would they doubt us? I knew Phillip had recounted the very same story. The cops had told me as much.

"Don't worry, little lady," the older of the two, a grizzled, red-faced guy with silvery hair and a big broom mustache, had said kindly, patting my wrist. It was all I could do not to snort; did grown-ass men still actually call women things like "little lady"? "Your boyfriend is going to be just fine. The gunshot wound wasn't deep, and he didn't hit an artery."

I wanted to see Phillip for myself, though. I needed to see with my own eyes that he was alright. I needed to touch him, to smell him. To know that he was still here with me. Lydia had said he couldn't die, at least not easily, but why should I believe her?

Who was she, anyway?

I'd had time, sitting in my uncomfortable, narrow hospital bed, to think about all the people I'd encountered since the spell, and what part they played in all of this. Lydia was married to Guthrie, and even though she claimed she hadn't seen him in a decade, she was tied into this somehow. It was no coincidence that Phillip and I had been magically bound and then me abducted right out of her front yard. I thought back to her cryptic answers to our questions, her weird, fragile demeanor and how seemingly at odds she'd been with herself – defiant and belligerent one moment, empathetic and concerned the next – and realized that she reminded me of someone. Someone else who seemed at turns empathetic and apathetic, willing to harm one moment and help the next. Lee Courtenay.

The nurse left, dimming the lights as she went, and I was alone in the room with my thoughts. It was only a matter of hours before I'd be allowed to check out, she'd said. It was just a minor concussion. Once the results from the blood test were back, I would be free to go. I didn't want to go back to the motel without Phillip – all those police and their questions to answer – and I was scared. What if Lee was there, waiting for me? Surely, he'd heard what happened to his right-hand man by now.

But as it turned out, he didn't go to the motel. He came to the hospital.

I was drifting off with Judge Judy on mute playing on the TV in the corner, when he let himself into the room. He came in so quietly I almost didn't notice him, just thought he was one of the nurses or doctors, until he cleared his throat and I came to.

My blood rose in alarm, but then I realized I wasn't scared anymore. Not after what had happened. I levelled my gaze on him, as much as I could, since my head was still making me woozy.

"You've got a lot of nerve, showing your face here," I said finally.

"I wanted to make sure you were okay," he said. He did look slightly guilty.

"Oh yes, I'm sure. I'm sure you also stopped in to check on Phillip, too."

"I didn't," he said. "It's you I worry about, not him."

"He's a person, you know," I spat. "A human being."

"I think I know all too well who is human and alive and who isn't, Stormy," he said, his voice edging close to bitterness. I had no idea what he meant by such a weird statement, or why his face twisted the way it did, and I didn't care. "And who is in need of my help."

"How absolutely philanthropic of you. Do you say that to all your kidnapping victims?"

"I told you before," he said. "You're in danger. I did what I did to try and save you, as fucked up as it sounds."

"Tell that to Phillip's shot-up arm."

He looked at me in surprise. "He's...wounded?"

"That tends to happen when you get shot," I said nastily. "And speaking of, did you happen to check in on your henchman?"

"He's not my henchman," he said. "But yeah. The two of you fucked him up pretty good, but I guess he probably deserved it." He sighed and ran a hand through his light hair. "I'm sorry about all this, Stormy. It's been handled badly."

"All this," I repeated, the words tasting sour on my tongue. "I don't even know what 'all this' is. I thought for a while that Phillip did, and he was just protecting me, but now I don't think even he knows. So why don't you enlighten me, Lee? Tell me why you keep following us around, and why you care so much about my well-being but don't give a fuck if Phillip lives or dies? Why won't you just leave us alone?"

"I can't," he said. "I wish I could, but I can't."

"Are you going to tell me why?"

"I'm not supposed to," he said.

"Let me guess," I said, holding a hand to my pounding head. "Mommy Dearest told you not to."

He looked at me in surprise. "What are you-"

"I'm not stupid. I figured it out," I said. "I can see the resemblance. You have the same whiff of self-loathing."

He winced.

"My head hurts," I said, closing my eyes, wanting him far away from me. "Can you leave?"

"I'll go. I just hope that…that one day I can explain. And

that you'll remember that I tried my best to keep you out of this."

"I'd prefer not to remember you at all," I said. "Now fuck you very much, bye."

"I'm sorry, Stormy," he said in a low voice, his expression stricken. He came toward the bed and held out something to me - my cell phone. Then he turned on his heel and walked out the door, without a look back, shutting it behind him with a gentle but firm *click*.

I lay there for a long time, staring at Judge Judy and drinking the orange-tinted dregs of ice from the bottom of my long-gone cup of juice, moping. There was something about Lee that did not make sense. He didn't seem to have a vengeful, manipulative bone in his body. Everything he'd done seemed to be thrust upon him, and his bitterness at having to carry it all out was pretty clear. And he had feelings for me, too – what kind of feelings I didn't know. It could be anything from a crush to pity, but whatever it was, it wasn't hate. He didn't want to hurt me. I could feel it – his *intention* – coming off him in waves, and he did nothing to try and hide it from me. He didn't want to involve me at all, but he seemed to have to. I wondered why.

Was it his mother, Lydia? I wondered if she'd orchestrated my kidnapping that day, entertaining Philip and me in her living room as a ruse, a distraction to keep us occupied until Lee and Shank could get there? But that didn't seem right, either. Oh, she was shifty and creepy and definitely a few cards short of a full deck, but I didn't detect outright malice in her. And her warning to Phillip, when she'd poked her feathery head out of her front door, had felt genuine. I'd felt her, then, the same way I felt Lee – her intentions had been good. What was it about these intentions – it was as though we could feel them, bouncing around in the air, threads that just needed to be picked up and followed.

Lydia had been fascinated by Phillip. I'd felt her sparked interest, her longing to examine him, pepper him with questions, take him under her wing. She felt protective toward him too. Whoever she was, she didn't want to cause either of us harm. And as angry as I was at him, I knew now that neither did Lee.

But I knew one thing: as soon as we were released from this festering shithole of a hospital, Phillip and I were high-tailing it back to Jekyll, even if I had to hog-tie him and throw him in the back of my truck in a burlap bag. We were *leaving*.

Judge Joe Brown was on now and I drifted off to sleep, still tasting oranges on my tongue, grateful that, for once, there was nobody lurking in the doorway to disturb me.

I AWOKE SOME TIME LATER, the sky pitch dark outside the heavy-curtained window, with the sense that somebody was in my room.

I reached for the "Call" button on the side of my bed, having had my fill of unwelcome visitors; I didn't care who the hell it was this time, I would go down fighting. But as the figure emerged from the darkness, my heart leapt. It was Phillip.

His face was ghostly pale in the darkness, his black hair a shroud around his head. His arm was bandaged up in a sling, stark white against the black of his shirt. He put a finger to his lips. "Are you alright?" he asked.

I nodded.

"I've got to go, Stormy," he said, taking my hand. His skin was a little cold. "If you don't feel up to leaving yet, I'll come back for you. But I have to get out of here, now."

"What's wrong?"

"I'll explain later," he said. "No time."

"I'll go with you." I sat up. The pain in my head was minimal, for which I was thankful. The scratchy hospital gown caught on the bedside table as I sat up, and I cursed. I rubbed a hand over my head, which was throbbing less than it had been. "Would you hand me my clothes? They're over there."

"Are you sure you're okay to get up?" he asked.

"Phillip, you got shot and you're asking me if *I'm* okay?" I smiled and gingerly started to put on my shirt.

"I didn't get a nasty bump on the head."

"Something tells me that if you did, you'd still be fine," I teased. He offered me an arm and I stood, pulling on my jeans. He leaned down, one-armed, to help me with my socks and shoes, and my heart filled with tenderness.

He smiled faintly and stood back up, doing a quick sweep of the room. I handed him my cell phone, which he pocketed, and we made our way toward the door. I didn't feel sluggish anymore, and my head and my legs were no longer shaking. All that was left was the faintest of headaches. I touched a finger to the bump gingerly, wincing when I felt the scabbed flesh.

He craned his head to the door and listened. He nodded to me silently and I nodded back, opening the door as quietly as I could. I peered out into the hallway, formulating a plan to tell the nurses I was just hungry if they apprehended me. It wasn't a lie; the hospital food they'd offered me – a hockey puck that was apparently Salisbury steak and a glop of icy cold rehydrated mashed potatoes – had sat untouched all night on my plastic tray. Luckily there was nobody in the hall. Phillip and I eased out together, walking carefully to the stairwell just off to the right of my room. It was too risky to take the elevator out in the main lobby, I understood that without him having to tell me. Phillip went in first, then beckoned to me with his long, thin fingers. As soon as we were heading down the stairs, he whisked off his arm sling and stuffed it in his pocket.

"Phillip, what are you doing? You probably need that-"

"My arm's fine," he said in a loud whisper, not slowing. "I just left it on in case they saw me."

"What do you mean, your arm's fine?" He'd gotten shot, for god's sake. I knew he was tough, but Jesus Christ.

"They got the bullet out early this morning," he said. "It was a clean shot, no fragments or anything. Didn't hit an artery. I'm good."

I pulled on his shirt, making him stop. "Let me see." I carefully pulled up his sleeve, bracing myself for the sight of a gunshot wound in his perfect, muscled arm. When I didn't see a bandage, I looked at him in surprise.

"I took it off," he said. "I'm fine."

"But you need to let it heal-"

"It's healed."

"But it must hurt-"

"No." He pulled the sleeve all the way up and I stared in surprise. The skin was smooth and white and soft. There was no bandaging, no bullet hole, no scar - no sign that he'd ever been hurt at all.

"Jesus," I said. "I'm beginning to get really sick of all these super-powers of yours."

He made a face and beckoned me to continue. We started down the stairs, me staring at the back of his head in awe. I almost tripped over my own feet and grabbed onto the banister.

"I guess I see now why you had to leave so fast," I said. "If they'd seen how soon you healed...well, there would be some questions."

"And I doubt they'd believe, 'my girlfriend raised me from the dead and now I have super human strength, psychic abilities and I heal from gunshot wounds.'"

He had called me his girlfriend. My cheesy grin didn't

seem appropriate, considering all that had happened and how much danger we were in, but it was hard to stop. He said nothing, just kept trudging down the steps in front of me, but I felt a vibe come off him, and it felt like laughter. I stayed quiet, though it didn't matter. Psychic abilities. He was probably reading my every thought right now, the bastard.

"I'm trying not to," he said with a chuckle. "But you think so *loud.*"

Navigating the lobby was stressful. We both did our best to blend in and look like visitors rather than patients, but it was difficult, me shuffling along, sleepy and with a headache, and him in his pale, 6'5" glory. We probably looked like two junkies on a drug bender, but thankfully, nobody milling around the elevators or gift shop gave us a second glance. We had to dodge one cop, but he was on his cell phone and didn't notice us as we dashed behind the map board.

"How are we going to get back to the motel?" I asked him when we were safely outside.

"We aren't. Too many questions to answer, and all that damage? No. Let Shank be on the hook for that, I'm not going back there."

"But what about our stuff? Our clothes, your phone, the money..."

"We can buy new clothes. Same with the phone." He smiled. "And the money is locked up safe and sound in your truck."

"Which is in the motel parking lot," I pointed out glumly. "I'm sure they have cameras all over the place."

"Good thing I snuck out of here two hours ago and went ahead and got it before I came to get you," Phillip said with a dangerous grin. "Your truck is parked right over there in the parking deck." He extracted my keys from his pocket and dangled them in my face, looking very pleased with himself.

Fifteen

Phillip moved around the kitchen like he still owned it, pulling open cabinets, digging an old kettle out from below the island, boiling water for tea. I sat at the counter, watching him and trying to digest all that had happened. My head was reasonably clear now, but I was confused and more than a little down in the dumps. The moment we were safely in the confines of my truck, I'd wanted to immediately head back to Jekyll; do not pass go, do not collect $200. But Phillip had insisted we should get at least one night of rest before making such a long trip. I supposed I saw the logic of that, but honestly, I was just ready to be free of Boston all together. I wouldn't feel safe or like myself again until I was back home. It all felt so heavy. Phillip poured me a cup of tea, dumped in a few spoons of sugar, and passed it to me, his face full of loving concern.

"Drink that," he said. "It'll make you feel better. My grandmother always used to say that nothing is more comforting than a cup of tea."

I smiled wryly. "It's so weird to hear something so poignant and vanilla coming from a junkie rock star who used to snort coke off of girls' butt cheeks."

His color rose and he managed to look offended. "That was one time," he said, turning to rinse off the sugar spoon. "And I had a cup of tea afterward, as I recall."

I snorted. The tea was hot, strong and sweet, and I had to grudgingly admit that I did feel better.

"I'm making you a meal," he said, rummaging through the pantry. "And I don't want to hear any arguments out of you. You need to eat; you can't keep living off Swedish Fish and crackers. You need your strength. What can I make you that's vegan?"

"I don't know," I said unhelpfully. I didn't feel hungry at all.

"Spaghetti?"

"Ok," I said dutifully. "Just leave off the parmesan cheese."

He nodded and set to work. I noticed as I drank down the hot tea that he was pulling out cans of crushed tomatoes and spices from the top of the pantry. He pulled a pot down from the island and a knife from the cupboard. He was going to make the sauce from scratch.

"Don't go to any trouble-"

"Shut up. I want to," he said, then winked at me, heading toward the kitchen door. "We used to keep fresh basil out back when I lived here." He disappeared for a moment, then came back inside holding a bright green bunch in his large hands.

"Is there anything you can't do?" I asked, watching him with pleasure.

"Yeah," he said. "I can't work a cell phone."

I giggled. "That's true. So," I said, looking around the room, which was total 80s kitsch, complete with blue-ribboned geese and gingham curtains to match, "this is where you grew up."

"Yeah. This is my house," he said, leaning up against the counter. "Or was. Now it's Jason's."

"What did you tell him?" I asked. I hadn't met Jason yet, but I knew he was here somewhere. Phillip had spoken to him quickly and furtively before ushering me into the house. So far it appeared that we'd been lucky and had lost the cops. We had a clear view of the driveway from the kitchen window, and Phillip had been periodically checking around back. What Jason felt about all of this, I didn't know and didn't want to ask, though secretly I was dying to meet him.

"Just that we were in a little trouble and I'd explain more later. He didn't really ask," Phillip answered, running a hand through his long, dark hair. "He's not as bad today as he was when I saw him before. I think the shock of seeing me has him going straight. But still – he's not at all like you remember from our glory days."

"And here I was thinking you'd talk shit about me behind my back."

Phillip and I both turned to the doorway. The man standing, leaning against the door frame, had skin that was pale and a little sickly, but the smile on his face was wide and real. He had shaggy mid-length brown hair that was slightly curly, cool, light-blue eyes that were pretty and almond shaped, if somewhat bloodshot, and a five o'clock shadow covering boyish, soft cheeks. Jason had always had a baby face. Doing the math in my head, I knew he had to be in his fifties, but he didn't look a day over thirty-five. Short and wiry in stature, especially compared to Phillip, he still had a presence about him, an aura. I supposed it came from years of being on stage and in front of cameras. There was a warmth to him, something genuine. He exuded a purity, a calm, that was the perfect foil to Phillip's dark, cynical, thunderous dynamic. I supposed Phillip's memories of the guy must be quite different, but I thought he looked remarkably well, considering. His skin had a pallid sort of look to it, but I thought Phillip had exaggerated when he'd said this guy was on death's door. I knew from all the photos I'd seen over the years that he had looked much worse before, especially in the few years after Phillip and Kim's deaths. He looked much more robust than the last paparazzi photo I'd seen of him. Though we were inside, he was wearing a brown corduroy coat with wool trim around the collar – I hadn't seen a coat like that since the mid-90s and I could easily imagine he'd had it at least that long.

He extended a hand. When I took it, it was warm. "Hi, Stormy," he said, his voice deeper and clearer than I'd expected. "Don't believe a word that tall piece of shit says."

Phillip was both right and wrong. It was true that Jason was a shell of his old self, but I could still see the enigmatic guitar player shining through his eyes. I'd never known him in person, after all, so it was easy to imagine him as he once was, young and vibrant, standing beside Phillip on stage, backing Phillip's baritone with his warbling, clear-throated alto. His laugh was musical, his pursed lips full of bemusement, and I liked him immediately.

"Hi, Jason," I said, feeling the flush creep into my cheeks. Being around Phillip for days hadn't done much to quell my status as a fangirl. I shook his hand eagerly. "I'm so happy to meet you. And please forgive me for saying this but – I'm a huge fan of yours. I have been for twenty years."

"Thank you," he said, appearing not even a bit embarrassed. Phillip's eyes had shifted to the side – he still hated the fawning – but Jason clearly relished it.

"I know it's weird to say-" I smiled, a big, cheesy grin that I couldn't contain. "-but it's just so – it's like a life's dream realized, you know? Not just to meet Phillip, but now to meet you too...well, I'm just so happy to see you both here, together. My favorite band. Wow." I burst into giggles.

Phillip's brows furrowed as he looked at me curiously, but

he wasn't angry. *What's come over you,* his eyes seemed to say. All I could do was shrug and try to stop the giggles, which were still erupting from my mouth. It was weird, but somehow seeing Jason Langley, seeing him as *real,* standing there in front of me – made Phillip seem more real, too. I thought I might burst from the hilarious, wonderful, weirdness of it all. For the first time in days, I felt something other than terror.

"I appreciate it," Jason said easily, still laughing, though he did look a bit weak. A sheen of sweat had broken out on his forehead and he took a breath. "I haven't met a fan in such a long time. I don't get out much, and they stopped coming to look for me, so it's nice to meet one again. Especially one Phillip is so fond of." He gave his friend a sly smile.

"Don't get any ideas, Jase," Phillip said in a mock warning, stirring the sauce he'd thrown together. It was already smelling heavenly in the kitchen. "Those days of two guys, one groupie are over."

I opened my mouth to protest hotly, but he burst out laughing. "Oh, pull your panties out of your ass, Stormy," he said with a laugh. "I'm just kidding. We never did that."

"Well, not more than once, anyway," Jason said, also laughing, but he headed toward the living room and slumped down in a chair in the corner. I wondered if he was okay. "Join me in here, Stormy?"

Seeming to read my mind as always, Phillip murmured near my ear, "He's alive. There's still hope. Right?"

I nodded, meeting his deep green eyes, and made myself smile for his benefit. He returned it gratefully. I rose to join Jason. "Your cup of tea is sitting on the table, ice-cold," Phillip said to me with a fake scold and made his way toward the kettle. "I'll make us all another cup and I'll join you guys in a minute."

"Just what he needs," Jason said from his chair, and I walked over to sit beside him. "Him and his fucking tea."

"Yeah, this side of him came as a surprise," I agreed. "Especially after years of watching YouTube videos of him upending whole bottles of wine onstage."

"Oh, he loved his wine and liquor, imagine he still does," Jason answered. "But any time of day you could catch him with that stupid mustard-yellow ceramic mug of his, filled with black tea, brewed strong enough to pour in your gas tank." He leaned closer to me, smiling. "I have a demo that's never seen the light of day in the basement. The song's called 'Earl Grey.' Wanna hear it later?"

"Jesus fuck, yes."

"Later, then. Don't tell Phil," he said, lowering his voice. "I told him I threw it away. At the end he yodels."

"*No.*"

"Yes ma'am."

I arched my neck toward the kitchen, where an apron-clad Phillip was pouring steaming hot water into mugs and tried to suppress a giggle. "I like it," I admitted, letting the laugh escape. "The little quirks. Like the tea. The apron. It makes him seem so...normal and human. So ordinary."

"I know," he said, facing me, "all about the spell. I told Phillip I knew, the first day I saw him here, digging up the money. He tried to pretend, to make up some dumbass story. Then he tried to tell me I was just high, hallucinating him or some shit. Fucking asshole." He shook his head. "But I know. And I wish you guys had come here first and talked to me. I could have saved you a lot of trouble."

"What do you mean?"

"I know Guthrie. I know his wife, too. Let's just say that they've sniffed around here more than once. This obsession with Phillip didn't start with you, Stormy. They're bad news, man."

"Don't suppose you know how to get us out of it?"

He shook his head sadly. "I'm still wrapping my head

around the fact that somebody did that fucking spell and it worked. I mean, all these years I've expected to see him walking through the door – I never had any doubt that he would, but-" He rubbed his hands over the stubble on his jaw. "Now that he's here, I can't seem to believe it. I remember when he put it in the liner notes. I thought it was fucking stupid. I told him so. He was shitfaced, we all were. 'Gotta put something there,' he said. 'It's either this or that photo of me with my ass cheek hanging out.' As you can imagine, we agreed to the spell."

"And the ass cheek picture still made it out to the public." I laughed.

"Oh, of course it did. Who do you think leaked it? He always pretended that photoshoot embarrassed him, and he wouldn't even talk about it interviews. He'd get all bent out of shape, claim the photographer was a hot chick who got him stoned and tricked him. But he's full of shit. He made sure every one of those pictures got out. He always was vain. Meanwhile the rest of us in the band are looking like gargoyles. Me with that crusty ass eyebrow ring and my hair dyed neon red..."

"Oh, I remember that." I was still laughing. "That eyebrow ring was as big as your actual eye!"

"I never took care of it, either. I was too blitzed." He pointed at his eyebrow, and I could see a little scar streaked in one brow where there was an absence of hair. "You don't want to know what it looked like when they took it out."

"Please don't make my girlfriend puke, you fuck." Phillip entered the room, holding a tray with three steaming cups on it. The tray was gold, olive green and orange and had little mushrooms all over it – 70s style at its finest. He handed Jason and I both a mug of tea and took one for himself – it was mustard yellow, with a chip in the rim. Earl Grey. I looked at Jason and smiled.

"What?" Phillip asked, settling in a chair beside me, looking from Jason to me. "What is it?"

"I like your sweet little mug," I said, leaning over to kiss his cheek, enjoying the double entendre. "Unless you snuck in a generous pour of bourbon, I'd have to say that your rock star card is officially revoked."

"Fucking take it," he said with a grin. "I was a shitty fucking rock star."

"Fuck you, man," Jason said, wiping at his brow. "You had it down to a science."

Phillip raised an eyebrow but didn't argue. He sipped his steaming tea.

Jason went on, "Look at you, you dick, still sitting there in those tight black pants and combat boots. Not even death could take it off you. You always lived the shit. You looked the part because you were the part. Didn't even have to try. And all that tortured, 'I don't want to be famous' stuff? That's part of it, too. Every big-time rock star says that shit, and most of them probably really feel that way, except for when they don't. You didn't fool us back then, Phil, and you ain't foolin' me now."

"Says the guy with all our platinum records hanging all over the living room and his guitar in the corner with brand-new strings, tuned and ready to go," Phillip countered. "And the stack of demos in the basement he said he destroyed back in '92."

"Yeah, so?" Jason mopped at his brow again. He really didn't look well, but his eyes were sparkling and happy. He seemed to be enjoying their banter. "I never claimed I didn't want it. You were the one always pretending you didn't."

"Well, if you hope to ever reclaim some of that glory, you're going to have to get clean, dude. You aren't gonna accomplish shit, strung out like you are," Phillip thundered, his bemusement suddenly turning to anger. I cringed.

"Phillip!" I protested, horrified, but he didn't look at me.

Jason had no answer, the smile disappearing from his face.

Phillip went on, seemingly oblivious to the sudden cold, dry air in the room. "Seems like losing two of your bandmates would have woken you up, but instead it just pushed you further down the rabbit hole." He shook his head. "Didn't you learn anything from our fuckups? Anything at all?"

"What the fuck, dude. We were just having a pleasant conversation and you come at me out of nowhere like-"

"It isn't out of nowhere," Phillip said, his voice softening somewhat. He glanced at me, unsure; he knew he'd gone too far. "It's just...I don't like seeing you like this. You're so... changed."

"Yeah, well, twenty-plus years have passed, and I got old. Imagine that. You know what? Just leave me alone, Phillip," Jason said bitterly. All the spry happiness from before drained away from him as he looked at Phillip, his expression both sad and angry. His tea sat on the coffee table, untouched. "You weren't here. You were *dead*. You don't have a clue what it's been like without you here, what we've had to fend off." He fixed an eye on me and said with venom, "And don't for a minute let him convince you it was a fucking accident. King Doom standing here trying to act like he's a cautionary tale when we all know he checked out willingly-"

"Jase-" Phillip's voice held a note of warning, and I looked at him with wide eyes.

"Death as art. C'mon. You left us. Fuck that, man. Fuck *that.*"

"Come on, Stormy." Phillip was on his feet in seconds, pulling me with him. "Let's leave him to it."

I was still holding my hot cup of tea and its contents sloshed on the hardwood floors. "Phillip-" I protested, as he dragged me toward the kitchen where the sauce was in danger of boiling over on the stove. I wanted to tell him that he was overstepping, that he was being unfair, but the thunderous look on his face stopped me. This wasn't about me, it wasn't my fight. Better to leave them to it.

I followed him from the kitchen into a bedroom, which seemed small under his impressive height. The top of his head was near the ceiling; he ducked as he passed under the ceiling fan. The light in the room was dim and the furniture was coated with a sheen of dust.

I sat on the double bed, which was lumpy and creaked under my weight. It was covered with a scratchy, olive green duvet that I ran through my fingers absently as I watched him, surprised at how angry I was at him for attacking Jason. He paced through the room, reaching the end of it and back in two full strides, his fingers running through his hair. I could feel the stress coming off him in waves. I could almost see it, a deep reddish-brown aura all around his head.

"There's bound to be some things to work out between the two of you," I said slowly, trying to ease into the discussion.

His laugh was hollow as he stared out the window. "What he said back there was true, you know." His voice was hoarse.

"I know," I said. "I think I've always known."

"How you must hate me."

"Of course not," I said. "But you *were* a total choad back there."

The corner of his mouth turned up a little. "All that trouble to bring me back, only to find out that I threw my life away in the first place."

"It doesn't matter."

"It does."

"Not to me," I said. "I don't judge you. Believe me, I don't. But Phillip – you should extend the same courtesy to Jason. He has problems, but who doesn't? You don't have to be so judge-"

"You don't know him." He sniffed.

"Neither do you," I countered. "It's been over twenty years. Maybe if you'd let the guy get a sentence out, you'd-"

"You have no idea what it's like to see someone you love-"

"Don't I?" I thundered. "Or did you forget that my ex-husband – the one whose nose you broke – is also a junkie? That our marriage ended because of it?"

He turned to face me. "I guess I did. Just for a minute." He sighed. "I'm sorry. But the thing with Jason is diff-"

"God, you won't let *me* talk, either!" I was almost yelling. "Are you always like this, just bulldozing over everyone's words, and feelings?"

"Yeah," he admitted, coming as close to sheepish as I imagine he ever got. His sharply defined cheeks were turning crimson. "So I've been told. Sorry."

"What I was trying to say-" I continued, fixing him with pointed look, "-was that I know what it's like to love someone with these issues. Tess was a drug addict, as you know. And you know what? So were both my parents," I thundered, the words tumbling out of my mouth before I could stop them. "Junkies and drunks, both. My childhood was littered with people like Jason, in and out of our house and our lives. That's why I don't talk to my parents anymore. Because it's too fucking painful."

He looked at me in surprise. "You never told me that."

"You never asked."

He opened his mouth to retort, then sighed. "You're right. I'm sorry."

I softened. "It's not like we've had a lot of time. But Phillip…what's *really* bothering you?" I asked him. He didn't answer, only paced back and forth like a rat too big for its cage, covering the entire room in two strides, then turning around and doing it all over again. "Phillip," I said. "Come sit down."

He paced the room once more, then reluctantly sat down on

the bed beside me. It gave a loud creak and he smiled, though it didn't reach his eyes. "Can you believe I slept on this every night? I don't know how I could walk the next day."

"You were a kid," I said. "Kids' bodies are much more forgiving." Truth was, his body was more than forgiving now, now that he was whatever he was, but I decided not to bring that up.

"It seems like a million years ago," he said, looking over at the bookshelf in the corner, which was filled about 50/50 with comic books and vinyl. "God. To think I passed so much time here, just reading comics and listening to music. Practicing my bass, thinking about girls."

"I can't believe I'm in Phillip Deville's boyhood bedroom," I said. "I've got stars in my eyes."

"Oh, stop," he said, looking at me with a shy smile. "Surely the novelty has worn off now."

"Not really," I answered honestly.

"Even after I've gotten you in so much trouble?" he asked.

I leaned over and touched a finger to the tip of his nose. "All the trouble just makes you that much more handsome."

He groaned.

"I can tell it's hard for you, being here," I said softly. "I'm sure Jason understands that, too."

He swallowed. "You don't know the half of it. It'd be hard anyway, just because, you know, the last time I was here, so were my parents and my siblings..." He trailed off. "And they're all gone, and so is Barb, and so is Kim. So many ghosts here, so many memories. I never thought I'd see this place again, and all that's hard enough, but then I find Jason here, and he's not doing good. But at the same time, it's so nice to see him, to have him around."

I followed the direction of his gaze to a framed picture on the dresser. I recognized it from all the way across the room – a young man, with curly white-blonde hair and startling bright blue eyes. He was wearing a grungy, green plaid shirt open at the chest, revealing the key hanging from a black cord he'd always worn. He had his arm around a young Phillip, who was clad in his usual black t-shirt, but with shorter, spiked up hair. Both had on eyeliner. Both were laughing and holding cups of beer. Kim Reznik, who had no spells to bring him back, who was lost forever.

"You should talk to Jason," I suggested. "Without judgement. You owe him that much."

His face was solemn and pensive. It hurt my heart to see him looking so melancholy. "You're right," he said finally. "I guess I'm just afraid of what he'll tell me. That I'll be even more angry with him, or-" he bit his lip "-worse, myself."

"But you'll talk to him?"

"Yes," he said, holding his fingers up in a scout's honor gesture. "I will."

I took his hand in mine and kissed it, then tucked it into my lap. "Did you ever have a girl up here?"

He laughed and turned his head. "I'm gonna have to plead the fifth on that."

"Damn," I said. "I was hoping I'd be the first."

"But I haven't had a girl up here since I was fifteen," he admitted. "I moved out not long after that. And I can tell you, Stormy," he pulled me close, his breath mingling with mine, "you're the only girl I've had up here that's mattered."

"That's not very nice to the other girls."

He placed a lingering kiss on my lips. "I'm sure they'd say the same thing about me."

"I doubt that. You are famous, after all."

"*Was* famous. In my other life." He kissed me again, long and slow, and pulled me close to him. I wrapped my arms around his neck and drew his face in closer, breathing in his smell, tasting his warm, salty skin. He reached his large hands up and ran them through my hair, loosening it from the clip, letting the strands run down my shoulders. He deftly avoided the bump on my head, his fingers caressing my scalp, something nobody had ever done before. Such a simple, almost nurturing movement, but it felt so good that my skin erupted in goose-flesh. His hands were so huge, he cradled my whole head in them as he bent his mouth to mine and parted my lips with his teeth.

His kiss was long and deep and full of need. I could feel the tension melting away from him, his shoulders relaxing, as he kissed me. His hands were still in my hair. I ran my own up his chest, to his shoulders, and up his neck, resting my fingers behind his ears, feeling the exquisite bones of his jaw. He was so strong, so perfect. I found myself wondering, not for the first time, if he'd always been this other-worldly, or if it was the spell. It didn't matter – he would have been perfect to me regardless.

We broke apart, both coming up for air, and he traced his lips down my collarbone, stopping to whisper in my ear, "I want you so bad." His voice was full of intensity, his hands rough and frenzied, running over my clothes, fumbling, urgent.

I pushed him back on the bed, resting on top of him, straddling his waist. I leaned down and placed a kiss on his lips. His hands trailed up my hips and under my shirt, resting on my bare lower back, warm and electric. "I want you too." I leaned down and kissed him again, letting my lips linger against his, teasing, gentle, until he groaned and kissed me back, hard. His hands fiddled with my pants, finally unbuttoning and unzipping and getting them down to my knees.

"What's the rush? We've got all night." We had both forgotten all about the sauce bubbling over downstairs.

"And I intend to make use of every minute of it," he said to me, laughing, his green eyes sparkling like emeralds. With one swift movement he'd lifted me off him, placed me on the bed beside him, reared up, whipped off his pants and lay there expectantly, propped on one elbow, his face full of bemused longing. I laughed.

"You're so beautiful," he said. "I'm so lucky."

"I could say the same back to you," I said, pulling off my pants, then my shirt. I unhooked my bra and lay beside him, nestling into his warmth. He caressed my side, his warm, calloused hands like heaven on my skin. "To think I had posters of your face all over my walls."

"Explain this to me," he said in a teasing tone, his hands still roaming all over my body. "The teenage girl experience...the rock star thing."

"Shouldn't you know?" I laughed. "We made you a rich man, didn't we?"

"Be that as it may, I can't say I understand it," he said, pulling me close to plant another kiss. "I never did then, either. Girls screaming and hollering for me, putting up posters with my ugly mug, throwing panties at me onstage."

"Your mug is anything but ugly," I said with a laugh. "But I think it's like... It's a fantasy, like Prince Charming, but with an edge. It's dangerous, because you're the bad boys, you know? But it's also safe, because we'll never attain you."

"Except you did." His voice was low and sexy in my ear.

"Except I did." I wrapped my arms around him and placed a soft kiss on his jaw. "I still can't believe it. I can't believe my dreamboat is right here. And he's done some very inappropriate things to me."

"I plan to do more."

"I plan to let you."

He gave a mock growl and slapped my backside. Then his face turned wistful. "I don't know how in the hell you managed to bring me back," he whispered, his lips finding me again. "I may never figure out how all of this worked. But I'm so glad you did. Even if – even if I'm gone tomorrow and this is all I ever did with my second chance, was meet you, get to know you, make love to you, well, that's more than I could have wished for."

"Don't talk like that."

"It's true."

"But you talk like it's goodbye."

He didn't answer, but his arms were around me, pulling me close to him, far into him, his hair feather-light around my face. I caressed him gently, my hands starting at his stomach then down to his navel, and finally to his delicious warm hardness. He gasped when I touched him, and his body responded, pushing closer and closer toward me, not able to get close enough. He moaned softly. But I pulled away.

I looked into his eyes, seeing desire there, but also something else. Worry. His face was a cold thundercloud, dark and foreboding, his brows furrowed over his eyes, which were misty with tears. It was a contrast against the warmth of him, the wonderful feeling of his hands, which were still caressing my skin, pulling me toward him even as he glowered. I grabbed his cheeks in my hands and pulled him to me, pressing my mouth against his in a kiss that reassured more than words ever could.

He relented against me, softening, kissing me back, exploring my mouth with his tongue. Fervently he pulled me against him, freeing himself from his clothes with one hand, pushing himself inside me urgently, and I moaned against his mouth. My arms locked around his neck and I rested my head against his shoulder, wishing I could be inside him the way he was inside me.

When it was over, I lay against him, both of us sweating and panting. I could hear sounds from the kitchen below. Jason had taken over the spaghetti that we'd forgotten.

I propped my head up and peered into Phillip's eyes, which were still glossy and sad. I didn't want him to feel that way.

Not about me. Not about us. Not when I was the one who had brought him back, brought him here.

I looked deep into his eyes, my hands splayed out on his chest, over his heart, his mouth inches from mine, and whispered, "I release you."

His eyes widened and he pulled back with a jerk, his hands going out in front of him, grabbing my shoulders, his mouth an "O" of surprise. "Stormy, what-"

"I release you," I said again, clearer and slower this time.

"Stormy, no-"

"It's okay, Phillip," I said firmly. "It's done."

Sixteen

We'd been lying on the bed, silently, for about five minutes. I stared at the wall, waiting for Phillip to say something, anything, but he hadn't spoken, not since I'd uttered those words. The shocked look on his face had pretty much said it all.

I knew I needed to speak, to explain, to make him understand why I'd done it, but I couldn't seem to find the words. Anyway, wasn't he always in my head? Didn't he know?

So then why did I feel anger and hurt coming off him in waves?

From downstairs I heard the clang of pots and pans and a voice from the bottom of the stairwell. "Phillip, you fuck, you forgot the spaghetti! You guys stop boning and come down and eat!" From the gaiety in his voice, it sounded as if he'd gotten over his hurt feelings.

I smiled despite myself and turned to Phillip, running a hand over the warm skin of his belly. "Shall we go down?"

"I'm not hungry." His eyes were faraway, his face haunted.

"Phillip…" I pressed, wishing he'd look at me. "I know you're upset, but we need to eat. All that talk about getting our strength back, that applies to you, too. And Jason's waiting."

"I want you all to myself," he said, starting to get his old self back. He was trying, anyway.

"Too bad," I said with a laugh, rising to dress. I knew we'd have to talk, but for now, I was starving. "I want that spaghetti. And anyway, I never said I was opposed to two guys, one groupie. Jason has always been my second favorite."

THE HOUSE WAS VERY quiet and still when I woke up the next morning, the sun streaming through one tiny window over by the desk, a beam of light hitting me right in the eyes.

I was tucked into Phillip's large arms, my skin coated with a light sheen of sweat, the result of our mingling warmth. I reluctantly pulled myself from him and sat up, rubbing the sleep from my eyes and the hair from my face, looking down at his sleeping form.

I had already fallen in love with the way his lips formed a pout when he slept, the way he always had one impossibly long leg bent beneath him, the way he held himself so still. I stared down at him, memorizing the lines in his face, the beautiful, strong bone structure, the inky black impossibility of his eyelashes. When he woke up, he might no longer feel the same way about me now that I had released him.

I didn't regret it. It seemed wrong, to be tied to a person in such a way. If that was black magic, I didn't want it. I loved Phillip. I didn't want to manipulate him, control him, or tie him to me by wayward means. I wanted him to be happy, not running around trying to save my neck, or trying find his way out of a mess I caused. If he woke up and saw me differently, so be it. I'd go back home to my trailer and try to resume my life without any regrets, because when you loved someone you gave them the opportunity to fly.

After a spaghetti dinner with wine and soft, fresh rolls, and a dessert of chocolate cake and more cups of tea, a novelty that I'd never get used to as long as I lived, Phillip and I finally talked about what I'd done. I explained as best as I could, fighting back a slew of embarrassing tears, trying to convince him that I'd done it as a kindness, out of love. "I can't bear the thought that you're tied to me through the spell," I'd explained as we sat out by the firepit in the backyard, watching the bright-orange embers crackle and burn. "I wanted you to have a choice, to be in control of your own destiny. And if you still love me in the morning," I'd said, swallowing the lump in my throat, "then I'll know this is real."

At that, Phillip had leaned over, his puffy black coat – apparently it had been his, many moons ago, and was still hanging in the coat closet- soft against my cheek and pulled me into his arms. I wanted to weep at the sweet, poignant nostalgia Jason obviously had carried for his old friend. I knew he was scared; scared about what this meant for not only us, but me specifically. Would I be in more danger without him rummaging around in my head, sensing danger? "What if we no longer love each other," he'd said sadly, his dark eyes meeting mine, "Now that the magic is gone?"

"That's what I worry, too," I'd said against his shoulder, squeezing him with all my might. "But fear isn't a reason to hold onto someone."

He had considered this, then slowly nodded in agreement. "I'll still love you," he said, tucking a stray bit of hair behind my ear. "I will."

I knew I'd done the right thing. Phillip knew it, too. I just hoped that I wouldn't end up regretting it.

Phillip stirred. His eyes flickered under the lids and he sighed and rolled over, his arm moving in his sleep to try and find me. It rested on my thigh and he settled back into sleep. My breath caught in my throat.

After a time, I stopped staring at him and gingerly lay back down, slowly, trying to be quiet so as not to wake him. He needed his rest, and I was afraid of what might be different, or how different things might be when he woke up. I nestled into him, resting my head below his chin, into the crook of his neck, feeling his pulse there, steady and strong. His skin was like a furnace. I tucked myself into him, small and quiet, waiting.

His breath was slow and steady, and I was almost asleep again myself when his low voice murmured in my ear, "I told you I'd still love you in the morning."

I WAS IN THE SMALL, cozy kitchen later that morning, making myself toast and coffee, trying to get up the motivation to do the dishes, when Phillip strode in. All the tension had come back into his shoulders, and his large, strong body was as jumpy as a cat's. I sighed, wishing the peaceful warmth we'd felt earlier could have lasted longer. Yesterday had been perfect, almost, even with the fight between him and Jason, which they'd managed to bury over plates of spaghetti and lots of laughter. They were like brothers and it did me good to see them together. "What's happened now?"

He leaned over the table and placed a long, lingering kiss on my lips. "You taste like bread," he said with a smile. "Don't worry, baby, it's not you." I smiled; he'd never called me *baby* before. "But…"

"What is it?" I passed him the plate and he took a slice absently, taking all but a corner of the toast in one bite.

"I know you're in a hurry to get back but…" He chewed

thoughtfully, looking at me. "Jason and I've been talking, and Stormy…I think I need to go back and talk to Lydia one more time."

"Really?" I gave an involuntary shudder. The woman's house was a dust-filled study in terror; after all, I'd been bound and kidnapped from there.

He sighed. "Yeah. I want her to answer some questions. Namely, why her son is stalking us, trying to snag you in broad daylight. Where the hell Guthrie is. What your powers truly are." He fixed his green eyes on me. "I have to know these things before I can pack up and go back to Jekyll. I hope you understand."

The toast was dry in my mouth. "Yes," I said, finally.

"You don't have to go with me," he said. "I completely understand why you wouldn't want to go back there."

"I don't mind," I said, pushing the plate away and standing up. "Actually, I do mind. I'd rather eat glass than go back to that woman's house. But I'm damned if I'm letting you go without me."

"Are you sure, Stormy?" His brow furrowed. "I don't like the idea of you setting foot there, honestly."

"Of course I'm coming with you," I said, drinking my last dreg of coffee, relishing the undissolved sugar granules on my tongue. "When do we go? Now?"

"Later today," he said, also standing up and coming over to me, his face full of unease. I looked up at him. He was so tall that I had to stand on tip toe just to reach him for a kiss. I was surprised to feel he was trembling, and when I touched his arm he jumped. He touched the side of my face, his expression softening. "We don't have to go right this minute. I have plans for you this morning, and all of them involve my bedroom."

"Mr. Deville, how scandalous," I purred, rising to meet his mouth with my own. He wrapped his arms around my waist and pulled me upwards, and I caught his long black hair in my hands. He carried me all the way upstairs despite my laughing protests. How long were we going to put off going home, I wondered absently, as he transported me upstairs. A small, nagging voice in my head that I couldn't silence said, *if you make it back at all.*

PHILLIP SAT on the edge of the bed, his back to me, shirtless, his long hair hanging in tangles down his back. I moved from my cozy spot, buried in the covers, and inched down the creaking bed, which I was quickly getting used to, to touch him lightly on the shoulder. "Are you okay?" I asked, running a hand over his pale skin.

"Yeah." He turned his head a little, smiling in my direction, but his gaze was faraway and remote. I wondered what he was thinking. Gone was the playful mood from before. After making love he'd turned inward again, working something over. His face was full of dread, an expression I'd never seen in person, but it chilled my blood because I *had* seen it – in interviews, in magazine spreads, the occasional paparazzi shots of Phillip from years ago. That look of dread, of almost-bitterness, and apathy had followed him for the last couple years of his life.

I could look at any picture of Phillip Deville and tell you what era it was from. Some of it had to do with his various hairstyles and colors, the slope of his body – gangly in his early years, giving way to hard muscle later on, starting to soften just a bit when he hit his thirties – but mainly it was his facial expressions that made it so easy to pick out the approximate year. In the beginning he'd had the cocky, excited energy of a young guy with his entire future ahead of him, full of possibility. Later, some of the excitement had gone, but he was still plucky, confident and hot as hell. But toward the end, right before his death, around the time of the last album, all his photos took on a sad, bitter edge. His eyes no longer shone, but were haunted and sad, his dark hair often wrapped around his face like a security blanket, his cheeks gaunt, and the tight line of his mouth showed his unhappiness. I didn't really like pictures from that era. I'd always preferred the ones from his earlier days, even though he was more handsome as he got older. It made me too sad to see him so obviously miserable.

It was how Phillip looked now.

I wanted to insist that he tell me, to force it out of him, but I knew him well enough by now to know that'd have the opposite effect. And anyway, I knew what he was feeling without having to ask. Whatever power he had of knowing my thoughts and feelings, I had some lesser version of that same power. After releasing him, it had started to feel stronger, which was weird, because I'd assumed the opposite would be true. In severing the magical cord, I'd managed to strengthen the cord between him and myself.

Looking at the back of Phillip, I suddenly remembered a dream – no, a nightmare, or I supposed, a daymare, since it had occurred right before I woke up – that I'd been having as I dozed in his arms. I closed my eyes, trying to pick out the threads of the dream, which was fading quickly from my memory. A beach, several shades below overcast, gray and moody, the waves sweeping over the beach like cooled lava, thick and slushy, blanketing the hot, clammy sand. A man, off in the distance. A sound, loud and cracking like thunder, causing him to turn and crane his head. His expression quizzical, his movements jerky and sinister. A bright flash of forking light from the sky. Smoke. Screaming. Pain. A bright, colorful light, almost like an aura, a haze, shimmering over everything, sparkling like glitter, raining down on me along with the rain.

And then nothing.

I shuddered and stared out Phillip's window. It was a beautiful, sunny day with no hint of rain, much less an approaching storm. I was nowhere near the ocean, and it was probably just a dream. I shook my head, clearing out the sense of foreboding, telling myself to stop worrying so damn much. I had enough on my plate without adding more helpings.

Phillip's expression was faraway. I wanted to pull him back to me, back to us. I reached out and touched the hair at his temple, pushing it behind his ear gently, my fingers getting caught in the tangle of black. Since I'd been with him, he'd carefully brushed his beautiful hair every morning, but it stayed tangled anyway. Today, it was the worst I'd ever seen it; a mess of snags and knots that would take forever to loosen. I realized as I touched his strands that it was curlier than I'd thought. It was thick and dense and unruly. It was unusually heavy on his head today; I could almost feel the heaviness wearing at him, giving him a headache. I leaned closer to him and gathered the soft black mass in my hands. Instinct told me he was too sensitive for a brush, so I parted it gently into three parts and set to work without one. I worked soundlessly, mindlessly. It was though my hands had imparted, outside of me, that they were to do this, and set themselves to the task.

Phillip sighed and leaned into me, his skin warm against my shoulder. I smiled and continued working, enjoying the soft-yet-brittle feel of his hair on my fingers, the warmth that radiated through me. I was filled with a feeling of *gold,* bright and gleaming, warm and sound. I braided his hair slowly, letting my hands caress the strands, the back of his neck, his ears. I remembered from childhood how good it felt, how relaxing and safe, to have someone braid your hair. When she hadn't been too drunk to hold a brush, my mother would sit me in the kitchen, gently and methodically dividing my hair into parts, taking her time to French-braid my blond hair, her fingers soft and ticklish and comforting. My entire body would buzz with wellbeing when she did my hair, all of it an experience of bliss, from the clicking of the little plastic barrettes to the gentle slope of the soft baby-brush she used well into my teen years, to the murmurs of apology when she'd accidentally hit a snag. I remembered how it felt, for someone to focus their attention on something so delicate and personal. It was one of the few times in my life I'd felt my mother's love, strong and poignant, and as I held Phillip's hair in my hands, I took that love from deep in my soul, that warm, glittering feeling of *gold,* that bright light, and imparted it to him. I felt it moving from deep within me down the length of my arms and into my hands, flowing forth from my fingers in an invisible stream.

Phillip's breathing slowed and he closed his eyes; he might have dozed. His weight was heavy and solid against me. When the braid was finished, I fished a hair tie out of my own hair, letting it fall over my shoulders in a messy cascade, and secured the braid behind his back. "There," I said, leaning over his shoulder to place a gentle kiss on his cheek. "Now it won't be in your way."

"Thank you," he said in a soft voice, still staring straight ahead, but he seemed lighter now. "It was bothering me. It felt...heavy."

"I know." I put my arms around his shoulders and pulled him into me, placing another kiss on his cheek, then one on his ear, his temple, and the top of his head. He sighed and leaned into me further. I held him tight.

"Don't go away from me," I said.

"I'm right here."

"You know what I mean." I rested my cheek on his large shoulder. "I can feel you...drifting."

He said nothing, only placed an absent kiss on my arm. I felt my heart catch.

"Promise me," I said. "That if you ever leave me, it's

because you want to leave, because it's over, and not because you think you have to."

He sighed and reached for me, pulling me into his lap, cradling me there. His large arms wrapped around me completely, and I nestled into his embrace. He returned my kisses, placing one on my cheeks, my forehead, and finally my mouth. His braid fell into my face, grazing my cheek, as he closed his mouth on mine, opening against me, tasting me. His lips were salty.

The kiss lingered, and I felt my body erupt into flame, and I instinctively pulled him closer, not able to get close enough. "You didn't answer me," I murmured when my lips were momentarily free. But he kissed me again, silencing me. He wasn't going to make me that promise.

He pushed me back onto the bed where we'd just lain together minutes before, ready for me again, and I was ready for him, too. It was amazing how much I wanted him, how I never felt satisfied, like we always had more to give each other. I'd never felt that way with Tess. Just the sight of Phillip filled me with fire, made me burn. I couldn't stop touching him. I loved the way his skin felt, both warm and cool all at once, how deep his green eyes were, how rough his mouth was, how big and strong his hands were. He was so very real, big and tangible and alive.

His weight pinned me down, but it was a steady, comfortable weight, and the delicious woodsmoke-scent hit my nose and made me woozy. He bent to kiss my neck, his lips trailing up from my collarbone to behind my ear. His breathing was rough, the breath hot on my skin. His hands were exploring the rest of me, stopping here and there at points all over my body, making me wild with passion.

We would have to talk about this. He couldn't do this every time I brought it up. "You're not being fair," I said out loud, placing my hands on his bare shoulders and pushing him back so I could look him in the eye.

"I'm sorry," he said, bending down to kiss me again, rough. "Do you want to stop?"

"No," I said, and he smiled. With one deliberate thrust he was inside me, and our bodies fit together, seemingly made for each other, thigh flat against thigh, his arms tangled up with mine, his weight bearing down on me. He moved against me, slow at first, then rougher, faster, and we both cried out. He kissed me, muting the sound, and I opened my mouth to his, wanting to taste him, to bite him.

His face was in my neck again, and I felt wetness there. Was it tears? And he murmured in my ear, "I love you." That was as much as he would give me.

WE EMERGED from the bedroom a while later and trudged down the stairs. There were voices in the living room. I followed Phillip, noting that the tension in his shoulders was back. He pricked an ear to the right as we rounded the kitchen. Then he stopped just outside the door, and turned to me, his face white.

"I know that voice," he said, his eyes searching mine, almost scared.

I craned my neck, listening. Jason was laughing with someone over the sounds of the stereo. He was playing a Bloomer Demons record, but it wasn't one I'd heard before. It sounded like a live cut. "Who is it?"

"Nate," he said, still pale.

"Nate?" I whispered in surprise. "As in Nathan 'Ollie' Green?"

He nodded. "Fuck," he said, "Fuck, fuck, *fuck.*"

I held in my shriek, the fangirl trying to pop out of me unbidden.

"Phil? That you?" The voice wasn't very familiar, but I could almost recognize it, mined from years-worth of memories of YouTube interviews and concert footage. He didn't sound at all alarmed. "You gonna come in here or keep hiding in the kitchen like a scared puppy?"

"Fuck," Phillip said again, then squared his shoulders and stalked into the living room. I didn't know what else to do, so I followed, holding my hands to my face, trying to quell the broad grin that was busting out on my cheeks. *The band's all here,* I thought to myself giddily. Well, what was left of it.

Jason was sitting on the couch, a bottle of ginger ale on the coffee table in front of him. Beside him was a slightly-older version of the man who completed the Bloomer Demons outfit – second-string guitarist and sometime keyboard player Nathan Green, affectionately known to fans as "Ollie" due to his love of skateboarding. I stared at him for a moment. He had changed a lot in twenty years, but he was still handsome as the devil. He didn't appear to have aged, his dark skin and deep brown eyes as youthful and smooth as ever, but gone were the long, butt-length dreads he'd had all through the band's career, as well as the piercings that had once studded his nose, ears and lip. A blue button-down shirt with the sleeves rolled up to his forearms covered up most of his tattoos, and his hair was in a full, natural afro. The only thing that reminded me of the old Nathan was the shoes – black-on-black high-top Vans, providing a sharp contrast to the light colored thin-legged slacks he wore.

As I entered the room, he greeted me first. "Hey," he said with a nod. "I'm Nate."

"Stormy," I croaked out, full on star struck and feeling like I might faint. "Oh wow, Ollie, I'm a huge fan-"

"Don't let her get going, she won't stop," Jason said with a laugh, but he winked at me. He looked at Phillip. "Bro, it's okay. Nate's known since the day I saw you out back, digging up the ground like a body snatcher. I called him as soon as you left. He's cool. He's not going to say anything."

"Sure," Phillip said, his voice brittle and wavering, his hand trembling in mine. "Until he tells...who? Barb? Our old manager? Some fan? A member of my *family?*" he sputtered. "I can't let this get out. Don't you understand there's no way I can function if people know-"

"Shut up, fuckface," Jason said, unruffled. "You chose to walk your dead ass back here to this house, and if you think for one second I'm going to house you and keep you safe and *not* tell our other best friend, you're a fucking idiot. You know damn well you can trust Nate."

"Phil." Nathan stood up and walked over to us. He held out his arms and pulled Phillip into an embrace. "I'm so fucking glad to see you, man. So fucking glad. Never in this life did I think-" His voice caught, and he pulled back and looked at Phillip, his eyes glistening. "Phil, I swear on my life – and yours, however many you got, dude – that I won't tell a soul. Don't you remember? When you started writing out that stupid spell you made all three of us cut our palms and make a blood vow that we would never breathe a word."

"More lives than mine are at risk if anybody-"

"Phil." Nathan clapped him on the back and led him by the shoulder over to the couch where they both sat down, Phillip's face like stone. "I swore and I fuckin' meant it. So did Jason. Forget about it, man. Losing you and Kim was the fucking worst. I'm just glad to have one of you back. We want to help you, and your girlfriend, too."

"Jason isn't in any position to help anyone," Phillip thundered.

"Cut me some fucking slack already," Jason said, acid in

his tone. "Unless you want to take it outside and I'll teach you some fucking respect. I haven't used in days-"

"If you think for one second you could take me, you fucking little twerp-"

"Kim isn't here to break it up this time, man. I should have shown you what was up years ago-"

"Sitting here in *my* house like king shit, like you're gonna show *me-*"

"My house, you mean. I paid for it. Big ogres like you, Lurch, fall down quick. You're slow and dim-witted. I've kicked your fucking ass before, and I can do it again-"

"Fuck you if you want to fuckin' try." Phil started to get back up from the couch. "We'll be sending your teeth back home in an envelope to your mother-"

I was getting ready to intervene with the water hose I'd seen on the back porch when suddenly, the yelling stopped, and all three remaining members of the Bloomer Demons were embracing and crying in a jumble of tattoos, piercings and black-clad arms and legs. Phillip's arms were around them both, holding them to his chest like little brothers, his face wet with tears. What should have been a foursome was only three, but I had no doubt all of them were thinking of Kim.

I sat back and watched, fighting the perverse urge to grab my phone and snap a picture. I didn't know if I wanted to laugh or cry, so I just shook my head, and thought, *men.* What a spectacle, and yet they always said we were the emotional ones. The scene in front of me was bittersweet and made me ache, but not only because I'd grown up loving them, not only because their dear friend Kim wasn't part of it. I watched them, soaking in the brotherly love, the beauty of their reunion, the purity and the ludicrousness of it, and then stepped backward out of the room, their show of friendly love reminding me that I hadn't talked to Sloan in days.

Seventeen

I started to get the shakes as we pulled up to Lydia's house later that afternoon. The memory of Phillip, frozen in the truck, his hands clutching the keys, and my own immobile limbs just before I'd felt a heavy, blunt object smack me in the head, then my world going black...I did not want to be back here. But Phillip had questions he needed answering, and neither of us were eager to leave the other after all that had happened. I exited the truck and slipped my arm through his, grateful for the warm pulse I felt, strong and steady.

I was already keyed up. Earlier, when Phillip was reuniting with Nate and Jason, I had gone upstairs to text Sloan. I'd sent her a brief message. *"Hey, haven't heard from you in a while. I've sent a couple of messages. You ok?"* After ten minutes passed with no response, I'd sent her a snapchat, a silly clip of me wearing one of Phillip's old bandannas that I'd found on his dresser. Then I'd PM'd her on Facebook, and finally given way to the thing I never did, and actually called her. The phone rang once before it went to voicemail. That meant she'd seen it and silenced me. I was angry. How dare she do that to me after all the times she'd complained about the same thing? If she'd been out of town, and I hadn't spoken to her in days, I would have rushed to answer the phone. I called her again, then one more time. Every time - voicemail. I was beginning to worry. What was going on? Was she mad at me?

I had the sense, just a niggling thought in the back of my mind, that something was going to go wrong today. The dream I'd had about the beach, how dark and terror-filled it had been. The sense of danger had been so real, so palpable. Somehow, some way, I felt that it involved not only me and Phillip, but maybe Sloan, too. Her silence really worried me. As nosy and meddling as she was, it wasn't like her to not check in, especially when she knew I was on a dangerous road trip.

As we walked to the porch slowly, like two inmates heading to their doom, I paused, whipped out my phone and tried to dial Sloan one more time, but the phone's screen froze. I rebooted it, giving Phillip a cursory, sly glance as if to say *this is your fault,* and dialed again, clutching the phone to my ear with tight, anxious fingers. I was stalling, trying to avoid walking up onto Lydia's porch and into what I felt must be an abyss of black magic and danger. I hoped she'd answer so I could go back to the truck and have a conversation and avoid the whole thing. It was really beginning to rankle me that I couldn't reach her – she was taking care of Blinken, after all. He was probably fine, but an update would be nice. But the phone didn't even ring one full time before going to her voice-mail. *"This is Sloan. Leave a message, bitch,"* her tinny, pre-recorded voice said in my ear. Then, instead of the usual beep, I heard, "Mailbox is full." I took a deep, shaky breath and slid the phone into my pocket, biting my lip and tasting blood.

Well, no sense in putting off the inevitable. I needed to focus. The last time I'd been near this woman's house I'd been kidnapped. What did she have in store for me this time? I couldn't be distracted, worrying about people and things back home when I needed to be on guard. I reached into my jacket pocket and fingered the tiny switchblade knife that Phillip had pressed into my hand earlier. It wouldn't do much, but it made me feel safer.

"Don't worry," Phillip said under his breath as we walked up onto the stoop. "I won't let her lay a finger on you. If she so much as looks as you sideways, I'll-"

"You'll what, Mr. Deville?" The screen door opened, and Lydia's now-familiar, white, frizzy head poked out. "I expected you'd come back."

"This is as far as we go," Phillip said in an angry voice, clutching my arm tight. "I need some answers, and I need them now. But if you try to bind us, or send your goon-"

"I won't be doing anything to you, boy," she said from behind the door in a gesture of defiance. I rankled at her calling him *boy*. The nerve, the disrespect. She held up a shaking but firm hand as though she'd heard me, as if to say *be quiet, girl.* "But I won't be answering any questions out on my front stoop, either."

"You will unless you want a police report filed for kidnapping and assault against my girlfriend."

"Who was kidnapped?" she said smoothly. "I'm not aware of any kidnapping. You're both here, fresh as life. I've not so much as touched anyone."

"But your son did," I said, raising my chin in defiance. "We both know you did some spell to bind us, and as for the kidnapping and assault, Lee and his friend Shank did both."

"Shank." Her face was a picture of disgust. "I never did like him. No brains at all. I always told Guthrie the man was an absolute boar."

"Enough," Phillip said, his face twisted in fury. "Tell us why your son has been following us since Jekyll Island. Why you bound me here and let them kidnap Stormy. Why they're so eager to get her alone. Why you claim you haven't seen or spoken to your husband in a decade when we both know that's bullshit."

"I won't answer anything on the front stoop," she said again, but her voice betrayed her nerves. "I have very nosy neighbors."

"Lydia," I said in a wavering voice. "Did you know your son came to see me in the hospital? After all he's already put me through, he had the gall..." I trailed off when Phillip gave me a sharp look. I hadn't told him that. "He'll be on the security footage..."

She sighed. "Fine," she said. "I'll have to bring out my oxygen tank. And can you pull up a few chairs from the table in the yard? I can't stand for long periods."

Phillip did as he was asked, though his face was still murderous, grabbing three chairs from the side yard and lugging them up onto the stoop where he placed two across from one, none too gently. Lydia made her way out onto the stoop, taking her sweet time, shuffling along with her oxygen tank pulling behind her, dressed in a cyan housecoat that had little centaurs on it. She looked even older and more weathered than the last time I'd seen her; she seemed very tired. As I sat across from her, trying my best not to look too closely at her because she unnerved me, I could *feel* her exhaustion, almost taste it. It was like an aura emanating from her, pale-blue and wispy, as though she were turning to a ghost in front of my eyes.

She situated herself in a chair and immediately lit one of her long, skinny cigarettes.

"Should you be smoking with that thing?" I asked her, gesturing to the tank.

"Don't feign concern for me, Fee," she said, reverting to the nickname she'd given me last time. "I'm an old woman and I'll do what I want. It isn't as though I have anything left to live for, anyway."

If she was expecting sympathy, she got none from Phillip. "I want answers," he repeated, crossing his legs impatiently. They were so long he had to tuck them to the side to avoid kicking her. "I want to know why Stormy's being followed, why your son is so obsessed with her, why she was hurt, and why you lied about Guthrie."

"That's a lot of 'why's," she said. "With which one should I begin?"

"At the beginning," he said impatiently.

"First, let's talk about magic," she said maddeningly, taking a long puff on her cigarette. That's what she'd said last time, too. She held back a cough; I watched her mouth and chest constrict with the effort. "Obviously Fee here has no idea about the magic she possesses or how much she has or how much is out in the world, ready to be tapped into."

"Nor do I want to," I said, though I was beginning to wonder if that was wholly true.

Lydia looked at me, one eyebrow cocked. She winked at Phillip. "Imagine – your first spell is necromancy, bringing someone back from the *dead* and then to say, 'oh, I'm done...'" She cackled, smoke emitting from her dry lips in a ring.

"I didn't mean to do the spell," I said defiantly. "I was a non-believer. I just thought it was a joke. I was drunk and in a bad place and I had no idea it would actually take root-"

"Don't you tire of hearing yourself tell that story?" she asked with a curious look at me. "It's a lie. And even if it wasn't, you've reaped the benefits."

"What benefits?" I demanded. "Being followed around, run off the road, beaten and kidnapped?"

"You've fallen in love," she said simply, and I fell silent. Phillip's hand found my own and clasped it tightly. His skin was warm and clammy.

She continued. "Magic has to go somewhere. It's energy just like anything else – it needs a conduit. A place to go and a medium by which to go through. Whether or not you called it, or it found you, doesn't matter. You're the conduit, and you've used those powers to reanimate dead flesh." I shuddered and she smiled. "Oh, don't carry on. It isn't as though you're Victor Frankenstein, robbing graves. It's not so morbid as all that. You've breathed life into a vessel that was lifeless. It's a miracle, really. True magic; Mary Shelley herself would've given her eyeteeth for such a chance."

"Black magic," I whispered, feeling dread.

"That again." She snorted. "Yes, there are rules...and you've broken some. But your intention was pure, which is why you haven't seen the whole host of things you *could* be seeing. Had things gone differently, you might already be dead for your errors. However, what you did was done in pure ignorance, and with an innocent, loving heart." She nodded, as if affirming her own words. "It is my belief that you'll be forgiven for your transgressions, and even be allowed to continue using your powers, should you decide to."

"I won't," I said firmly, but even as I said it, I felt an odd, electric tickle of desire course through me. Phillip must have felt it too, because he dropped my hand and cut his eyes to me with a startled look.

"You have the power to reconcile life and death," she said. "Given to you from the goddess herself. That isn't to be taken lightly. Why would you denounce it?" My cheeks burned, but whether it was from shame or desire, I wasn't sure. What goddess, I wondered. I vowed to find out more about that one day.

"Where's Guthrie?" Phillip demanded suddenly, breaking the subject. "Why did you lie?"

"Oh, who knows," she said dismissively. "I haven't seen him in years. That part was true. When we separated, I swore a blood vow that he'd never darken my doorway again. There was a rumor that he'd died. Probably be the best thing for him. He was a miserable man. A terrible father."

"He's the father of your child. You can't honestly expect us to believe that-"

"Guthrie is not important," she said loudly, interrupting Phillip. "Don't you understand that? He was never what was important. He's a meddler, a trickster, a complication. Stop giving him power."

Phillip took my hand again and clutched it tightly.

"There's no need to feel revulsion for what you've done," she continued, ignoring Phillip. "The spell is one that has been used before. There are others out in the world…" She paused for a moment, puffing on her cigarette, seeming to weigh out something within herself, then took a dry breath and continued in a low tone, "…those who are like Phillip."

"Like Phillip?" I said, startled. "You mean who have come back to life?"

"Yes," she said, puffing on her cigarette.

"Currently?" I asked. "Do you know these people?"

"I know one other," she said matter-of-factly, stubbing her cigarette out in an ashtray that had mysteriously appeared from her pocket. "And so do you."

"And who is this other undead person?" Phillip asked, his voice wearing thin on patience.

"Undead." She sniffed. "What is this, a cheap horror film?"

"Who?" I repeated, squeezing his hand.

"My son," she said, smirking under her wrinkles, as she saw the expression of horror appear on my face. "Lee."

Eighteen

Phillip and I turned to each other, the shock in his eyes mirroring my own. "I..." I fumbled for words. "You're telling me that Lee is like...Phillip? He died and was brought back?"

"Yes," she said simply, lighting another cigarette even though she'd just put one out. Her expression was almost bored, as though this were a subject she discussed daily and was sick to death of. "I'm the one who brought him back."

"With the same spell?" I asked. I knew she had magic. I'd somehow known, from the beginning, that she'd been the one who bound Phillip and me. So why had we assumed that the spell had been Guthrie's? It was as though I could see the strands of it in her aura, the almost imperceptible light-blue haze that seemed to float around the porch. She caught my stare and I looked away first.

"Yes," she said. "When he died..." her voice caught. "...I didn't even think twice. There was no way I could let my son go. He was too young; I couldn't bear it. Such a stupid acci-dent." She didn't elaborate, but I closed my eyes, suddenly overcome with images that seemed real...a car pushed into the wrong lane, crushed metal and flames, blood in the road, mingling with tiny shards of glass, glinting in the late-day sun, the sounds of ear-splitting screams and the wail of an ambulance siren. A shock of pale, sandy blond hair over a lifeless face. I shuddered and opened my eyes. Lydia was staring at me intently, her face full of a deep sadness.

"How long?" I asked, though I wasn't sure it mattered.

"He died five years ago," she said. "When he was twenty-two."

I marveled. That explained why Lee seemed so young to me; his boyish face, his gentle nature. He might be nearing thirty, but in some ways, he was stunted as a young man of twenty-two. Yet another thing I'd wondered about but hadn't brought up to Phillip yet. Would he age? Now that his clock had started back up, would it move forward? Or would he forever be young, destined to watch me grow old, like some kind of bloodless vampire?

Lydia cut into my thoughts. "Oh yes, they age. Don't worry. They aren't immortal." She puffed on her cigarette. "But it's slower for them than it is for us. The second time around, it seems you get longer."

Phillip was oddly silent next to me, digesting this new information.

"The problem, Fee, is that there's only so much of this magic. It's not infinite, but a resource that can be exhausted. And the magic is running dangerously low."

"I don't follow."

"Not every witch can be a necromancer. It's not something we all know how to do. Guthrie is a warlock, but he was never able to do it. I could." Her chest puffed out proudly. "I think a part of him never really believed I had the power. Thought I was just holding something over him, exaggerating my abilities. That's why he was so free with them, giving them away. When I found out he'd given my spell to Phillip here, over something as base as *drugs,* I was furious. When I found out the fool had put it on an album cover…" She looked at Phillip with deep disdain. "It was one of the many times I left my husband."

"So Guthrie didn't take it any more seriously than Phillip did," I said.

She nodded. "It wasn't until Lee died and I brought him back that Guthrie understood that I'd had this power for real, that it was legitimate. He suddenly realized that all along I'd been the powerful witch, and he the novice."

"Sour grapes?" I asked.

"You don't know the half of it," she said with a rueful smile. "Men never take it well when they find out their women are more powerful than them. And yet, so often, it's true." She paused. "Oh, once he knew I was legit, he tried to get back in touch, tried to reconcile his relationship with his son. I told him where to shove it."

"Lee didn't, though."

"Lee loves his father, despite knowing his failings. He's young and can't be blamed." Lydia's mouth was pursed and uncomfortable. I could understand why she felt so protective of her son. Any mother would but added to the mix was the fact that Lee was like Phillip, and therefore even more in need of her protection. Still, from what the woman had said, Guthrie was an opportunistic, manipulative shithead who had never taken her powers seriously. I could see why Lee would feel forced to do his father's bidding, but why had Lydia helped if she hated Guthrie so much, if he'd disrespected her so?

Phillip looked at me with a grim smile; he was thinking the same thing. He leaned over and kissed my forehead, his hair tickling my face. His lips were cold. "So I think we're up to speed - the spell is yours, Guthrie is an asshole, I'm an asshole, Stormy tapped into the magic by accident, blah blah – poof, here I am." He tapped at his knee impatiently. "Why is Guthrie hiring goons to follow us around, and if you hate him so much, why are you helping him? Because we insulted your magic or the goddess or whatever? Because we stole from you?"

"No," she said. "I'm not helping *him*. I'm trying to set things right. Because you've upset the balance."

"How?"

"I was so angry when he gave that spell to you," she said, her face taking on a dreamy quality as though she hadn't heard us. "But even I figured it wouldn't be a problem. I never dreamed that anyone would be powerful enough, or smart enough, to decipher it." She glowered at Phillip and turned back to me. "It's so rare an ability in a witch that we figured there was no chance someone would find it, know what it was, recite it and actually have the power to bring it to fruition."

"But Stormy did it," Phillip said in a low voice.

She nodded. "Yes, she did. As I've said, there is only a finite amount of this magic available. You can't just repeat that spell willy-nilly and bring back a dozen people. I don't know why that is, if it's the universe trying to regulate or balance its energies or what, but there can only be so many reanimated people at one time."

"So?" I said.

"So," she said, looking at us as if we were the dumbest people alive, "I was planning to bring myself back. Now I can't. Because of you two."

I stared at her with my mouth wide open. Phillip's hand in mine had started to sweat.

"I'm in very bad health – I have cancer, in case you didn't realize, though I figure you can see it in my aura – and I doubt I'll last another month. I've hung on as long as I can, but I can't hang on much longer, and after I die, Lee is going to bring *me* back. I've been training him for that very purpose."

I stared at Phillip in horror. His face was grim, but he didn't speak.

"Only there's not enough magic left in the spell now. And

because of this unexpected..." She gestured at Phillip again. "...snag...well, I'm in a bit of a dilemma."

Phillip was quiet for a long moment, but I could feel his anger coming off him in waves. She must have felt it too. He was quietly seething. After another moment, he said in the same low voice, "So let me get this right. Your husband stiffs me out of some cash and gives me a spell in payment because he has such little respect for his wife or her powers that it's immaterial to him. Turns out the spell actually works, and here I am, brought back, alive and well, and somehow you seem to think it's Stormy's fault? For doing a spell she had no idea came from you with no real feeling behind it? This total fluke is all at her feet? Even though you've used it already to bring somebody back? You were going to be so greedy that you were going to use it again?"

"It's my spell," she said defiantly. "I wove it, I wrote it. It's *my* magic, and I-"

"You allowed it to be given away. It's not Stormy's fault that this happened," he said.

"I never said it was her fault," Lydia said, for the first time seeming less sure of herself. "But she's opened up something that can't just be shut again. And that's what she's trying to do. She's borrowed on my magic and now refuses to pay the debt."

"The *debt?*" I shook my head. "Are you serious?"

"I can't very well bring *myself* back," she said. "And Lee isn't experienced enough to write a spell on his own. He's very green, even more than you, Fee. He can borrow on my magic now, but once I'm gone, he won't be able to."

I was confused. None of this made sense. "You could try and pool your energy with mine to see if we can't build the banks back up." Even as I said it, it sounded ludicrous.

She made a face. "That's not how it works. You don't even know how. I can see how green you are from here."

"So we know what *you* want from her," Phillip thundered. "What is it that Guthrie wants?"

"To use her magic for his purposes, I assume," she answered calmly. "I believe he sees her as just another potential 'friend' to do his bidding. He has so very many, including my son."

"Every time I've seen Lee, he's just urged me to go back home to Jekyll," I said angrily. "He's never said one word about you or the spell or using my magic to help you. *Or* about helping his father, either."

"I know," she answered, stubbing out her second cigarette. "He doesn't care about building up my magic. He worries, thinks it'll exhaust me too much. He doesn't want me to suffer." She fixed an eye on me. "He wants to see you safely away and hidden so I can't beg you for help and so Guthrie can't bother you. He thinks he can do it on his own – save me, appease his dad, keep you safe, save the world." She smiled wistfully. "But he can't. He can't do any of it. I love my son, but he's useless in this, and he's putting himself in danger. I need *you* to help him, Stormy."

"No." Philip stood up, still holding my hand. "You all have some fucking nerve. As if she asked for this. As if I asked for it!"

"You may not have," she answered him calmly. "But Fee did, when she recited that spell."

"Stop calling her that."

"Sidhe and Fee," she said. "Such a pair."

"You and Guthrie," he sneered, "are much worse."

"Indeed," she said. "We did not part on good terms. Lee comes and goes – he does some work for Guthrie, and I don't ask, because I don't want to know. You want to talk about black magic, dark magic – that's Guthrie's sort. That's what he's drawn to. Only he doesn't balance it out." She fixed an eye on me. "I don't know what he wants with you, girl, and that's the truth. But what I *do* know is that he's far more dangerous than I could ever be; not because of any great power of his own, but because he's able to get so many people to do his bidding. His charm, his ability to invoke fear…those are *his* powers." She shook her head sadly. "I may have sent Lee after you, to try and talk a bit of sense, but it's Guthrie who hired Shank, and Guthrie who gave him the go ahead to drug you and beat you."

I squeezed Phillip's hand, hard. A feeling of dread had begun to course through me. She was telling the truth. I didn't trust her, but I believed her. And I had to admit, a small part of me liked her. In another life, I might have thoroughly enjoyed sitting on her dusty couch, learning about spells and hearing about the no-doubt colorful, mysterious life she must have led. I wouldn't have minded hearing more about Lee, too; I'd never tell Phillip, but I found him almost as curious as I found his mother.

I felt Phillip tense beside me; I hadn't been guarding my thoughts carefully enough. I'd never get used to the loose connection between all our brains. I squeezed Phillip's hand harder, a silent warning not to boil over, but inside, I was smiling. Lydia was charming me despite myself. I could see now how Lee managed to be so disarming while doing all sorts of shady things. He had inherited that quality from his parents, one of whom had, in the small space of ten minutes, managed to almost turn me over to her side.

"I'll tell you one thing more," she said to me, her small eyes fixing on mine. "And you should heed it, because it's a strong message I'm getting."

"Oh, now you're an oracle, too?" Phillip's tone was nasty.

"Really, Sidhe. I must ask you to get control of yourself. And they say women are too emotional." She rolled her eyes and turned back to me. "You played around with the tarot a bit, didn't you, Fee? And now a certain card has shown itself to you twice."

I gaped at her. "Ok, I'm listening."

"The tarot is just fools' magic, a wayward spirit having a bit of fun. It's nothing to be overly concerned about, only..." She looked at me curiously, lighting another cigarette. "So many people misinterpret the death card. They see it and think it literally means death – that someone is going to die, or that they themselves are dying." She took a puff. "I imagine you saw it and interpreted it as Phillip – an omen of death himself, standing on your doorstep."

I nodded. That was exactly what I'd assumed.

"That's all wrong, Fee. Generally, the death card *does* mean death – but not the death of a person. Rather, it's the death of something important, something you thought was finite. It represents a closing, an ending. Often a tragic or unexpected one."

"Like what?" I asked. "Like losing my job?" I didn't think Jean would fire me over my short vacation, but who knew.

"Could be," she said. "But not in your case, I think. Something more personal, something you thought was steadfast, unbreakable. It could be anything, really. The end of a marriage, a betrayal from a friend...even losing one's home."

I sighed. "Well, one of those things has already happened." I didn't mention Tess. She didn't know him, and anyway, she'd probably already seen it in my aura. At the thought of him, my heart felt a little pang. God, how long was it going to take to get over it already? I'd thought maybe I had a shot at moving on until I'd discovered he was now working for Guthrie, being paid to terrorize me; now the pain was fresh and raw again. It didn't seem fair.

"Just keep your eyes open," Lydia said, still puffing away. "The card wants you to heed its warning. Be careful who you trust."

"I don't trust *you*," Phillip cut in. "I want to know how I can keep Stormy safe. That's all I want. For her life to go back to the way it was."

"As if that were possible, Sidhe."

"*Stop* calling me that," he growled. "And yes, it is possible. I'm going to *make* it possible."

She looked at him with a small, quiet smile, and said, "*You, my long, tall fairy, are no witch.*"

His eyes flashed in anger. "But I'm the wild card in this game and Stormy is the one holding the deck, right?"

"In a manner of speaking." Lydia fixed her eyes on him, a look of curiosity on her wrinkled face. "Though it's hardly a game."

"And if she hadn't brought me back, and I wasn't here, alive, walking upright-" he gestured to himself "-you'd leave her alone?"

"*I'd* have no reason to bother her," she said. "I can't speak for Guthrie, though. I assume-"

"I get it." Phillip stood again, pulling me to my feet with him. He turned to me, cradling my face in his hands, and suddenly pitched forward, planting an unexpected, tender kiss on my lips. Then he kissed both of my cheeks, his lips rough and hurried on my skin, pushed my hair from my face with his long, graceful hands, and smiled. His deep green eyes searched mine for a moment, full of tenderness and unspoken words, then he kissed me again, even slower this time, his mouth searching mine as if he was trying to find the answer to an unspoken question. I kissed him back, but my hands were on his shoulders, half-heartedly trying to push him back, to ask him what was going on, but the soft, sweet feel of his mouth against mine was too much to resist. Lydia was watching us. I could feel the heat of her gaze as Phillip finally pulled away, his eyes still on mine, the expression on his face both sad and resolute. I opened my mouth to ask what he was doing, but his look silenced me; his eyes said *no*. He stared at me, silent, for a few beats, his eyes moving all over my face, seeming to memorize me, and then he bit his lip and turned to Lydia.

I watched as Phillip reached in his pocket and produced a pair of kitchen scissors, ones I recognized from his old family house. I'd seen them that morning when he'd cut open the bag of loose-leaf Earl Grey tea; always the damned tea. They were sharp and glinted in the sunlight as he held them up.

Lydia and I both looked at him, aghast. "You say bringing me back upset the balance," he said, reaching up and pulling his long braid – the braid I'd lovingly plaited with my own hands, infused with my love and care and yes, my magic - out in front of him, "so let's remove me from the scale." My eyes widened and my hands flew to him, but he was too fast – with one swift movement he opened the scissors, enclosed the long, messy black braid between the blades, and snipped. Lydia and I reached out, shouting, but we were too late. Phillip had just enough to time to blow me a kiss.

The braid fell to the porch soundlessly, followed by the loud *thud* of Phillip's tall, heavy body as he tumbled to the porch floor.

Nineteen

"Phillip!" I was by his side in an instant. His skin was clammy under my fingers, his eyes closed. I pressed at his face, pushed him, shoved him, shook him, but he didn't wake up. Lydia had said his hair was his armor and if he cut it, that was the end. It didn't seem possible that someone so large and strong and full of life moments ago could now be lying lifeless on a dusty old porch, all from cutting off his hair. But he wouldn't wake up.

"If he's dead, I swear I will-" I screeched at the old woman, who had stood up and was peering down at us, her face full of weary concern.

"He's not," she said, but her voice was shaking. "He breathes. See?"

I placed my trembling hands under Phillip's nose, and waited. Sure enough, I could feel a faint, shallow trace of breath on my skin. "Phillip," I said, tears prickling behind my eyelids. He was as still as a statue, and his skin was growing colder by the minute; too cold. "Phillip, wake up!"

"You must be a stronger witch than I realized," she said

thoughtfully behind me. "Cutting his hair should have ended the spell immediately, but he lives."

"Then why won't he wake up?" I moaned. "Oh god, Lydia, is he dying?"

"I don't know." Her words chilled me to the bone.

Then I knew. The knowledge just came to me – I could feel myself standing up, looming over him, my hands and fingers extending as if they were apart from myself, full of muscle memory and intention that I could barely control. Only I could wake Phillip, but I couldn't do it by shaking him or yelling in his ear. I would have to use magic. It didn't matter if I knew how or not; my body knew. My spirit knew.

I bit my lip and looked down at his silent form. His dark eyelashes were a deep contrast against the paleness of his face. He was fading fast. His skin had taken on an almost gray undertone. I needed to work quickly.

"He wouldn't want you to," Lydia said, intuiting my intention, her body stiff and tense beside me. I heard her lighting yet another cigarette. The smoke trailed around my face. "He cut his hair for a reason – to free you. He did it so quickly, without even a thought – it's what he wanted, to sacrifice. What love he must have felt for you."

"You're just saying that because you want the spell for yourself."

"That doesn't make it any less true, Fee."

"No."

"He didn't want to live the first time, either," she said, though her tone wasn't cruel. "Some people just aren't meant for this world."

"Shut up," I spat. I wasn't in the mood for her platitudes right now; besides, she had an agenda. One hell of an agenda.

She didn't reply, only stood there, hovering over me, watching as I thought fervently what I could do to save him. She offered no guidance, but I could feel her quiet presence beside me, could almost hear her wrestle with a thought, then come to a resolute decision. It was unspoken, hanging in the air –an invisible-but-solid reinforcement – Lydia was with me. She might not have much magic, but what little she had, she was pooling it with mine. Even in my frantic and distracted state, I knew this was extraordinary. There must be some hierarchy of magic; surely someone as old and experienced as her was at the top, and I resided somewhere at the lowly bottom – for her to put aside her own desires and cast her lot with me – well, that was something indeed.

But I didn't have time to think about it now; Phillip needed saving. I placed my hands on his cold skin and tried to infuse warmth into his body, but he was like ice I tried to formulate a spell, a prayer, but words failed me. As I cried in frustration, I heard the crunch of gravel on the driveway and didn't bother to look up. I knew it was Lee. Whether his mother had called him, or he'd just known, I didn't know. And for once, I didn't care. I stared down at Phillip's nearly lifeless form. Lydia was right, dammit, he *wouldn't* want me to do this; he'd said as much many times. If I hadn't done the spell, if I hadn't brought him back…He'd been blaming himself for everything pretty much since he'd drawn a fresh breath. I knew that making this sacrifice for me was him trying to even the score, to thank me for what I'd done by giving me a chance to live freely again. If I took that sacrifice away, would he be able to forgive me?

But if I didn't save him again, would I be able to forgive myself?

I set my mouth in a firm line, stretched my limbs and rolled my head, preparing myself. There was no choice; I had to save him. And it needed to be right away. Phillip's skin felt so cold; foreign, unnatural. He'd always been so warm. I had to get that warmth back, into his blood, his heart, his body. I wouldn't allow him to die again; if he hated me for it later, then so be it.

Bracing myself against any attack – physical or spiritual – I focused all my energy, imagining it forming into a bright yellow ball inside my chest, and envisioned propelling it outward, over my shoulders, down my arms and into my fingers, where it would flow forth into Phillip, setting his cool body alight, with golden, shimmering magic, warming him up and reviving his cold, still vessel. He didn't move. I crouched back down, gingerly putting my hands on his cold form, pulling his dead weight into my arms, murmuring silently. "Wake up. Wake up, Phillip." I cocooned him in the yellow light in my mind, imagining him blanketed with it, caressing his skin, his hair, letting it seep into his pores, infiltrating his very blood, his muscles, his bones. Reheating him. Reanimating him. Then I bent down and placed my lips to his – they were ice-cold and turning blue – and let my breath mingle with his own. I pictured a perfect storm; a meeting of cold and warmth, icy blue breath and golden, warm life.

"It's not too late to stop, Stormy," Lydia cautioned, and I felt a warm hand touch my shoulder. I ignored her. "He doesn't want this. He didn't then and he doesn't now."

"Then why are you helping me?" I asked.

She sighed. "Because I can't not help you."

"What's going on?" Lee was stepping onto the porch. "Ma, what's going on?"

"I've told them everything. Phillip did the noble thing and took his exit," she explained in a low voice. "And now poor little Fee is trying to bring him back – *again.*"

"She can't do that," Lee said, stepping over to me. My lips were still pressed to Phillip's, and I didn't look up. I barely registered them talking. I was still holding him in the light, afraid to let it go for even a moment. "Can she?"

"Let her try," she said, stopping him from moving toward me. Her voice had taken on a dreamy quality. "It won't come to anything but let her try. It's been so long since I saw another witch at work. Can you see her aura? It's so golden! Oh, she's so much more powerful than I-"

I felt a sudden *zap* in my fingertips, reminding me of the feeling I'd had when I'd touched the electric fence that housed the cows when I was little. A feeling of pure power, traveling through my fingernails with a jolt; not painful, just...*big*. It flew out of me and seemed to form into a ball, much like the one I was imagining in my head, aimed at Phillip. I watched, transfixed, as the odd ball of light hovered in front of my eyes for a moment, and then suddenly traveled backward, shimmering and quick. The next thing I knew both Lydia and Lee were in a heap against the front door, and the disconcerting smell of sulfur was in the air.

"What did you *do?*" I heard Lee's voice rather than saw him. I was still focusing all my energy on Phillip.

"Oh, Goddess." Lydia's voice was small and seemed to contain both awe and revulsion.

I laid Phillip's head down gently on the porch, and stood up, facing them. They were still huddled against the front door. My hands *ached.* I looked down to discover that the tops of them were bright red, like a bad sunburn.

I looked at Lydia helplessly. Her wide, shocked eyes stared back at me. "What did I *do?*" My voice was a croak.

"I don't know," she said, her voice shaky. "Fee...oh Fee... you are a very powerful witch."

I stared at her in horror.

"Ma," Lee spoke up, scrambling to his feet, offering her his arm. Had my power actually blown them backward into the door? Could I have really done that? "We need to get you inside. We need to call the police. He, uh...he's still..."

"Give it a moment, son," Lydia said, taking hold of his arm and rising on her shaking, weak legs. "See what she's done."

I was afraid to turn around. Instead, I stood there, trembling, watching as they looked past me, their eyes wide. I heard him before I saw him.

"Stormy Spooner." My eyes closed at the sound of his voice, low and measured, but full of gravel. With a deep, shaking breath, I turned to face him.

Phillip was standing behind me, his newly shorn hair a messy halo around his head, his cheeks flushed red with life and vigor, his face absolutely murderous.

Lydia had hobbled back toward the door, pulling her oxygen tank behind her. "Lee, help me inside." Her voice was a wail. "He'll blame me for this, and I haven't the strength… help me inside, son."

Phillip's hair was in spikes all around his ears, still black as ink, but with a sheen it hadn't had before. He ran a hand through it, feeling it, realizing the scope of what had happened, and his eyes turned dark. "Listen to your mother, Lee," he said, his eyes never leaving my face. "Quick. Before I change my mind."

The door slammed behind them. I heard the deadbolt turn. The porch was suddenly eerily silent. I rushed to Phillip, gingerly stepping over the shorn braid, my exhausted arms ready to embrace him, but he stopped me with a raised hand. I might be the one with the magic, but his raised hand held all the power and fury of a resurrected god, and I stopped in my tracks, feeling my cheeks burn so hot they might as well have burst into flame. Phillip's darkened face was full of barely controlled rage. He could pull a bolt of lightning from the sky and smite me with it, and I'd have no trouble believing it at all.

He took one last look at me, his eyes flashing with fury, his other hand clenched by his side, and wordlessly turned and walked down the steps, his heavy boots thundering on the old, rotting wood underneath. He walked past the pickup, his newly short hair whipping around his ears from the force of his movement.

I rose my shaking voice and called to him, feeling tears starting in my eyes. "Phillip, where are you going?"

He didn't answer. He'd already reached the front gate and turned to walk out into the street. Fuck, he wasn't going to take the truck?

Without turning, he reached into the pocket of his black jeans, pulled out a wad of metal keys, and tossed them backward onto the grass.

I stared open-mouthed behind him as he walked down the road, his black combat boots thudding against the concrete, hands jammed in his pockets. The brilliant, golden sunny sky of an hour earlier had gone; the horizon behind him had turned a cold, defeated gray, and a low, rumbling thunder had begun far off in the distance. Another storm was coming, right on time. Phillip disappeared down the sidewalk, fading into the trees as I stood there, still watching, seeing nothing but the gray sky. I turned toward Lydia's front door, wishing stupidly that she'd come out and tell me what to do, offer me some comfort, anything. The curtain in the window moved ever so slightly.

"I told you he didn't want it, Fee." Her weary, haggard face appeared in the dusty window, full of a million different expressions. "May the goddess have mercy on you. And me." I took one last look at her, stepped off her porch with a sigh, and walked to my truck, alone, wondering if Phillip Deville would ever, ever forgive me.

TWENTY

I sat in Jason Langley's kitchen, clutching a cup of tea I'd made for myself. I didn't want it, but I needed comfort. Nothing had gone as expected. Not just today, either. Nothing had gone as expected this entire time, ever since I'd done the stupid spell and set the whole mess in motion. Shit, if I really admitted it, things were going wrong even *before* that. I couldn't remember the last time I'd made a responsible, *good* decision.

Every time I thought things might be going back to normal, something else happened, and it seemed that no matter how hard I tried to do the right thing, I kept doing the wrong thing instead. Was that the curse, the underside of all the magic? That I became a total idiot?

What *had* I expected, exactly? For Phillip to fall into my arms with gushing thanks? I kept hearing Lydia's small voice from behind me on the porch, "I told you he didn't want it." She was right. Every fiber of Phillip's being had made that clear to me. I'd disregarded his choice and brought him back anyway - used more black magic, which of course would have consequences - and now he probably hated me. I'd never forget the awful look he'd given me before turning to stalk off into the evening. I'd never seem him look like that, and never wanted to again: an overwhelming mixture of fury, disappointment, and absolute heartbreak. The way he had loomed over me, his fists clenched, his face dark. There had been no love on that face, not for me.

Maybe releasing Phillip *had* released the love we'd come to feel for each other. Or maybe he'd done it when he'd taken those scissors…

Or maybe it was just as simple as I'd disregarded his feelings and broken his trust, and that was reason enough.

I sat at the little kitchen table, my fingers working over themselves nervously, waiting. I'd been sitting here long enough to make two cups of tea that had both gone cold. Jason had come in and placed a kind hand on my arm, saying nothing, and had retreated out onto the porch, his usual hang-out place, realizing I didn't want to talk. At least, not to anybody but Phillip. How long would he make me wait? It wouldn't surprise me if he didn't come back at all.

I heard voices on the porch and turned my head to listen. I heard heavy footsteps, then the unmistakable low, deep voice of Phillip. My heart began to pound, and I stood, walking over to the sink to rinse my cup, needing to do something, anything, with my damned hands, the hands that had taken over and done their magic and made Phillip hate me. I heard the front door open, his boots hitting the welcome mat, and the sounds of him rummaging around behind me. I sat the cup on the drying mat, squared my shoulders, and finally turned around.

Phillip was sitting at the table where I had just been, his head in his hands. I couldn't see his face because his back was partially to me, but I could tell by the way his broad shoulders shook, the way he kept pushing one hand to his eyes in a furious, boyish gesture, that he was crying.

The silence was unbearable, but I stood by the sink silently, giving him time to collect his thoughts, giving him the space and respect I'd refused him before. I watched him as he sat there and cried, wishing I could see inside his head the way he saw in mine, wishing I could ease some of his pain. Finally, he stood and whirled to face me, and in the harsh light of the old-fashioned kitchen, he seemed even taller. His dark hair, newly shorn, fell over his ears in an unruly mess. It suited him, gave his eyes an even wilder look, framed his chiseled face in just the right way. He was so damned handsome, even trembling the way he was, even with tear-streaks on his rugged cheeks. I began to shake. I'd never seen him so wild, so undone.

"You brought me back," he said. "Again. Why? Answer." The way his voice boomed, the clipped intensity of his questioning, made me shake harder, but then I collected myself, raising my chin and eyes to face him head on, a sudden anger rising up in me.

"Don't talk to me like a fucking child," I said hotly. "And why do you think?"

"You knew I didn't want you to," he said, his gaze unflinching despite his watery eyes.

"Maybe you don't get to decide everything," I countered, walking over to him.

"When it's my life, I do."

"And my life? Is that of any consequence? Do you think you can just exit stage left and leave me to pick up the pieces?"

Stalemate. We stared at each other, both breathing heavily, as though we'd been in a physical altercation, when in reality, there were yards between us. His eyes were wet with tears, but his mouth turned up in the slightest smirk. He was still angry, oh yes, he was so angry he could spit, he could hit something, break something. Instead, his green eyes bore through me like liquid fire. I stared back at him, defiant, daring him to say one more thing, to question my motives, to question my love for him and the depths to which I'd go to keep him alive.

It took him less than two steps to get to me, and then his arms were around me, crushing me against the counter, my arms splaying out, accidentally knocking over the cup I'd just rinsed. It hit the floor with a clatter but didn't break, and Phillip picked me up and carried me to the stairs, his mouth already on mine with a fury and a passion I'd never felt before.

I was halfway to swept away, but I managed to pull back, putting my hand on his chest, making him stop. "No," I said fiercely, pushing at him. "Put me down."

He deposited me on the step immediately, his expression puzzled. "I'm sorry," he said, his fury gone, his voice uncertain. "I thought you wanted-"

"I do," I said, my hand still on his chest, my nails scraping at the skin through his thin black shirt. I let my fingers trail down, finding his nipple, running my nails over it. "But I'm capable of walking myself up the damn stairs, Phillip Deville."

His mouth curved into a smile, and I knew I was forgiven.

PHILLIP ROLLED OVER IN BED, clutching a pillow to his naked chest, and asked softly, "How did you do it?"

"I don't know," I answered honestly. I lay in bed beside him, pecking at my phone, sending another text to Sloan. I still hadn't heard from her. I didn't know whether to be hurt, pissed off or worried. Either she was ghosting me, which would be truly shitty at a time like this, or something was wrong.

"Surely you must remember what you did, or at least a little bit," he said, reaching over to push my hair behind my ear. "I just want to know. Lydia was so sure it'd be permanent, and in, like, five minutes, you brought me back. Again."

I sighed, putting down the phone. "You should have seen the look on her face, Phillip," I said, loving the feel of his hand in my hair. "She was shocked. She didn't know I could do it, either."

"So what'd you do?"

"I just…like…" I positioned my hands to show him what I'd done, and described the ball of golden light, how I'd focused on enveloping him in it. "All I know is it *felt* different this time. Back home, when I did that spell, I had no sense of it working. I just felt silly afterward. But this time, I could feel the light building up, I could feel it responding to me. It was all unconsciously done. I didn't recite anything; I wasn't even thinking clear words. I was so frantic. I just sort of…sent it – the feeling, the magic, whatever… - toward you." I cleared my throat. "You're welcome, by the way."

He chuckled. "I'm still not quite at the point where I'm willing to thank you. It's just weird…I'm trying to under-stand." His eyes fell on me, the intensity of his gaze unnerving. "According to her, the moment I cut my hair, it should've been over. Boom, dead, you know? Lydia was very clear on that. And I knew, deep in my being, that it was true." He ran a large hand through its shortened length and sighed. "Remember how I didn't want to get a haircut back in Brunswick? I instinctively knew my hair was my protection."

"When you cut it, you hit the ground like a lead balloon," I said, shuddering at the memory. "So Lydia *was* right, in a way."

"Well, I hit the ground, and I was like, *out* or something, but I wasn't gone," Phillip said, his face thoughtful. "I could hear you, feel you. I felt your magic flowing into me, and it gave me strength. But it didn't bring me back because I was never gone."

Suddenly I knew. "It's because I released you," I said. "When I released you yesterday the magic left you. It was no longer in you, and therefore no longer in your hair. Remember when you said it felt so heavy? It's because all the lightness was gone, all the power." Lydia's Samson and Delilah comparison had been eerily close to the mark. I bit my lip, remembering. "And then, when I braided it...well, I kind of infused it, infused you...with my love. With warmth. I didn't exactly know what I was doing, but I...I think I put a protection spell on you." I remembered the feel of his hair in my hands, the feeling of *gold. Light.*

"So you cancelled out the old spell and put me under a new one."

"I think I did, yeah," I said sheepishly, putting my hands up in mock surrender. "Oops."

"Fuck," he said. "That's the stupidest shit I ever heard. Magic fucking hair. My life's a fucking joke. It's a goddamn b-movie straight to VHS."

I began to laugh.

"What exactly about this fucking situation is funny to you?" he demanded, suddenly angry again. He was still clutching the pillow to him as though his life depended on it.

"Honestly?" I looked at him. "All of it." I laughed. "The question is, what *isn't* funny about this situation? I just had sex with a zombie rock star with epic, magical hair. And I'm imagining you as a goth Charlton Heston in some biblical biopic, dressed in long, flowing robes."

He didn't crack a smile.

"Without all the guns," I added.

Still nothing. His eyes blazed and I shuddered under their intensity.

"You shouldn't have brought me back, Stormy. I was trying to help you. To save you. From them. To make all this right. You fucked it up."

"Good."

"I'm serious."

He glared at me. "Oh, just shut up," I said, grabbing the pillow from him and whacking him with it. "Stop pouting.

We've been over this already. Who are you to decide what's best for me, anyway? In the scheme of things, you're a week-old baby. And at the moment, you're acting like one."

His mouth fell open and he stared at me in shock. After a moment, he threw back his head and began to laugh. Then he pulled me to him and kissed me roughly on the lips. I started to push him away, still angry, then I caught his scent and lost all composure. On instinct, I put my hands up into his hair, getting a momentary shock at no longer feeling the long, silky strands. I was still so angry with him, and he was still so angry at me, but we couldn't stop kissing each other, devouring each other.

He pulled me to him, crushing me to his chest. "Do you know why I did it so fast? Why I just cut the fucking braid so quick without even looking at you a second time? Because if I hadn't, I never would have been able to do it. I couldn't bear the thought of leaving you, but I had to, to give you a chance at a normal life." His lips grazed my temple, both rough and soft. "You don't understand, Stormy. They won't leave you alone. Lydia might've taken a shine to you, but Guthrie…Lee…he won't ever…"

"He will." I sniffed, pressing my face against the warm firmness of his chest. "I'll make him."

"You can't," he said. "He's tied up in you, obsessed. It has something to do with your magic. It's like a scent to him, one he finds irresistible. I suspect that his fascination with you stopped being about his parents a long time ago."

I buried my face in his shirt. He was right. I knew it. I had known since before we left Jekyll Island, though I hadn't known why. It was a naked hunger, visible and obvious. An attraction that couldn't be denied. And if I was honest, there was a small glimmer of me that found Lee Courtenay attractive, too, enjoyed flirting with the danger. His pale eyes, the dotting of freckles that made him so impossibly boyish, even the air of self-loathing about him, it was all very attractive and familiar. I didn't want it to be, but it was like a moth to a flame; no matter how guilty I felt about it, no matter how dangerous I knew he was, I kept flitting by him, just enough to singe.

And now I knew why. I was a necromancer – a witch. The same magic that came alive when Phillip was near me was awakened when Lee was near me, too. Their very bodies spoke to the magic within me. The only difference between Lee and Phillip was that I loved Phillip. The base reaction, though, was the same. The thought gave me a shudder. It was magic, that's all. My magic mingling with his, trying to find a common ground. The real attraction, the real love, was right here in this room, with Phillip.

Lee meant nothing at all.

"Whatever it is," I murmured into his chest, "we'll figure it out. Together. I don't care about them." I looked up into his eyes, which were full of concern, but tenderness, too. "I want to be with you. If you want to leave, I will never force you to stay. But if you're going to leave, do it because you want to, and not because you think it's what's best." I wrapped my arms around his neck and pulled his face down to mine.

With a swift movement, he rolled me over and positioned himself on top of me, a small, curious smile on his lips. With the shorter hair, he looked slightly older and impossibly sexy. His green eyes flashed in the dim of the room.

"I hope you mean that," he said, putting his hands on his angular hips, "since you no longer have an escape route."

"What?"

"If I piss you off, which I inevitably will, you can't just take a pair of kitchen shears to my head." He laughed. "I'm here for good, it looks like. And if I'm here, I want to be with you."

I pulled him close to me, breathing in his familiar scent and nestling my head in his neck. His skin was so warm, and I could feel his pulse, strong and steady. "I love you, Phillip," I said again, grazing his skin with my lips.

He was breathing fast. His hands fumbled with my clothes, but he whispered, "Not just because I'm your favorite dead rock star?"

"That's only the main reason," I said, fumbling with his belt buckle. "There are so many other great ones to choose from. Like this one, for instance."

Then our clothes were in a heap on the floor and neither of us said anything else.

Twenty-One

THE PHONE RANG, SHRILL AND LOUD IN THE QUIET OF PHILLIP'S old house, the opening bars of *Bloody Good Fun* echoing through the room. I rolled over, groaning, cursing myself for not putting it on silent before falling asleep.

"Change that ringtone immediately," Phillip grumbled from where he was buried under a pillow. He unearthed himself and wiped the sleep from his eyes, his hair was sticking up all over his head, making him look about twelve years old, despite the heavy five o'clock shadow on his strong jaw. His eyes were as bleary as mine no doubt were. We'd stayed up half the night, talking and doing other things that definitely didn't involve sleep. "The last thing I need to wake up to is my own fucking voice. I always hated that song."

"It's one of your best," I said, giving him a sassy look, leaning over him to grab the phone off the night stand. His skin was warm, and I fought the temptation to pull him back down under the covers with me. I looked down at the phone; the number was unfamiliar, but the area code was for Jekyll. It was probably Sloan. Thank goodness — I was beginning to go out of my mind, not hearing from her. "Totally underrated. And I know your music better than anybody. I'm your biggest fan, remember?"

He muttered something sarcastic in reply and planted a whispery kiss on my shoulder, then was out of bed, pulling his black boxer briefs over his muscular thighs. I dared a quick glance and a wink, and then hit the green button with my finger. "Hello?"

"Stormy." The voice on the other end of the line was familiar. "It's Lee. Don't hang up."

"Jesus Christ, Lee-"

"I've left town," he interrupted. "And I don't want to bother you. I just...I wanted to check if you guys were okay – you…and Phillip."

"We're fine," I said, watching Phillip's retreating naked back as he walked into the little blue bathroom. All the tension had finally gone out of him, and he was standing straight, posture straightened, no longer weighted down. He was whistling the bars to a song I didn't recognize. Was he writing again? "Better than fine. We're leaving today. Not that it's any of your business. And I trust that your mother won't be bothering us anymore."

"I'm glad to hear it. And no, she won't. I'm sure you hate her, and I guess you have good reason, but she was just trying to...well. You know. She isn't a bad woman. But I guess it doesn't matter now. I assume you and Phillip are done with all your searching, anyway."

"For now, I guess," I answered distractedly. "We know about all there is to know about the spell, don't we? I can figure out the rest on my own. I don't hate your mother, for the record, but no offense, I'll be glad to see the back of all of you. Even Guthrie, though I've never met him." I sighed. "I hope I never do. I'm happily going back to Jekyll, out of all of your hair forever." I almost giggled at the word *hair,* which would forever have new meaning to me now.

There was silence on the other end of the line. I heard Phillip turning on the shower, the knobs squeaking, the pipes grinding on.

"Stormy." Lee's voice had lowered and sounded weird. "How dumb can you be?"

I bristled. "What are you talking about?"

"Guthrie *lives* on Jekyll Island." There was a pause. "You seriously haven't figured that out?"

I sat there in shocked silence, unable to speak. I had seen the area code right there on my phone but when I'd answered… Lee's phone was registered in southern Georgia. I'd met him at the Brunswick Farmers Market. He'd snooped around my house so easily because *he lived nearby.*

With his father.

Guthrie.

"Stormy?"

I stammered. "But your mother said she didn't know-"

"She doesn't. She doesn't want to know where he is; she's happier in ignorance, so I've never told her," he said. "But you should know the truth."

"All this time he's been there?" I was dumbfounded. "On *Jekyll?"*

"Yes."

"But..." I stammered. "Phillip and I drove all the way to Boston to find him! You knew where we were going and why! You let us go on a wild goose chase knowing all the while that he was back where we started?" My heart began to pound. "All that talk about getting back to Jekyll because I was safer there – you *lied!"*

"I had orders," he said.

"You lied," I repeated, desperate. "Or you're lying now."

"Who do you think hired Tess? How else would Guthrie know him if he didn't live nearby?" Lee argued. "Why do you think *you* of all people could tap into the spell? Did you think all of that was a coincidence? No, it's because of where you're from – your proximity to Guthrie." I noticed he didn't call him *Dad.* "You've never understood the scope of this. I tried to warn you…he's nearer to you than you could ever realize."

"No," I said, angry. This was supposed to all be finally over. "No."

Lee went on as if I hadn't spoken. "When Ma finally kicked him out for good, years ago, Guthrie went to live near his sister in South Georgia, my aunt. He's always wanted Mom's magic. She told him she'd hex him if he so much as came near her again. This thing with Phillip and the spell has been a bone of contention between them for over twenty years. So Guthrie has been trying to find other ways to tap into the magic all this time. He'll use anything – and anyone – at his disposal."

"How did he find me?"

"I don't know." Lee answered, and I sensed he was telling the truth. "I wish I did."

"Lydia told me," I said. "That you're…like Phillip."

He was silent for a moment before answering. Then in a quiet voice, he said, "It's true. I'm like Phillip – well, that's the only way I'm like him." There was bitterness in his tone. "But I wasn't talking about *me.* I was talking about you. And your loved ones. Guthrie will do anything to tap into the magic." His voice was tired, but also frantic. "Look, Stormy, ignore everything I said before. It's best for you to stay away. As in, stay away from Boston *and* from Jekyll. I love my parents, but I can't protect you from them forever."

"All this time you kept telling me to go back to Jekyll, and now you're changing your tune."

"That was before," he said, "Now that I know you plan to use your magic, it's different."

"I won't," I said fiercely

"Yes, you will," he replied. "Both Ma and I could see it in your aura, clear as day. Deny it all you want, but it shines in you." He paused, his voice tender. "If I'm being honest, I could see the shine right from the beginning, starting with the day I met you. You were glowing that day – really pretty."

Jesus, how stupid was I? I had run into Lee – literally –the same day I'd seen Phillip. He said he was visiting his aunt. And I suddenly knew, with absolute certainty, that his aunt was the Goat's Milk Soap lady. The woman who had sold me the bundle of sage. The one I'd used in the spell. I remembered seeing her holding out a delicate pink soap to Phillip, who had been watching me. None of this had been a coincidence. Fuck. FUCK. It had all been smoke and mirrors, to use Phillip's term. It had all been by design, all part of an elusive, enormous trap. None of us had any choice in anything at all, it seemed. It seemed that everybody in my orbit, in one way or another, belonged to Guthrie. "I'll never use magic again. Ever."

"Oh, Stormy." Lee's voice was tired and sad. "You can't un-ring a bell."

I ripped at the skin around my fingernails, my mind in a whirl. "Why me?"

After a moment, he continued, as though I hadn't asked the question. "I wish you all the happiness in the world. I hope to see you again, in this lifetime or another." There was a click and I dropped my phone in my lap.

As I heard Phillip's razor-velvet voice echoing among the spray of the shower, I looked down at the phone at my list of received calls, the Jekyll Island area code, and over to our already-packed bags, and let out a long sigh.

THE FIRST HOUR of driving had just been me sitting in my truck, hands gripping the steering wheel tightly, trying to swallow my tears. My undersized suitcase was sitting on the seat beside me, looking forlorn and small without Phillip's large black suitcase beside it.

Lucky for me, my cell phone was now working perfectly, and my GPS was telling me where to go, because I didn't have the first clue how to get from Massachusetts to Georgia. The furthest I'd even driven on my own was Fort Lauderdale, and I'd been nauseated with panic the entire time. I didn't do long distances. I make more brave souls, like Sloan, who have no logical fear of death, do all that shit for me. But this time I hadn't had a choice. Or had I? I supposed it didn't matter now.

Spotify was working now, too. Of course it was. The source of the disturbance was no longer there to interfere. I was listening to *God is Dead* by the Bloomer Demons, which was the absolute last thing I wanted or needed to hear right now, but it was my self-inflicted punishment.

I was doing the right thing, but the guilt in my heart demanded a punishment anyway.

He would never, ever forgive me.

My truck was making a horrible rattling sound and I prayed to a god I didn't believe in that I could at least make it back to Georgia before the thing finally died a slow and painful rusty death. If I could just make it home, if I could just get back – I could hopefully make everything right again.

Not right for me – no, I would never be right again, not without Phillip – but right for him, and even for Lee and Lydia, though they didn't deserve it. Right with the world, even and settled and no longer askew. Then I could crawl back to my shitty little trailer and live my lonely, divorced life with Blinken and my library books and try to forget that all this had ever happened.

As if I could forget.

I gripped the wheel even tighter, blinking my eyes against the oncoming dusk and fatigue that seemed to be making my vision blurry. It wasn't tears. I would not be shedding tears.

My phone rang. With a quick swipe of my finger, I muted the call without so much as looking at the number, and kept on driving, the music pounding in my ears like a lover's accusation.

Another hour passed, and I stopped at a gas station to fill up. It was one of those truck-stop gas stations with a greasy spoon built in, and I figured I needed to put something in my stomach to keep up my strength, so despite my better judgement I popped inside, wincing at the acrid smell of over-fried bacon and eggs cooked in butter. I slid into a booth and ordered a cup of coffee.

I rubbed at my bleary eyes as the waitress wrote on her pad. "Do you know if the apple pie is vegan?" I asked.

She blinked. "I'm not sure."

"Is the crust made with margarine or butter?" I felt like a burden, an annoyance. It seemed to be a theme with me lately.

She blinked again. "Margarine."

"I'll have a slice, then," I said. "Thanks."

She wandered off and I put my head in my hands, exhausted. I was tempted to just lay my head down on the Formica table and go to sleep, but I knew sleep wouldn't come. My nerves were frayed, and my stomach was doing somersaults. What was he feeling? Was he angry? Had he cried? Did he hate me or was he relieved? Despite by best efforts, my mind went back to the note I'd left in Phillip's old room, the note he no doubt found right after getting out of the shower. I'd left it on his suitcase, being sure he'd see it when he went to dig out his clothes.

PHILLIP,

I'M SO SORRY.

WHEN YOU SEE THIS, I'll already be gone. That is, if I'm able to get out of here fast enough. I hope I can because I know you'll try to stop me, and I can't let you do that. Thank god you take the longest showers of anybody I know.

I LOVE YOU. But you don't belong on Jekyll Island with me. When I did the spell, I never dreamed it would work. But it did. And now you're here with another chance at life. Bringing you back a second time was selfish. You were right to be angry. As long as you're with me, risk and danger will follow, and you deserve better. You really do. Seeing you in your boyhood home made me even more certain – it's where you belong, with your best friends and your memories and a chance for happiness.

I LOVE YOU, Phillip. But this is for the best. Please don't follow me.
    Stormy

THE WAITRESS SAT the plate and cup down on the counter with a loud clack and I almost jumped out of my skin. I sat up, rubbed at my eyes, and thanked her, pressing my debit card into her hand to pay the bill before she had a chance to walk off.

She tapped her pad. "I warmed the pie for you and put on whipped cream. We use the fresh stuff, none of that tub junk. I'll be right back with your receipt."

I stifled a groan, looking at the mound of fresh dairy cream on my now-ruined pie. I pushed the plate away with a sigh. The coffee was oily and bitter. It was no more than I deserved.

I wondered what Phillip was doing right now and bit the thought off with another sigh. I didn't deserve to know. Not after what I'd done.

I ROLLED BACK into town what felt like a hundred hours later, feeling like something the cat had dragged in. It was a miracle I hadn't fallen asleep on the road, but I'd managed, with the aid of five cups of coffee and a huge box of Swedish Fish that had tasted like plastic sadness. When I'd passed the "The Peach State Welcomes You" sign I had started to cry and had continued to sob for the next two hours. I was thoroughly dehydrated and half insane, but I was home.

As I turned onto the familiar road to my house, I was torn. What to do? Go home and sit in the silence of my little trailer? As though nothing had ever happened? The thought seemed impossible. I'd never be able to sleep, no matter how exhausted I was. My place might as well be filled with ghosts, for the last time I'd been there Phillip had been there, too, and I couldn't imagine walking back into that dark quiet, my old life, alone. Not after I'd left Phillip behind. I'd rather die.

I picked up my phone and dialed Sloan's number. It had been days since we'd spoken, and whether or not she was mad at me, I was pissy that she hadn't even bothered to update me on my cat. She was supposed to be watching him, and she knew what that damned cat meant to me. I prayed she'd finally answer and wouldn't send my call to voicemail. My little quip about her love life had been nothing compared to the shit she'd given me in the past…if she was seriously that salty over it, well, I couldn't help it. I'd been through hell; the least she could do was answer her damn phone.

I couldn't be truly angry, though. I was too tired. And too sad. And too lonely. Maybe she'd meet me somewhere and come home with me, or better yet, let me spend the night at her place. I really didn't want to be alone tonight.

She picked up on the second ring and all the blood rushed to my face in relief and surprise. "Hey."

"Hey." My voice came out a croak; it had been hours since I'd spoken, and I'd cried myself to the point of dehydration. "Where the hell have you been? I've been calling and texting you for days!"

"Sorry," she said, and paused. "What's up?"

"I'm on Piedmont Street," I said, brushing past her lackluster reply. Evidently no explanation was forthcoming. "Dreading going home. Are you at the house? I thought I might stop by."

"No, I'm not," she said. "Sorry."

"Oh." I waited for her to say more, but she was quiet. I took a shuddering breath, hating myself for being on the verge of tears, for wishing she sounded happier to hear from me. "Are you busy?"

"Not really," she said. I waited for her to ask why, but she didn't. Something definitely wasn't right. Sloan usually never shut up.

"Phillip isn't with me," I said finally, and the floodgates opened. I started to cry.

"Oh, honey." She clucked, after a beat. "Did you two break up?"

"Yes," I said, relieved that she cared, though I could hear something odd in her tone. "Can you come?"

"I'll meet you at your place," she said. Her voice was no longer clipped and cold, but she still sounded odd. "It'll take me a few though. I'm actually on Jekyll, so I'll have to go over the toll and everything. Twenty minutes?"

She was on Jekyll. Why? The only person she knew out there was Gus...ah. It all clicked then. Her shortness, why she wasn't seeing Dan, why she hadn't been answering my calls. She was back with Gus and was afraid I was angry with her. As if I could judge her, after all I'd done. At the moment, all I felt was relief at hearing her voice. I forgave her everything, right then and there. I just needed her. If I could just see her, talk things through, it would all be all right.

"Okay." I sniffed, trying to get myself together. "See you then. And thanks."

"Of course." She hung up.

I wiped at my eyes and began to drive home. I felt better already, knowing that she'd be there with me. The ache in my heart had grown with every mile I'd driven away from Phillip, and now that I was back home, back in my old town, my old life, without him, the pain was unbearable. It wasn't just being away from Phillip that was breaking my heart, but the knowledge that I'd betrayed him. Left him while he was taking a shower, in the middle of the morning, with a shitty, abrupt note that offered no real explanation. After all the things we'd said to each other the night before. After all we'd been through.

I hadn't seen any other way around it. When Lee had called and dropped the bombshell that Guthrie wasn't only alive, but living just a few miles away from me, something in me had snapped. I didn't know why I'd been used as a pawn, and I might never know. But it was obvious how very little power or control I had over my own situation where him and his odious family was concerned. I might never be free of them. But there was one thing I could control - I could keep them from Phillip, and I intended to.

I was going to confront Guthrie and do whatever was necessary. And I was going to do it alone.

But first, home. And Sloan. And a good night's sleep, if I could fall asleep. In the morning, I would work the rest of it out. I was going to secure Phillip's happiness – even if it meant I never saw him again.

Twenty-Two

At least dear Blinken had the good sense to be waiting for me, right by the front door as I shuffled in and flicked on the light. "Oh, my sweet kitty," I exclaimed, picking him up even though I knew he hated it, and nuzzling my face into his soft fur. He allowed me to hold him for about five seconds – a record for him – then wrenched himself free, sauntering into the kitchen with an irritated swish of his tail. "I'm sorry I left you," I said to him, my voice still full of tears. I deposited my purse and coat on the couch and followed him. "But it looks like Sloan took good care of-"

As I flipped on the kitchen light, I saw that I'd spoken too soon. Both of Blinken's bowls were empty, and he'd tipped over the large bag of cat food (I bought twenty-pound bags at Sam's to save money) and chewed a hole in the side; that wasn't usual behavior for him. He must have been starving and desperate to do that. I crinkled my nose, smelling the familiar strong ammonia stench of the litter box. As I pulled the sliding door to the laundry open, my suspicion was confirmed: she hadn't changed his litter in days. "I'm so sorry, Blink," I said again, picking up the plastic scooper from the peg with a sigh.

From the looks of it, she'd maybe only been over once to take care of him, if at all.

I'd left the front door unlocked when I'd shuffled in the house, bedraggled and exhausted, not giving a damn who followed me in. A serial killer could have crept right up behind me and dispatched me unceremoniously without a fight. I cleaned Blink's litterbox, gave him fresh food and water, and a few contrite chin scritches, and set myself to making tea. I needed something hot to drink to try and clear my head, to shake off the funk that had settled into me on the long drive home. The feeling of desolation, of rock-bottom, was so strong it made me physically weak.

Sloan slunk into the kitchen unannounced sometime after me, looking like a guilty ghost. "Hi," she said by way of greeting, sitting down at the kitchen table and regarding me with a wan smile.

I was boiling water on the stove since I'd never owned a kettle. I turned to her, knowing what a mess I was – puffy, irritated eyes, flushed red cheeks, greasy hair- and waited for the inevitable, "You look like shit" - one of her usual greetings. But it didn't come. She just regarded me with a wariness that put my already frayed nerves further on edge and sharpened my irritation to a fine point.

"What's up, Sloan?" I said tiredly, turning back to my water. "Sorry the place stinks." I turned to her with a pointed glare, but if she took any notice of my anger, she didn't acknowledge it. Christ, did she even remember that she was supposed to be watching my fucking cat? A little contrition would be nice, for once. "You know, since the litterbox was overflowing when I got home."

I saw a brief flicker of acknowledgement in her eyes, then it was gone. She raised her chin, oddly defiant. It unnerved me; I suddenly felt like we were in a battle I wasn't aware I was having. I turned back to my pot of boiling water, biting my lip.

"What are you doing?" she asked.

"Boiling water. For tea." I rummaged in the cabinet above me, sure I had some bags of black tea leftover from Tess. He had liked his sweet tea like every good Georgia boy.

"Since when do you drink hot tea?"

"Since now."

"I could make a pot of coffee."

"Not unless you want some."

"Okay." She didn't get up. There was silence in the kitchen while I poured the boiling water over the tea bag and let it steep, my bleary, tear-soaked eyes watching the dark brown tea pooling into the boiling hot water like ink. I grabbed a spoon and stirred in some sugar; too much sugar. Phillip had barely put any in. I remembered he'd told me if you brew a good cup of tea, you don't need the sugar. In a mad frenzy, I tossed the contents into the sink and started over, this time with no sugar, watching Sloan regard me silently.

I sat down across the table from my best friend, the two of us in our usual spots where we'd sat with each other for years and years. Didn't matter the table, this was always our position, across from each other, hands folded, a beverage in front of us – vegan fraps, wine, coffee, and now, apparently, tea – ready to lay our secrets bare.

But something had shifted in the time I was gone. We wouldn't be sharing any secrets this evening. The person sitting in front of me was brooding, bitter – and for some reason, scared. How had she undergone such a change, I wondered, when it had only been a few days? I could tell by the way she wasn't looking directly at me, but rather at a point above my eyes.

"Are they jacked up again?" I said, managing a small smile.

"Huh?" She was confused.

"My eyebrows," I said with a laugh. "You're staring at them."

"Oh." She let her shoulders ease a little and smiled back. "No. They're fine."

"Thanks for rushing over," I said. "I just didn't want to come back here alone. You know, after..."

Her face softened. "Yeah. I know." She reached across the table and gave my hand a nudge. "I could tell how much you liked him. I'm sorry. But hey, he was a rebound, right? That's what rebounds are for. Hot sex, adventures. And then you move on to the next *real guy*, right?" She smiled at me kindly. "I'm sure he's just around the corner."

Her choice of words poked at me. Real? That didn't even sound like Sloan, but at any rate, it wasn't comforting and wasn't welcome. I'd just left Phillip the day before, for Christ's sake. And she'd known me my whole life. She knew what the man meant to me. Even without the context, she had to know that I'd be devastated. But I kept myself in check. She probably hadn't meant it the way it sounded. "Yeah," I said finally, taking a sip of scalding tea, not caring that it burnt my tongue. It was flat and bland, and I wished I had a cup of Earl Grey, Phillip's tea, with its comforting, floral bergamot. "What about you and...Dan? Are you okay?"

"Oh, yeah," she said absently, picking at an invisible crumb on the table. "We were never serious. It was just a few dates. I mean, I liked him but..." She looked at me with a small smile. "He was a total bigot, so. I had to cut him loose."

She was staring at my eyebrows again. I had known Sloan for twenty something years. I knew when she was lying. But I said nothing. Maybe the pain was simply too great, like mine was, to elaborate on it. Maybe she was trying to be strong for me. "Okay," I said softly. I didn't have the energy to push further, and I hoped she felt the same way.

The silence at the table became a chasm. Years of

comforting each other and suddenly we felt like strangers. Was it me and all that had happened in the past few days? Maybe it was coming off me like a cancer and she could sense it. Maybe I was the problem. I pushed my cup of tea away and stood. "I'm so tired. I probably should go to bed, get some sleep. I'll be in much better shape to talk tomorrow." As lonely as I felt, I suddenly wished I'd never asked her to come over.

"Me, too." She yawned and threw her arms up over her head. "I'll bunk down on the couch."

"You know where the blankets are."

I was halfway to my bedroom when she called to me from down the hall. I stopped and turned, and her face was sad in the dim light of the living room.

"I really am sorry about Phillip." she said, and it was almost as if, for a split second, she knew everything.

"Thanks," I said, and went to my bedroom, shutting the door behind me.

Before settling down in my old, familiar bed, I pulled out my phone to see if I had any missed calls or texts. There was nothing. *Good,* I told myself, pulling the covers over my head. *I'm glad.*

Sloan would have been able to spot the lie easily.

"YOU ONLY JUST GOT BACK LAST night," Sloan said, spreading almond butter on a piece of whole grain toast. I poured us each a cup of coffee and sat in my usual spot, pushing the sugar bowl and the creamer toward her. I was in the mood to drink mine black. "Why do we have to rush out to the farmers market?"

"There's someone I need to see," I said, pressing the

steaming cup to my lips and relishing the burn of the ceramic on my bottom lip.

"Who?"

"Just a person I know." I wasn't sure how to explain to Sloan, not without telling her everything else. "Are you coming or not?"

"I will if you buy me a *pain au chocolat* from that cute Latino guy who bakes all the yummy vegan treats. What's his name? Juan?"

"Yes, it's Juan." I smirked beneath my cup. "And yes, I'll buy you one. I might buy myself one, too."

"You should," she said. "Didn't Phillip feed you? You look like you've lost ten pounds."

I blanched. She noticed my expression and frowned. "Sorry."

"It's okay." I managed to smile. I must really have looked rough - Sloan never apologized for shit. "I wasn't gone long enough to have lost weight. Though I had a hard time finding vegan fare. He did make me the most amazing spaghetti one night." My cheeks flushed as I remembered the spaghetti Phillip had started, then forgotten, because we were upstairs, wrapped up in each other. Jason had finished that spaghetti and he'd teased us about it during the meal. We'd toasted Phillip with good red wine and Phillip and Jason's wide smiles had both been so genuine, so full of joy, me sitting in the middle, just watching them, deliriously happy, while Phillip's hand had caressed my thigh under the table. "And anyway, it was Blinken who was apparently starving." I wasn't planning on letting it go, whatever she thought.

"Yeah, sorry," she muttered, having the good sense to look down at her feet. "I did feed him, but I didn't come as often as I should have. My bad."

My bad? Really? A few choice words sprung to my lips, but I bit them off with a placating smile, deciding it wasn't the time to start a fight. Later, though, for sure. The old doormat Stormy was gone for good.

Sloan regarded me with curious eyes.

"So are you going to tell me what happened?" she asked. "With Phillip?"

"Yeah," I said, letting out my breath in a long sigh, though it was a lie. Sad as it made me, I wasn't sure I wanted to entrust her with everything that had happened, with all my newly obtained secrets. "Eventually. What about you?"

"Same," she said. "Eventually."

And that was that. We finished our coffees, got dressed, and an hour later were in my poor, abused truck heading to Brunswick to the market, back where I'd started. The day was sunny, but the air was cold and windy. I could smell the salt in the breeze. The truck was still making the knocking noise and I made a mental note to check my funds and take it into the mechanic on Monday, if I could afford it. Along with the note that I couldn't bear to think about, I had also left Phillip's money sitting on his suitcase. I didn't want it. I never had.

What I wanted I could not have, not without bringing more trouble to the man who had dealt with enough of it already.

The market was surprisingly dead for a Saturday morning and Sloan and I didn't even have to stand in line to get fresh, warm chocolate croissants from Juan. Two more steaming hot coffees and a loaf of ciabatta later, we stood over by the picnic tables, wiping crumbs from our mouths. I handed her my little bundle wrapped in parchment paper. "I can't eat mine," I said, pushing it at her. "I don't have any appetite."

"But these are so fucking good," she protested.

"You go ahead. I can't." My stomach was doing somersaults.

"So who is this VIP we're here to see? The gluten free lady? Because if you think I'm going to start eating cakes made with chickpea flour-"

"No, it's not her," I said.

"Ooooh, I know. That cute avocado farmer you told me about. Yes! Get right back on that horse, that's the spirit! Where is he?" Her eyes danced. Gone was the weary, abrupt Sloan from the night before. I wondered, again, what was going on with her, why she was being so weird, so flaky.

"No, it's not him, either," I said. "But if I'd been smart, I would have jumped on that before...everything."

"There's still time."

"Nah," I said. "I'm not interested."

She rolled her eyes. "Fiiiiine. So who are we here to see then?" She popped the last bite of *pain au chocolat* in her mouth and licked the chocolate from her fingers.

"Her." I pointed down the middle row to the little table that held the goat's milk soaps, bundles of sage, bottles of random items – the "Pagan Priorities." Sitting in a folding chair with a green canvas was a stooping woman with long, red hair with streaks of gray, in two messy braids, and clad in a pink sundress – if I remembered right, the same one she'd been wearing when I'd last seen her, handing a delicate little soap to Phillip. I felt a pang in my chest. "If you want to stay here, I'll go talk to her. You don't have to come."

Sloan craned her neck, looking. "I don't even see who you're talking about. That row is so clogged. The lady with the hibiscus jam or the one beside her with the hemp purses?"

"Neither." I pointed again. "The Goat's Milk Soap lady – the one with the Pagan Priorities sign."

Sloan followed the direction of my finger, then went visibly pale. "Uh." She bit her lip with a little gasp and shook her head.

"What's wrong?"

She tried to recover herself somewhat. "You go talk to her. I'll stay here."

"Do you know her?" I asked. When she didn't answer, I asked again. "Sloan?"

"I need a bottle of water," she said, shaking her head again. "That croissant got stuck in my throat. I'll meet you at the truck." Then she was barreling out of the market and toward the parking lot, digging her phone out of her purse as she went.

I stared after her, baffled, and then shook my head and moved toward the makeshift table, squaring my shoulders. I'd worry about Sloan later - she was being weird as fuck, but I didn't have time for it right now. I was here, and I was going to talk to this woman and find out what I needed to know. I swallowed down the butterflies and took a deep breath, telling myself not to take any bullshit. I would take care of this once and for all. For me. For Phillip.

When I reached the table, I had to stand and wait while she bagged up four waxy, fragrant bars of soap for a woman in a hideous long, flowing dress that seemed to be made entirely from burlap. They exchanged a few pleasantries and my brain screamed, ready for this to be over with. If I had to wait much longer, I'd lose my nerve.

Finally, she was free, and turned to me with an impersonal smile, the one reserved for all her customers. Her eyes were the same icy glass blue as Lee Courtenay's, her face was covered in freckles, and her red hair was like spun gold. The family resemblance was extremely strong. I knew, if I ever met the infamous Guthrie, his evil-ass face would be covered in freckles.

"What can I get for you, hon?" she asked after a moment, those pale eyes fixed on my face.

"Do you know me?" I asked.

Her brow furrowed. "Did I sell you some soap a while back? The hy-absinthe one? Or no, wait. I sold you some sage, right? Not too long ago?"

"Well, yes," I said. "You did. But I wondered if you knew me...if you recognized..."

She stared at me. She really didn't seem to know, or she was the best liar ever. I decided to just out with it.

"I know your nephew," I said. "Lee. And in a manner of speaking, I know your brother, too. We haven't met, but he and I are...we know of each other."

"Guthrie?" She blinked dumbly. "You two are friends?"

"We aren't friends," I said firmly. "But I have business with him. I need to see him. I know he lives with you – Lee told me. Can you tell me how to get in touch with him? It's important."

She shook her head rapidly; her hair flew around her face. "I'm afraid not, hon. I don't just go around giving out my address and phone number to people. I don't know you, you see. And my brother wouldn't appreciate that. He is a very private man."

"I understand," I said, trying to be patient. More flies with honey than vinegar. "But as I said, Lee is my friend."

"If Lee is a friend of yours, can't you just ask him?" she said.

I didn't have an answer for that. I decided to try another tack.

"I have things of an, er, delicate nature, that I can't discuss here." I gestured around us. "I think you must know what I mean."

Her dumb stare gave nothing away. Her eyes were as fierce and unwavering as diamonds. Suddenly her face didn't look half as kind.

"I think they may be in danger. I need to warn them. But I can't do that if I don't know how to get in touch with them."

"The best I can do," she said, with a conspiratorial whisper, leaning toward me, "is pass on your information to *them.* Maybe Guth or Lee would call you back. Beyond that, I'm sorry, but I can't help."

"I guess that will have to do." I sighed. They already had my information. They knew where I lived, my phone number, everything about me. They'd followed me all the way to Boston. But I still dutifully scribbled down my cell number on a business card and pressed it into her wrinkled hand. "Just tell them it's important – and um, tell them -" I thought for a moment. "Tell them I'm on my own. That it's just me. They'll understand."

She stared at me for a moment longer, then put the card into her apron pocket and turned back to her soaps without another word.

I stood there for a second, waiting for some other confirmation, a word of goodbye, anything, but it was as though I never existed. Finally, I turned on my heel and left her table, and stalked out of the market, back toward the truck where Sloan was waiting for me.

I was halfway to the car when I stopped, just before reaching the parking lot, my heart suddenly beating fast.

What had his sister called him? Guth? I'd heard him called by that nickname once before, when Phillip had said it. I hadn't paid it any mind at the time, but it had stuck in my memory. It was short for Guthrie, obviously, but it was a weird nickname, one you didn't hear often. It was closer to a term of endearment, something a loved one would use. And it was definitely a rare name for a person, something that you'd not be likely to forget. If someone wanted to hide their involvement with a guy like that, they'd likely change the name to something a little more innocuous.

I stood there, biting the inside of my lip, my blood feeling like ice in my veins, realizing that *Guth* sounded an awful, awful lot like *Gus*. And then I was running, as fast as my legs could carry me, back to my truck.

Twenty-Three

Sloan was silent as I began the drive back to my trailer, and the paleness hadn't left her face. I looked at her out of the corner of my eye, deliberating. Her profile was the same – same old Sloan. Any person who happened upon the two of us wouldn't think anything was amiss; just two old best friends out for a drive, enjoying the comfortable silence between them. But I knew better. I could feel her tumultuous emotions under the surface of her decorum.

I held off speaking for as long as I could, trying to stay calm, to formulate some kind of plan, to make sense of everything. I made it three miles down the road before I couldn't take it anymore. I decided to play dumb at first. "Sloan, what's wrong with you?" I asked. "You're not yourself. Did something happen when I was gone? Other than you breaking up with Dan?"

She shook her head. "No." She was staring out the window like an angry, sullen teenager. I pressed her.

"Come on, Sloan. I know you better than that."

She started to say something in protest, but then her phone rang, the familiar bars of Aerosmith's "Love in an Elevator" blaring loud in her pocket. She pulled the phone out with a groan and hit the silent button. She shoved it back in her pocket and resumed staring out the window. She clearly couldn't wait to get out of my vehicle. I'd not only lost Phillip, but I'd lost Sloan, too. I set my mouth in a firm line, beating back tears. When had it happened? When had she turned on me? And why?

Lydia's words came back to me, her warning. The death card in the tarot. The death of a relationship...a betrayal of trust...The signs had been there all along, and I'd ignored them. I had assumed it meant my marriage, or even losing Phillip. I'd never thought the dying relationship would be mine and Sloan's.

I decided when we got back to my house, I'd open a bottle of wine and just lay it all out there, tell her I knew the truth, and then beg her to stop this, whatever it was. If she needed to come clean about something, she should. Before I had to find out another way.

Her phone rang again as I was wiping away one wayward tear, hoping she wouldn't turn and see. With a sigh, she pulled the phone out of her pocket and stared at the screen, deliberating. Finally, she answered. "Yeah?" I watched her fingers stray to the volume button and turn the sound down. She didn't want me to hear whoever was on the other end of the line.

She said nothing, only listened, giving a small nod now and then. Finally, she sighed, closed her eyes, and put the phone in her lap, then said, with her eyes still closed, "When you get to the light, head toward the bridge. We're going to Jekyll."

"Why?" I asked.

Her eyes were still closed. "He wants to see you."

"Oh," I said, unsurprised. "So it's all going to happen sooner than I thought. I finally get to meet the infamous Guthrie, aka Guth, aka Gus."

She opened her eyes and looked at me. "How long have you known?" she asked, her voice low and shifty. Her posture was tense and stiff, like a bratty teen who just got caught coming in late; I half expected her to open the truck door and fling herself out.

"Since about five minutes ago when I got to the parking lot and figured it out."

She looked at me in surprise. "You mean you didn't know before? Wasn't that the point of going to see Renee?" *Renee?*

"I knew she was Guthrie's sister," I answered. "But I didn't know that Guthrie and Gus were the same person, and I certainly didn't know that you were in cahoots with him this whole time to betray me."

"I didn't -" she started. "I never-" She flushed deeply. Apparently, I'd rendered her speechless for the first time in... well, forever. "Well, anyway, he got your message. And he wants to see you."

"Lucky me." I couldn't keep the bitterness from my voice. "It's all coming up Millhouse today, isn't it? I lose the love of my life and my best friend in a twenty-four-hour period. And now after weeks of manipulating me from afar, a drugged out, evil, crazy man is summoning me to his house. I can hardly contain the excitement."

"He isn't *evil,*" she said, swallowing. She looked guilty as hell. "I mean...I don't *think*...he doesn't want to hurt you or anything. He said he just wants to talk." She chewed her fingernail. "And anyway, wasn't that what you were hoping he'd do?"

I didn't answer. The truth was, I wasn't sure what I was trying to accomplish by advertising my presence to Guthrie. I only knew that I was tired of hiding from him, tired of Lee popping through like the Kool-Aid man every time I exhaled, telling me to go here or go there to stay safe. Coming home and "turning myself in," so to speak, had been an act of protection for Phillip more than anything else, though I did have a few ideas up my sleeve. Sloan didn't need to know about those, especially not now. Now that she'd betrayed me.

I turned onto the road that led to Jekyll and concentrated on driving. "How long have you known?" I demanded. It was getting dark. I flicked my lights on, a sudden sense of unease filling me. For two years she'd said as little about the man as possible, her affair with him the one secret she'd ever kept from me, and I'd just let her. I'd never pushed her to reveal more about him or asked any questions. My chest felt tight.

"Known what?" she asked.

"Who he was, what he wanted with me. About him and Phillip...and Lee and Lydia..." I stuttered. "All of it. How long have you known?"

Her face softened a little. "Just a couple of days, actually," she answered. "I'm sure it must seem...you must think I... But no, I didn't know. I tried so hard to keep you apart from him, because I was ashamed." She stared out the window again, but I could see her pained expression. "He did ask about you sometimes, but it was casual, like he was just showing interest in my life, you know? He said he wanted to meet you, but I always put him off. I was embarrassed. About what you'd think. He's so much older, and he deals drugs, and he's still married to his crazy ex-wife." I thought back to Lydia and smiled grimly. I could only imagine the stories Sloan had heard. "But I swear, Storm, I never knew that he had such a fixation on you. I never knew about Phillip, or the spell, or any of it. He kept me in the dark. He only told me about it the night you left. I went to see him that night and I mentioned that you'd gone to Boston, on a trip with some guy, and he hit the roof. He started screaming and yelling, and the next thing I knew he'd called in Tess and Shank and his son, Lee. He had us all lined up like little ducks, and he was screaming at everybody. I didn't know what was going on."

"Then what happened?"

"Lee pulled me aside and told me everything. He told me that he'd kept your trip from his father to give you time to get away. I didn't believe him at first – it all just seemed so crazy. But his story matched the one you tried to tell me, you know, the night we got pizza. He told me how Guthrie and his mom knew Phillip from back in the day, how they'd given him that spell, and how the two of them had basically been fighting over it ever since, with him caught in the middle. And then you did the spell and all hell broke loose."

"I know what Lydia wanted with us," I said bitterly. "But as for Guthrie, I'm still in the dark."

"You'll have to ask him," she said. "I don't know, either. But I do know he's obsessed with you. He knows so much, Storm. He's been watching you for a long, long time. He's had Tess feeding him info, and I didn't know it, but he was getting stuff from me, too. He's been grooming you for this from afar. He knew you were going to do the spell long before you ever decided to. It's so fucked up." That was the truth; I felt it in my bones. But how? It was impossible, but every cell of my body felt it was the truth.

"What happened after he got everyone together?" I asked, gritting my teeth.

"Guthrie sent Lee and Shank after you guys. He told Lee he'd better fix his mistake, or he'd answer for it. He sent Tess and Roberta, too." I wondered if she'd really known Roberta all along, had known Tess worked for her boyfriend, and just hadn't wanted to tell me. "Lee didn't want to go, he pleaded with Guthrie to leave you be, but he insisted. He told them to get you and bring you back here – without Phillip. By any means necessary." She swallowed. "Did you know that Lee was the one who knocked on your door that night when I was there?"

"I had assumed as much."

"He kept trying to warn you. He was so desperate for you not to do the spell. But when I answered the door, he bolted because he knew I'd recognize him. And then after you'd done the spell, he tried to warn you again. He wanted you to get away from Guthrie, but you wouldn't be any safer in Boston, really. Not with his mom there. He was really upset. He wants to see you safe, but he keeps fucking shit up. I think...I think he has a thing for you."

"Poor thing," I said, not bothering to hide the acid in my tone.

She didn't seem to notice. "Guthrie's been making me stay at his place in case you got in touch with me. I've been keeping my phone dead on purpose so I wouldn't get your calls and texts. After a couple of days, though, he noticed, and made me charge it. He changed, Stormy." Her face was wistful and sad, but there was something else there, too, something furtive and calculating. I wasn't sure if I was getting the whole story, the truth, even now. "He was a cool guy at first, but after a while he just wore me down. I tried to get out of the relationship, but he kept drawing me back. But nothing in the past two years compares to what he's been like this week. I never knew he could be so...awful." She shuddered.

"I guess that explains why you totally abandoned my cat with no food or water," I retorted.

"I couldn't exactly get to your house, as I've just said," she shot back. "But he's fine, Stormy. He's a cat. He can take care of himself. It's not like you were gone a month."

"Still, you gave me your word-"

"Gus was basically holding me hostage, Stormy!" Her voice rose; she was almost yelling now.

"Did he hurt you in any way?" I asked, my heart softening a little bit. I could tell she was really upset.

"No," she said, "Not yet. I worry though, now that you know..."

"He's not going to hurt either of us," I said firmly. "I'm going to end this shit once and for all."

"He knows things about you, Stormy," she said. "Secret things, private things, things that only me and your parents would know. Like, from your childhood. Things about your parents, Storm, things you've only ever told *me*. And some things you've *never* told me. Things about you and Tess. He used me. He'd done all these things to try and, like, reel you in. That vinyl at the flea market, sending Lee to your house. I bet he got Renee to sell you stuff for the spell." Her voice wavered. "I never even made the connection until you dragged me to the farmers' market today. I never even paid attention, never noticed that Renee had a booth there. And I've been in the woman's house dozens of times! I've been such a fucking idiot. You must hate me."

"No," I said. "I don't hate you." *But I sure as shit don't trust you anymore, either.*

"It was Guthrie who ran us off the road," she said. "Guthrie and Shank."

That explained why the person I'd seen in the rearview mirror had kind of looked like Lee. I wasn't surprised. So Lee had been telling the truth when he said he hadn't done it. I smiled in grim relief; a small part of me had hoped he wasn't capable of real violence.

"After he told me that I realized, really realized, how big this all was. He could have killed us that night. Gus claims you have powers, powers that are like his or something, that the two of you together can...I don't know. I don't know what I believe. But I do believe he's obsessed with you. That he wants something from you. And he's willing to hurt you to get it."

"Why did he care if I did the spell in the first place?" I wanted to know.

"Why else?" she answered with an obvious shrug. "He wanted to see if you *could.*"

I wasn't sure what hurt the most. That this man who I'd never even met had involved my ex-husband, my best friend, or that he had hurt Phillip, all to get to me. And why?

"Turn onto Beach Road," Sloan said, gesturing. "Storm, I know what it looks like, but I swear, I didn't *know.* Gus can be shady, but I just thought it was the nature of our job, you know? I never considered he was actually, like, a *bad guy.* He always kept us in the dark, because-"

"What do you mean 'our job'?" I asked.

"That's how it started," she said miserably. "I met him at Beachy Keen, remember? He asked me if I needed money. I thought he was propositioning me at first, but then later..." She saw my stricken expression and rushed to explain. "I never did anything horrible, I swear, Stormy. I never hurt anyone. I just sold a little reefer for the guy. A pill or two here and there. And after a couple of months I told him I couldn't do it anymore. Just the weed." She looked ashamed. "I was just so *broke.*"

"But you were seeing him, too."

"Yeah," she said quietly. "There's something about him. I fell for it. I'm not proud, Stormy. But every time I tried to get out, every time I'd meet somebody new, somebody nice, it was almost like he – he sabotaged it. Every time. Like he had some kind of power over me, he could make everything just crumble in my hands. It's gotten to where I just don't even want to try anymore."

"I get it." I sighed. And I did. "But Sloan, it was goddamn shitty of you not to warn me about all of this. You couldn't have sent one text?"

"He threatened me," she said, her voice giving way to tears. "The things he said he'd do to you – to Phillip – to Dan – I couldn't risk it, Stormy."

"Is that why you dumped Dan?"

"Yeah," she answered. "I had to protect him."

Rage burned inside me. It was one thing to mess with me.

Another thing still to mess with the man I loved. But to find out the extent he'd manipulated and threatened my best friend? I would tear him limb from limb.

"Take the next right, Franklin Road," she said, wiping a tear from her eye. She really did look miserable. "And it's number 5099, on the left. Big blue house with white shutters. Five minutes, tops."

"That's right across from Driftwood Beach," I exclaimed. "Less than a mile from the trail I always take, near the dunes."

She stared at her lap, her face full of guilt.

Realization hit me with a jolt. "The man," I said, more to myself than Sloan. The memories came back to me in a flood. Out on the beach. The day of the storm. He'd been standing right there when that massive thunderclap hit, then the hail, then the bolt of lightning, striking a foot away from me, such a force of pure electricity that it had split the dead tree in half and thrown me into the sand. I had felt the force of it in my fingers, the current jolting through my hands like scalding-hot water, like a child touching an electric fence. Guthrie had been there, off in the distance. Standing, watching. Had he *made* it happen?

I knew, suddenly, without a doubt, that he had.

Sloan's voice was quiet in the dark car. "I'm sorry I didn't believe you, Stormy. About Phillip."

"Oh, that's okay," I said. "Who the fuck would have?"

"I thought you had lost your fucking final marble," she said. "I really did. I was ready to ship you off to the funny farm."

"I wish you had," I said. "While I still had a chance to get away from all of you."

I'D EXPECTED some huge monstrosity covered by dark trees, with peeling paint and haunted, dark windows, like a smaller version of Hill House, or something out of a southern gothic mystery, but Guthrie's two-story home was the same cracker box house with a garage underneath, high, reinforced porch and palm trees in the yard as every other beach house on Jekyll. I parked the truck under one of the trees and got out, not bothering to take a moment to collect myself or even think about my game plan. I was too angry, too eager to see this man, look him in the face and tell him exactly what I thought of him.

Sloan led the way up the creaking steps to the top of the porch. I followed, looking around, memorizing my surroundings. The shades on the windows were drawn, but I could see a dim light peeking out. The sounds of a football game were coming from the house, and I could hear voices. A scraggly, skinny black cat with one white patch on his chest darted out of our way as we reached the front door and scurried off the porch.

"That's Tito," Sloan said, and then lightly rapped her knuckles on the front door, which had recently been painted white – I could still see the streaks of gray underneath.

"Who?" a curt voice on the other side of the door asked.

"Me," answered Sloan in a voice unlike her own. It seemed her rudeness was in place here.

"Come in."

She pushed the door open and turned to me with an "after you" gesture. I was suddenly without desire to go inside, after everything I'd done to facilitate this meeting, but I squared my shoulders and went in anyway.

I was standing in a small living room, filled with blue-suede couches that were faded and worn and covered with cat hair – from the scraggly beast I'd seen outside, no doubt – and two men sat on the biggest one, facing the TV, both holding

Xbox controllers. The football game I'd heard outside was not an actual game, but rather a video game. One of the men playing was Lee, his light-blond hair shoved under his usual baseball cap. The other one, with a large stick-on bandage covering the bridge of his nose, was Tess. When I entered the room, Lee put down his controller and turned to me with a large smile. Tess did not acknowledge my arrival. For the first time, I felt no pain in his presence.

"Hi, Stormy," Lee said, his voice welcoming but his eyes giving away his wariness. He had warned me to stay away, and I had ignored him. I found myself smiling at him, genuinely glad to see him despite the circumstances. I opened my mouth to speak to him, then the man standing near my right shoulder, half hidden in the hallway, caught my eye. I turned and looked at him, my chest filling with dread.

So this was Guthrie. I squared my shoulders and evaluated the man. He was short, shorter than I'd imagined, though that shouldn't be a surprise since Lee wasn't that tall, either. I guessed his height at maybe 5'10, 5'11 on a good day, since I myself was 5'9" and we were practically eye to eye. He was balding just at the top of his head, but what hair he did possess was a ruddy golden-red, much like his sister's, with a brushing of white at his temples. His beard was also reddish, but his eyes were that same icy blue as Lee's, and he had that same smattering of freckles all over his face, just as I'd suspected. His eyes were a disconcerting shade. In certain lights, it was almost as if the eyes had no color at all, devoid completely of emotion and feeling. I'd only seen it in glimpses with Lee, who was always amiable and charming, even in the most stressful of situations, but with Guthrie, it seemed to be his natural state. Those eyes had no feeling as they looked me over, and despite the warm smile his mouth was making and the jovial, familiar way that he extended his hand to shake mine, I knew without a doubt that this was a very, very bad man. He might look a little like his son, or an aging, genial Opie Taylor, but he was not a nice man, a good man. I shook his hand and suppressed the shudder that went through my body when his skin touched mine.

"So you're Stormy Spooner," he said with friendly grin. "Finally, I get to lay eyes on the woman who has entranced everybody I know."

What utter horseshit. I smiled benignly. "But you've seen me before, haven't you? Just across the road, on the beach? Remember? The day of the storm?" He shook his head, feigning confusion, never losing his smile. "The infamous Guthrie. I can't say I know your last name."

"And I can't say that I want to tell you," he said with a laugh. "I prefer just Guthrie. Or Gus, if you want." He had a lisp. When he said "Gus" it sounded like "Guth." Now it made sense, though I wondered how anyone – Sloan, Phillip, Lee, or anyone else- had felt comfortable enough to tease this man with a nickname. Everything about him – his posture, his eyes, his very aura – was oozing with malignity. And yet, I wasn't afraid. Not anymore, when I had nothing else to lose.

I looked him over with cool eyes. "I met your wife," I said.

"I apologize." He laughed again. "She's not a very warm person. And I heard that she made things a bit difficult for you." When I didn't respond, he put a hand on my arm, to try and disarm me. My skin tingled where he touched me, and it wasn't a pleasant feeling.

"Can I sit?" I asked coolly, gesturing to the couch where Lee and Tess were perched, and he nodded.

"Of course you can. I know you must be tired. I heard you drove all the way from Boston yesterday." He leaned past me to embrace Sloan quickly and gave her a kiss on the cheek. I clenched my fists; I wanted him to keep his hands off her, though she made no indication that she was uncomfortable.

"Hi, darling. Can I get you both a drink? I've got beer, wine, water, tea..."

"Did you want a tea, Storm?" Sloan asked me, a wide smile on her face. "I can make a pot."

"No, thanks," I said, walking over to the love seat and sitting down so I was catty-corner to Lee and Tess. I wanted to keep my eye on the door at all times. "I'm good."

"I'll take a beer," Tess said, tearing his eyes from the video game, but he still didn't look at me. He was trying his hardest not to from the looks of it. I stared at him warily; any love or desire I'd felt for him had finally shuffled off to die. What I was looking at was a coward - a shrunken, dejected, shell of the man he used to be. I pitied him.

Sloan ignored his request and so did Guthrie, who had sauntered over and took a seat beside me. Sloan sat in the corner in a burgundy colored easy chair with a blue afghan. She curled her legs up under her, obviously familiar with this house, comfortable here, but she looked so miserable and frightened that I couldn't bear to look at her. She was going to make me lose my nerve.

Guthrie took no more notice of her than he had of Tess. He only had eyes for me, it seemed. "I'm glad to finally meet you, Stormy. But I must say, I'm surprised you reached out to me. After all this time, trying to see you under cover of darkness, you come right out into the light. What brings you here? What can I do for you?"

I took a deep breath. Now or never. Might as well lay it all out there. I was sick of these people. I wanted to go home and sleep for two weeks.

"I have a proposition for you."

"You do?" Guthrie didn't look surprised.

"Yes." I steeled myself and dived in. "I think I know what you want from me."

He smiled. "And what's that?"

"Access to me, my power...whatever you want to call it," I said. "You want to see what I can do – paired with you." I looked him square in the eye. "And I'm prepared to give you that."

"Are you?" He smiled. "I'm a bit surprised. I thought you were quite uneager to-"

I cut him off again. "Don't you want to know my terms?"

"By all means."

"You'll leave them alone. Forever. Forget they exist." He stared at me, emotionless. "You'll release Sloan from your employment, and from whatever...relationship you've got her trapped in. You'll get out of her life for good." I gestured to Lee. "And him, too, if that's what he wants. I know he's your son, but he doesn't want to work for you, either. He's trapped between you and Lydia and he's fucking miserable." Out of the corner of my eye I could see Lee's shocked expression.

"What about me?" Tess piped up, finally acknowledging I was in the room. "You gonna release me, too?"

"No," I said, not bothering to look in his direction. "You're on your own." I heard a laugh bubble up from Sloan in the corner.

Guthrie was smiling through tight lips. "I hardly think-"

"I'm not done," I went on. "I imagine you know your wife Lydia is dying. And I'm sure you don't care." Sloan's eyes widened. "But if...when...she succumbs to her illness, I'd like to bring her back. It was what she wanted, and I'm prepared to do it." If he was surprised, he gave no sign. I felt butterflies in my stomach as I talked. It was only yesterday, on the long drive home, that I'd even begun to consider helping Lydia. I hadn't fully decided I would until I'd stood in Guthrie's foyer. Then I'd known, without a doubt, that I wanted to help her. Living with this man for years could not have been easy, and despite her gruff, abrasive demeanor and shady dealings, I knew she'd done everything she had to try and protect Lee.

Plus, I had a lot to learn, and who better to learn from?

"You've got quite a list of demands, don't you, doll?" he said smoothly.

"I'm not your doll," I spat. "Lastly, you'll leave Phillip alone. I want him to be free to live his life – a real second chance. It isn't his fault that any of this happened. He didn't ask for it, not really. He didn't know what he was asking. He's...*good*. But he thinks he's not, and that's partly your fault." I felt tears prickle my eyelids and willed them away. I didn't want to cry in front of this man. "I will need your *word* that you'll leave him alone – forever. Or the deal's off."

"My dear, you don't have the first idea of what you're talking about. You don't even know half of your own powers, much less mine. We need to sit down and talk about all of this before-"

"I don't care," I said, meeting his cold blue eyes. "I don't give one single solitary fuck. I know the most important thing. Me, my magic, whatever it is, is important to you. Important enough to stalk me, have me kidnapped, spied on through the people I love. I'm important to you. So make the choice, *Guth.* Me, or all your little henchmen."

"You just want me to release them all?" he asked. "And you'll give yourself over to me." I felt a chill as he said the words.

"Yes."

"I'll require a contract," he said after a moment. His face, somehow old and young at the same time, was thoughtful.

"Fine." I wanted this to be over.

He smiled a slow, chilling smile and stood up. "Give me just a moment." He left the room and I turned, triumphant, relieved, until I saw the looks on the faces of both Sloan and Lee, who were staring at me in horror. Even Tess looked vaguely uncomfortable.

"You don't know what you're doing," Lee said in a quiet

voice. "Stormy, rethink this. He's much more powerful than you know. You have no idea what he-"

"It doesn't matter," I said, shaking my head firmly. "I don't care. All that matters to me is getting the people I love out of harm's way."

"By putting yourself in our place?"

"If that's what it takes," I said steadily.

He shook his head, beginning to say something else, but was interrupted by a loud banging on the front door. Sloan jumped about a mile in the air. The four of us sat there, frozen in the living room, waiting for Guthrie to reappear and answer the door, afraid to move or breathe. Something had come, and it was *angry*.

Twenty-Four

The banging resumed, loud enough to wake the dead.

"Christ," Lee muttered after a moment, and wrenched himself off the couch, heading for the foyer. "I'll get it." He pointed a finger at me. "But we're not done, Stormy. You can't do this…this…madness."

The banging continued, louder now. "Fuck!" Lee reached the door and threw it open. "For fuck's sake, where's the fucking fire-"

He was literally thrown backward, landing on his ass in the hallway, dazed, as three men thundered into the room, the door going back on its hinges so hard it knocked a fist sized hole in the drywall. I shrank back instinctively, my hands going out in front of me.

He was by my side in a flash pulling me up off the couch with one arm, drawing my face forward to meet his glittering dark-green eyes, which were full of fury and fire. His black hair was wild, shaggy and unbrushed, and the five o'clock shadow on his jaw told me what I knew without a doubt – he had left his house for Jekyll before his hair was even dry, fresh out of the shower, my note folded into his pocket. He had come to find me the moment he knew I'd gone. *Phillip*.

He held the note out to me now, shaking his head, fixing a haughty gaze on me, eyes flashing. "If you wanted to break up with me," he said, pushing the note into my hand, "why didn't you just say so?" I caught the hint of a smile at the corner of his mouth.

"I…"

"Cat got your tongue?" he asked with a smirk. He hooked an arm around my waist. "Fuck if I'm going to let you get rid of me that easy."

"Oh, Phillip," I breathed, and threw myself into his arms.

Those strong arms closed around me, and for a moment everything else fell away. I could hear shouts – Lee, who had picked himself up from the hallway floor, and Tess, who had seen Phillip and immediately moved toward the door, a somewhat confused Jason Langley, who was trying to block a seriously pissed off looking Nathan "Ollie" Green, who had changed out of his business casual attire, from ripping Tess apart, and Sloan, who had jumped up from her chair in the corner and was pleading with someone.

I didn't register any of them. Phillip. Phillip. Phillip. I could smell him, feel him, and he was so real. How could it have been barely twenty-four hours since I'd last laid eyes on him? It had felt like a lifetime. And here he was, with me, holding me tight and I was damned if we'd ever, ever let each other go again.

But he was here to stop me. And I couldn't let him do that.

I pulled away from him, feeling the ache in my chest, unable to look at him but finding it hard to look away. I smiled and he smiled back. His face was full of so many emotions – fury, confusion, heartbreak, relief – but most of all, it was full of love. "I'm sorry," I whispered, leaning up to plant a gentle kiss on his lips. "I love you so much. But I have to do this."

"No. You don't," he started, but a shadow in the hall stopped him.

Guthrie emerged from the hallway, holding a stack of papers in his left hand. In his right, he held an old, tarnished looking gun, which he pointed casually at Phillip, as though he was showing it to him at an antique fair. "Nice to see you, Phil. Been a long time. But first thing's first. Stormy, come over to the table and sign the papers. And then your friends can be on their way. Unless..." He smiled, his cold eyes meeting mine. "Unless you've changed your mind."

"No," I said, pulling away from Phillip and walking over to him. "I haven't."

"She's signing her fucking life away," Lee said, his voice full of bitterness. "For you."

"And for you," Sloan reminded him. "And me. For all of us."

"'Cept for me," Tess chirped bitterly from the corner. "She don't give a fuck about me."

"It's just paper," I said, my eyes on Guthrie, who was still holding the gun, making me seriously uncomfortable.

"No, it isn't," Lee said. "It's magic. Those kinds of contracts are a whole other kind of binding, Stormy."

"Don't do this," Phillip warned. I'd never heard him sound so desperate, so scared. "Please don't. There are other ways we can-"

Guthrie was still pointing the gun, and dread pounded in my ears, a sense of foreboding thrumming along with my heart. The gun was going to go off...it was going to hit some-one...it was inevitable. I could read it, right there in his dark, ugly aura. I needed to make a move and do it fast.

"No," I said firmly. I grabbed the pen and stack of papers from Guthrie's outstretched hand, looking into his pale face. I couldn't control the laugh that bubbled up from my lips. "A blue Bic pen? Didn't you know that Phillip Deville, the sexiest fucking rock star on the planet, once famously signed his recording contract in his own blood? And this is the best you can do? How embarrassing."

I put the papers down on the wooden table by the wall with a flourish and braced it with my hand. I clicked the pen and bent down to sign. Guthrie stood over me, his shallow breaths moving my hair. I wished he'd back up. I could feel the eagerness coming off him like magnetic waves, the darkness of his aura hovering over me, mingling with mine like an oil slick on warm ocean water, making my stomach roll over. No time to read the contract. Fuck it, it was now or never.

I put the pen to the paper. I scrawled out a shaky "S." Then all hell broke loose.

Phillip was on me in a second, pouncing down upon me, ripping the paper from my hand and tearing it in half. He wrenched the pen from my fingers and snapped it in half, too. Then he turned. It was just a moment – his arms, raised, moving toward Guthrie, who had slunk back against the wall, his voice shouting, his oddly pale eyes flashing, his aura pulsing, and then a loud *bang*. My eyes widened, still fixed on Guthrie, shrunk against the wall, holding the gun out from him, the gun which he'd just fired, the gun he'd pointed at Phillip...

Then there was another, even louder bang, and I hit the floor.

Twenty-Five

"Stormy." Sloan's voice, full of tears, was near my ear. "Fuck, Stormy, come on. Wake up. Wake *up*." There were other voices, too, all of them frantic and scared.

"Give her a minute. Just one more minute."

"What are we going to *do?* If she doesn't wake up, we need to call an ambulance, the police..."

"Just give her another minute."

"Goddammit, does she ever eat?" Sloan again. "She's wasting away. I never see her eat. No wonder she faints at the drop of a hat..."

Then a voice, blissful near my face, full-throated and defensive. "I tried to give her some of my steak. I tried to buy her a Big Mac. It's not my fault I fell in love with a fucking vegan who lives on coffee."

"You could have taken better care of her-"

"Like you did? Lying to her all this time? You might oughta back up and give me some space."

"Is she gonna be ok? Y'all, Stormy ain't gonna die, right?" Tess. So he did actually still care, somewhere deep in there.

"I'm on parole, y'all. If I get busted in a house full of dead folks, I'll go to prison." Then again, maybe not.

"How many times did I warn her? I told her to get the hell away, for her own safety. Did she listen?"

"Stop making excuses and help me *get her up.*"

"Where the hell are you going, Tess? Oh, for fuck's sake."

"If she doesn't make it, I swear to Lucifer I'll-"

"What? Kill yourself a third time? Shut up and *help.*"

I opened my eyes.

Phillip was staring down at me with his beautiful, almond-shaped green eyes, his face full of worry and love and fury. Sloan and Lee were hovering behind him, all three faces lined with concern, Sloan's with a side of super-pissed.

I reached a shaking hand out to my love, toward his face, and he grabbed it in his own, clutching at my fingers, as he leaned down to kiss me. His cheeks were glistening with tears.

"How...?" I croaked, trying to sit up. He brushed my hair from my face. I tried again. "I saw him...he shot you..." I gestured to get up, my head still swimming, my belly still rolling, as Phillip helped me up into a sitting position. The room seemed uneven, out of balance, like the foundation had fallen.

Phillip cradled me, pulling my head to his chest, moving my hair out of my eyes. He kissed my forehead. "He didn't shoot me, Stormy."

"He didn't?"

"Well, he shot, but he missed. He..." His voice cracked and he pulled his hands away from my face. The rest of the room came into view. "*Jason* jumped in front of me." I looked around the room. Sloan and Lee were still hovering, Sloan's face full of tears and Lee's shell-shocked. Nathan was standing off to the side, his hands behind his head, pacing back and forth, muttering. I suddenly realized why the room felt so off kilter.

There were two bodies on the floor in the corner. One was Guthrie, still slumped against the wall, his oddly empty eyes even more vacant. The second was Jason Langley, sprawled out peacefully like a kid in bed who had thrown off the covers, his beautiful curly brown hair falling over one blue eye. They were both dead.

"Lee shot him," Phillip said in a quiet voice. "But it was too late."

The magnitude of it hit me and I began to wail. Jason had given his life for Phillip. Lee had shot his own father. All of this had happened because of me and the deal I'd tried to broker. The deal I'd thought would save them all. The death card. I kept pulling it, again and again. It would never stop.

"Where's Tess?" I asked, tears flowing down my face.

"He ran," Sloan said, pushing her hair back with a shaking hand. She gestured to the front door, which was standing wide open. I could hear the sound of crickets chirping in the night, and off in the distance, the faint sound of crashing waves. "Right out the front door. Like the coward he is."

I swallowed hard, staring at the open front door, beyond which lay the cool, peaceful darkness, the open sky, the soft, powdery sands of an empty Driftwood Beach, stark with bleached, skeletal tree limbs like beckoning fingers, calling me to the rolling ocean…and far off in the horizon, the pale moon, cold and soundless, steadfast and true.

"Tess always was a fucking coward," I said. I surveyed the scene, grave. Then I stood up on trembling legs, Phillip holding my arm steady. I used both hands to wipe the tears from my cheeks with one movement, feeling the strength in my fingers, knowing without knowing what they needed to do. I took a deep, shaking breath. I leaned forward and planted a gentle kiss on Phillip's beautiful mouth. Then I clasped my powerful fingers and cracked my knuckles outward, shaking my head to clear all of it away, all the distractions, the chaos, the outside noise. There was no time for it now. I had work to do.

"Right," I said, surveying the two bodies on the floor. "I guess I'd better get started."

Acknowledgments

My deepest, darkest thanks go to:

First and foremost, to my friends Jennifer Babineau and Elizabeth Tankard, my go-to-gals: you guys are always there when I need you, whether it's for a beta read, a thoughtful critique or a boost, and on those days when imposter syndrome is at its worst, I know I can reach out to you for hilarious gifs, great ideas and best of all, loyal friendship. Beth, I think you might love Phillip Deville even more than I do, and that's saying something! In this very online world of ours, one of the perks is that your chosen family can be far away, and still close as ever. You guys are family.

To my soul twin, Ellen Burke, who partially inspired this book: thanks for all the years of friendship, the endless conversations about everything under the sun, from metal and grunge, celebs and cults, murder and mayhem, all the "bless your hearts" and everything in between. You, too, know what it is to walk through the fire; here's to us coming out on the other side. You get it. This novel would not exist if not for you and I owe you a case of Code Red.

To my friend Amanda Wright for taking a chance on a guy named Phillip Deville; to Jennia Herold D'Lima, rockstar editor, for your notes in the margins; and to Elle Beaumont and the rest of the Midnight Tide team for giving these stories new life!

Additional thanks to Lauren Emily Whalen; Cydney Flanigan; Cate Short; Kelley Lawson; Amelia Ross; Melanie Stodghill; my parents John and Teresa; my brothers Jonathan and Chris; my chosen-sister Jessica "Marge" Campbell; Nonna Anita; Papa Clark; and finally, to Blake and Cal: all the coffee and tea and cake I consume, the crazed-evenings spent pecking away at keys, the frenzied, insane look in my eyes: it's all just the perks of living with a writer. I do it all for you.

In loving memory of Dot, Julia-Ann, Jesse, Mike, and Jackie; and, in memory of Nathan "Nate" Rodriguez: it's been twenty years, but I'll never forget that adorable grin, or those obnoxious JNCOs. You're always in my heart, my friend, where we are forever 17.

Last, but certainly never least – thanks to my favorite dead-rockstar, the Green Man, Peter Steele.

About the Author

Lillah Lawson is the author of novels Monarchs Under the Sassafras Tree (2019; nominated for Georgia Author of the Year 2020); So Long, Bobby (February 2023); The Dead Rockstar Trilogy ('20-'24); and Tomorrow & Tomorrow with Lauren Emily Whalen (October 2023).

Lillah enjoys writing across genres, specializing in historical fiction, southern gothic, and horror. She also writes a monthly column for her local newspaper. In addition to writing, Lillah works at a non-profit, is a genealogist pursuing her BA in History and English Literature, and proudly serves as secretary on her local library's Board of Trustees. An avid music lover, she's happiest at metal shows. She lives just outside of Athens, Georgia, with her husband, teenager, and two fur friends.

facebook.com/LillahLawson

instagram.com/LillahLawson

Also by Lillah Lawson

The Dead Rockstar Trilogy

Dead Rockstar

The Wolfden

Driftwood Dreary (August '24)

Standalones

Monarchs Under the Sassafras Tree

So Long, Bobby

Tomorrow and Tomorrow

Doomed Girls of Jefferson (January '25)

The Vamp (September '25)

The Hex Next Door by Lou William

What's a little necromancy between family?

For the Crow Witch, Icarus "Rus" Ashthorne, Moondale seemed the perfect hiding place. But like they always say, you can't go home again, and Rus finds out quickly that nothing is how she remembered, while at the same time very little has changed. Then she comes face to face with the only woman she's ever loved, Az Elwood, and... well, things get messier than she thought they ever could.

The Elwoods are a staple of Moondale, respected, feared, powerful, and Azure Elwood was always happy with her place amongst them. Happy to play the part of the good little witch, until Rus Ashthorne. Eleven years ago, Rus got on a bus and left Azure behind, but she's back, with two little girls trailing her like ducklings, and enough unspoken things between them to drown the town.

Now witch hunters are knocking at their proverbial door, the council of magic is being a real pain in the ass, and Rus

wonders how much magic it'll take to protect the people she
loves from herself and the danger following her.

Available Now